Most Ardently

SUSAN MESLER-EVANS

Entangled Publishing, LLC
2614 South Timberline Road
Suite 105, PMB 159
Fort Collins, CO 80525
rights@entangledpublishing.com

Embrace is an imprint of Entangled Publishing, LLC.

Edited by Candace Havens
Cover design by Bree Archer
Cover illustrations by 7romawka7, aekikuis, and mayalis/GettyImages

Manufactured in the United States of America

First Edition October 2019

embrace

For Kat – the Lizzy to my Charlotte.

Chapter One

In Which Elisa Benitez Meets the Most Obnoxious Girl Ever

It is a truth universally acknowledged that a single woman in possession of a good fortune must be...*difficult.*

"Difficult" was the word Elisa's mother used when she really wanted to say "ridiculously, impossibly infuriating." It was also the first word that came to mind when Elisa met Darcy Fitzgerald.

Of course, more than one person had claimed that Elisa could be *difficult.*

Maybe this is karma.

It had been, overall, a terrible first meeting. And the argument that ensued had started the way many arguments do: in a college classroom, over a book by a guy who was too dead, she presumed, to care.

Elisa had been on a college campus precisely once before, when her older sister Julieta had graduated with her Associate's. At the time, the students of Steventon Community College had seemed apathetic toward everyone around them and the campus appeared small and easy to navigate. It was a different story now that she was a student there herself. Suddenly, everyone was staring at her, the map on the website was completely useless, and her breakfast was threatening to reappear.

Even so, Elisa got to class ten minutes ahead of schedule and was surprised to find that she wasn't the only one. Sliding into an empty seat in the front row, she cast her brown eyes around, surveying the other early birds. She was clearly the youngest person there, though not by much—she was eighteen, and most of the others looked to be in their twenties or so. A couple of jocks sat in the back row, huddled over someone's phone, and three girls sat in the row behind Elisa, chattering away about their summer vacations. The professor, it appeared, wasn't there yet.

Another girl, who couldn't have been much older than her, sat alone at the end of her row. With her warm brown skin and wavy hair, she was...

Well, I certainly don't use the phrase "prettiest girl I've ever seen" lightly.

She'd brought a book with her and seemed determined to not look at, much less make eye contact with, anyone else in the room.

Elisa, deciding to take her chances with the only other unaccompanied person in the room, offered the girl a smile and a small wave.

"Hi," she said. "Is it your first day of college, too?"

The other girl's dark eyes left the book she'd brought with her, and Elisa got the impression she hadn't noticed her until just now. "No." Her voice was lower than Elisa had expected, and so soft, she almost wasn't sure she'd said anything. "I started last semester."

"Did you go to Steventon Public High? I don't think I ever saw you. I'm actually a senior there. I finished all my credits already, so they said I could start here early if I wanted."

When the school had offered Elisa the chance, she'd had three thoughts at once:

Hey, being a teacher's pet who never goes outside finally paid off.

Wait, does this mean I don't have to do the application essay?

I never have to fight through the demonic circle that is the west hallway to get to my locker ever again? TAKE ME NOW.

"I wish I'd done that," the other girl said. "I don't miss high school at all. But to answer your question, no, I just got into town last week."

"Oh, do you like it here?"

"Not really, no."

Elisa wasn't entirely sure what to say to that. So she just went with, "Ah."

Five minutes passed, and the professor still hadn't shown. Some students seemed perfectly happy with this arrangement, continuing to talk or text, while others squirmed in their seats and glanced at their watches, asking the others if they'd possibly gotten the start time wrong.

Elisa cleared her throat and threw an idea out to the room: "Maybe we should call the registrar's office or some—"

One of the jocks in the back row cut her off. "You know, there's a rule that if the professor doesn't show up after fifteen minutes, we can just leave."

She bristled. There was no such rule. She had checked.

"But if ever the prof really is fifteen minutes late," her father had said, "leave anyway. That's what I always did, and I graduated with a three point eight."

Before she could say anything, the girl who'd brought a book with her spoke. Her eyes didn't leave the page.

"I don't think that rule is official, and even if it were, it hasn't even been fifteen minutes yet." Man, her voice had a way of quieting a room. "And don't interrupt people. It's rude."

The jock rolled his eyes and droned, "Thanks, *Mom*, I'll keep that in mind," which earned him a few laughs from the other students. Even so, Elisa noticed the red creeping up his cheeks, and she smiled.

"Thank you," she whispered to the girl, who didn't respond beyond a small nod.

Sitting in a room full of people—all older and at least outwardly more comfortable than her—was doing a number on Elisa's nerves. She hadn't loved high school—especially not since her best friend had graduated two years earlier—but at least she'd known what she was doing.

Here? No idea. Totally flying blind.

Maybe this was a bad idea.

Okay. Wow. I've been here less than fifteen minutes, I've spoken to two people, and I'm already spiraling. Get it together, Benitez.

On that thought, she reached into her pocket for her brick of a smartphone, which was a few years out of date but worked okay and was basically indestructible. Seriously. She could probably take someone's teeth out if she threw it at them hard enough.

She reread the text her father had sent to her that morning.

Good morning, college student. Let me know how your first day of classes go. Remember: confidence, eye contact, and it is virtually always cheaper to find PDFs of your textbooks somewhere online. Legally bought PDFs, of course. You DEFINITELY shouldn't look and see if anyone's put them up for free someplace. And, on that note, you absolutely should NOT Google your homework questions to see if anyone's put up a cheat sheet for the full assignment. That would be irresponsible of me to explicitly encourage. Love you.

Elisa smiled. Papa had a way of easing the knots in her stomach, even over text.

Finally, nearly ten minutes after class was supposed to begin, the door opened and a woman rushed in, throwing her briefcase onto the desk.

"Good morning, everyone." The professor had unkempt hair and her blouse was buttoned up wrong, but she was making an effort to be energetic and cheerful anyway. Elisa offered a small smile in return. The girl at the end of the row just grimaced as she put her book away. "I'm Professor Maya DeCaro, and this is Introduction to Literature. While I get my roster pulled up, why don't we go around the room and share a little about ourselves?" The suggestion was met with stray groans. "You." She looked directly at Elisa, and she felt her stomach twist. Even though she knew exactly what her professor was about to say, she still prayed that she wouldn't. But then came the cursed words: "Go ahead and get us started, will you? Your name, your age, something about yourself."

"Um—" Crap. "Okay." *Crap.*

Elisa stood, trying her best to smile and look somewhat convincing. Every eye in the room was on her, including those of the girl at the end of the row.

"I'm Elisa Benitez," she said. "I'm a senior in high school, actually—and, um, I'm... I'm the second of five girls."

"Oh, would I know your sisters?" Professor DeCaro asked, looking up from her computer.

"Julieta, maybe. She graduated with her associate's degree a couple years ago."

"Oh, Julieta Benitez, of course." The professor's face lit up with a fond smile. "She was such a lovely girl. Smart, too."

Elisa nodded, smiling back. That didn't surprise her much—Julieta could get along with anyone. Any professor who'd taught her was guaranteed to like her. It was impossible not to. Even Lucia, her youngest sister, looked up to her.

Elisa sat back down, and they moved on to the other girl. She stood, but she didn't so much as crack a smile.

"I'm Darcy Fitzgerald."

Elisa barely kept her jaw from dropping, and she wasn't the only one who was surprised. Two girls in the row behind them immediately began whispering to each other, their eyes wide. Elisa distinctly heard one of the guys in the back row mutter, "Holy sh…"

Elisa couldn't really blame them. It was as if a Hilton or a Kardashian was sitting in their classroom. Everyone knew the Fitzgerald family. Elisa had been aware that they lived in the general area of Steventon, Ohio, but she never imagined she'd meet one. Elisa rarely left town, and the Fitzgeralds were always off doing…

Well, she was never sure *what*, exactly, it was that they did. The family had been well-known since her parents were teenagers, maybe even before that. These days, they were simply famous for being famous.

The Fitzgeralds were almost offensively rich. So, what the hell was their prodigal daughter doing in a community college in Steventon?

"I'm nineteen," Darcy continued, voice inflections barely changing. "And I'm the oldest of two, unless you count my older cousin, with whom I was raised."

She sat back down before anyone could comment. The professor apparently got the message because she swiftly moved on to the next person.

Elisa glanced at her, trying not to be too obvious. Darcy seemed committed to the whole "I'd rather be anywhere else," vibe she had going on. Dark clothes, including a pair of shoes that probably cost more than all of her textbooks combined, matched her mood, her lips twisted into a semi-permanent scowl.

She's hot in a mean-girl sort of way. And so out of my league.

And Elisa's "interesting fact" was that she had sisters. She wondered why of all possible things to say, she'd chosen her birth order. Her excuse was that her sisters were really the most exciting thing in any given day. The Fitzgeralds had *plenty* going on.

The class got through the introductions, and the professor told everyone to get out their copies of the first book: *Lord of the Flies*. When she saw it on the book list for the semester, Elisa had groaned out loud. She'd had to study it in high school and had often found herself wondering if the teacher was punishing the class for something.

"Has anyone read this book?" Professor DeCaro asked.

About half the hands in the room went up, including Elisa and Darcy's.

"What did you think?" the instructor asked, then paused before saying, "Not that it'll change anything—we're reading it no matter what."

Crap.

"I liked it a lot," Darcy said. "I thought it was really well-written, and I think it's a very accurate message, especially given our current political climate."

Elisa spoke up before anyone else had the chance. "Oh, come on—that's a little cynical, don't you think?"

Now Darcy was looking at her. "Maybe."

"I'm not wild about our political situation, either, but I have to disagree," Elisa said.

"Your disagreeing doesn't keep me from being right."

"*Wow.*" Elisa actually had to laugh. "Come on. You can't honestly believe people are all bad."

"History proves that, given enough of a chance, humans will tear each other to shreds."

"But the message of the book—at least, the way I was taught it—isn't as clear-cut as 'humans are bastards.' I thought the point was that people who are relatively privileged—in this case, English schoolboys—aren't any better than anybody else, and that they're capable of doing awful things when they're removed from consequences and authority figures."

Darcy gave this some thought. "I think things would've eventually gone to hell even if all the students in *Lord of the Flies* were female," she said. "Although the details probably would've played out differently. It's an interesting point, to think about how changing the genders would change the story."

A guy in the back row threw out, "Man, I'd hate to be on *that* island. Groups of girls are crazy. Away from civilization, it'd be anarchy."

Both girls responded at once, looking away from each other to glare at him. "I'm going to pretend I didn't hear that," Elisa said, while Darcy said, "The idea that women can't get along is a myth, which you might know if any woman anywhere would give you the time of day."

Professor DeCaro tried to intervene. "Hey, now…"

The guy had gone red, but he defended himself. "I was just joking," he said. "I make one joke, and suddenly I'm the jerk?"

Elisa took a sharp breath. "Yes. Exactly. Glad we agree."

"That's not f—"

"Okay, rule of thumb: if your joke's punchline is 'women be crazy, amirite?', it's not a very good joke, and you're probably just an asshole."

"*Hey.*" The professor's voice was sterner now. Elisa cringed.

"Hey, *what*?" Darcy asked, eyes sparking as she looked

at her. "I think she was imparting some very good advice."

Did she just mouth off at the teacher? On the first day? Toto, I don't think we're in high school anymore.

Professor DeCaro had the look of someone who was counting down the days until retirement. "Let's keep personal insults, gender stereotyping, and profanity out of our class discussion, okay, ladies? And that goes for you, too, gentlemen."

Darcy shrugged. "Fine by me. Where were we?"

"Whether or not humans are evil," Elisa said.

"Right. Thank you. Anyway, Golding wrote the book to make a point," she said. "The point was that *no* group—be it sex, race, financial background—is immune to savagery, under the right circumstances."

"Well, yeah, of *course* no one is immune," she conceded. "But I think hard times bring out the best in most people, much more than it brings out the worst in others. I think if you give people a fair chance, most of them will try to help. People are inherently good."

"I disagree."

"Your disagreeing doesn't keep me from being right."

Darcy's face gave away nothing, but there was a flicker— just a flicker—of emotion in her eyes. Whether it was amusement or annoyance, Elisa couldn't tell. With Darcy, there probably wasn't much difference.

The professor hastily called on someone else, not giving them an opening to start up again, and Elisa flipped through the pages, resigning herself to reading the book *again*. She glanced over at Darcy once more and caught her looking over at her. Both girls quickly turned their gazes back to their books, pretending they hadn't noticed the other.

Okay, Elisa, you've got a pretentious classmate who is so pretty it's just not fair, and a book you hate. But it could be worse. You could be back at the high school. Remember the locker? The square-dancing unit in gym class? The cafeteria food?

It could always *be worse.*

. . .

Elisa didn't have any other classes on Mondays, which meant she was back home by noon. Of course, it balanced out because she was on campus from ten in the morning to five in the evening on Tuesdays and Thursdays, with only ninety minutes free in the early afternoon to rush home to eat lunch. *At least the campus is only a twenty-minute drive.*

She lived with her mother and sisters in the Longbourn Apartment Complex, which had issues of its own. Longbourn probably looked downright appalling to those that hadn't been there all their lives and had time to get used to it. It had a recurring problem with rats that resurfaced every three years or so, the washing machines in the laundry room only worked about half the time, and the landlord actually had the nerve to jack up the rent recently. But, still, it was home. Elisa had lived there, in the same apartment, for her entire life. And even a rat-ridden, overpriced pit had its upsides.

The best of those was in the lobby when she got there, on her phone.

"Yes, sir. Yes. Yes. Right. You're right. I'm sorry. My fault."

Charlene looked up when Elisa walked into the building, and she waved but didn't stop talking to whoever was on the other end of the call. Elisa was slightly disappointed to notice that she was in her work attire of a pencil skirt, high heels, and a blouse. Charlene was *supposed* to be able to stay home that day, but apparently, that wasn't happening.

"I'll call him," Charlene said, keeping her voice so chipper it was very nearly convincing. "You're right, sir. Yes.

I'm sure. I promise."

She made eye contact with Elisa, rolling her eyes and pointing at the phone.

Work. Sorry, she mouthed.

"It's cool," Elisa whispered. Charlene's job always had her dealing with some disaster or other. She'd bet her friend was the most competent person at work, but as a secretary with no college degree, she was treated like a glorified coffee machine on the best days.

On the worst days, the higher-ups treated her like their personal maid, emotional punching bag, and occasional therapist. It was one of life's greatest injustices that a smart, ambitious woman like Charlene could be ignored while idiots like her boss lived off her hard work.

"I'll fax it over as soon as I can," Charlene said. Her tone was polite and cheery, but her eyes gave her away. Her boss was lucky he wasn't in the room with her; he would not have survived the conversation they were currently having. "Yes, of *course* I mean within the next hour. Have I ever let you down before?"

"Want me to kick his ass for you?" Elisa whispered. Her friend grinned but swatted her on the arm, shushing her.

"Yes, sir, understood. I'll have it to you by the end of lunch. See you then. Goodbye." She hung up. "Hey," she said, wrapping her arms around Elisa in a quick hug.

"I thought you had the day off," she said.

"Yeah, so did I. Doesn't appear to matter." She rolled her eyes. "Looks like I'm putting in a half day today."

"That sucks."

"Yeah, but, hey." She forced a smile. "A job is a job. I'm glad I have it."

"Don't use your customer service voice on me, Locke."

Charlene laughed. "Okay, okay, work sucks. But enough about that. How was class?"

"Ugh, could be worse. Beats the high school." She shrugged. "The professor seems nice, but the first book we're reading is *Lord of the Fuckboys*. And there's one girl that just...*argh*."

"Ditzy?"

"No, not really," Elisa conceded. "She seems pretty smart. But stuck-up. And hot. She's annoying, but she's really hot. Why are the cute ones always the ones who make you want to rip your hair out?"

Charlene laughed at that. "Yeah...that does *not* get better after graduation."

"Guess what her name is?"

"How would I know what her name is?" Charlene asked, rolling her eyes.

"Darcy Fitzgerald."

She raised her eyebrows. "Really? Are we sure she's *that* Darcy Fitzgerald?"

"As far as I know, there's only the one."

"Maybe you should try and get on her good side. You know, just in case."

Elisa snorted. "I don't think she *has* a good side."

"Oh, come on, you've only met her once. Besides, pissing off a Fitzgerald probably isn't smart."

"Yeah, would've been good to know that an hour ago."

Charlene laughed, shaking her head. "Well, be nice."

"I'm nice," Elisa said a little too loudly.

"Of course you are, Lisa. Look, I gotta go," she said. "My boss will probably rip my head off if I'm not over there soon."

"Go kick ass. I have some reading to start."

Char was two years older but had grown up at Longbourn, too—for most of their lives, she had lived in the apartment above the Benitez family. Her parents and younger sister, Molly, were still there. But after graduating high school, Charlene had insisted to her parents that she needed to get out of their hair and start being independent, so she'd moved into another apartment.

Sometimes Elisa's sister Julieta admired what Char had done and thought about moving out, too. But her job as a website designer, while doing admirably well for a small startup, didn't make her nearly enough to live alone, and she knew it. Fortunately, their mother, Alejandra, would've been distraught if she left, and was very open about how much she enjoyed having her there.

Though, of course, if Julieta left to get married, Alejandra wouldn't complain.

"Elisa." Alejandra hurried to greet her daughter at the door as soon as it opened. Like her daughter, she was short and fat—though Elisa was proud to say she now officially had half an inch over her. "Do you know what Charlene's mama told me when I saw her in the laundry room today?"

"That Charlene's boss is robbing her of her hard-earned days off?" she guessed.

"No, she told me that empty house in Netherfield Park just sold."

Elisa nearly groaned but managed to keep it in. *Of course it's something like that.* Netherfield Park was the richest neighborhood in Steventon—the kind that didn't even have a bus going out there because if you had to take the bus, you definitely couldn't afford to live there.

"That's great," she said, not making much of an effort to sound sincere.

"Guess who bought it?"

"Who, Mom?" If she said "Darcy Fitzgerald," she'd probably scream.

"*Robert Charles II,*" Mom said, as if this was supposed to mean anything to her.

"Who?"

"Have you *always* been this oblivious?" Alejandra looked

appalled at Elisa's very reasonable question. "Mr. Charles is one of the youngest millionaires in the world. His father owns a movie production company—well, owned. He retired a couple years ago, and now it's his son's."

"Did they make any movies I'd know?"

"Oh yeah, loads." She waved her hand. "*Camp Massacre, The Flutist, Camp Massacre 2,* that version of *Hamlet* where Horatio was a dog, *Camp Massacre 3: Todd Kills Yet Again…* That's all I got off the top of my head, but you get my point."

She laughed. "Oh, wow, you should've told me we were dealing with Oscar-winners."

Mom rolled her eyes, but she was smiling. "The world becomes a brighter place with every slasher movie, and you know it."

She chuckled. "Can't argue with that." She'd seen pictures of her mother in her childhood bedroom, covered in posters for all the bloodiest, most disgusting horror flicks of the day. According to her father, she'd made him watch *Child's Play* for their anniversary one time. It was apparently quite romantic.

"Why would Robert want to live out here?" Elisa asked, moving toward the fridge, which forced her to squeeze between her mother and the room divider. Until the year before, she had shared her room with Julieta, the oldest Benitez sister, and Lucia, the youngest. But then, Lucia had decided that she deserved her own room, and had bought a room divider, put a sign declaring "Lucia's Room" on it, and closed off a little part of the living room to be her own.

She even moved her bed in there herself. Mom had decided it was easier to just let her rather than argue, which was par for the course when it came to Lucia. Elisa was a little irritated that her sister got her own space when no one else did but was mostly just glad to have her out of her hair. Or at least out of her room.

"Even Netherfield probably isn't as nice as what he's used to."

"Who cares?" Mom said. "He's only twenty-five, single, very good family, very well-off."

Elisa let the fridge door shut with a small slam, emerging from the kitchen with a tube of Go-Gurt. Eating without a spoon was necessary, because Lucia had blown off her turn at doing the dishes. Again.

"Mom," she said sternly. "*No.*"

Please, Lord, don't let her go there, not this early in the day.

"I'm just saying, you or Julieta could do worse."

Oh, come on. Really? I haven't asked You for much.

"*Mom…*"

"Look, Elisa, I know you hate it when I try to set you up but keep an open mind. Would it really be so bad if one of you girls married a wealthy man to take care of you? O-or woman, in your case, dear," she hastily added, smiling.

Elisa cracked a smile despite herself. When she'd come out as bisexual two years before, her mother and sisters had accepted her with open arms. Mom had also been accepting when the second-youngest sister, Camila, had come out as trans the year before that. She didn't always understand things, and she sometimes said something so outdated it was cringe-worthy, but Elisa and Camila could both rest easy with the knowledge that their mother's love was truly unconditional.

Her requirements for a spouse for one of her daughters, meanwhile, had plenty of conditions. This magical person had to make at least $80,000 a year and have a "good family," whatever that meant. They needed to own, not rent, a home, and must be able to travel whenever they pleased. The last one was strange, but her mom liked to dream big. But the caveat to all of that was their significant others didn't necessarily have to be male.

Dealing with the extended family had been a bumpy ride, especially on her mother's side. Some, like her brother, accepted Cam and Elisa as easily as she had, while others, like her parents, didn't understand either of them. She said that Abuela and Abuelo still loved them just as much as they did before—they just needed some time to adjust their worldview. If they weren't used to it by now, they probably never would be.

"I'm not saying money isn't nice to have," Elisa said, "but it's not really something I'd think about before I got married."

Alejandra snorted.

"*Mom.*"

"I know you're a romantic, dear, but finances in a marriage are *very* important. You want to be sure there's money to take care of your children when you're gone, and money to enjoy yourself with while you're still around."

"You married Papa when you were both flat broke," Elisa said without thinking. She regretted it as soon as it was out.

Her mother turned away from her as soon as she mentioned her failed marriage. Elisa's parents weren't the sort to publicly argue or even slight each other in private— well, her dad did, sometimes, a little—and hadn't even had to go to court to settle custody. Her mother had full custody, but her father was free to see his daughters anytime.

"Look how that turned out," she said curtly.

"I'm sorry, Mom," Elisa said, moving closer. "I didn't mean to bring that up."

"It's all right, dear," she said, though Elisa could tell she was still upset. The way she refused to meet her daughter's eyes gave it away. "It was fifteen years out of my life. We can't pretend it never happened."

As much as you'd love to. "I'm gonna started on my homework. Love you, Mama." She pecked her on the cheek and headed to her room before her mom could bring up Robert Charles II again.

As a freelancer, Julieta worked from home. From nine a.m. to five p.m., the room she and Elisa shared was her office. When Elisa came in, Julieta was sitting up on her bed, her laptop balanced on her knees. It had been a Christmas gift from their father. He was delighted she wanted her own business and told her that it was an "investment." Elisa and her other sisters had laptops, too, but they were discounted models that were about four years out of date.

"How's the latest client?" Elisa asked, tossing her bag on the floor and sitting on the bed on her side of the room. Her side was disorganized and had no aesthetic or theme to speak of. Julieta's was pristinely organized, with furniture, bedding, and accessories in her favorite shades of pink.

"Demanding," Julieta said, tearing her gaze away from the screen long enough to give her sister a warm smile. "He's asked to change the layout *five* times so far."

Elisa groaned. "It's like, make up your mind."

"The customer is always right," she said with a small shrug. Even so, her smile became ever-so-slightly strained.

"Does that still apply when the customer's an idiot?"

"It applies *especially* when the customer's an idiot."

Elisa dug through her bag for her book. "Did Mom tell you about the house in Netherfield Park?"

Julieta gave a tiny laugh, shaking her head. Her hair, black and wavy, fell in front of one eye, forcing her to push it back. It was only then that Elisa noticed that Julieta hadn't even changed out of her pajamas or brushed her hair. That figured. Even unkempt, her older sister looked beautiful. "Only a thousand times."

"I wonder how she expects us to meet him, anyway. It's not like he runs with our crowd."

"I'm sure Mama will find a way. She always does."

"Well, she fully expects one of us to marry him, I think, soooo... Not it."

"Gee, thanks. Can I count on you to be my maid of honor?"

"Only if the best man is cute."

Chapter Two

In Which the Benitez Sisters Attend a Wedding

It had taken less than a week for her mother to find a way.

Even for her, that was impressive.

It turned out, as she explained to her daughters over a Saturday morning breakfast of frozen waffles and canned peaches, that since getting into town, Robert Charles II happened to frequent the same bookstore as their father. When he wasn't working, Elisa's dad basically lived in the stacks of tomes, even when he was between paychecks and wasn't actually going to buy anything. The workers had resigned themselves to his presence.

"So, what, you went over to 'randomly' run into him, nineties rom-com style?" Camila asked, pouring about a gallon of maple syrup onto her plate. On Saturdays, it was rare for the Benitez family to have breakfast before ten, and today was no exception. Camila had been the last to rise from her bed, finally appearing at the table sometime around ten thirty in a flowered bathrobe and Hello Kitty slippers. The smell of waffles was a surefire method to wake her up. Maria had been, as usual, the first sister awake, and had wasted no time expressing her annoyance with her for being so slow.

"Don't be silly, that'd be way too awkward," Mom said. Elisa relaxed a bit. "I just called up your dad, explained the situation to him, begged him to help me until he agreed to shut me up. Your father says Robert's going to a wedding next weekend. And your dad is a friend of a friend of the groom, so he managed to wrangle us some invitations. All six of us, and Charlene, too—turns out her boss is a groomsman."

That last part was no doubt an attempt to stop Elisa from getting too annoyed with the whole thing. It didn't work.

"How'd you even know where Robert goes?" she asked with a small frown.

Mom stood, going to get the butter out of the fridge. "Oh, don't pretend you've never dug through anyone's social media before."

Elisa set her fork down with a clatter, gaping at her. "Mom."

"It's not my fault his privacy settings aren't very good," she defended herself. Sitting back down, she gave her daughters a sly grin. "He's posted about a dozen pictures from that store since getting into town. I got to see what he looks like. You know, he's awfully cute. So many of those millionaires *had* to become rich to make up for ugliness, but not Robert Charles II, that's for sure. If I were ten years younger…"

"*Mom!*" Elisa, Maria, and Camila shouted in unison.

"What kind of cute are we talking here?" Lucia asked, dark brown eyes sparkling as they always did whenever a hot, rich guy was mentioned. Which, with Lucia, was 95 percent of the time. "Like, 'reads to homeless orphans on the weekends' cute or 'has probably stabbed a guy and we love him for it' cute? Or is he somewhere in-between?"

Elisa stared at her. "What in the hell are you talking about?"

"There are seven distinct levels of attractiveness," her sister said. Elisa looked over to Maria and Julieta and was glad to see she wasn't the only one running on confusion. "Everyone falls on a tier somewhere, and everyone has their own preferences for where they want their boo to land."

"Does anyone still say 'boo' when they mean 'boyfriend or girlfriend'?" Maria asked.

"I do. It's cute, it's easy to say, it's gender-inclusive, and it reminds me of ghosts. Win-win-win-win."

"Can't argue with that logic," Elisa said with a small smile. "Mom, did you have any cute little nicknames you used to call your boyfriends?"

Mom nodded. "Mostly it was 'sweetie,' 'hon,' or 'dumbass.' You know, flirting."

"Anyhoo," Lucia said, "I call it the Benitez Sliding Scale of Cuteness. Patent pending. Cam helped me perfect it. It's all *totes* scientific."

"Your mind is a labyrinth, Lulu," Elisa said.

"Thanks. But, of course, I'll need to study Robert at closer range to know for sure where he lands..."

"Don't even think about it, missy. He is too old for you," Mom said, which was true. Lucia, although the tallest of her sisters at five foot ten, was only fourteen—a fact that often seemed to escape her. "And, for the curious, he's one hundred percent on the 'reads to homeless orphans' end of the scale."

Elisa was never sure if she envied her mother's ability to follow Lucia's thought process or not.

"Is he too old for *me*?" Camila asked with a playful grin.

Mom gave her a stern stare. "*Absolutely.*" Camila just laughed and went back to shoveling peaches into her mouth by the spoonful.

"Mom, just because he's cute doesn't mean he's worth our time," Maria said. At seventeen, Maria was the middle child, and by far the most introverted. Having come along only eleven months after Elisa was born, they'd been mistaken for non-identical twins more than once. Elisa privately thought her parents were crazy for having another kid so soon, but of course she would never say that, especially not to Maria herself. "Most cute guys are huge dicks."

"*You're* not the one he'll be after, anyway," Lucia said. Elisa kicked her under the table.

"Don't be ridiculous, Lulu, there are plenty of men out there who would love a smart, dependable girl like Maria," Julieta said, giving her an encouraging smile.

"Smart, dependable..." Maria muttered. Elisa gave her a sympathetic glance.

Mom made a valiant effort to keep the conversation on track.

"You could at least give him a chance," she said. "And we're going, so that's final."

Elisa and Maria groaned, exchanging a mutually exasperated look, but the other three seemed pretty excited about it.

"Who's getting married?" Julieta asked. "We should bring them a present."

"No one we know," she said, clearly not getting why most people would deem this a reason to *not go*. "So...soap basket it is. That's not the point. The point is to get a chance to introduce ourselves to Robert without it being awkward."

"And crashing a wedding isn't awkward at all," Elisa muttered.

Mom whacked her on the back of the head with a spatula.

• • •

The wedding was being held in a park near Netherfield. Mom had insisted, much to Elisa's aggravation, that they park the family minivan at least five blocks away. "If we show up in this thing, we may as well hold up a giant neon sign that reads, WE'RE BROKE," she explained, forcing Julieta to drive past the park and turn around so they could find someplace to hide their sticker-covered, maroon-colored chariot of shame.

"I thought the fact that we're poor is the whole reason we're doing this," Maria said, voice strangled from where she was squeezed between Lucia and the window.

"Yeah, but we don't wanna let *them* know that," Lucia said, in the "oh my God you are such a moron" voice only a self-centered fourteen-year-old could pull off.

And right on cue, Camila echoed: "Yeah, obviously." Despite being a year and a half older than Lucia and a grade ahead, she tended to copy her. Julieta and Elisa had, on separate occasions, tried to persuade Camila that she didn't need to imitate Lucia, but she seemed to encourage it. She liked having someone want to be like her. It was nice to be admired, Elisa supposed, as Lucia reached over and squeezed Camila's hand, grinning at her.

Julieta found a place to park, and the family spilled out of the van. Elisa stumbled slightly as her feet hit the sidewalk, unaccustomed to walking in heels. Charlene, who had to wear them daily to work, grabbed her arm, steadying her a bit.

"Think Mom would give me grief for taking these off for the walk over?" she asked.

"I think she would decide that the sight of your bare feet would make everyone think you're even poorer than you really are," Charlene laughed.

They could hear the wedding before they could see it. The actual ceremony wasn't supposed to start for another half hour, but plenty of people had already arrived, and all their voices were blending together. It was impossible to pick out any individual words unless you were really working at it. As they got closer, Elisa could hear classical music playing from speakers set up for the occasion.

"Whoa, did they rent out the entire park?" Maria asked as their mother presented their invitations to the man at the gate, who checked the guest list to make sure they weren't party crashers. "I expected it to be in the gazebo or one of the shelters or something."

"We're in rich people territory," Elisa said, desperate to find a seat. Her feet were killing her. "They probably *bought* it."

Maria and Camila both laughed, but Julieta tossed her a pleading look. "Please don't antagonize anybody before we've even talked to anyone."

"I'm not," she said defensively.

"Elisa…"

"Okay, okay. I promise I will be the picture of perfect manners."

Charlene snorted. She elbowed her.

Upon seeing the size of the crowd that had turned out for the wedding, Elisa suddenly understood how her father had managed to get them in so easily. There was simply no way the bride and groom knew *all* these people personally. When her cousin Vega had gotten married, her mother had forced her to invite every single distant cousin and friend of a friend of a friend. Vega had known maybe an eighth of the people at her own wedding. Elisa had the sense it was the same deal here, which at least took some pressure off. She probably wouldn't be expected to pretend she actually knew the couple at all.

"Look at the ice sculptures," Lucia squealed, embarrassingly loudly, actually pointing. Ignoring the people glancing at them, Elisa turned to get a look.

She was about to comment on how pretty the ice sculptures were, when something caught her attention.

Darcy was here.

Of all the people she would've expected to see, Darcy

wouldn't have even cracked the top twenty. Was she imagining this?

She blinked. Nope. She was still there.

"What the *hell*?" Elisa said aloud, before she could stop herself. Her face heated as a couple of guests gave her odd looks, but she was glad that Darcy was not one of them. She was standing by the sculptures, wearing a deep plum dress that she pulled off effortlessly, her wavy hair pulled back for the occasion. Her wealth seemed more much obvious here than it ever had at school. She seemed as displeased to be here as she did on campus, though. Her eyes flicked around the vicinity, apparently looking for someone.

She cast her glance to Elisa, and a spark of recognition lit her eyes.

Crap.

Elisa politely waved at her, unsure what else to do.

"Who're you waving at?" Charlene asked. "Someone we know?"

"I do," Elisa said. "Darcy's here."

"That snotty girl from your class?"

She nodded. "She's over there," she said, gesturing as subtly as she could.

Charlene turned to look, and she was glad to see that she was no longer looking at her. Instead, she was talking to a group of people, apparently having found whoever it was she was waiting for.

"Who're they?" Charlene asked.

"No clue."

She didn't think they were Darcy's family—these people were all white, blue-eyed, and golden-haired. They were definitely related to each other, though. The entire group was tall, with round faces and cute, button noses. There was the mother, two twin girls who didn't look like they were that much older than them, and...

"Robert Charles," Alejandra said, barely keeping her voice to a whisper.

Robert Charles, the man her mom was determined to get one of her daughters to marry, knew Darcy Fitzgerald. And, judging by his smile and the way she allowed him to hug her, he knew her pretty well.

It freaking figures.

"Is that him?" Julieta asked, peering over the top of Elisa's head to get a look.

"Oh, he's cute," Camila said brightly.

He *was* cute, Elisa had to admit. And he didn't give off the snobby vibe that Darcy and his sisters did. He looked like the sort of guy who went to farmer's markets, and who rescued cats from trees.

Before Elisa could say anything, Mom was hustling Julieta over to where Darcy and Robert were, and everyone else followed, whether out of morbid curiosity or a desire to do damage control, Elisa was unsure.

They were within ten feet of Robert, but he hadn't noticed them yet.

"Okay, honey, just relax and let Mama handle this," Mom was whispering to her eldest daughter.

"Handle wh—*oof*—"

Julieta hadn't finished her sentence when Mom gave her a nudge—well, more like a forceful shove—in Robert's general direction. Julieta fell to the ground, more surprised than hurt, but it got everyone's attention. Including Robert's.

Because just saying, "Hi, welcome to the neighborhood," is too close to what normal people do.

Eh, normal families are probably boring, anyway.

Julieta hadn't been on the ground for two seconds when Robert rushed forward, offering her a hand to help her to her feet. She took it, clearly embarrassed, but he just smiled at her.

"Sorry, I'm so clumsy," Julieta said. She wasn't, but that would probably leave a better impression than "my crazy mother decided to manufacture an epic love affair between us." Once she was on her feet, she was able to smile back.

"Don't worry about it," Robert said. "You're not hurt, are you?"

"No," she said, "not at all. Thank you."

"No worries. We haven't met, have we?"

"No—no, we, um, we haven't. I'm Julieta Benitez."

"Robert Charles," he said, as if they didn't already know that. He finally let go of Julieta's hand to gesture to the people with him, and that's when Elisa saw it in Julieta's eyes. A flicker of disappointment.

Here we go.

"This is my mother, Amelia, and my sisters, Cora and Louise," Robert was saying. "And this," he gestured toward Darcy, who'd witnessed the entire interaction with a scowl, "is my best friend, Darcy Fitzgerald. She's like a sister to me."

"Pleasure," she said, in a tone that indicated that it wasn't. Julieta smiled graciously at each of them before introducing her entire "entourage."

"These are my sisters, Elisa, Maria, Camila, and Lucia, and Elisa's best friend, Charlene Locke...and my mother—"

"Alejandra Bello," their mother announced, thrusting her hand forward. Elisa cringed a bit, but Robert didn't seem to mind, shaking her hand politely. "We're delighted to meet you, Mr. Charles."

"Don't call me that, please," he laughed. "Just call me Bobby. Being called Mr. Charles reminds me of work."

"All right, Bobby it is," she said, looking elated to be on a first-name basis with him so quickly. Never mind that he probably told *everyone* to call him that. "So—bride or groom?"

"Bride. Sort of," he said. "She's Darcy's...uh..."

"Second cousin," Darcy said.

"Second cousin. That's right. Darcy asked her to let us tag along so we could meet people."

"How funny," Mom said. "Julieta's father got us invited to the wedding for the same reason." Elisa nudged her in the side, but she ignored her. "He's a friend of the groom but was unable to attend."

Probably because he barely knows him.

"Truth be told, my Julieta barely knows anyone here outside of us," her mom said.

Of course, neither did her other daughters, or Charlene, but she didn't seem too concerned with that particular detail.

"I know how that feels," Bobby said. "Everyone's very nice, though. You know, if you don't already have plans for the reception, you're welcome to sit with us."

Her mom smiled. "We have no plans whatsoever."

Elisa couldn't help but feel a bit bad for Bobby. He was trying to be nice, and had no clue what he'd just done.

"Bobby," Darcy said, a hint of irritation seeping into her tone, "the ceremony is supposed to start in five minutes. We should find our seats."

"Oh, right." He gave the Benitez family one last smile. "See you at the reception, then."

As the Charles family and Darcy headed in, Mom did a little victory dance once they weren't looking, her plan having gone perfectly.

"Was shoving her really necessary?" Maria asked. "Life isn't a dating sim."

"*Your* life may not be," she said. "But that's only because you don't let me meddle."

"Mom, I think I speak for all five of us when I say I would literally rather eat cement."

Elisa tried and failed to fight a grin, even as Mom shot Maria her most withering look. "We should probably find our seats, too," she said. She just hoped that they weren't near Darcy.

They weren't. They were in the very back row, which she suspected was a side effect of being an afterthought on the guest list. She smoothed out the skirt of her pale-blue dress, trying to appear vaguely interested in the ceremony.

Julieta, meanwhile, wasn't even pretending. She was too busy stealing glances at Bobby.

• • •

The reception was beautiful. By the time the wedding was finished, the sun had begun to go down, the sky streaked with scarlet, and the park was lit with little twinkling lights. A string quartet had been hired to play for the guests, and there was even a little area to dance. Elisa could tell that her mother was hoping Julieta and Bobby would put it to good use, but they'd spent the entire reception so far back at Bobby's table, talking to each other—and only to each other. A bridesmaid approached, reaching for Bobby's arm and inviting him to dance with her. He got points for shaking his head and turning back to face her sister.

"They *are* kind of cute together," Charlene said. She and Elisa hung out by the fountain, watching the rest of the party. This was how they spent most parties they attended—off in a corner, watching the action unfold. Being alone in a crowd wasn't so bad if you had a friend to be alone *with*.

"Yeah," Elisa admitted. "I haven't seen Julieta that happy since before her last boyfriend dumped her."

"How can you tell?" It was a fair question—Julieta projected an image of happiness and friendliness at all times.

Before Elisa could respond, her friend had grabbed her arm, a look of dread in her eyes. "Uh-oh. Incoming," she whispered.

Elisa looked up to see what she was talking about and barely repressed a groan when she saw Colin Burger headed toward them. He'd gone to their middle and high school and was Charlene's age. He'd been determined to win Elisa's friendship for years. And he was a *huge* pain in the ass, a fact that had always escaped him. The girls put up with him simply to avoid trouble. He wasn't mean, really, or even truly harmful. He was just...*Colin.*

"Charlene and Elisa—the dynamic duo," he said upon reaching them. He immediately pulled them both into a big, inescapable bear hug.

"Thanks for asking permission," Elisa muttered into his shoulder. He didn't seem to hear her. He hugged her so tight she could smell his cologne.

Unearned Confidence and Desperation. He must have bought it by the case.

"What—what are you doing here?" Charlene asked.

"I just love weddings, don't you?" Colin asked. "I have to admit, I usually prefer church weddings—there's something about the tradition of it all. But this was just a lovely ceremony. You know, I'm majoring in theology at Gardiner University, and you learn all sorts of interesting trivia. Not just in your classes, but listening to other people talk. Like, for example, did you know that the original purpose of the best man was to fight to the death? Back when arranged marriages were normal, sometimes the bride's actual boyfriend would turn up to 'kidnap' her, so the groom would hire the best swordsman he could afford to stop him. Isn't that just fascinating? I think so, anyway. Wait— I'm sorry, I've forgotten the question."

"What. Are. You. Doing here?"

"Oh, right. Well, it's actually a family affair. The bride, the lovely Miss Hannah Rollins—or, as I suppose I should now be calling her, the lovely Mrs. Hannah Cooper—is actually my second cousin. I was unsure if I should take the time out of my busy schedule to pay my respects to a distant relative who I've only met once or twice, but my mother convinced me that it would be a good opportunity to relax and get to know my extended family a bit better. And she was right—well, she usually is. I'm really enjoying it."

They blinked at him. Leave it to Colin Burger to answer a simple question with a novella.

What did he just say? She rewound the convo in her head.

"Wait, second cousin?"

"Why, yes. Hannah and I are related through…let's see, I believe our great-grandfather Lucas—"

Elisa cut him off. Not to be rude but because with Colin, that's what it took to get so much as a word in. "Do you know Darcy, by any chance?"

Colin, for the first time since he came up to them, allowed the smile to slip from his face, ever so slightly. "Yes," he said, noticeably less than pleased about it. "Her mother was my aunt. We saw each other pretty frequently when I was growing up, but, if I'm being honest…? She's kind of…scary."

Elisa had to laugh. "I can see that. We take a class together."

"How are you enjoying college so far? I've found that it is so rewarding to be studying in a field that interests me. I did extremely well in high school, but it was so difficult to concentrate in a crowded classroom. My mother had wanted me to attend a private academy, but my father thought that public school would be good for me, since everyone at my elementary school was from the same background as me. I pride myself on mixing very well with people from different economic backgrounds, and now that I'm studying theology, I'm learning how to interact with people from various cultural backgrounds, as well—"

"It's great," Elisa said, more than a little exasperated. "College is great."

"That's good to hear." Colin said. "Anyway, I was wondering if you would do me the honor of a dance?"

He held out his hand, waiting for her to take it. Elisa's brain basically short-circuited. *Just say no.* But she couldn't. Colin was just tolerable enough that she didn't want to insult him.

"Actually, Elisa promised her mother she'd be available whenever she needed her," Charlene lied. "Family stuff, you understand."

"Oh, I wouldn't keep her long."

"Still, Alejandra's word is law."

"That it is," Colin chuckled.

"I would be happy to dance with you, though," Charlene said, taking his hand.

"Right this way, then."

Charlene cast a glance over her shoulder to Elisa as she went.

Thank you, she mouthed.

Charlene smiled back.

Best friend ever.

Elisa glanced around. Julieta was still talking to Bobby, and she could tell that she was already enamored. Her mother was making small talk with his mother and, judging by the look on Darcy's face, doing a crap job at it. *Should I go over there and help her out? Or should I keep avoiding Darcy like a coward?*

Then she found Maria, Camila, and Lucia.

Coward, it is.

Her three younger sisters were by the snack table and the string quartet, and each was causing a scene in her own unique way.

Maria was talking to the violinist and was giving him a lecture on what he *should* be playing in lieu of the covers of popular love songs he had been hired to play. Camila was hitting on a waiter who was about twice her age, and she was failing miserably, judging from the amused pity on his face.

Lucia had found the Jell-O shots. *Oh. Hell. No.*

"What the hell kind of wedding has Jell-O shots?" Elisa muttered to herself, arriving just in time to stop Lucia from taking a drink. She snatched the shot glass out of her hand and chucked it into the nearest trash can.

"*Heyyy*," Lucia protested.

"You're underage," she snapped.

"I can handle one little drink."

"Yeah, that's what you told Papa at the last work Christmas party he took us to. And we all know how *that* turned out. And you—" She whirled around, grabbing Camila and dragging her away from the waiter, who very wisely took the opportunity to escape.

"Stop flirting with people who are *working*. It's rude." She then rounded on Maria, who was clearly enjoying watching her two younger sisters get lectured. "And *you*. You do not make requests at a wedding. The music is chosen by the couple, not some girl they don't know who just showed up."

All three of her sisters were glaring at her, though Camila had the decency to look at least a little embarrassed.

"Every time I turn my back on you three..." Elisa massaged her forehead, wishing either Charlene or Julieta were here to give her some backup. Lord knew her mother wouldn't be much help. "Can we please get through one social gathering where you don't embarrass the family?"

"You mean, where we don't embarrass *you*," Maria muttered.

"I heard that," she said sharply.

"You were supposed to."

"Just—" She sputtered for a moment, trying to think of something that would occupy their time and wouldn't cause a huge scene, but that they'd also agree to. Which was, in her experience, like trying to find a girl in Steventon who was also into girls, and who she could actually stand the thought of dating. That was the problem with living in such a tight-knit community—there were only so many lesbians to go around. "Just…go eavesdrop on Julieta and Bobby, okay? Mom will want updates. And be discreet."

Camila, Maria, and Lucia all ran off, then, unable to resist the chance to spy on their elder sister's love life. They pretended to read the drinks menu, leaning in to try and overhear what Bobby was saying to Julieta.

If this is them trying to be discreet, I might actually cry.

Finally, after a few minutes, Bobby got up from the table, and headed toward the snack table, where she stood. For a second, she thought he was coming to speak to her, but then she realized he was looking to her left.

Darcy.

Um. Nope.

She ducked behind the nearest tree, hoping she could just stand there until Darcy and Bobby left.

Yep. Super-mature, super-smooth. That's me.

"Darcy, you haven't spoken to anyone all night," Bobby was saying.

"And are you really so cruel as to make me break my streak now?" Darcy said.

"Come on, you must be getting lonely."

"I prefer my own company over that of anyone else. You know that."

"Even mine? Or your sister's?"

Darcy didn't say anything.

"Everyone's having a good time. I'm not saying you have to make a new friend, but I wouldn't want you sulking all by yourself."

"I am not *sulking*. I am brooding while in the vicinity of others. It's a completely different thing."

Elisa clapped a hand over her mouth to keep the laugh in. When she peeked back out, the corner of Bobby's mouth was quirking up in a repressed grin.

"Well, would it kill you to brood in the vicinity of someone you can talk to?"

"It might," she insisted.

"Why don't you go hang out with that Colin guy? He's your cousin, right?"

"We have never gotten along. If we talk now, there may very well be a brawl at this wedding," Darcy said. "Is that what you *want*?"

Elisa disliked them both so much, she wasn't sure who she'd even root for. She was willing to bet Darcy could pick Colin up and toss him like a ragdoll, though. A light breeze probably could've knocked him over.

Bobby let out a sigh. "Okay...what about that Elisa? Julieta's sister?"

"What about her?" There was now a layer of ice coating her tone.

"You said you have a class with her, right? That's at least something to talk about."

"Look, Bobby—I know you mean well, but I also know you want to get back to Julieta. Don't stay here and fuss over me. You've found the only pretty girl in this town, so there's no point in trying to get me to find one. Elisa is...fine, I suppose, but not nearly enough to sway me. And her other sisters have been causing problems all night. Do you know I saw one of them arguing with the violinist about what to play? And that's not even getting started on their mother. Basic manners seem to escape them. I can hardly imagine Elisa is much better."

"Darcy, come on. I've been talking to Julieta all night, and she's great."

"Well, congratulations. You found the only normal one."

Her jaw clenched as her hand curled into a fist, nails digging into her palm.

Nice to meet you, too, Darcy. Welcome to Steventon, enjoy your stay. Asshole.

He sighed. "Fine. Suit yourself," he said.

"I'll be headed home soon. Don't feel obligated to leave when I do."

It's a good thing *she* left. Elisa may not have been able to hold her temper much longer. Who was Darcy to criticize *her* family? Sure, Elisa had given her sisters an earful for being rude, but she was their sister. That was her *job*. Darcy was just some random girl who didn't know them.

And I'm fine. Ugh.

Unclenching her fists, Elisa sighed and shook her head. Darcy was not going to ruin this night for her. She was going to have a good time if it *killed* her.

And, honestly, it probably would.

Chapter Three

In Which Elisa Spends an Entire Party Sulking

An after-wedding party at Colin Burger's was not Elisa's idea of fun. But she wasn't ready to go home. Bobby invited Julieta out for drinks with him, and she'd accepted, which meant their mother wouldn't talk about anything else until she fell asleep—which, since she was hopped up on cake, wasn't likely to be any time before midnight.

Even if Elisa went to bed, she'd still have to hear about it. It was a small apartment, and her mother's voice tended to carry. She was glad Bobby turned out to be nice. Julieta's blush said it all. Her sister was happy and excited.

But that didn't mean Elisa wanted to listen to their mom talk about it for hours.

So when Colin invited Charlene and the remaining Benitez sisters to his apartment in Hunsford, the token "rich but not as rich as Netherfield Park" neighborhood, she agreed. Her mother had been skeptical about Elisa and her sisters being out so late but had relented as soon as she found out that some of the handsome, single groomsmen would be in attendance, too. The possibility her daughters might meet a future husband was all the encouragement her mother needed.

"This is going to be so much freaking fun," Lucia said, practically bouncing off the walls of the minivan after the girls dropped Mom off at Longbourn Apartments. They'd left with the promise they'd be home by one a.m., which left them with a solid three hours to spend at Colin's party. Elisa just hoped Mom would be asleep by the time they got home.

"Remember, we're all underage, so no drinking," Elisa said, reminding herself just as much as anyone. Only because she had to stay in control if she wanted to watch out for her sisters. "Colin will probably have some liquor there, but if anyone offers, say, *no*."

"Jeez, do you ever stop nagging?" Lucia asked.

"She only nags because she cares about you," Charlene chimed in from the passenger seat. Elisa gave her a smile.

"You don't have to worry about us, Elisa," Camila said, leaning forward to talk to her. "We'll be fine, honest."

"I'll always worry about you," she said, now allowing a hint of fondness into her voice. "Even when you're married with three kids."

Elisa had never been to Colin's place before, but she assumed his parents were paying for it. He was in school full-time, and he never stopped posting about it. If he'd had a job, she definitely would've heard by now. He posted about every part of his life, which was almost as boring as hers.

She was surprised by how nice the apartments were. Unlike the McMansions in Netherfield Park, she could see herself living in one of these…in a parallel universe where she had money.

Colin answered the door when they reached his apartment, and he hugged them. Lucia and Camila didn't seem to mind.

"Thanks for inviting us," Camila said. "Here I thought the party was over."

"I'm always happy to have people here," Colin said, ushering them in. Elisa could see the kitchen and into living room, with about a dozen people scattered throughout. Most of them were wearing bridesmaids' dresses or groomsmen's suits, with drinks in hand.

While Colin droned on and on about the virtues of his apartment, he'd taken the girls' coats and hung them up, and offered them all drinks. Elisa was glad that he at least had the good sense to offer them Coke and juice. Colin was underage, too, for another few months, so the booze must have come with the bridesmaids.

After listening to him for ten minutes straight, though, she wished he'd offered anything that would dull the throbbing in her head.

"Thanks," Elisa said, taking a can of orange soda from him.

"This place is beautiful," Charlene said, interrupting Colin. Finally.

Of course, Catherine Burger, Colin's mother, would put her little boy up in the nicest apartment she could find. His older sister Anna was currently living the dream in a London penthouse, on her parents' dime. The Burgers were seriously rich, though Elisa had never known how. *Maybe* his father did something with the stock market, but she wouldn't swear to it.

He was related to Darcy.

Why am I even thinking about her? Wrong. So wrong. Anger twisted in her gut.

"E, are you okay?" Charlene asked, nudging Elisa. "You look like you're mad about something."

"Let's find a seat, and I'll tell you," Elisa said. "I overheard Darcy and Bobby talking back at the wedding."

They found a seat on the huge windowsill overlooking the street below. Charlene sipped a wine cooler, since she wouldn't be driving and, allegedly, didn't have work the next day. Eyebrows raised, she waited for Elisa to tell her what she'd heard.

And she did, relaying the entire conversation. She hadn't meant to get so worked up over it, but by the time she finished...

"I mean, can you *believe* her?" she finally snapped, crumpling up her soda can in her hand. "She barely even knows us, and she's already made up her mind to hate us."

Charlene looked amused. "You really want to talk about someone making snap judgements, Elisa?"

"Oh, come on," she said. "I decided I hate Darcy because she's a snob. She decided she hates me because... because my sisters are idiots. It's *totally* different."

"They *were* being pretty rude. Not—not that I agree with Darcy," Charlene hastily added when Elisa glared at her. "I'm just saying. She doesn't know them as well as we do. She doesn't know that they're not always that bad."

"She doesn't want to get to know them. That's the problem."

"Well, did you want to get to know *her* after that first day of class?"

"Well—*no*, but—"

"I'm not saying she isn't ridiculous. But you're getting awfully worked up over basically nothing. I mean, you don't even like Darcy, so who cares what she thinks?"

"I care, because she was badmouthing us to Bobby."

"Since when do you care what he thinks?"

"Since I realized Julieta actually likes him."

Charlene sighed. "Fair enough," she admitted. "Well, if he likes her back, he won't let Darcy screw it up."

Elisa shrugged, fingers playing with the fabric of her

skirt. "I dunno. I mean, Bobby said they're best friends. Those opinions matter. I'd ask for your opinion before I got serious with anybody."

"And I'd always do the same with you," Charlene said. "But first impressions can be misleading. He seems like a smart guy. He'll look past it if he really likes her."

"I hope you're right."

"I'm *always* right."

"Don't get ahead of yourself, Miss Locke," Elisa said, smirking.

Before Charlene could reply, Colin forced himself in between the two.

"How are you two enjoying the party?"

How would we know, we've only been here five minutes. "It's great, Colin. Thanks again for inviting us out."

"I am always delighted to be in your company, Elisa. And yours, too, Charlene, of course. But, Elisa—I feel that even though we essentially grew up together, we don't spend that much time one-on-one."

I'm thinking he doesn't understand the reason for that. "I suppose we don't," Elisa said, barely keeping her tone nice.

"I'd like to change that."

Oh no.

"Elisa, I was wondering if you'd ever be open to the idea of having dinner with me."

Charlene took this as her cue to leave, saying something about needing another drink.

Thanks, bestie.

"Uh—Colin. That's, uh…that's really nice of you to offer," she said, "but I am just…so busy with school right now. The semester just started, and I'm in all these clubs." She wasn't in a single one. "I barely have time for Charlene, let alone…"

"Oh. I—I understand. Maybe some other time, then." For

the first time in years, Colin seemed to be without words, and he looked downcast, though he was clearly trying to hide it.

Feeling a tiny pang of sympathy, Elisa said, "But thanks again for offering. That's very sweet."

Colin nodded, attempting a smile, which was more of a smirk. "Well...have a good night, Elisa. I better go check on my other guests... A host never gets to stop and enjoy his own party."

As he left, Charlene returned, sitting next to Elisa again. "Well, he wasn't crying, at least not here," she said. "I take it you let him down easy?"

Elisa nodded. "I mean, it's nice that he's interested, I guess. I don't hate him or anything."

"Ringing endorsement."

"Well, you *know* how he can be."

"Yeah, I do," Charlene said. "Honestly, I'm kind of surprised it hadn't happened sooner. I think he's been thinking about it for a couple months, at least."

Elisa groaned, running a hand through her black hair. "Don't...don't tell Mom I turned him down, okay?"

"What kind of fool do you take me for?"

Colin had always been persistent in befriending Elisa, but in the past few months, he'd become much harder than usual to avoid. He'd popped over to the apartment "just to say hello," and had messaged her and commented on all her social media posts far more often than he used to. He'd also invited her to almost every event he'd hosted. It had taken Elisa a while (and Charlene interfering) to figure out what the sudden extra attention was about, but once she did, she took every precaution to keep her *mother* from figuring it out, too. Mom also thought Colin was annoying, but she'd be willing to overlook that if he showed interest in one of her daughters. His bank account could make up for almost anything, as far as she was concerned. Elisa didn't see it that way. No doubt that whoever Colin wound up with would have a very comfortable life and would probably be able to go on all sorts of fun, exciting vacations and live in a huge, expensive city, with all the fast cars and fancy clothes their heart desired. But the price for all that would be actually putting up with him 24/7. No amount of money was worth that.

The apartment was huge, so even though there were at least thirty people in attendance, it didn't feel too crowded. The music drowned out almost all conversation from Elisa's standpoint, and it was easy to lose track of time as she sat there, chatting with Charlene about everything from the wedding to Charlene's soul-sucking job. Before she knew it, they'd been sitting there talking for almost a full hour.

"Hey, where are your sisters?"

Crap.

"Hell," she muttered. "I'll be right back, Char."

She quickly searched the rest of the apartment. It was like herding cats every time they went out together, and her sisters had a way of leaving chaos behind.

I love them. But sometimes I wish someone else was the prison warden.

Maria and Camila were sitting in the room Colin referred to as the lounge, chatting with a couple of bridesmaids from the wedding. When Elisa asked, "Where's Lulu?" Camila and Maria only had shrugs, but one of the bridesmaids piped up.

"She's the tall, skinny one with pink streaks in her hair, right?"

"Right," Elisa said. "You've seen her?"

"I think Jamie was talking to her in the kitchen."

"Thanks," she said, hurrying off, not bothering to ask who Jamie was. Whoever he was, Elisa was willing to bet that Lucia was way too young to be talking to him.

She was right. She found Lucia and Jamie, who was, as

it turned out, one of the groomsmen—and one of Elisa's classmates. They were in the spare bedroom, making out on the bed. *I'm going to murder her.* Elisa charged in, turning on the light and shouted, "Stop." Other than Jamie's jacket, which was laying on a chair, they both seemed to have all their clothes on.

At least there's that.

"Elisa—" Lucia was blushing furiously, pushing some hair out of her eyes. "You could knock."

"Oh, hey, Elisa," Jamie said, clearly not getting why Elisa was upset. "I didn't know you two knew each other."

"She's my sister," Elisa said, putting her hands on her hips. "My *fourteen-year-old* sister."

Jamie went paper-white, and jumped up from the bed, grabbing his jacket and quickly saying, "I'll see you in class, Elisa. Lucia, delete my number from your phone, please," he said in one breath before hurrying out.

"We're going home," Elisa said. She grabbed Lucia by the arm and forced her to her feet. "Once Mom hears about this, you won't be allowed to leave the apartment for a month."

"Please don't tell her," Lucia pleaded, trying to force her wrist out of Elisa's grasp. "We were just having fun."

"You are too young for *that* kind of fun. Especially with a guy *that* age. Lucia—those laws exist for a reason."

"Age is just a number."

"Yeah, and jail is just a room." Elisa let go of her wrist to bring her hand up to her forehead, massaging it. Her head hurt. "Lulu, you *need* to stick to guys your own age. For your own good, and everyone else's. Jamie could've gotten into serious trouble if you two had done anything."

"Guys my own age suck."

"I guarantee, the kind of adult man that would do that with a fourteen-year-old girl sucks *way* more. The only excuse is that you didn't tell him how old you were."

Lucia crossed her arms, raising her chin in defiance. "I'm mature for my age."

"First of all—no, you're not. Second of all—if it was maturity they were interested in, they'd be going for women their own age. Not *children*."

"I am not a—"

"Yes, you are. Legally, mentally, and in all other aspects. You are a child. So *be* a child. You don't have to pretend you're this mature, experienced adult when you're not. There's nothing wrong with just being fourteen."

"You always said you *hated* being fourteen," Lucia said.

"Yeah, but I still had to go through it. And so do you. No amount of drinking or hooking up with older guys will change that."

Lucia glanced away, lip trembling slightly. Elisa sighed.

If she thinks she can start crying and soften me up, then she is…totally, completely, 100 percent right. God dammit.

"Okay. That's my lecture. I won't tell Mom about this," she said. Lucia looked up, then, meeting her eyes for the first time since she had walked in. "But please think about what I said. You shouldn't be in any rush to grow up—and this isn't the way to go about it."

Lucia didn't respond right away, tearing her gaze away once more. "I'll think about it," she said quietly.

"Thank you." She let out a sigh. "I'm just doing this because I want to keep you safe, Lulu. You know that, right?"

"Yeah. I know."

Elisa smiled and wrapped an arm around her sister's shoulders. "C'mon. Let's find Char and the others and get out of here."

• • •

Tiptoeing past the room where Mom slept, the Benitez sisters hurried off to bed. Lucia had gone into her section of the living room, unusually quiet, while Camila and Maria slipped into the room they shared. Elisa was last, locking the front door behind them, before going into the room that she shared with Julieta. As she expected, the other bed was empty.

She had nearly drifted off to sleep when Julieta returned an hour and a half later, quietly slipping into the room and preparing for bed. She was humming a love song that she had heard on the radio approximately six thousand times that week.

"Jules," she whispered, "I was wondering when you'd get back."

"Oh, did I wake you? I'm sorry, I didn't mean…"

"You didn't." Elisa sat up. "How was it?"

She was beaming, looking bashfully down at her feet. "It was great. He's so sweet. He gave me a ride home and even kissed me before letting me out."

Elisa grinned. "A kiss on the first date? Why, Julieta Benitez, you skank," she said playfully.

Her sister blushed, shaking her head as she laughed. "Oh no, no, it…it was very G-rated, just on the cheek. I don't think this even counted as a date. But," she added, "he did give me his phone number and email, and he told me to add him on social media."

"So, do you think there's something there?"

Julieta nodded. "I do. I really do."

She paused. "How can you tell?"

Her sister ran her fingers through her hair, a smile still playing around her lips. "I can't explain it. It just felt like—like the more we talked, the more it felt like we've always known each other. And there weren't any awkward pauses, or any moments where I said something and then was immediately like, 'Why did I say that?' We just *clicked*, you know? I mean, yeah, *maybe* it was the alcohol, but I really don't think so.

I know you hate to give Mom the satisfaction, but…maybe there's actually a future for Bobby and me."

"Don't tell him that," she advised. "Guys are notorious flight risks."

"I won't. I'd like to keep him around for a while."

"I'm glad. G'night, Jules."

"Good night, Elisa."

She rolled over and tried to fall back asleep, listening as her sister's breaths became soft and steady. As her eyes closed again, she thought about what Julieta had described. She'd heard of that sort of thing before, of course, but she'd never known it to actually happen in real life—until now.

She was happy for her sister. So, so happy—Jules deserved this more than anybody else she knew. But she couldn't help but feel a twinge of jealousy.

When's it my turn?

Chapter Four

*In Which the Benitez Sisters (and Charlene) Crash a
Birthday Party*

Elisa had gotten used to her and Darcy being the first ones to
arrive at British Lit every Monday and Wednesday. Normally,
her strategy was to ignore her, but after what she'd overheard
at the wedding, she couldn't just sit there and say nothing.

"Hello, sunshine," she said, as Darcy took her usual seat
at the end of their row. The professor didn't technically keep
a seating chart, but everyone stuck to the chairs they'd picked
on the first day of class, anyway. "Decided to come to school
with the rabble?"

"Why so sarcastic this morning?" she asked, not looking
at her as she searched for something in her bag. "And you
should know that being passive-aggressive doesn't suit you."

Elisa felt her jaw tighten. She sucked in a sharp breath,
before forcing her voice to come out even. "I heard what you
were saying to Bobby about me and my family. And, frankly,
I don't appreciate it."

Darcy's fidgeted in her chair. "Do you often eavesdrop

on private conversations?"

"I don't know, do you often make fun of people you barely know?"

"I wasn't making fun of you. I was…observing."

"Well, maybe keep your *observations* to yourself. People might start thinking you're a stuck-up jerk."

She didn't say anything and refused to meet her eye. That was good enough for Elisa. She'd planned on being snarky all day—maybe all week—but there was one thing Darcy was right about: being passive-aggressive really *didn't* suit her.

As it got closer to time for class to start, other students began to trickle in, Jamie among them. The second he and Elisa caught each other's gaze, he went scarlet. She only met him with *the look*, which she'd inherited from her mother. He looked away, mumbling out a "good morning" before dashing to his seat, which was safely on the other side of the room.

Darcy's eyes flicked from her to Jamie and back again. "What was that about?" she murmured, scooting her chair closer.

"Nothing."

"You looked about ready to rip his head off. That doesn't seem like nothing."

"Just…he was with one of my sisters last night—I mean, I got there before anything could happen." *Why am I telling her this? We're not friends.*

She frowned. "Not Julieta?"

"No, no." She shook her head. "She was with Bobby. It was, um, it was Lucia." When Darcy's eyes widened and she sat up, opening her mouth to speak, Elisa continued. "I mean, in his defense, he didn't realize how old she is. When I told him, he ran off right away."

The tension dropped out of her shoulders. "I'm assuming that's the only reason he went home with his balls still attached?"

A snort erupted from her before she could stop herself, and she clapped a hand over her mouth. Poor Jamie must have heard and been able to guess what they were talking about, because he just blushed harder and sank lower into his seat.

Fighting a smile, she said, "You're damn right it is."

Darcy wasn't smiling back, but something in her eyes had softened. "Well, if you change your mind about sparing him, let me know. I might be able to provide some assistance."

"Don't tell me. You have a hitman on your payroll."

"No. I have a *dozen* hitmen. I mean, what am I? Poor?"

She said it with such a straight face that Elisa couldn't stop herself from laughing. Even with the snobbery, she was actually pretty funny. Maybe that was why Bobby liked her. Or maybe it was just the fact that they'd known each other for so long.

Nah, that can't be it. I've known Colin for years, and he still drives me insane.

If Bobby and Julieta worked out, then that meant Darcy would be around to drive her insane for a long, long time.

Now there's *a cheerful thought.*

• • •

As Elisa predicted, Mom was over the moon that Julieta and Bobby had hit it off. She had hoped that this would be enough to get her to stop worrying for a little while, and just let things run their own course. Which only proved that she truly was an idealist at heart. A total of thirty-six hours passed before Mom went right back to obsessing over Julieta's love life.

Elisa honestly didn't know what she'd expected.

"It's been too long," she was saying to Elisa as the two of them did laundry one evening. The laundry room at Longbourn was dim, claustrophobic, and smelled like a combination of old soap and cigarette smoke. Elisa couldn't help but wonder how clean their clothes were *really* getting. "Why hasn't she seen him yet?"

"They've been IM'ing basically nonstop," Elisa pointed out in an attempt to placate her.

"IM'ing is not the same. They need to be face-to-face. She needs to wear that sexy little number I got her for her last birthday—"

"That's why you got her that dress?"

"—and she needs to up the ante if she wants to trap him."

"Your concern would be a lot more touching if you didn't make it sound like she was planning to *eat* him."

"This is the twenty-first century, Elisa. Women can trap men if they want to. It's feminism."

"I...I am one hundred percent sure that's not what feminism is."

Mom slammed the washing machine lid shut. "I swear, if Julieta just took my advice, she'd have him, hook, line, and sinker by the end of the month."

"Mama, I want them together, too, but I don't think rushing it is the solution. Romance works best if it's left to do its own thing."

"That statement, Elisa, is proof you know nothing about love," she said, heading for the door.

Elisa didn't like that glint in her eye. Her mother was planning on being clever again. And when Alejandra Bello decided to be clever, things at home usually became *much* more complicated.

. . .

Saturday was typically the only day Julieta allowed herself to relax.

Their mom had other ideas.

"Julieta, dear, have you seen Bobby lately?" she asked. Elisa immediately looked up from her book. Mom knew perfectly well that Julieta hadn't seen him yet. They all did. *What is she playing at?*

"Not since the wedding, Mama. But we've been texting a lot," Julieta said, repeating the same thing she'd been telling her mother all week.

"Have you thought about what you'd say if you were to bump into him someplace?"

"What do you mean?" Now she looked nervous.

Mom went to sit in between her daughters on the couch, taking Julieta's hands into her own.

"I'm just saying, it's always good to think ahead. Like, suppose, for instance, you ran into him while at a fancy restaurant, in your best dress and highest heels, looking even lovelier than normal. He'd, of course, be too stunned to talk, so it'd be up to you to do the talking. It couldn't hurt to have a game plan."

Julieta looked about as suspicious as Elisa felt. "When do I *ever* go to fancy restaurants?" she asked.

"Maybe you should start," Mom said, as if Julieta had been the one to think of it. "Hell, start tonight. You've been working so hard on that business of yours that you deserve it. Why not check out that new restaurant on Fourth? It's called Eclipse, isn't it?"

"Mom," Julieta said slowly, "what are you up to?"

She finally dropped the act and leaned in close. "Darling, Bobby will be at Eclipse tonight with some friends and family. I was thinking it couldn't hurt if you were to...spontaneously run into him."

Elisa and Julieta both responded at once, Elisa saying, "You've officially reached a new level of nuts," at the same time Julieta exclaimed, "*Mom.*"

"Just think of this as an excellent opportunity, Julieta."

"An opportunity to what, provoke a restraining order?" Elisa asked. Her mom smacked her in the stomach without even turning around.

"Mom—I don't think…" Julieta began saying, but Mom cut her off.

"Jules, I know you're worried about being too forward, but nothing ever happens in this world if you don't take the initiative. You wouldn't have your business; Elisa wouldn't be working toward a college degree; Lucia wouldn't hold the current Steventon High record for 'most times of being sent to the office without actually getting detention.' Initiative is a powerful, powerful thing."

"Mom, I can't just *show up* where Bobby is. That's not taking initiative, that's stalking." Suddenly, she frowned. "How'd you even know where he'd be tonight?"

Mom looked away.

"You dug through his social media *again*?" Julieta cried. "Mom, you *promised*. No more cyberstalking."

"Well, I had to do something," Mom huffed. "If you had your way, you'd still be flirting over Instagram captions in a year."

"Mom, I'm twenty-two. I'm an adult. I can handle my own relationships."

"If you're an adult, why do you still live at home?"

Julieta flushed, clearly hurt, but said nothing. Elisa felt her jaw tighten, and her next words flew out before she had a chance to consider them.

"Mom, that is *beyond* not fair, and you know it. Julieta's working, she pays for the groceries at least half the time, she helps pay the bills, *and* she's trying to save up as much as she can," she said. "If she could move out, she *would*. Besides, she's working on much more important things than winning over some guy."

"Robert Charles is not just *some guy*. Jules really likes

him, isn't that right?"

Julieta wasn't meeting either of their gazes. "I do," she admitted, "but...Mom, you know I love you, but you can be a bit...single-minded when it comes to marriage. And yeah, I want to get married one day, but there's more to life than that."

"Well...well, of course there is, but...Julieta, this is about your happiness. Money or no money, I wouldn't approve of that man if I didn't think he was a good match for you. You know that."

"Yeah. It's just...well...sometimes you can be a bit... pushy. In the best way," she hastily added, seeing her mother's jaw set.

Elisa shifted uncomfortably as they fell into silence. Small arguments and disagreements were common in their family, but it was rare that anyone—least of all Julieta—was that blunt with Mom.

Most of the time, it felt like all of them against the world.

But sometimes, it became the Benitez sisters against their mother. And it was not a nice feeling.

Mom looked between the two of them and let out a sigh. "I'm just saying that if things work out between you and Bobby..."

"We haven't even been on a date," Julieta said. "Not a proper one, anyway."

"Then it's time to get to your first proper date," she said. "Come on, what's the harm in trying? It's not like he'll have any reason to suspect you planned it. The worst that could happen is he'll just say 'hi' before going back to his own table. At least you'll get a nice meal out of it."

"A nice, *expensive* meal," Julieta pointed out. Then, she sighed. "You're not gonna let this go, are you?"

"Nope."

Julieta squeezed her eyes shut. "Okay, fine, I'll go," she

whispered, as if the words were physically painful to say.

Mom beamed at her, jumping up from the couch. "I knew you'd see it my way," she said, looking very proud of herself. "I'm going to go pick out some options for what you can wear."

She ran off to Julieta and Elisa's bedroom, looking like a kid rushing to the Christmas tree.

"I can't believe you let that happen," Elisa said, mostly pitying, but also kind of snickering. "You used your Assertive Voice and everything."

"I *know*," she groaned, burying her face in her hands. "This is gonna suck." She looked up. "Could you come with me? And maybe Charlene, too. That'll make me feel slightly less like a stalker...and if Bobby doesn't want to hang out, at least I'll have someone else to talk to."

She shrugged apologetically. "I'd like to, but Char and I are both broke."

"I'll pay," she offered.

"Are you sure? Eclipse is expensive, even for just one person."

Julieta bit her lip. "If we all drink water and just get appetizers..."

Lucia flew out from behind the divider that separated her room from the rest of the living room. Elisa groaned a little bit. She hadn't been aware she was even home—and, judging from the look on her face, Julieta hadn't either.

"I'll totally help foot the bill, sis," she said, jumping up onto the couch.

"Uh, who invited you?" Elisa asked.

"Oh, come on, you can't have a girls' night without me." She pouted.

"It's not a girls' night, it's Mom's latest ridiculous matchmaking scheme."

"Uh, since when were those mutually exclusive?

Remember our last spring break?"

Elisa was suddenly haunted by memories of the trash-littered beach they'd visited, the sound of her mother encouraging Julieta to pretend to drown in plain view of the handsome lifeguard, and the nauesating, inescapable smell of the peach schnapps her older sister had gotten sick on.

In spite of how objectively horrific the whole thing was, though, it had actually been kinda fun.

"Okay, good point. But you're not going."

"Jules," Lucia said in her sweetest voice, "if you let me go, I'll split the bill with you. I'm totes loaded right now. I just won a hundred dollars off of Nadine in a bet. She thought that I was exaggerating when I said I don't have a gag reflex—but guess what?"

"How did you even prove—ugh, wait, no," Elisa said, shaking her head. "Eclipse is super-expensive, Lulu. You'd probably end up spending a sizable chunk of that...hard-earned cash."

"But I've wanted to check out Eclipse for forever."

"It's only been open a month."

"Yeah, and I've wanted to check it out for that whole month. Ergo, *forever*."

Julieta looked like she was thinking very hard. "Okay, fine, you can come, too. But no alcohol—not a *drop*. And no talking to older guys. You can hang out with us, and with Bobby and his family if Mom's plan actually works."

Lucia grinned. "Deal," she said, and she and Julieta shook on it.

· · ·

"I feel like I've been tricked, somehow." Julieta sighed as Maria and Camila got into the minivan after Lucia, Elisa, and Charlene.

"You got Lucia'd," Elisa said. "It happens to the best of us."

After Julieta had relented and said Lucia could tag along, she had run off and told Camila about the planned girls' night. And then Camila had wanted to come, too. Lucia, of course, said that she wasn't about to go on a girls' night without her "most favorite older sister and number-one BFF." Julieta had caved, as always. And then, Maria had found out about the plan, and even Elisa had to agree that taking the other two but not her would just be unfair.

"Now have fun, and remember, Julieta—you were blessed with the Bello beauty gene, so use it where it really counts," their mother said, reaching into the window to smooth Julieta's hair one last time.

"Yes, Mama," Julieta said.

"And remember to text as soon as you're there," Mom said to the car in general. "Gotta keep tabs on my babies."

"Yes, ma'am," the entire car responded.

Julieta started the engine and they were off, headed toward Eclipse.

"I'm glad *my* sister didn't catch wind of this," Charlene chuckled, buckling her seatbelt.

"I wish she had," Elisa sighed. Molly Locke, Charlene's sister, was Lucia's age, and actually acted like it. Her days were spent watching anime and getting into arguments over her favorite TV shows on Tumblr, which could be annoying in its own way, but at least no one was at risk. Elisa lived in pretty much constant fear that Lucia would one day go too far, and someone would get hurt. Molly was a good influence on Lucia, but her little sister called Molly "too vanilla."

"So, let's be real. Am I gonna be able to afford anything at this restaurant?" Charlene asked, pulling her carrot-orange hair back into a bun. This was one of the few times outside of work that Elisa had ever seen her wear makeup.

Eclipse was one of those places where looking like a normal, tired, overworked person was *not* an option. All of the girls had worn their best party dresses, and Elisa had even allowed Lucia and Camila to do her makeup. Or, more accurately, attack her face with eyeliner and lipstick. They did a beautiful job, but they were not gentle about it.

"God only knows. Julieta said she and Lucia could foot the bill, though."

Charlene shook her head. "I could never ask her to do that."

"You didn't ask. She offered."

"I just don't feel comfortable letting Julieta spend that kind of money on me," she said.

"Suit yourself," Elisa said, sighing at her friend's stubbornness.

The valet at Eclipse's parking lot did a double take at the maroon minivan the girls rolled up in. But still, he took the keys from Julieta and left the six of them standing on the curb in front of the restaurant. Well, half restaurant. The other half was more like a nightclub, from what Elisa could see through the glass doors and tall, clear windows. There was a DJ and a dance floor and even some strobe lights. The windows shook ever so slightly from the music inside, the bassline audible even from out here.

It was also packed to the walls.

"How on Earth are we even supposed to get in?" Maria asked as they made their way inside.

"Just let Jules handle it," Elisa said, pulling out her phone to text her mother.

Just got inside. It's crowded as all hell in here. See you at home later. xoxo —E

Just as she slipped her phone back into her purse, Julieta made her way to the hostess.

"Hello, may we, uh, get a table, please?" she asked, shouting to be heard.

"Do you have a reservation?" the hostess asked.

She looked like she'd swallowed something sour, and even Elisa paused for a second, caught off-guard. Of *course,* they needed a reservation. The place had just opened. They were probably booked until Christmas. She wasn't sure who she was angrier with for not thinking of that—her mother, or herself.

"Um...check under 'Benitez,'" Julieta said, trying to save face. She paused, then added, "Or 'Bello.'" Maybe her mother had thought ahead and called them.

The hostess typed on her computer, then looked back up at her, shaking her head sympathetically. "I'm sorry, I'm not finding anything. When did you call? Maybe the computer deleted your reservation by mistake."

Julieta was about to bite the bullet and admit they had no reservation when the clouds parted, and the sun shined through the storm.

Or, in layman's terms—when Bobby walked out into the lobby, on his phone.

"Okay, ma'am, can you hear me now?" he was saying. "Yeah, I just had to step out. Now why were you calling? What? *No,* I don't need a coupon for a massage. Yes, I'm sure. I'm sure. Thank you. Thank you. I'm sure. Goodbye."

He hung up and was just about to head back in when he saw the group.

"Julieta," he said, looking delighted. He walked over and pecked her on the cheek.

"Hi, Bobby," she said, smiling despite the situation. "We were just trying to find a table, but..."

He thought quickly. "Oh, I'm sorry—I should've told you to ask them to look for a reservation under *my* name." He turned to the hostess. "They're with me—Charles."

Elisa could tell from the look on her face that the hostess knew perfectly well he was bullshitting. But she apparently decided it was more trouble than it was worth to argue, because she just smiled and said, "Okay, follow me. I'm so sorry for the confusion."

"Oh no, it was my fault," Julieta said, grinning at Bobby. As soon as the hostess was out of earshot, she said, "It's a good thing you got that phone call. What was it for, anyway?"

"Telemarketer," Bobby shrugged. "Offering some kind of promotion for a massage parlor."

Elisa frowned. "Did they say which one?" she asked.

"Uh… Massages by Cassandra, I think."

Elisa and Charlene exchanged exasperated glances. *That figures.* Massages by Cassandra was where her mother worked. Of course Bobby just *happened* to get that call and have to step out into the lobby right after Elisa texted her mother to let her know they were there.

"I wonder what she was planning to do if he'd taken her up on the offer," Charlene whispered into Elisa's ear.

Elisa shrugged. "I don't think she was thinking of anything except how to get us in here."

"Not us. Julieta."

"I guess I can't knock the plan," Elisa admitted. "It *did* work."

Bobby took Julieta's hand into his own as they reached the table where Bobby's party was waiting. It was a long table against the back wall, but still with a clear view of the dance floor, and fortunately, there were just enough empty seats for the new additions to squeeze in. There was Bobby's mother, and his sisters, a few people Elisa had never met, and *Darcy*. With her comments from the wedding ringing in her ears, Elisa had to fight the urge to turn around and run away.

There was also Colin and his mother, Catherine, for some reason. She knew they were related to Darcy, but she didn't realize they knew Bobby, too.

Okay, if this is some cosmic joke, it's not funny.

Darcy and Colin both looked surprised to see Elisa, but while he smiled and got up from his seat to greet her, she slumped back in her own chair, looking uncomfortable.

"I wasn't aware you'd be joining us this evening," Colin said, hugging her as soon as he reached her.

"Neither were we," Elisa said.

Then he guided her to a chair between him and Darcy.

Oh. Joy.

"I'm surprised to see you Benitez girls in this restaurant," Catherine said. She always sounded like she smoked about a pack a day. "It seems so…sophisticated compared to what you're used to."

Elisa's jaw clenched, but she restrained herself from snapping back and causing a scene.

"We enjoy a nice meal in a nice club as much as anyone, Mrs. Burger," she said, barely keeping her tone even.

"Still, I wouldn't want you to break your bank account just to have a nice meal," she said, voice dripping with that faux concern that drove her crazy. "I don't imagine your mother makes what one could call a livable wage as a… *masseuse*."

"I think you and I just have different ideas of what constitutes a livable wage," Elisa said, her hands tightening into fists on her lap. She'd only seen Catherine Burger a handful of times in her life, and the woman had never failed to make her disdain for them known. The first time they'd met, Catherine had made a passive-aggressive comment toward her mom about "having more children than is fiscally responsible." The ensuing fight had led to Mom getting kicked off the PTA for throwing something at the vice president.

Elisa caught Darcy looking at her with a curious expression. If it was pity, she didn't want it. Just thinking about the idea of Darcy pitying her made her even angrier.

Colin spoke up before his mother had a chance. "The Benitez family has proven themselves many times to be quite resourceful with their money, Mother."

Huh. Okay. That was nice of him—score one point for the mama's boy.

Catherine gave Colin a look that probably could've killed a small animal.

He shifted uncomfortably in his seat, stumbling over his next words. "I—I'm just saying, I'm sure if Ms. Bello thinks they can afford to be here, it's all right. I mean, simply the arrangement of their apartment shows how ingenious they can be, being able to fit six people into such a small space—"

Elisa cut him off. "Y'know, tiny homes are the thing these days. Use fewer resources, gentler on the planet." Colin was trying to stick up for her, and she even appreciated it, a little, but she really didn't want him to get into the details of *how* tiny her apartment was.

"What's the occasion for you guys?" she asked. "My sisters and I—and Charlene, of course—are here celebrating Julieta's business doing so well."

Well, she *had* just celebrated her thirtieth client.

"It's Cora and Louise's birthday," Darcy said. "Bobby invited all his cousins and told me to invite mine, too, to 'balance it out.'" She huffed, fiddling with her napkin. "I wish Willow had been available."

Elisa flushed. "Oh. We—we didn't mean to crash a birthday party, we just—"

"Oh, there's always room for one more," Colin said brightly. "Or, you know, six more, as it were. Besides, Mother and I barely know the twins, either."

"And I suppose that if Bobby says it's okay, I'll have to make peace with the situation," Darcy muttered, taking a sip of her drink.

Elisa rolled her eyes, but Darcy didn't appear to notice.

The waiter came by, and Elisa ordered water and a relatively cheap appetizer, as did Julieta and the others, even after Bobby said he'd pay for them. Although it was nice of him to offer, and they would be smart to take him up on it, Elisa half hoped her sister would refuse. They might have been broke, but they still had some pride.

At the other end of the table, Julieta and Bobby were holding hands and talking only to one another, apparently forgetting that there were other people present. To be fair, if she were sitting next to Charlene, Elisa was sure she'd be doing the same thing. It was so easy to ignore everyone when you were talking to one of your favorite people on the planet.

Elisa was between two of the biggest annoyances in the known world.

Colin rambled about the latest project he was doing for his theology degree, going on in explicit and thorough detail and completely missing how everyone except his mother was utterly bored by the time he got through the first sentence.

Darcy hadn't said much, but she kept at Elisa. It wasn't one of her nasty looks, but she didn't exactly seem happy to have her there, either.

Elisa ate her food, pretending to listen to Colin, desperately wishing for the waiter to come by with the check, when she heard the DJ announce, "These next three songs are gonna slow us down a little bit, so grab your best girl—or best guy—and make your way to the dance floor for couples' dancing."

Julieta and Bobby rose to their feet, walking over to her end of the table.

"We're going to go dance," Bobby said. "Darcy, you want to come with us?"

"It's couples' dancing." Darcy's brown eyes flicked up to Bobby's face, and she made no move to get up. "I'm single. Ergo, I will not be joining you."

"Darcy, come on. You could find somebody to have a couple's dances with you."

"Doubtful."

Julieta chimed in. "Elisa, you could dance with her, couldn't you?"

Murdering a sibling—that's number one on my list when I get out of here.

She was about to say "no," but then she glanced on her other side. Colin was grinning at her. Wanting to avoid a repeat of the awkward moment at the wedding, Elisa took a deep breath and forced out, "Want to dance?" in Darcy's general direction.

She stared at her for a moment before saying, "Yes. Thank you."

Industrial lye is how you get rid of a body, right?

Figuring she may as well do this properly, Elisa got up, offering Darcy her hand, which was surprisingly warm. Darcy took it, standing up from the table and letting Elisa lead her out to the dance floor.

"I think you should lead. You're a head taller than me," Elisa said.

"I suppose I should."

The only dance Elisa had any knowledge of was the middle school slow dance: wrap your arms around your partner's neck and their arms around your waist, sway in place—and leave enough room between you that the chaperones won't write you up for inappropriate contact. Fortunately, Darcy seemed to know what she was doing, so Elisa more or less followed her lead.

"So…" Well, this was about as horrifically awkward as she'd expected. "Um…where are you from? I remember you said you just moved here."

"I grew up in Columbus. I still live there. But after Bobby bought his home in Netherfield, he offered to let me stay for a few months. I figured I might as well be doing something, so I enrolled in the college. But since we're only two hours from Columbus, I still go down to see my sister on the weekends sometimes."

"Oh," Elisa said. "I can't imagine being able to just visit someone for months. I'd be worried about overstaying my welcome."

"I've never had to worry about that with Bobby. He and I have been friends since I was a kid."

"Still, doesn't it feel a bit weird to live with someone for months on end?"

"Well, there are advantages to having a huge home."

"I guess so."

"But minimalism is very popular right now, and I'm with you about the tiny houses thing. My friend has a gorgeous one on the beach in Malibu."

That was…*so* not the same thing. "Cool." *Oh, whatever, you didn't need to impress her anyway.*

They fell into an uncomfortable silence, each avoiding looking at the other's face out of sheer awkwardness. Finally, Elisa cleared her throat and tried again.

"So, um…do you like it at the college? I know you said you were just trying to kill time, but…"

"Well, actually, I decided to go because one of the professors was a friend of my mother's," Darcy said. "It seemed a bit silly to take only one class, so I signed up for the literature course, too."

"Which professor?"

"Greer. He teaches philosophy. I'm in his Philosophy of Language course."

"Oh yeah, I've heard of that. I didn't even know freshmen could *take* that class." From what she'd heard, it was pretty advanced. She'd gotten confused just reading the course description online.

"Normally, no. But exceptions can be made."

"Like when the prof was your mom's friend?"

Darcy let out a small chuckle. "Yeah. Like then."

They fell back into awkward silence.

"Do you like dancing?" Elisa finally asked.

"No."

"Oh."

"There are countless other ways I'd prefer to be spending my time."

Now Elisa was getting irritated. "You know, you didn't have to say yes."

"You didn't have to ask."

"I was trying to be nice."

"So was I. I thought that was what we're doing right now. Trying to be nice."

They had stopped moving and just stood on the edge of the dance floor, eyes locked.

"Well, 'nice' usually involves making conversation instead of making the other person do all the work," Elisa said.

Darcy looked surprised. "I have been making conversation. I've been answering your questions."

Elisa rolled her eyes. "It's not my job to explain basic people skills to you," she said.

"If you want to discuss basic people skills, how about the fact that you and your sisters and your friend showed up to a party uninvited?"

Elisa flushed. "Bobby invited us to sit with him. It's just a coincidence that we were here when you were."

"Forgive me for assuming, but crashing a party aligns perfectly with the impression of your family that I got at Hannah's wedding."

"First impressions can be misleading," was all Elisa could think of in response. Even though what Darcy was saying was the absolute truth, she would not allow her to run her mouth. Only *she* was allowed to say mean, accurate things about her family.

"I find that that is rarely true," Darcy said. "For instance, my first impression of you is that you are a proud, overly-optimistic person who's too sarcastic for her own good. And I'm right, aren't I?"

"So, by that logic, *you* are a conceited, pretentious jackass?" Elisa snapped.

Darcy's eyes flashed. "No one's ever called me pretentious."

"Maybe they should start. No one's ever stood up to you in your life, have they?"

"I don't consider myself someone who needs standing up to."

"Then maybe you could do with some self-reflection," Elisa said. "And I'm *sorry* that there are a thousand other things you'd rather be doing than dancing here with me, but rest assured, the feeling is incredibly mutual. I like you about as much as you do me. But your best friend and my sister are...something, so I thought we could at least be cordial. But I guess that's beyond you."

She let go of Darcy.

"Thanks for the dance," she added, not even trying to keep the edge out of her voice as she turned to head back to the table.

"Elisa—wait."

She turned around, crossing her arms. Darcy was shifting awkwardly on her feet.

"I didn't mean to upset you. I... I didn't mean that I'd rather be doing anything than be with you, specifically. I just hate dancing, that's all." She hesitated before her next words came out, quiet and mumbled. "I'm sorry."

She rolled her eyes. "Thanks for the apology, I guess, but

you obviously hate *me*, too."

Darcy tilted her head, brow furrowing. "I don't hate you, Elisa," she said, as if this were the most obvious thing in the world.

Elisa stared at her, at a loss for words, but before she could think of a response, she saw Camila, Maria, and Lucia out of the corner of her eye. They'd all found dancing partners. Maria was dancing with one of Bobby's cousins, who at least looked to be close enough to her in age. The other two danced with two random men Elisa had never seen before. How they'd even managed to find them, she had no idea. But they both looked college-aged—i.e., way too old for them.

"Crap," she muttered, hurrying off to intervene before anything further could happen. She didn't bother saying goodbye to Darcy.

Darcy stood alone on the dance floor, staring after Elisa for a moment before returning to her seat.

Interlude: In Which Charlene Overhears Some Very Compelling Bathroom Chit-Chat

Charlene had gotten stuck dancing with Colin again. Well, maybe "stuck" was the wrong word. He'd been very polite about asking, and he was actually a pretty good dancer. And they'd been right next to a speaker, so the music drowned out most of his latest speech.

She had ducked into the bathroom and was about to leave her stall to wash her hands, when the door opened again, and three sets of feet walked in. They all stopped at the mirror, doing their makeup. And gossiping.

"I can't believe Bobby has been talking to her all night," a familiar voice said. It was either Cora or Louise, but Charlene had no idea how to tell them apart. "It isn't *her* birthday."

"I know. And she's not even as pretty as his last girlfriend," the other twin said. "And her *family...*"

"God, I *know*. I'm embarrassed *for* them. Even the one that's not actually related to them."

"The middle sister is so boring. And *ugly*."

Charlene felt her chest tighten on Maria's behalf.

Option 1: Burst out of the door and scream at them both for being judgmental brats…and probably prove their point.

Option 2: Stand here and do nothing.

Ugh. This is bullshit.

"And the youngest… God, what a train wreck, am I right?"

Both twins laughed.

"She's a teen pregnancy waiting to happen. I hope Bobby gets over Julia or whoever soon. Then he can go back to girls actually worth his time, right, Darcy?"

That explained who the third girl was.

"I don't do gossip," Darcy said.

"Oh, come on, we're alone." Charlene barely repressed a snort. "You can be honest."

"Yeah, didn't you get stuck dancing with the fat one?" the other twin asked.

"Her name is Elisa," Darcy said, her voice suddenly sharp. "And I wasn't *stuck*. I could've said no."

"We saw her screaming at you earlier."

Oh, Elisa, what did you do now?

"She wasn't screaming. It was just a disagreement. Very mature."

"She looked really pissed off." There was a pause. "What are you thinking? You have that look on your face."

It was a moment before Darcy answered. "Not much. Just the…joys of a spirited girl and a pair of fine eyes."

One of the twins snorted. "*Man*, you're weird. Who talks like that?"

"I knew getting her that word-a-day calendar was a bad idea," the other said. "Come on, Cora, let's go dance. I think they're back to *good* music."

Cora and Louise left, and Darcy was quick to follow. Finally free, Charlene popped out of the stall and washed up as quickly as possible so she could find her friend. She couldn't stop thinking about what she'd overheard. She'd had a bad vibe from Cora and Louise right from the start, but she'd tried not to judge too much. (She'd leave that to Elisa.) But it looked like, in this case, her first impression had been correct. Darcy, however, had been a surprise. Not only did she not participate in trashing the Benitez family, she'd even kind of stood up for them. Well, for one of them.

And Charlene was willing to bet all the money she had that she knew exactly which spirited girl Darcy meant, and who those fine eyes belonged to.

She paused, going back-and-forth in her head. She'd never meddled in Elisa's love life before, but that was mostly because she had no love life to speak of. Her first instinct was to let her know she had an admirer—but given that the admirer wasn't her favorite person, was that wise?

But they *did* have a lot in common.

Those two dating would be kind of amazing. Or it could lead to the end of human civilization.

Win-win.

She slipped out of the bathroom and scanned the dance floor for Elisa. No easy task, since the club was incredibly crowded, and the lighting was dim, with only occasional bursts from the strobe lights to allow her to see where she was going. Charlene almost had to laugh. Here she'd thought this would be the sort of fancy restaurant you saw on TV, with candles, chandeliers, and snooty French waiters. This was trendy, but not old-school fancy.

She found Elisa, berating her younger sisters as she led them back to the table. She didn't even know why she was surprised.

"We were just dancing," Camila protested.

"Yeah, what are you, a nun?" Lucia added.

"I just wanted to say, Elisa," Maria said hastily, "that this wasn't my idea, Lucia and Camila talked me into it—"

"Traitor," Lucia said.

Elisa looked about ready to strangle them. "Just sit down and keep your hands to yourselves. I can't take you three *anywhere.*"

"If they were just dancing, maybe you should let up a little," Charlene murmured to her, quiet enough that her sisters couldn't hear. She was trying to stick up for them a little bit, but she also couldn't undermine her best friend.

Elisa glared at her.

"Or maybe not," she quickly added.

Elisa slumped down into one of the chairs at the table. Bobby, Julieta, and the others were nowhere to be found. Probably still on the dance floor.

"Where's Colin?" she asked.

"Getting a cab for his mother, I think. She looked about ready to leave," Charlene said. "Her nerves aren't so good."

Elisa chuckled, but still looked stressed.

"I overheard something interesting in the bathroom."

"Hm?" She didn't seem all that interested, but she turned to listen, anyway.

"Darcy, Cora, and Louise—"

Elisa groaned automatically.

"No, it was…" She trailed off. She couldn't very well say it was *all good things.* "It was interesting. Darcy was talking about a girl she likes."

"Darcy's a lesbian?" Elisa said, looking surprised.

"Or something." She shrugged. "Whoever she was talking about, it was definitely a girl."

"Huh. Man, I have *terrible* gaydar. Who's the unlucky girl?"

"She didn't say. She just said she was 'spirited' and had a pair of 'fine eyes.'"

She watched Elisa closely to assess her reaction and see if

she'd reach the same conclusion Charlene had.

She didn't. She just snorted.

"'Spirited.' I'm not sure I've ever heard someone use that word in conversation."

"It's what she said."

"Oh, I believe you. It goes with her whole 'I'm too smart to use one word when I can use twelve' shtick."

"Come on...you're not even a little curious about who she was talking about?" she pressed.

Elisa shook her head. "Nah. It's *Darcy*, what do I care about her love life? Except maybe to give the girl a heads-up..."

Charlene wanted to find the nearest wall and hit her head against it repeatedly.

Chapter Five

In Which Julieta Bursts Like a Fire Hydrant

The success of Operation Eclipse, as it became known around the Benitez household, had given Julieta enough confidence to call Bobby and ask him for a proper date. Elisa supposed that if their relationship had survived Mom interfering to speed things along—not once, but *twice*—then maybe they really were right for each other. And he did make Julieta really, really happy.

Four weeks later, she and Bobby had gone on five whole dates. They'd officially moved up the ladder from dancing and kisses on the cheek to Julieta coming home suspiciously late with her makeup and hair messed up.

Elisa was happy for her. It was high time *someone* in this apartment got a love life. Maria never dated at all, and Lucia had only had one proper boyfriend. For all her bravado, when it came to guys, she missed *far* more often than she scored. Camila had had a girlfriend or two prior to transitioning, and had been on a few dates since then, but never anything serious. Elisa personally thought that this was all right—Camila was only sixteen. But everyone deserved to have someone special in their lives.

Elisa had never actually been on a date. Except for that time Wyatt Berkowitz took her to the Snow Ball in middle school and gave her a very awkward, very hesitant first kiss. But she was pretty sure that didn't actually qualify.

If your mom had to do the asking for you, it didn't count. And if your mom asked by calling *his* mom, it *especially* didn't count. So, in a way, it was kind of fun to watch Julieta's relationship play out.

It was like getting all the excitement of a new relationship without actually having to deal with the stress of being *in* one.

And no one was living vicariously through this whole thing quite like their mother.

"It's almost nine," she commented, glancing out the window at the darkened sky.

"Julieta said she'd be late," Elisa said from where she sat at the kitchen table, reading the latest book Professor DeCaro had assigned. They'd made it through *Lord of the Flies*—praise the goddess—as well as *Go Set a Watchman*, and were now reading *A Clockwork Orange*. Elisa liked it but wondered if she'd get her literature nerd card revoked for saying the movie was better.

"It's not like her not to call," Mom said, but she didn't sound worried. Instead, she sounded *delighted*. "She and Bobby must be *busy*."

She groaned, looking up. "Okay, Mom, I'm happy for them, too, but this has officially gotten weird."

"Oh, come on, I'm allowed to be happy. Julieta's very responsible, it'll be fine," Mom said, waving her hand. "Besides, if she weren't, Bobby seems like the type of man who'd have the decency to marry her if it came to that." She thought that over for a second. "Say, there's an idea..."

"Mom, *no*."

"I'm kidding, I'm kidding. I promise I'm not *that* desperate."

"Yeah, somehow, I'm not convinced," Elisa said, shaking her head.

There was a knock at the door. They exchanged surprised glances.

"Who'd be coming over this late?" Mom asked.

"Maybe Julieta forgot her key."

Alejandra went to the door and opened it.

It was Bobby.

Immediately, her mother flushed red. Elisa was pretty sure she knew why. The apartment wasn't a wreck, but, well... when you had six people living together in such a small space, all of whom were working or in school full-time, sometimes things fell through the cracks. Mom had changed out of her nice work clothes and into a pair of sweatpants and an old T-shirt, and she'd piled her hair on top of her head in a messy bun.

Bobby didn't seem to mind at all. "I'm sorry for coming over so late, Ms. Bello," he said. "May I come in?"

"Where's Julieta?" Mom asked, reluctantly standing aside to let him into their "unsightly" home.

"Back at my place," Bobby said. "She got pretty sick while we were out today. It was...messy." He grimaced. "Being in a moving car is pretty awful for her right now, so I told her she could stay at my house until she feels better."

They both stared at him.

"In one of the guest rooms," he added quickly. "Don't worry, Ms. Bello, it's all very appropriate."

"How long do you think she'll be there?" Mom asked.

Bobby shrugged. "The doctor said it's a virus that's been going around—it could last anywhere from three days to three weeks, depending on how bad she got it."

"The doctor?" Elisa said, alarmed. "Did she have to go

to the hospital?"

"Hm? Oh no, no, no," Bobby said. "It's not that bad, I don't think. My family has one on call, so I had him come over to check her out."

"Oh," Elisa said. She should've just been glad Bobby had a doctor available for Julieta at the drop of a hat, but mostly she just felt jealous. Her family tended to put off seeking professional help until they'd exhausted all other options— she was sure none of them had been to a routine checkup in years.

The only sister who saw the inside of a doctor's office with any sort of regularity was Camila. Starting at her fifteenth birthday, she'd seen a small handful of experts and physicians so she could begin hormone therapy. Their mother's brother, Javier, footed the bill, which was the only way they could afford it.

"Anyway, Julieta sent me over to get her things, and I figured I'd tell you all when I got here," Bobby said. "I should've called ahead. I'm sorry, but I just didn't think of it. I'm sure she would've wanted to call you herself, but she's so sick, she basically just quarantined herself into one of the bathrooms."

"I understand," Mom said. She tugged at a loose lock of her hair—a nervous habit she'd passed on to all of her daughters. "Elisa, go help Bobby get some things out of her room."

Elisa nodded, gesturing for him to follow her.

"Jules mentioned you two share a room," he said, as they stepped inside. "I'm going to guess that... *this* side is hers." He pointed to the neater, cleaner, more aesthetically pleasing side of the room.

"Correct," Elisa said, stepping over the pile of books she had on the floor next to her bed. "We share the closet, but she got some colored hangers, so we can tell whose clothes are whose. Hers are pink, mine are blue."

"She's very organized, isn't she?" he said.

"She has to be. Oldest of five, running her own business—if she didn't have some system to keep things straight, she'd go insane."

Bobby reached to unplug Julieta's laptop and put it into its case. "Speaking of her business...do you think there's any way I can talk her out of working while she's sick?"

She let out a lovingly exasperated laugh, shaking her head. "Nope. Last year when we all got the flu, she was working on her latest client's request while curled up in six blankets and drinking hot tea."

"I believe it. She was still throwing up when I came over here, and when I asked if there was anything specific from home she'd like to have, she just said 'bring my laptop and work spreadsheets' in between heaves."

He was smiling fondly as he spoke. So he still liked her, even when she was vomiting. That was a good sign if there ever was one.

"That definitely sounds like my sister. But bring her quilt, too. She'll be glad to have it while she's away from home." Elisa stepped away from the closet, four days or so worth of clothes in her arms. "You can always come back and get more clothes if she's there longer than a few days. Plus, I assume you have a washing machine."

"We'll make it work." He paused to look at the small bookshelf on Julieta's side of the room. "What are her favorite books? She'll have to take a break from work sometime."

"I wouldn't count on it. But anything by Terry Pratchett is a good bet."

Tossing a couple of *Discworld* books onto the pile on the bed, he said, "Am I selfish for being glad Julieta's staying with me? If she weren't, I'd be over here twenty-four/seven to check on her."

Elisa smiled. "That's not selfish. That just means you like her."

He went slightly pink, but said, "I suppose that isn't much of a secret."

"Just don't say so to my mother. She's already embarrassingly supportive. I don't think Julieta could stand the shame."

He grinned. "Not a bad problem to have, if you ask me."

"You clearly don't know my mother."

. . .

Julieta had been at Netherfield Park for a week. She'd been online semi-frequently, but usually had her status set to "busy." Fortunately, Bobby texted Elisa with updates every few hours, so she knew that Julieta was better, and that the puke-per-day average had gone down significantly but she was still mostly staying in bed.

Still, texts weren't quite the same. Elisa missed her big sister's voice. Especially when her only company for most of the week had been Lucia, Maria, and Camila. She loved them dearly, but being the acting oldest sibling was *exhausting*. She didn't know how Julieta did it.

So, a week after Bobby had come over to fetch Julieta's things, she decided to see if she was up to talking on the phone.

Bobby picked up, even though she had called her cell.

"Hey, Elisa—Jules told me to go ahead and pick up for her, she's in the shower."

"Are *you*?" Elisa asked.

He sputtered for a second before saying, "No—no. I'm standing outside the bathroom door. I just heard her phone going off in her room—"

She laughed. "Relax, I'm just teasing you. I was calling to

see how Julieta's doing."

"She's... Well, she's still feeling pretty crappy," he said. "And I know she misses you." Suddenly, his voice brightened. "Hey, why not come over to visit for a couple of hours? I'm sure she'd love to see you."

"Are you sure that's a good idea?"

"Pretty sure. Her fever's down. The doctor said that the meds he gave her are working, so you shouldn't catch whatever this is."

Elisa paused, then said, "Okay. I'll be over soon. What's the address?"

"Eighteen thirteen Lancaster Drive. See you soon. Bye."

"Bye."

She and Bobby hung up, and she went to find her mother.

"Mama, can I borrow the car?" she asked, sticking her head into the kitchen.

"Sure," Mom said, not looking up from what she was doing. "Where are you headed?"

"Bobby invited me over to visit Julieta."

She looked up. *"No."*

"What?"

"I cannot have you over there interfering. Not when those two lovebirds are finally getting some real, quality alone time."

"Mom, she's *sick*. She's spent most of her time there curled up in her room."

"With him taking care of her, fetching things for her, catering to her every need. Come on, Elisa, you've read enough romances to know where that's going." Elisa felt the heat rush to her face as her mother shot her an amused glance. "Yeah, I know what's in that shoebox underneath your bed."

"That's not the point," Elisa said quickly. "Julieta's probably homesick. I don't see how my being there for a couple of hours could hurt."

"You are not taking the car over there."

"Mom—"

"Don't *'Mom'* me. You're not taking the car. End of discussion."

And she went back to what she was doing without another word.

Elisa hesitated.

"Okay. I won't take the car," she said.

She grabbed her coat, her phone, and pulled on her favorite pair of boots, then headed out the door before her mother could work out what she was doing.

According to Google Maps, it was a three-hour walk to Netherfield Park, and she still had a solid four hours before it got dark.

The things she did for her sister. And to spite her mother.

Okay—mostly to spite her mother.

Chapter Six

In Which Elisa Enters Stepford (Or Close to It)

The sky was streaked with pink by the time Elisa reached Bobby's house. It had rained for about half an hour a while back, but her hair was nearly dry as she walked up the sidewalk to ring the doorbell. Her feet were killing her, and she was sweaty, despite it being October. On top it all, a car had gone past her about twenty miles over the speed limit and splattered her with a tidal wave of mud.

A maid opened the door.

"Sorry, I think you have the wrong address," she said, beginning to close it again.

Elisa quickly stuck her foot in the doorway to keep the door from shutting. "I'm Elisa," she said. "Julieta's sister."

"Oh. Oh, yes. Mr. Charles mentioned you were coming. Three hours ago."

"It's a long story."

"Follow me, Miss Benitez. And please remember to wipe your feet on the doormat before you step inside."

Deciding not to comment on how weird it was to be called

"Miss Benitez," she stepped into the house—after getting most of the mud off of her boots. The inside of the house was beautiful—white marble floors with a high ceiling, a chandelier glittering in the entry hallway. She looked around, trying her best not to gawk. The maid took her coat from her before leading her into the lounge, where Bobby, Cora, Louise, and Darcy were all playing a video game.

Oh, right. Darcy is staying here. Elisa had forgotten about that.

"Your guest has arrived," the maid said, presenting Elisa to the others. She shifted on her feet self-consciously.

"You look like you've been hit with a truck," one of the twins said.

She rolled her eyes on instinct but couldn't really get offended—it was true. "It was a long walk."

Bobby looked appalled. "You *walked* here all the way from Longbourn?"

She shrugged weakly. "Mom needed the car," she said. *The truth miiiiiight freak him out a bit.*

"Why didn't you call? I would've sent a car to pick you up," he said.

"I did think of that about halfway here," she admitted.

"You must've gotten caught in the rain."

"I did."

"Your feet must be killing you."

"They are."

"It looks like you got splashed with mud."

"Yep."

"And you *still* didn't call?"

"Nope."

"Why not?"

"To prove a point."

Bobby gave her an odd look before shaking his head, apparently deciding to leave it at that. "Would you like to see

Julieta?"

"Yes, please."

He gestured for her to follow him. She only got a glance at the others before she left the room. Cora and Louise were both staring at her as if she were something disgusting that they'd found on the bottom of their shoes. Darcy simply watched her with the slightest curve of a smile around her lips.

Fortunately, the McMansion Bobby lived in had an elevator, and Bobby had correctly guessed that she was in no mood to take the stairs. Elisa, for her part, couldn't quite wrap her head around the idea of an elevator in a *house*. Even the one back at the apartment complex was broken half the time.

"All the guest rooms are on the east side of the second floor," Bobby explained. "My family and I—and Darcy—all sleep in the west side."

"Isn't Darcy a guest, too?" Elisa asked.

"She's *never* a guest," he said with a smile. "We've known her way too long for that. She's family."

Elisa smiled, too. *No wonder she's nicer to him than anyone else.*

The elevator opened with a pleasant *ding!* and Bobby led her down a long hallway. Elisa cringed when her still-damp feet left a trail. Feeling sorry for whoever would have to clean up the mess, she followed behind him. Every closed door looked the same to her, but he seemed to know where he was going.

Finally, they reached a door that was cracked open. Bobby knocked lightly, peering inside.

"Jules, you awake?"

"Yeah," came her croaky reply.

"Your sister's here." He opened the door wider so Elisa could step in.

Julieta had dark bags under her eyes, and a trash can next to her bed, but managed to sit up, brushing some hair out of her face. "Elisa," she said, opening her arms for a hug. In spite of her aching feet and her exhaustion, she grinned, rushing forward to sit on the bed, hugging her sister. "I figured you weren't coming today after all."

"Mama needed the car, so I walked," Elisa explained.

"All the w—"

"Yes, all the way. Yes, in the rain."

Julieta laughed. "Well, Mama's stubbornness had to go somewhere, I guess. But Bobby would've given you a ride if—"

"If I'd called. Yep. I know."

Bobby chuckled before pecking Julieta on the cheek and saying, "I'll be right back."

After he left, Elisa told her *why*, exactly, she'd walked to Netherfield instead of taking the car. Julieta groaned, looking embarrassed but not surprised.

"I'm glad you came anyway," she said, "but Mom's gonna kill you."

"Yeah, her texts to me said as much."

"What'd you say?"

"Well, I ignored her for as long as I possibly could, and then I texted back that I had already walked halfway there, so there was no point in telling me to come home now unless she wanted me walking through our end of town alone at night," Elisa said. "And then she said, fine, if I was that determined, I could go, but I shouldn't expect her to come and pick me up. I said I could live with that, and I'm sure that one day, we'll be on speaking terms again."

Julieta laughed, shaking her head. "Lisa, you didn't have to do that. I don't want Mom mad at you."

"She hasn't yelled at anyone in nearly a week. One of us was due to piss her off. Figured I'd give Cam and Lulu a break."

"Well, you didn't need to go to all that trouble," Julieta said, though she was still smiling, "but I am very glad you're here."

"What's it like, being a guest in Netherfield Park? Is it like visiting with royalty?"

She blushed, looking down at her lap. "Bobby has been lovely. He's the only person I've seen much of for the past week. The others tend to go out or hang out downstairs. Darcy did keep an eye on me for Bobby when he had to deal with work for a few hours yesterday, though."

She grimaced. "Ugh, being under the watchful eyes of Darcy Fitzgerald. What was *that* like?"

"It really wasn't bad," she insisted. Elisa gave her a look. "Really, it wasn't. She's not as…considerate as Bobby, but she was genuinely trying to help, I think. She held my hair back when I got sick, and she tried to get me to stop working for a little bit. Said it wasn't good for me."

"See, that is so *like* Darcy," she said. "Who is *she* to tell you when you can or can't work?" She paused and then reluctantly added, "It *was* nice of her to sit with you, though. But she still shouldn't have told you what to do."

Julieta tilted her head, not even trying to hide her amused smile. "I seem to remember a certain someone hiding my laptop so I'd get some sleep when we had the flu last year," she said. "Now don't try and tell me that was Darcy, because she wasn't even in town yet."

"W-well, no, but…" Elisa stumbled over her words for a second, before giving an exasperated, "You *know* what I mean."

"Elisa, is it possible—just *possible*—that maybe you're being a little hard on Darcy?"

"No," she said stubbornly.

"I know she made a bad first impression—"

"And second, and third."

"—but she's been Bobby's best friend for years. You like Bobby, don't you?"

"Yeah, but..."

"If he likes her, then she can't be that bad, can she? Not all the time, at least."

"I think Bobby is like you," Elisa said. "Too nice. Too forgiving."

"Being forgiving is a good thing, Elisa."

"Yeah, in moderation."

Julieta sighed, leaning back against the pillows. "Well, one of us has to be," she said. "You can be practical and cynical, and I can be naive and forgiving, how about that?"

"Sounds good to me."

Bobby returned, then, carrying a small tray of food.

"Here you go," he said, setting the tray on Julieta's bedside table. "I wasn't sure if you wanted fish or roast beef, so I brought you a little of both. And there's vegetables and bread if the meat is too much for your stomach." He ran a hand over Julieta's hair, kissing her on the forehead, before turning to Elisa. "I'm sorry, Elisa, you just missed dinner— I'm sure our chef wouldn't mind fixing you something if you're hungry, though."

"I'm fine," she said. "I ate before I came."

"Still, that was hours ago..."

"I promise, I'm fine. I can just hang out here with Julieta."

"Actually, about that..." Bobby said. "It's already starting to get dark out. Why don't you stay the night? We have plenty of room, and you can spend the day here tomorrow, too."

"I don't want to be a bother," Elisa said. She really didn't want to leave, not when she'd only just arrived. "I can Uber home and come back tomorrow." Though, she had exactly five dollars in her pocket, which might get her to the end of the road he lived on.

"Don't be ridiculous. You're always welcome. You can stay as long as you like."

He flagged down a maid who was in the hallway and asked her to take Elisa to a room. Promising Julieta she'd come right back, Elisa followed the maid, leaving Bobby to fuss over her sister.

The guest bedroom was amazing, almost exactly like Julieta's, except with a forest green color scheme instead of a dusty rose. There was a queen-sized bed with at least ten pillows, a flat-screen TV, a bookshelf, a desk, and even a huge walk-in closet. If this was where they kept guests, she could only imagine what the *real* bedrooms looked like. (She made a mental note to ask Julieta.)

"I think you'll be very comfortable in here," the maid said, fluffing one of the pillows. "I just changed the sheets in this room a few minutes ago, and Brenna vacuumed and dusted earlier."

"It's perfect," Elisa assured her. "Thank you so much."

"My name is Cassie, by the way. Call me if you need anything."

"I will. Thank you, Cassie."

After she left, Elisa slipped back down the hall to see Julieta. Bobby was still there, and his face lit up with a small smile as soon as she walked in.

"Oh, I was just about to go check on you," he said. "Do you like your room?"

"Very much," she said. "Thanks again for letting me crash here. I should probably call Mom so she doesn't worry, now that I think of it."

"Actually, about that... Julieta and I were talking, and she—well, we—were wondering if you wanted to stay until she's feeling better?"

They both looked at her hopefully. Elisa almost laughed out loud. With Bobby sitting on the bed, holding Julieta's hand, they looked like they were married already. And his asking as if she were a guest at *their* mansion, not just his, didn't help.

"I wouldn't want to impose," she said. "I mean, Bobby—I'm sure you didn't intend on having me over for longer than a few hours. And since Julieta is feeling a bit better, I can take her home tomorrow."

He frowned and pulled Julieta's hand to his chest.

"Elisa, have you seen the size of this place?" He laughed. "I've gone for a week without seeing my own sisters in here. I think I'll live. It's no imposition at all."

"If you want to go home, I understand," Julieta said. "I mean, honestly, I'm getting kind of homesick." She glanced at Bobby and hastily added, "Not that I don't love being here. I just miss my sisters. And Mom."

Elisa couldn't deny that the idea of staying in a relative stranger's mansion for what could potentially be weeks on end seemed a bit weird and awkward to her, but Julieta seemed to have enjoyed her stay there, even with being sick. And, honestly? A vacation away from their mother and other sisters didn't sound half-bad.

And she *had* really missed Julieta.

"If you're sure I won't be overstaying my welcome...then yes. I'll stay," she said.

Julieta grinned. "Oh, Elisa, that's great."

"Since you'll be staying over," Bobby said, "how about I drive you to your apartment real quick to grab some clothes, fill your mother in, that sort of thing?"

"Okay," she said, as her heart hit the bottom of her stomach.

Bobby hurried off to grab his keys and jacket, and as soon as he was gone, Julieta said, "What's wrong? You have that 'sudden moment of existential dread' look again."

"*Mom*," she said. "She'll never let me stay here. She

thought my visiting for a few *hours* would somehow wreck your relationship with Bobby. Imagine how she'll react when I tell her I'm staying for at least a few more days."

Julieta, much to Elisa's surprise, didn't look worried. In fact, she was smiling.

"Elisa, I've had a whole twenty-two years' worth of experience in dealing with our mother, and you didn't think I'd think of that?" she asked, pretending to be offended. "Why do you think I insisted *Bobby* drive you over instead of one of the chauffeurs?"

"What does that have to do with—*oh*."

"I think you'll be surprised at how agreeable Mom can be, under the right circumstances."

• • •

Elisa and Bobby arrived back at Longbourn Apartments less than a half hour later. After seeing Netherfield Park, she felt somewhat embarrassed at her neighborhood, though that was ridiculous. He had been there before and clearly didn't mind. It wasn't a slum, exactly, but most of the houses were boarded up, and the only businesses still operating within walking distance of the apartment complex were two liquor stores, a gas station that ran out of gas to sell with annoying frequency, a thrift store, a strip club, and one surprisingly amazing food cart. She had never been thrilled with the neighborhood she called home, but being outright *embarrassed* by it was new to her.

Alejandra came to the door almost immediately after Elisa unlocked and opened it. She did a double take when she saw Bobby and forced a charming smile. Evidently, she'd decided to wait on throttling Elisa until he was gone.

"I was wondering when you'd get back. Thank you so much for giving her a ride home, Bobby," she said. "How's

Julieta feeling?"

"She's better, but still pretty sick," Bobby said. "Actually, Ms. Bello, I invited Elisa to stay until Julieta's feeling better."

She stared at him for a split second before her eyes flicked to Elisa, saying *what the hell are you doing.*

"You don't have to do that," she said quickly.

"Please, it's my pleasure. Julieta said she's been missing home, and I think Elisa staying would help a bit."

Julieta, you absolute genius.

"Elisa's in school," Mom said, clearly thinking on her feet.

"Oh, that isn't a problem. Darcy commutes there all the time from the house, she said the drive isn't bad at all. In fact, Elisa can even commute with her on the days they have that class together."

Elisa froze for a second. She really, *really* needed to quit forgetting about Darcy. She guessed that the college was a half hour's drive from Netherfield Park—which was actually shorter than her normal commute, so fine. But a half hour in a car twice a week with *Darcy*? And she hadn't even thought about how she'd be living under the same roof as her.

If she'd thought this through all the way, she would've said no. It was one thing to come over for a couple of hours, avoid Darcy during that time, leave, and return the next day. Actually *living* there would make avoiding her outright impossible, even without counting the commute.

She couldn't change her mind and disappoint Julieta or let her mother win.

Ah, karma. You're a bitch.

Bobby was still talking.

"I promise, Ms. Bello, I'm happy to have Elisa stay with us. And I'm sure Darcy will be glad to have some company that isn't me or my sisters."

Yeah. No.

Mom's eyes flicked between Bobby and Elisa. Elisa had to give Julieta some credit; she definitely knew their mother. She would never refuse Bobby's very generous offer, especially not when he was her eldest daughter's kind-of-sort-of-maybe-almost boyfriend.

"If you're sure. Elisa, I'll help you get a bag together." Her tone was pleasant, but her eyes said "murder." Bobby didn't seem to notice.

Once they were alone in Elisa's room, her mother's smile dropped off her face, and she gave her most withering look.

"Clever," she said. "I'll give you that. But understand that if you screw anything up for Bobby and Julieta, you are grounded until the third coming of Jesus."

"You mean second."

"Oh, you *wish*."

Elisa barely repressed an eye-roll. "Mama, *they* invited *me*, remember?"

"Why didn't you say no?"

"Because Julieta hasn't seen any of us in days, and she's obviously lonely over there. I mean, Bobby's been great, but she's been stuck in bed for a *week*."

Alejandra threw up her hands. "Julieta should know better."

"Maybe love is clouding her judgment," she said dryly.

"One can only hope." She sighed and began picking out clothes for her to bring with her. "You know, your other sisters are gonna miss you."

Elisa rolled her eyes as she grabbed some books to bring. "Oh, come on. A few days with no nagging older sisters? They'll be thrilled."

"*I'm* gonna miss you."

Her expression softened ever so slightly. "You know you could always come over to visit Jules," she said. "I know she'd be happy to see you."

Mom sighed, shaking her head. "Believe me, I'd like to. But I've been working all these extra hours, and then next thing I know it's nighttime, and I'm exhausted and in no state to be talking to anyone... I call her, though. I can usually manage that on my lunch break." She sighed, running a hand through her messy hair. "I'd love to take the afternoon off some time and visit, but it's just not doable."

"Mom, don't beat yourself up. You work hard to support us. Julieta understands that. We all do." Elisa pecked her on the cheek. "And I promise to call you, too. It's not like I'm moving across the country. Just staying across town for a few days."

"Netherfield Park may as well be a different planet."

She nodded. "You have no idea."

"Listen—if you're gonna be there, then you're gonna help, okay?" Mom said. "I mean it. Imply that he should ask Julieta to be exclusive, give him tips on what kind of presents she likes, arrange a private candlelit dinner for them as a surprise, pop in a Beyoncé CD when they're alone in a room, lock them into closets together—the whole nine yards."

Elisa chuckled. "I'll see what I can do."

• • •

Elisa overslept and missed breakfast the next day, but that was okay, since that meant she'd missed spending a whole meal with Cora, Louise, and Darcy. When she went to check on Julieta, she found her curled up on her side, groaning. The trash can was within arm's reach, though it luckily looked like she hadn't hurled. *Yet.*

"It's always the worst in the morning," she mumbled half to herself as Elisa came to sit in the chair next to her bed.

"I'm sorry, Jules," Elisa said, biting her lip. "Want me to get Bobby?"

She shook her head. "No, it's not that bad," she said. "It just feels like there's a rock in my stomach."

"That *sounds* bad."

"Earlier this week it was a snake. I'll take the rock. Besides, I don't want Bobby to spend all day fussing over me."

Elisa went to push a lock of Julieta's hair behind her ear. "Is there anything I can do?"

"Keep me company. I've been going a bit stir-crazy in here."

Elisa fetched some food from the kitchen to make up for missing breakfast, and then she was content to spend the day in her sister's room, watching TV while Julieta typed on her laptop—once the pain had lessened enough for her to sit up. It was almost like being at home…if home had a huge TV and the occasional maid popping in to see if there was anything they needed. Elisa wasn't sure what would take the most getting used to; being called "Miss Benitez," or being asked, "Can I get you anything?" every couple of hours.

Eventually, Julieta drifted off to sleep, still sitting up. Gently taking the laptop and setting it on the table, Elisa pulled a blanket over her older sister and tiptoed out of the room. She shut the door behind her just as Bobby came down the hall.

"Shh," she said, raising a finger to her lips. "Julieta's asleep."

"Oh, good," he whispered. "The past few days, her stomach has been killing her so much, she hasn't been able to get much sleep. I was just coming to see how she was doing."

"We should probably head someplace farther from her room," she said, glancing back at the door. "She's a light sleeper."

"Believe me, I know," he said, ushering her down the hall. "Since Julieta's asleep, you want to come downstairs and hang out with the rest of us? You don't have to stay holed up in your room the whole time."

Elisa hesitated. Truthfully, she *wanted* to stay holed up in her room the whole time. Bobby had been great, but the others...

"I wouldn't want to impose," she said.

"Nonsense. You're our guest."

She thought it over for a second, then nodded. She should be polite. Bobby had been so accommodating—well beyond the call of duty. Socializing a bit was the least she could do.

"Okay. What are we doing?"

"At the moment? Not much. We're all just hanging out in the lounge. Darcy's doing her own thing, Cora and Louise are doing their own things..."

"Ahh, ignoring everyone in the company of others," Elisa laughed. "One of my favorite social activities. In that case, would it be rude if I brought a book with me?"

"Not at all."

Feeling a bit better that she wouldn't have to talk to the others much, Elisa ducked into her room, grabbing one of her favorite books, *Annie on my Mind*, before following Bobby down to the lounge.

The lounge seemed to be the same thing as a living room, except without a TV. Darcy sat in the corner reading a novel that was so heavy, she probably could've knocked someone out cold with it, while Cora and Louise sat on one of the couches, playing a game of chess as they talked back and forth excitedly. The twins didn't even react when Elisa walked in, but Darcy's gaze was trained on her.

Elisa took a seat in one of the empty recliners and opened the book she'd brought. It was one of her favorites, and she'd read it at least five times. Everyone stuck to their activities in comfortable silence. Or, semi-silence—Cora and Louise were still whispering.

Just as she was starting to think that maybe staying here

wouldn't be so bad, Cora raised her voice.

"Bobby," she said, "what was the name of that girl Isaac used to go out with?"

Bobby looked up briefly from his laptop, forehead creasing in thought.

"Uhhh... Victoria."

"Why'd they break up, anyway?" the other twin asked. "Isaac didn't want to talk about it last time we saw him."

"He didn't tell me," he said. Elisa immediately got the sense that this was a lie.

"He finally figured out that she was denser than osmium," Darcy said, not looking up from her book.

Elisa didn't say anything, trying her best not to listen as she turned another page in her book.

"I don't know what osmium is, but she *was* an idiot," Louise said. "I'm pretty sure Gianna's smarter than she is."

"Gianna's smarter than most people," Darcy said, a slight bite to her voice.

"How's she doing, anyway?" Bobby asked. "I haven't gotten a chance to talk to her since I moved."

"She's well," Darcy said. "I invited her out here, but she's busy with her music teacher. She's started work on learning Chopin."

"Chopin?" Cora said. "Jeez. I can only play 'Heart and Soul.'"

"She's one of the most accomplished people I know."

Louise laughed. "Knowing you, that's probably a club of two."

"Give me a little credit. It's a club of five. Six, if I'm being charitable."

Elisa looked up, then. "Oh, come on," she said, glancing at Darcy. "That can't be true."

"It is," she said. "Gianna's incredibly accomplished. She's got a four-point-oh GPA, she's a classically trained musician, she—"

"That's not what I meant," she said, exasperated. Darcy gushing about her sister would've been sweet if it weren't at the expense of everyone else. "I meant you *must* know more than five or six accomplished people."

"I gotta agree with Elisa," Bobby added. "I think most people are accomplished, in their own way."

Darcy snorted.

"What it means to be 'accomplished' is subjective," Elisa said. "For instance, you may think yourself *very* accomplished, being rich and smart and pretty and all, only to find no one agrees with you." She paused, then added, "Hypothetically, I mean."

Cora chimed in before Darcy could say anything. "Disagree. I think there are a few requirements you need to hit before you can be considered accomplished. Objectively speaking."

"I have a feeling I'm going to regret this, but... Like what?"

"Well, you have to know something about music that isn't played on the radio. You should be able to dance and be able to discuss politics and art. You should speak more than one language. You should be able to appreciate foods besides local fast food chains. You need to have a goal to work toward. You have to be polite, intelligent, a good conversation partner, in good physical shape, you should have a job of your own—or pursuing education, I suppose—and you should have some kind of talent that sets you apart from the rest of the crowd."

Well, Elisa was right. She *did* regret it.

"You should also," Darcy added, "better yourself via extensive reading."

Because that list wasn't already long enough. Thanks, Fitzgerald.

Making a point to ignore Cora, she looked to Darcy.

"You actually believe this crap?" she asked, working very hard at keeping her voice level.

She shrugged. "I wouldn't call it 'crap.'"

"What would you call it, then?"

"Standards."

"Well, I still don't believe you've met five or six people who meet your definition of accomplished," Elisa said. "I think you've met *none*."

"Oh?"

"Believe me when I say there is no one alive who checks off every single box on that list. I think a lot of people—probably *most* people—get most of them, but not *all*. Besides, that list sounds more like a recipe for an annoying, pretentious hipster. No offense toward Gianna intended," she added quickly. She didn't like Darcy, but there was no reason to bring her sister into this.

Though Darcy seemed perfectly willing to insult *her* sisters...

"What I'm saying is—if someone's a nice person who you enjoy being around, who you get along well with and can talk to easily, isn't that more important than them meeting all the requirements on some stupid list?"

"I could never enjoy being around someone who *didn't* meet those requirements," she said.

"No wonder you always seem like you'd rather be anywhere than with other people."

The corner of Darcy's mouth quirked up into a small smirk. "Now you understand."

"That was *not* intended as a compliment," she snapped.

Bobby was just about to hurry in to change the subject, when they were saved by a maid coming in to announce that lunch was ready. Elisa was the first one out. She shouldn't have taken the bait. She should've just ignored Cora and Darcy both. But her annoyance had gotten the better of her, and now she had no choice but to stew in silence.

Fitzgerald: 1
Benitez: 0
Is it time to go home yet?

Interlude: In Which Julieta Begins Shipping It

Julieta woke up some time later when the door to her room creaked open. She rolled over and sat up, blinking the sleep out of her eyes. Bobby slipped inside, shutting the door behind him. She blushed and was all too aware of her tangled hair and groggy, sand-filled eyes.

"How long have I been out?" she asked, yawning.

"Couple hours," Bobby said. "Elisa came down to the lounge with the rest of us so you could rest. Your laptop's over there," he added, nodding toward her bedside table.

"Is she having a good time?" Julieta asked, grabbing the laptop and putting it back in its case.

He cringed, sitting down on the bed next to her. "Uh... I was trying to see to it that she would, but then my plan was very cleverly usurped by my sisters and Darcy."

She laughed. "Oh no. Darcy can't seem to walk three feet without pissing my sister off, can she?"

"Darcy pisses off most people, just by being herself," Bobby admitted. "It's a gift. Elisa's just the first person that she's *cared* about pissing off."

"What did she do this time?"

"Well, it was her and Cora, really—they were talking about what they thought made for an accomplished person. Elisa thought that the requirements were a bit too harsh. Honestly, so did I."

"What was the list?"

"I can't remember it all," he chuckled. "It was kind of long. She was already pretty annoyed with Cora, but then Darcy decided to chime in, and, well…"

"That only annoyed her even more," Julieta finished.

"Exactly. The sad part is, I think Darcy may have been trying to compliment her, but it…backfired. She said an accomplished person would have to be well-read."

"Elisa is certainly that." She tilted her head. "What about me? Do I fit Darcy Fitzgerald and Cora Charles's requirements for an accomplished woman?"

He smiled, leaning in to peck her lips. "You meet *my* requirements for an accomplished woman," he said. "Surpass them, actually."

She grinned. "Good enough." She pulled back, tucking some hair behind her ear. "So where's Elisa now? Sulking in her room to avoid Darcy?"

"How'd you know?"

"I know my sister. And where's Darcy?"

"Last I checked, sulking in the lounge, lamenting the failure her latest conversation attempt with Elisa."

"Well, she did kind of go about it wrong," she said. "I mean, she couldn't have just said, 'Hey, Elisa, I think you're really accomplished'?"

Bobby laughed, shaking his head. "Darcy doesn't do things like that. She just dances around the subject and hopes the people she likes will get the hint."

"So she does like Elisa? *Like her*, like her, I mean."

He hesitated, before saying, "Yes. But you *cannot* tell her you know. Do not so much as *hint* at it. And don't tell Elisa, either."

"Why not?"

"Because Darcy swore me to secrecy, and I don't want her to *kill me*."

Julieta chuckled. "Well, I think it's sweet. It's too bad Elisa's so oblivious."

"It *is* sweet," Bobby said. "I mean, I've known Darcy her whole life, and this is the first time she's ever really had a crush. She's had a couple of dates, but they always asked *her* out. I've never seen her try to go after someone herself... Probably explains why she's so crap at it." He let out a fond laugh. "But... I mean, I know it's none of my business, but, like—does Darcy even have a chance there? Is Elisa...?"

"Gay?" Julieta finished. She nodded. "Yeah. Bi, actually. She's been out for a couple years now. She doesn't really care who knows. Sometimes I think our grandparents think she *should* care, but she doesn't. I've always liked that about her."

Bobby cringed. "Are your grandparents really conservative?"

She sighed, fiddling with the blanket. "Yes and no. I think if Elisa had just been a lesbian, they'd have been okay, once they got past the initial surprise. But to them, the idea of being bi is so...out-there. It wasn't even really considered a thing when they were our age. So, I'm pretty sure Abuela thinks Elisa's just 'going through a phase,' and Abuelo... well, I can never tell what *he's* thinking. He's like a brick wall."

"I hope they come around someday."

"Yeah. Me too." Shaking her head, she tried to steer the conversation back into calmer waters. "For real, though... I'm not sure Darcy has a chance, anyway, with the way things have been going."

Bobby let out a small laugh. "Yeah. Taylor Swift, she

ain't."

"How'd you and Darcy meet, anyway? Isn't she, like, five years younger than you?"

"Six," Bobby said. "Her mom was my dad's best friend, ever since they were kids. I think our parents kind of hoped Darcy and I would end up together." He grimaced at the thought. "Luckily, Darcy being gay meant that plan was all kinds of dead."

"What'd your parents say to that?"

"Well, by the time she came out, my parents had already accepted that I see her as family, so even kissing her is basically incest as far as I'm concerned," he said. "And, well... Darcy's parents died before she even really knew herself."

"She was very young when they died, wasn't she?"

"Fourteen," Bobby sighed. "I know they would've been okay with it, though. They were good people, good parents. I wish you could've met Darcy's mom, especially. She was such a nice woman. She would've liked you, and Elisa."

"Was she like Darcy?"

"No. Gianna takes after her more, I think. Honestly, I'm not sure where Darcy got her...Darcy-ness from. But she's always been like that, ever since she was a kid."

"It is so strange, knowing you two are best friends," she said, chuckling. "It's sweet, but objectively, it makes no sense."

"I don't know if we would be if we weren't raised together," he admitted, "but I'm very glad we are. We've been through a lot together. Darcy's never turned her back on me, even when I felt like I had nobody."

"I know what you mean," Julieta said, thinking of Elisa.

"So, you like the idea of Darcy and your sister?"

"I do," she admitted. "But Elisa's stubborn. She's already decided to hate Darcy, and well, she's single-mindedly hated Armie Hammer for years because of *The Lone Ranger*."

"Well, I mean, I saw that movie, too. I can't really blame

her for *that*."

Julieta laughed. "But you see what I mean. Once she's made up her mind that she hates somebody…"

"Darcy's got her work cut out for her, huh?"

"*Oh* yeah."

Chapter Seven

In Which Darcy Tries Her Best (And Fails, Miserably)

"I could drive," Elisa offered, as she did every time she and Darcy got ready to make the commute to the college. "We don't have to use the chauffeur."

"He's here and getting paid for his time no matter what. We may as well employ his services," Darcy said, which was her response every time.

"Limo service makes me feel like such a douche," she muttered, slinging her backpack over her shoulder.

"It's not a limo. It's a town car."

Darcy, as she found out when she'd started staying at Netherfield, couldn't drive. Instead, they were driven to and from class each day by Jordan, a chauffeur. She liked Jordan, but she *didn't* enjoy being forced to sit alone in the backseat with Darcy.

"It doesn't matter what you call it," she said. "I still feel like a pretentious tool."

"Do you feel that way when your mom or your sister drops you off someplace?"

"No, but they're not hired to drive me around places. It's different."

"Not in my mind, it isn't."

Elisa sighed, shaking her head as they headed out the front door, where Jordan was waiting with the car. "Just—why didn't you get your license when you were sixteen like everyone else?"

"Cars are giant, metal contraptions of death," said Darcy, with the utmost seriousness. "If something goes wrong, I'd prefer not to be responsible."

"Thanks for the vote of confidence," Jordan said, rolling his eyes, but he was smiling. He opened the door for them.

"Thank you," Elisa said, climbing into the back. As always, the car was perfectly clean, as if new. The Benitez family minivan often went months between much-needed cleanings, but according to Darcy, all the cars owned by Bobby and his family got washed once every three days and were vacuumed twice daily. Elisa had at first wondered who on earth had the time for that, before she remembered that there were probably people on the payroll whose entire job was car upkeep.

Jordan turned on the radio like he always did, and they began the drive toward the campus. She leaned her head against the window, singing softly under her breath to the tunes she recognized. Jordan, despite being about Bobby's age, tended to favor 1970s funk and disco—the kind of music Elisa's mom liked to listen to while she was cleaning.

As they pulled onto the highway, Darcy turned to face her and cleared her throat. "Um—I was wondering, have you finished your essay for *A Clockwork Orange*?" she asked.

Elisa glanced over at her. "Yeah. Have you?"

"Yes. Yes, I, um, I finished it last night."

"Well... Good."

"Good," she repeated.

There was a pause.

"I enjoyed the novel a great deal," she said.

Elisa had no idea why Darcy was trying to make conversation. She'd seemed fine with riding in semi-awkward silence before. Still, it was best not to antagonize her. They were in a small space, after all—it wasn't like she could go sulk elsewhere.

"I liked it okay," she said. "I think I prefer the movie, though."

"I've never seen it. I don't watch films often. Books are always better."

Ah, a pretentious comment, right on schedule.

"Not always. *The Graduate, Jaws, Fight Club, V for Vendetta*—though that's a comic—sometimes the movie is better. Not always, but it happens."

"Did you know that the author of *Jaws* dedicated the rest of his career to helping sharks after he realized his book and the movie adaptation caused people to hunt sharks to near-extinction?"

"Yeah, I read that somewhere."

"Oh."

There was another pause.

"How are you today?" Darcy asked, sounding like the phrase was in a foreign language.

"Fine."

"Oh. Good. Um, I'm fine as well."

"Great."

Darcy sighed, slumping over slightly in her seat.

"What is it?" she asked.

"Nothing, it's just... I've exhausted my list of possible conversation topics for this car ride."

Weirdo.

• • •

"Hey, Elisa."

Elisa looked up from her bag. Professor DeCaro had just dismissed the class for the day, and they were getting ready to go and meet Jordan to head back to Netherfield Park. Kelly, a pretty, petite girl who sat behind them in class, had come over to their table.

"A bunch of us were planning to go get a drink. I know you're not twenty-one yet, but the bar has food and soda, too. Want to come?"

"Isn't it a bit early for drinking?" Darcy said.

Kelly ignored her. "It's that bar on Mansfield and Woodhouse."

"Sure," she said, "that sounds like f—"

"Elisa carpools home with me." Darcy cut her off, looking directly at Kelly.

"You can come, too," Kelly said, though she seemed noticeably less cheerful about inviting her. Elisa felt a pang of sympathy for Darcy—just a bit.

She turned to her. "Come on. I've wanted to get out of the house lately, anyway. It'll be fun."

Darcy hesitated before deflating a bit. "Okay, I'll tell Jordan to drop us off there."

• • •

If Elisa felt like a tool being dropped off to class by a chauffeur, it was nothing compared to how she felt being dropped off at a *college bar* by a chauffeur. Darcy, however, didn't appear to mind at all that some of their classmates were staring at them. She hopped out of the back seat and leaned in to talk to Jordan, who was still up front.

"Come and get us in an hour, please," she said.

"You got it," he said.

"Thank you, Jordan."

The bar, the Hangover, was nothing like Eclipse. It was small and crowded, with TVs on the wall running multiple sports channels, used jerseys and old alumni photos as decor, and a bulletin board covered in pictures of people who'd managed to eat the Hot! Hot! Hot! Party Platter in under ten minutes.

It was much more what Elisa was used to—cheap, greasy food, sticky countertops, and too much noise to hear yourself think. She'd come here a few times with her parents and had fond memories of watching whatever game was on and listening to them reminisce about their college days. Her father swore by the bar's platter of fried pickles and jalapeños as a hangover cure. Darcy, however, looked hilariously out of place. She visibly shuddered when she touched the countertop, immediately retracting her hand.

"Oh, sorry. I was just about to wipe this down," the bartender said, not looking too concerned. "Now, what can I get for you?"

"Coke, please," Elisa said, sitting on a stool next to a couple of her classmates.

"Same for me, please," Darcy said, looking like she'd rather be anywhere else.

Elisa spent most of the time chatting with Kelly and her friend Amanda. Darcy didn't say anything at all, except for a quick "thank you" when the bartender brought her drink. People had tried to invite her into the conversation, but either she didn't notice, or she was doing a really good job at pretending she didn't.

Elisa finally let it go and ignored her. If she wanted to sit there and not say anything, that was her choice. From what she could tell, the fact that she'd even gone out with the others was progress.

Eventually, Elisa got up to use the bathroom. On the way back, she passed the jukebox, which hadn't worked in years.

One guy, however, didn't seem to have gotten the memo. He stood there, pounding lightly on the top of the machine.

"Come on, *play*, dammit," he muttered.

Elisa repressed a giggle. "That thing's been broken for almost half my life," she said. "You think they'd put up an 'out of order' sign or something."

The guy glanced up. He had dark gray eyes, and a handsome, cheerful face. He looked like he was a couple of years older than Elisa and was taller than her by nearly a foot.

"Scale of one to ten, how much of an idiot did I look like just then?"

"To someone who didn't know the machine was broken? I'd guess a two and a half."

"And to you?" he asked.

"A solid eight."

"Well, make that the first time a girl has ever ranked me only an *eight* out of ten." He gave an exaggerated, smarmy grin.

She laughed in spite of herself. "*Oh* my God, how conceited can you get?" she asked, though she didn't doubt for a second that it was true. He looked a bit like Lucia's favorite soccer player—tall, muscular, and like he had to fight girls off with a stick.

"Hey, I have to brag about my beautiful face. It's all I have."

"All you have, huh?" Elisa asked, leaning against the wall, tilting her head to look at him. "Not even a name?"

He smiled. "I suppose I have that, too."

"May I have it, or have I offended you too much with my sad rating?" She'd never actually flirted with someone before, so she wasn't sure if she was doing it right or not.

He paused, pretending to think it over. "I suppose I can swallow my wounded pride just this once. George Sedgwick. Just call me Wick—everybody does."

"Okay, Wick it is. Avoiding confusion with another George?"

"Nah, I just never liked my name much. It's cute on a toy monkey or a kindergartner, but by the time I was thirteen, I wanted something that suited me a bit better," he said.

"Well, it *does* suit you."

"You know what would suit me even better? What I'd *really* like to have?"

"What?"

"Your phone number."

Elisa groaned aloud. "I should kick your ass," she said, giggles escaping her, even so.

He smiled. "Oh, come on. I know it's awful, but is it really awful enough to warrant physical assault?"

"You think I just give out my phone number to every idiot who punches a jukebox?" she said. "What do you think I am?"

"Well, if I can't have your phone number, can I at least get your name?"

"Elisa. Elisa Benitez."

"May I buy you a drink, Elisa, Elisa Benitez?" Wick asked.

Her heart hit the bottom of her stomach. "I'm only eighteen," she said, suddenly realizing she had no idea how old he was.

He winced. "Yikes. Am I a dirty old man for still thinking you're cute?" he asked.

"Depends. How old are you?"

"Twenty-two."

Elisa smiled. "That's not that bad. We're both college students, then."

"Oh, I'm not a student," Wick said.

"Oh, really? Did you graduate already, or are you not a college kind of guy?"

Wick looked away for the first time since the conversation started. "It's a long story," he said.

She wanted to ask, but she shouldn't pry—after all, they'd only just met.

"Anyway," Wick said, hastily changing the subject, "What do you study?"

"English, because apparently, a future of living under a bridge in a cardboard box is where it's at," she said, chuckling slightly. "I'm actually here with my British Lit class."

"Ooh, I love a girl who is well-read," he said, grinning at her.

Elisa rolled her eyes to cover up the fact that she was blushing. "You're shameless," she said.

"I consider it to be part of my charm. Is it working?"

"Maybe a little."

He smiled broadly. "I knew it."

"Don't get cocky," she said.

"It's probably too late for that."

"Probably."

"Is it such a crime to tell a pretty girl I like her?"

"There are worse things," she admitted, smiling. "You know, twenty-two and eighteen is okay if you go by the 'divide your age in half, add seven' rule."

"*Now* who's shameless?"

"Is it such a crime to tell a pretty boy I like him?"

"Pretty boy? Ouch." Even so, he was smiling. "Leave me some dignity, please."

"You were trying to feed a dollar to a machine that's been dead for nearly a decade. I'm not sure you have much to spare."

"Fair enough." He looked at Elisa intently. "The rule says it's okay?"

"Yep, I did the math."

"So, how about your phone number?"

"Okay."

Wick grinned victoriously, handing over his cell phone so Elisa could put in her number. She was just handing it back to Wick when Elisa crashed back to reality thanks to the sudden and highly unwelcome sight of Darcy across the bar. She was coming toward them, shrinking away from anyone that came within three feet of her.

Elisa groaned, and Wick turned to see what had caught her attention. As soon as he saw Darcy, he went pale.

"I, uh, better get out of here. I'll call you," he said. "It was nice meeting you."

"Uh—you, too," Elisa said. *What the hell?*

He hurried off before she could ask why he was suddenly in such a rush. Somehow, she doubted the fact that he'd seen Darcy and decided to run for it was a coincidence.

"Jordan will be out front in about five minutes," Darcy said, once she reached her. "I was wondering what was taking you so long, anyway."

"I met a guy," Elisa said, shrugging.

"Oh yeah?" She didn't sound too thrilled by this turn of events.

"Yeah. He said he'd call me." She couldn't help but smile. "He's nice. Cute, too."

"Congratulations," she said dryly.

They went out front to wait for their ride, Elisa still riding on the high of meeting Wick. Darcy, meanwhile, seemed to be in an even worse mood than normal. She could practically see the clouds darkening and the birds stop singing.

Just as Jordan arrived and the girls got into the backseat, Elisa's phone went off.

"He just texted me," she said, grinning from ear to ear.

"Desperate," Darcy said, rolling her eyes.

"No, sweet. I like that Wick's the kind of guy who is upfront about telling a girl he likes her. No head games, no playing hard to get—which, so far as I can tell, is speaking in goddamn code—Just talking."

Darcy stared at her. "Not George Sedgwick?" she asked.

Elisa looked up from her phone, then. "You know him?"

Was every aspect of her life going to be touched and ruined by Darcy Fitzgerald?

"I've known him for years," she said. "And, Elisa—listen to me. *Stay away.*"

"So he *did* leave because of you."

"Yes. And he was smart to do so—if I'd seen him face-to-face, I would have ripped his throat out."

Elisa raised her eyebrows. "You hate him that much?" Privately, she took this as a ringing endorsement in Wick's favor.

"I despise him. And I'm trying to protect you when I say block his number and hope you never run into him again."

"Why?"

Darcy hesitated. "I can't tell you," she admitted. "But—but trust me, he's *scum.*"

Elisa gave her an exasperated look. "Oh, come on."

"Listen, a lot of the reason why I hate him is not my story to tell," she said. "But do you really think I'm so spiteful that I'd try to turn you against him for no reason?"

"You really want an answer to that?"

She looked hurt. "I can't force you to believe me," she said. "If I could tell you the full story, I would. But you have my word—I'm trying to look out for you. Wick is bad news. Run fast, run far."

"We'll see."

Shaking her head, she turned to stare out the window. "Don't say I didn't warn you," she muttered.

• • •

Elisa and Wick texted for the rest of the evening, completely ignoring Darcy's glowering whenever she pulled out her phone. She was almost a little embarrassed at how giddy she felt every time her phone went off, alerting her to a new text. She'd only just met the guy, and here she was—practically tripping over herself to answer every message. If Lucia were here, she'd definitely give her an earful about how she should be playing "hard to get" and how she should stop throwing herself at him if she didn't want to scare him off. Personally, Elisa was more a fan of "if you like them, tell them so."

Elisa was about to head to bed for the night when she passed one of the studies. Inside was Darcy, on her phone. She would've kept walking if she hadn't heard her say, "Wick's here."

She stopped dead and stood outside the study door, holding her breath. Darcy was still talking to whoever was on the other end.

"I don't know how long he's been here... I haven't seen him since—yes, yes, since then... I don't know. I don't know..." It was strange, hearing her sound this uneasy. "Well, the good news is, at least he's not there with you... Look, try not to think about it... Has he tried to contact—no? No. Okay, good. Hopefully he'll keep his distance. I made it very clear to him he was never to interact with any of us again... No, he doesn't know. He was talking to Elisa... I tried. I *tried*, okay? She wouldn't listen to me." To her surprise, that did sound more like concern than like annoyance. "Look, she's an adult, she's free to ruin her own life any way she sees fit... Okay, I'll call tomorrow. Try not to worry too much, all right? I love you. Good night."

She'd never heard Darcy's voice so soft or so gentle before.

Elisa quickly slipped away before Darcy had the chance to leave the study, heading down another hall to avoid detection. Her mind reeled with questions. Who was that on the other end? Why did Darcy say Wick would ruin her life? Why would she tell Wick to stay away from her, and why did he listen? And what didn't Darcy want Wick to know?

Another text came through. It was amazing how easily one could be distracted by a flattering message. Elisa didn't dwell on those questions any further—at least, not that night.

Her only other thought on the matter before heading to bed was wondering why Darcy cared if she dated Wick or not.

And why do I care that she cares?

Chapter Eight

In Which the Benitez Sisters are Reunited

Elisa had enjoyed her stay at Netherfield Park, but by the time she'd been there for two weeks, she felt herself going a little stir-crazy—which, considering how huge the McMansion was, should not have been *possible*. Then again, it was hard *not* to go a little crazy when you were living under the same roof as someone you couldn't stand yet always seemed to run into.

And it wasn't just Darcy. Cora and Louise were as awful as ever and seemed to be getting more obnoxious by the day. She doubted they realized how irritating they were, but no way they even cared.

Bobby tried to keep the peace as best he could, but between his endless capacity to be accommodating, and Julieta's complete hatred of confrontation, Elisa often felt like she was the only one willing to call Darcy on her crap. She bit her tongue around the twins, since they were Bobby's sisters. But the way she saw it, Darcy was fair game.

It wasn't just the less-than-ideal company, though. The

guest room she had been put up in was lovely, and she'd enjoyed having her own space for once, but there came a point where she just missed her bed. She'd never spent more than a week away from her home before, and even though it was only across town, she really missed it. And she missed her mom, too. Phone calls weren't the same. Hell, she'd even begun to miss her little sisters. But she'd promised she'd stay until Julieta had recovered.

The second Julieta said she was feeling better, though, her patience wore out.

"Morning," Elisa said, slipping into Julieta's room. The past couple days had been a huge improvement. Julieta had begun joining the others for meals, and while she was still nauseous and unable to go out, she seemed a little less miserable, and she hadn't thrown up in a few days. "How are you feeling?"

"Better," Julieta said. "Much better, actually. I feel... nearly normal."

"Like...'ready to go home' normal?"

Julieta smiled, nodding. "I think so. Tomorrow we can—"

"Oh, to hell with tomorrow," she said, rushing to the closet and pulling down her suitcase. "We're going home *today*."

Julieta sat up, amused. "You're really that desperate to get out of here?"

"You're *not*? You've been here for almost a *month*. Seriously, I was starting to think you were either plague-ridden or pregnant."

"Elisa, I'm not—" Julieta cut herself off, face flushing. "I'm not... There's no way, okay? I've been very careful. Honestly, I think you just like a bit of drama."

"Oh, *please*, with our family? I think the desire for drama is in my blood. Besides, you've been throwing up for a month. I doubt I'm the only one who started to wonder."

"Pretty sure you *are*, actually. I just have a cruddy immune system is all. And it hasn't been all bad... I mean, it was a month with a guy I really like, being treated like royalty." Even so, she kicked off her blanket and got up, starting to get her clothes out of the closet.

"Bobby has been very sweet," Elisa admitted, "but I'm homesick. You must be, too."

"I am." She sighed. "And I'm sure that without me around to micromanage, Mom's been going nuts."

"Ooh, Mom. We should call her."

"I'm going to head downstairs and tell Bobby I'm ready to head home," she said, pulling on her bathrobe over her pajamas. "You go ahead and pack your stuff."

"On it."

Elisa practically ran down the hall to her own room and wasted no time in getting ready, shoving all her books and clothes into her bag, with no care for organization. She was nearly done when she heard a voice behind her.

"I heard a rumor you're leaving."

She jumped. Turning around, she was surprised to see Darcy leaning against the doorway to her room. Her arms were crossed, and she was glowering, as always.

"Julieta's feeling better, so we're getting out of your hair," she said.

"I doubt Bobby ever saw you as an annoyance."

"I think he may have been the only one."

Darcy didn't say anything, just glanced around the room. Her things were almost fully packed.

Finally, she said, "Well, I came to say goodbye."

"Um, thanks?" Elisa said, confused.

"I enjoyed having you here."

"Thanks," Elisa said again, mainly because she couldn't exactly say the feeling was mutual.

"I'll see you in Professor DeCaro's class, then," Darcy

said.

"I guess so."

"I look forward to hearing your thoughts on *Fahrenheit 451*."

With that, Darcy gave an awkward, almost comically formal nod, before walking off without another word. Elisa just stared after her. She couldn't exactly call the interaction *unpleasant*, per se, but it was...weird. Of course, almost all of Darcy's attempts at conversation were weird, when they weren't infuriating. Or both.

Sometimes, Elisa couldn't decide if Darcy was actually a naturally mean person, or if she just never quite got the memo on how human interaction worked.

If it's the latter...there might be hope for her yet. Maybe she's less stiff when it's just her and Bobby?

Julieta popped into the room shortly after Darcy left.

"Bobby says he'll drive us back over to Longbourn," she said. "You all packed?"

"Almost," she said, checking the bedside table drawers to make sure she hadn't left anything. "Darcy came to say goodbye."

Julieta's gaze flicked the bag on the bed. "Her body isn't stuffed in there, is it?"

She rolled her eyes. "Oh, shut up. I was nice." Julieta raised her eyebrows. "Okay, I wasn't *mean*."

Julieta shook her head with a small smile. "Well, hopefully, you can manage to continue to be not-mean long enough to finish packing and meet me and Bobby downstairs."

"I'll be down in five."

· · ·

Elisa called her mother from the car and told her that she and Julieta were on the way home. By the time Bobby had pulled up in front of Longbourn Apartments, she was already waiting out front. She hugged and kissed both of her daughters as soon as they were out of the car, before turning to Bobby, thanking him endlessly for letting them stay with him.

"It was no problem at all, Ms. Bello," he said. "They can come back anytime."

As soon as Bobby drove off, Mom seized Julieta's left hand, looking hopefully at her ring finger. When she saw it was bare, she deflated instantly.

"Damn," she said. "I was hoping you'd managed to lock him down while you were there."

Julieta laughed. "Mom, why would I get engaged and not call to tell you about it?"

"Oh, allow me to have a bit of hope." She grabbed one of Julieta's bags, and the three of them headed toward the elevator. "By the way, Elisa—a couple of your friends are up in the apartment. I may have posted on Facebook that you and Jules were coming back, so they just kind of...showed up."

Elisa smiled. "Good to know I was missed—wait. A *couple*?"

She wasn't a girl with many enemies, but she also wasn't a girl with many friends. She had Charlene, of course, and...

"Colin," she said, forcing a smile when she saw him waiting on her couch.

"Elisa," he said, looking much more genuinely enthusiastic. He threw his arms around her. "I've missed you the past two weeks."

"I've...missed you, too?" Oh, the lies she told to avoid confrontation.

"Hey, E," Charlene said. Once Colin released Elisa, she hugged her, too, though she was much gentler about it.

"Hey," she said, now with a genuine smile. "How've you

been? It feels like it's been ages."

"I'm good. Work is murdering me slowly, but other than that, everything's good. I missed you, though."

"I missed you, too."

Lucia, Maria, and Camila swarmed Julieta the second she came into the apartment. Their voices, high-pitched and overlapping, grated against Elisa's eardrums.

"Did he propose?" Lucia asked, bouncing up and down on her feet.

Julieta laughed. "You are *so* like Mom. No, I am still unengaged."

Lucia groaned.

"By the way, my stomach feels much better, thanks for asking," she added, rolling her eyes a bit.

"So what did you even have?" Maria asked. "You were there forever."

"Ugh, some virus that's been going around," she said with a grimace. "Be glad I wasn't here. I'm shocked I didn't give it to Bobby."

"Yeah, even for you, that one hit you hard."

"Honestly, I was starting to wonder if you had a more... *permanent* issue," Camila added, patting her stomach.

Julieta rolled her eyes, groaning aloud before saying, "I am not pregnant, oh my *God*."

Elisa just laughed, smugly saying, "See? Told you."

"Drama queens," Julieta said. "I am surrounded by drama queens. And Maria."

"*And* your mother," Alejandra added.

"I said what I said."

While Lucia and Camila continued to bombard Julieta with questions about Bobby, Charlene and Elisa sat down on the couch. Much to her annoyance, Colin sat with them. Unsure of how to politely tell someone to go away, she decided not to say anything.

"Anything exciting happen while you were over there?" Charlene asked.

"Well, I mean, there was Darcy, who was... Darcy," she said, rolling her eyes.

"I doubt she knows how to be anything else."

"Yeah, but she's so...so..."

"Darcy?"

"*So* Darcy."

"I know firsthand how irritating she can be," Colin said. "I remember when we were kids, she would entertain herself by dumping whatever she was eating or drinking at the time down my shirt."

Elisa sort of understood the urge but didn't say so.

"We spent a lot of time together as kids, though. I remember our mothers used to take us to the art museum in Columbus at least once a month..." He trailed off, before turning to Elisa. She suddenly got the sense he'd been planning whatever he was about to say next. "Say, I haven't been to the museum in a while, and I think you'd like it. How would you feel about making a trip there sometime? This weekend, maybe?"

Charlene, right on cue, jumped up from the couch, saying, "I'll see if Julieta needs my help unpacking."

Elisa stammered for a moment, before saying, "Colin, that's nice of you to offer, but I'm...uh..."

"Busy?" he asked, looking disappointed.

"Well—no, but, um—"

"It's a beautiful museum," he urged, "and I get in for free. I'm sure I could get you in free, too."

"It's not about the cost of the date, it's about—you know, I don't think you and I would make a good...team. Not like that," she said.

"I...understand," he said. The smile slowly dropped from his face, and the cheerful glint in his eye seemed forced.

Elisa was pretty sure he *didn't* understand but decided not to press the issue. "Thank you for inviting me, though."

He excused himself, and Charlene returned.

"Are you gonna run off every time he does that?" Elisa asked.

She shrugged. "Probably," she said. "I could choke on all the secondhand embarrassment, you know."

"*Good*." She groaned, putting her head in her hands. "I'm really trying to be nice to him, but he's pushing his luck."

"He's…persistent."

"That's one way to put it. I can't believe Mom let him in."

Charlene shrugged. "He's obnoxious, but he's not *mean*. Besides, he likes your mom's cooking. I think she enjoys the praise."

"Well, if he doesn't knock this off soon, I may lose my temper, and no one wants that. Besides," Elisa added with a sly smile, "he has competition now."

She sat up, suddenly interested. "You actually managed to meet somebody at Netherfield?"

"Yes. Well, no, not *at* Netherfield—at The Hangover. Darcy and I went there after class one day, and I met this guy there."

"What's his name?"

"George Sedgwick."

"Sounds fancy. He old money?"

Elisa laughed. "No. He said he works as a bouncer for local clubs and lives in a tiny studio apartment."

"Damn. You were so close to making your mother happy."

"I don't think I would've been able to stand the shame."

Elisa pulled up a selfie Wick had sent her and showed it to Charlene.

"He's cute," Char said. "You guys gone out yet?"

She shook her head. "No, just texting a lot. But get this—

he knows Darcy, and she *hates* him."

She raised her eyebrows. "The plot thickens. She say why?"

"No. She just told me to stay away."

"Maybe she was jealous."

Elisa felt her face warming up at the idea, but quickly pushed it away. *That's not what Char means, dumbass.*

"Doubt it. According to Bobby, Darcy's a hundred percent lesbian, so even if she *did* date him, she probably wouldn't care if anyone else did," she said, shrugging. "Wick ran off from the bar the second he saw her, though, so the feeling's definitely mutual."

"Darcy really didn't say *anything*?"

"Well, she said she was trying to 'protect' me when she told me to stay away from him."

Charlene frowned. "Okay, *that* sounds serious. I mean, it'd be one thing if she just didn't like the guy, but if she actually thinks you dating him would be *dangerous...*"

Elisa snorted. "Come on, he seemed totally nice."

"So did Ted Bundy."

"*Oh*-kay, that's...morbid."

"I'm not saying he's definitely a serial killer," she said, "but if Darcy says it's a matter of safety, don't you think you should at least find out why?"

"I tried to ask her. She wouldn't tell me."

"Have you tried to ask him?"

"No. I didn't want to make things awkward by bringing up Darcy," she admitted.

"Maybe you should. Get his side of the story, at least. Then you can decide for yourself."

"Okay."

Elisa pulled up her texts and typed out a message to Wick.

Hey, so, I've been dying to know since the day we met...what is up with you and Darcy? Darcy Fitzgerald, I mean. She said she knows you, but I got the impression you two aren't exactly...friends. —E

Wick texted back about ten minutes later. Charlene peered over Elisa's shoulder to read the message.

It's a long story. Way too serious. Wouldn't want to dampen the mood we've got going here. ;) —W

"What mood?" Charlene asked, suspicious. "And why the winky face? Elisa Jane Benitez, what have you been—"

"Don't ask questions you don't want the answer to," she said, starting on her response.

Sounds dramatic. Think it has something to do with the reason why Darcy told me to stay away from you "for my own safety?" —E

"Hopefully he's the kind of guy that finds the third degree sexy," Charlene said.

"Shut up."

Ugh. That is so like Darcy... Look, I like you a lot. You know that. But I don't think it'd be very gentlemanly of me to badmouth Darcy. We haven't spoken in years. Maybe she's changed. —W

Elisa and Charlene exchanged shocked glances.

"Ah-ha, so it's Darcy's fault," Elisa said. "Why am I not surprised?"

"Wait until you have all the facts," she said.

"Yeah, yeah..."

I understand. But if you ever change your mind... —E

Well, maybe I could be persuaded...with the right incentive. —W

"If he wants nude pics, say no and block him," Charlene said immediately.

"Oh, ye of little faith."

Oh yeah? —E

Have dinner with me next Saturday night. —W

Elisa's heart skipped a beat. She hesitated, then wrote back.

Deal. Where and when? —E

Place we met. 7 p.m. —W

I'll be there. —E

"Okay, Elisa, look," Charlene said, "I know your judgment may be clouded by his...admittedly impressive arms, but don't you think this is a little weird?"

"What do you mean?"

"I mean the whole... 'I'll let you unlock my Tragic Backstory for the low, low price of going on a date with me.'"

Elisa rolled her eyes. "Oh, come on. I like him. It's hardly a price as far as I'm concerned."

Charlene sighed. "You're an adult," she said. "So it's your choice."

"Okay, now you sound like Darcy."

"Hey." She whacked her on the arm. "Just keep your guard up, okay? And be careful."

"When am I ever not careful?"

Chapter Nine

In Which We Find Out the Walls Are Really, Really Thin

With a little over a week until her date with Wick, Elisa had allowed herself to fall back into her normal routine—aside from Colin coming over every single day since she'd returned home, which did, admittedly, throw off her game a bit. Luckily, on this particular day, he had to be home in time for his weekly bridge game with his mother and her friends, so he was out of the apartment and out of Elisa's hair by suppertime.

She was sitting on the couch, her biology homework on her lap. As she tried to remember what the difference was between prokaryotic and eukaryotic cells, and why she should care, her mother's voice drifted in from the kitchen.

"Yes, I'm aware of when the money is due, but I simply don't have it this week," she pleaded, her voice high-pitched and strained. "I can get it to you in part, but—yes, I understand that, but—look, is there anyone *else* I can speak to? No? Okay, is there *nothing* you can do for me...?" She sighed. "I understand. I'll—I'll figure something out. Thank you. Goodbye."

Elisa heard her mother set her phone down. There was a brief pause, and then a loud groan.

Elisa got to her feet and was standing the kitchen doorway by the time Mom looked up from where she'd placed her head on the table.

"How much of that did you hear?" she asked.

"Enough," she said, sitting in the chair opposite her mother. She paused before deciding to just ask. "You behind on your student loan payments again?"

She hesitated, then nodded. She ran a hand through her dark hair, pushing it out of her tired eyes. "Yeah. There's a minimum amount you have to pay every month, and well…" She sighed and shook her head. "Don't worry about it, Elisa. I'll figure it out."

"Is there anything I can do?" Elisa asked, feeling stupid even as she did. What could she do? She didn't have a job, not even part-time. She'd considered getting one, but to her surprise, her mother talked her out of it.

"As long as we can afford it, focus on school and school alone," she'd said. "I worked two jobs while I was in college, and I barely had time or energy to study. It probably would've made the difference between C's and A's."

"But I want to help," Elisa had replied. "I'm sure I can manage something on the weekends."

"Get a degree, and your choices will double."

"Are you kidding? I'm an *English* major."

Even so, she'd heeded her mother's advice. Her grades were great, but she was just as broke as everyone else in the house, and she doubted Mom would've taken any money from her even if she offered.

"No," Mom said. "Just let me handle this. I'm the adult." She stood and grabbed a can of soda out of the fridge. "You go to school for four years to get a degree to get a job, and then you spend the rest of your natural life using the job to pay off the degree. But if you *don't* have a degree, you can't find a job at all. It's a trap."

"You don't regret going to college, do you?"

"No," she admitted. "It was very important to my parents that I went, and I enjoyed my time there. I just wish I'd been able to get scholarships. Honestly, Elisa—if it ever gets to the point where scholarships won't cover your tuition anymore and you have to take out a loan, it may be worth it to take a break from school to get a job, after all."

"I know," Elisa said, sincerely hoping that wouldn't happen. She liked college, and it was a nice reprieve between the hell that was high school and the hell that awaited her in the workforce.

Seeing the look on her daughter's face, Mom quickly added, "But I doubt it'll come to that. You've always been good with school. I'm sure you'll be fine." She paused. "You've applied for scholarships for next semester, right?"

She nodded. "I sent in the general application last weekend."

"Good. Do *not* let yourself get trapped in the black hole of student loans." She smiled, trying to lighten the mood. "It's too late for me, so just leave me behind. Run. Save yourself."

Elisa chuckled. She paused, debating with herself whether or not it'd be wise to voice her next thought.

She decided to just go for it.

"If you're really behind," she said carefully, "I'm sure Papa would be willing to help."

Her mother's smile dropped immediately, and the look she gave her probably would've made lesser women shake with fear.

"Don't even go there," she said.

"I'm just saying—I doubt he could pay it all off, even if you asked him to, but surely he'd be able to help you make this month's payment."

"I'm sure he could. But I'm not asking my ex-husband for a loan," she said, words clipped.

"Mom, in nine years, has he *ever* missed a child support payment?"

"No. But that's money he pays to help support you girls. It's *very* different."

"But if you just talked to him, I'm sure he'd want to help you out. I mean, he still cares about you, and—"

"I have my pride."

"Okay, okay, fine. Fine…" Elisa said. She and her mother could argue until the Rapture if no one stopped them, but sometimes, she had to pick her battles.

Mom gave a short, exasperated huff. "It's not that I don't think your father would help if I asked," she said, "but the day I ask Miguel for a loan is the day I let you take a job in an Atlantic City strip club."

"You know, strippers can make really good money. Just saying."

Mom rolled her eyes, but she was smiling. "Like I said, Elisa—they're my loans, my problem."

"Okay. I just… I hate seeing you so stressed out about this."

"I'm the mother of five. I'm *always* stressed out about something."

Elisa sighed. "I'm gonna go finish up my homework, okay?"

"Okay," Mom said. She pecked her on the cheek. "Dinner will be in an hour or so."

She got up from the kitchen table and headed into the living room, accidentally bumping into the room divider as she moved toward the couch.

A muffled *oof* came from behind the wall.

Frowning, Elisa walked around, poking her head into the

closed-off section of the living room her youngest sister had claimed.

All four of her sisters were crouching on Lucia's bed. Camila had her ear to the wall.

"Hey, E," Julieta said, trying to look innocent.

"What the..." Elisa said, keeping her voice down. The last thing her mother needed was to know that the entire household had heard her conversation with the bank. She quickly slipped into the tiny, claustrophobic space, hands on her hips. "How long were the four of you eavesdropping?"

"It was Cam's idea," Maria said.

"Liar," Camila gasped.

Elisa rolled her eyes. "That's not what I asked. And seriously—*et tu*, Julieta?"

She shrugged helplessly. "I was worried, okay?"

"We all were," Lucia added. "I didn't know Mom still had loans to pay off. Hasn't she been paying them off for, like, twenty years now?"

"More." Elisa sighed, sitting down on the bed. It was crowded and cramped, but she made it work—she and her sisters had all forced themselves onto the same bed before. Whether Julieta was reading them all a bedtime story, or Elisa had just had the most awful day and needed a willing audience to rant at, or Camila had been scared by a thunderstorm and needed company, they'd managed to make it work. Granted, the last time had been when they were all much younger and much smaller...

"I still have some money left over from that bet I won against Natasha Bridges last week," Lucia said, looking like she was thinking very hard. "I mean, it's not much, but maybe it could help this month—"

"No," Julieta said, gently but firmly. "Mom would never accept money from one of us. Trust me, I've tried. I pay for my share of the groceries, and I help cover the bills sometimes, but she won't let me touch her loans. And I actually have a job—there's no way she'd take money from someone who doesn't."

"I wish she'd ask Papa for help." Camila sighed. "I mean, they're still friends, right?"

Elisa shrugged. "'Friends' may be a strong word. They don't hate each other or anything."

"Mama was devastated when Papa left her," Julieta said. "You're all a bit young to remember this, but she cried a lot for the first couple months after he moved out. Tío Javier moved in for a while to help with the rent and look after things while she tried to find a better paying job and get back on her feet."

"I'd almost forgotten about that," Elisa said quietly. Javier was her only uncle, and he lived in Chicago. She hadn't seen him in a couple of years, but now that Julieta had said it, she could remember him fixing dinner while Mom was out at interviews and driving the sisters to and from school.

Elisa had asked him once if he was angry at her father. At the age of nine, she was too young to really grasp the nuances of marriage and divorce, but she'd understood that there were a lot of complicated emotions for everyone involved.

"A little," Javier had replied. "I hate seeing Alejandra hurt like this. But I don't think I'll stay mad forever. He's your dad, and that's the most important thing." He'd looked at her then. "Are *you* mad at him?"

Elisa hadn't said anything at first, but, once she realized she really wouldn't be in trouble no matter what she said, she'd responded, "Yeah. Kinda. Everything was so nice before. Now it's all weird and sad. Mom's sad all the time, and Dad isn't here, 'cept when he picks us up on the weekends, and… I dunno. It just sucks."

"Yeah," he agreed. "But it won't be that way forever. You can be mad at him if you want. Just try and keep it from taking over, okay? That doesn't help anyone."

Elisa had nodded, feeling like she only sort of understood. At the time, she couldn't really imagine not being a little angry with her father, but mostly, she'd just been happy to be able to admit it.

"Mom doesn't like to talk about that time much anymore," Julieta said. "I mean, she's doing all right now—I think she knows the divorce was probably for the best. But at the time..." She sighed, shaking her head. "I'm not sure she could ever really be friends with Papa. Even if it wasn't *completely* his fault, he broke her heart. In the long run, it had to be done, but..."

"Doesn't make it hurt any less," Maria said.

"Yeah. And it's hard to be friends with your ex at the *best* of times. When you loved them as much as Mom loved Papa..."

"The higher they are, the harder they fall, huh?" she asked.

"Something like that."

Maria sighed, picking a piece of lint off of her jeans. "I'm never getting married," she declared. "*Never.*"

Julieta touched her younger sister's arm. "Come on, Maria, don't say that."

"I mean it," she insisted. "Look, it's not that I wouldn't like to find love or whatever...but all of my friends have divorced parents, like us. Half of those, the parents won't even *talk* to each other. My friend Isabelle, she said that her mom won't even see her dad. *Literally.* She goes to her dad's house on the weekends, and her mom drops her off a block away and has her walk over, so she doesn't have to see her ex."

"Most divorced couples don't act like that, though," Camila said. "I mean, Mom even has Papa come over for Christmas and our birthdays, and they never argue."

"Oh, they argue," Elisa said dully. "They just try not to

let us see it."

"W-well, that's still good," she said. "I mean, if they really hated each other, they wouldn't care about arguing in public, would they?"

She shrugged. "Maybe. I don't know."

"Divorced couples *can* get along," Julieta said, "and it's not like after you get divorced, you'll never fall in love again."

"Mom hasn't," Maria said quietly.

"No," she admitted, "not yet. But some people just take a long time to move on, that's all. And besides, she's so busy, with her job and us..."

"I don't see how a few years of happiness is worth who knows how many years of heartache."

"Not all marriages end like Mom and Papa's, though."

"Fifty percent of marriages end in divorce," Elisa pointed out.

She paused, flustered, before saying, "But if you assume your marriage is in the fifty percent, you're setting yourself up for failure. Being pessimistic can really screw you over."

"Being a pessimist rocks," Maria said dryly. "I'm always either right or pleasantly surprised."

This was met with some weak chuckles, but they faded away quickly. The sisters fell into silence for a moment. Elisa could hear Mom's voice, coming from her bedroom. She was on the phone again, probably talking to her brother or one of her parents; she was speaking Spanish. She didn't even bother trying to eavesdrop.

Unlike her mother and uncle, she and her sisters had not been raised bilingual. Mom had said that she'd always *meant* to bring them up speaking Spanish, but clearly, it hadn't worked out like that. Elisa knew enough to manage basic pleasantries, but anything more complicated than small talk was beyond her. The only Benitez sister that spoke it fluently was Maria, and she'd used an online course to teach herself.

This also had the side effect of making her the favored grandchild of their mother's parents, since she was the only one who could talk to them much.

Lucia brought her knees up to her chest. "I can't wait to get married and have kids," she said. "I always thought I'd make a good stay-at-home mom."

"No career plans?" Elisa asked.

"I mean, I've also thought about becoming an internet celebrity."

She snorted. "Combine those two and become a mommy blogger."

"I know you're being sarcastic, but if I can, I totally will."

"You're fourteen. You might be surprised what you actually end up doing," Julieta said. "I mean, I didn't think I'd end up running my own business, but I love it. And Bobby's a nice bonus."

"Let's be real, raising a family *is* a full-time job," Lucia replied. "Probably why Mom's always so tired. I guess I could be the one that works if my husband really likes kids."

"My plan is to stay in school for as long as humanly possible," Maria said. "College, grad school, the whole thing. After that, I might become a professor or something. Getting paid to force people to read books and write papers sounds great." She nudged Elisa. "I always assumed that was your plan, too."

"I don't have much of one," she admitted. "I'm taking it semester-by-semester. I wouldn't be surprised if I end up teaching, though."

"What do you *want*, though? Dream big."

"What I want…" She paused, thinking it over. "I want to travel. A lot. I'd love to be one of those people that has apartments in big cities all over the worlds. With books, lots of books… And, you know, if I happened to be able to bring my soulmate along for the ride, even better. Or Charlene.

Actually, screw marriage, I want to go on a worldwide road trip with my best friend."

"I already know what I'm gonna do," Camila said. "I'm going to do makeup for actors on movie sets."

"Really?" This was a surprise to her. She'd always known Cam had liked experimenting with different beauty products, and she was very good at it, but this was the first she'd heard of her wanting a career in the field. Actually, this was the first she'd heard of her wanting a career at all, except for that period where she'd wanted to be an Olympic archer when she was five.

"Totally. I'd be great at it, and those skills are always needed. Hair and makeup artists are the unsung heroes of the movie industry."

"Why do you think I let her practice on me all the time?" Lucia added.

"Huh." *Man, I need to listen to them more often.* "Hey, if it works out with Jules and Bobby, he could probably introduce you to some people."

"Don't jinx it," Julieta said. "I really want it to work out."

"Personally," Elisa said, "I'm only going to get married if I find the deepest, purest, truest love in the world. Which is why I'm planning my life around the assumption that I'll one day be the family spinster."

All her sisters broke into giggles. Elisa grinned.

"It's a hard job, I know, but someone's gotta do it," she said. "I'll overstay my welcome during holidays at Julieta and Bobby's mansion, give your kids questionable life advice, tell all the wild and embarrassing stories of our youths, be the one that teaches all the kids at family gatherings about sex and drugs and R-rated movies, drink vodka-laced coffee at the breakfast table... It'll be great."

"Can there be two spinsters in a family?" Maria asked, smiling a bit.

"I think, at that point, we cease to be spinsters and become 'maiden aunts,'" Elisa said. "Which would mean it'd be our job to house any unmarried children of our siblings to help them find husbands, lest they wind up bitter old crones like us."

"Wait," Lucia said. "You'd be the Spinster Sisters. You could totally start a band with that name."

Elisa laughed. "What do you say, Maria? If we're both still single when we're fifty, we start a band?"

Maria laughed, too. "Deal."

Chapter Ten

In Which Colin Does. Not. Get. It.

Three days before Elisa was supposed to go out with Wick, she was still stuck playing host to Colin Burger. He'd come over every single day after class let out, like clockwork. And no matter how desperately Elisa hinted to her mother that she didn't want to spend time with him, she kept letting him in.

Today, he had crashed dinner with Elisa, her mother, her sisters, and Charlene. The dinner table was too crowded at the best of times, but the addition of Colin made it feel even more cramped than normal. It didn't help that he was, as always, talking.

"So, then Mother and I began to check into our hotel," he said, "but our luggage hadn't arrived yet. So, Mother gets on the phone with the hotel's management to complain that the bellhop had lost our bags, when the bellhop himself appears behind her, just as she was demanding they fire him. With our bags in tow, no less. Of course, he took offense when he heard Mother's harsh criticism of him, and it showed on his face.

Just as I was about to pull Mother away from the situation, so she wouldn't say something she'd regret, the bellhop's boss comes over and—"

"Would you like more mashed potatoes?" Mom interrupted. Camila and Lucia both blinked out of their stupor. Elisa just continued staring at the wall behind him, which was how she'd fooled him into thinking she was listening.

"Oh, yes, please, Ms. Bello," he said, eagerly handing over his plate. "Your cooking reminds me so much of the cook we had back home, before I moved out, anyway. As glad as I am to be living on my own, there are times when I miss the way she would prepare meals…"

And he was off again. Elisa had taken to thinking about her most recent Introduction to Literature assignment as a means to ignore him. She'd escaped into her own head, thinking about the paper she had to write on *Fahrenheit 451*, when Charlene spared them all from his latest monologue.

"How's work going, Julieta?" she asked.

"It's going good, I think," she said. "Bobby told a few of his friends about my business, so I've gotten a rush of new clients."

Mom beamed. "Bobby really is good to you, isn't he?"

"In more ways than one," Maria muttered. Elisa kicked her under the table.

"Y'all going out anytime soon?" Mom asked.

She nodded. "He got us tickets to a laser show at the planetarium."

"Oh, I love those," Charlene said.

"I do, too," Colin said. He looked across the table, directly at Elisa. "Do you go there much?"

"Not much," she said, already sensing where this was headed.

"I'd like to go sometime soon. Would you do me the

honor of accompanying me?"

Charlene's hazel eyes darted to the kitchen door. She must have decided it was too far and too crowded for her to make a break for it because she stayed in her seat.

"I'm sorry, I'm very busy," Elisa said. Her voice came out much icier than she'd intended, but he didn't appear to notice.

"Oh, I'd be happy to accommodate your schedule," Colin said. From his expression, she could tell he wasn't being intentionally obtuse—he really was that oblivious.

It looked like she'd have to be blunt.

"Uh... Colin, could we talk alone, maybe?" she said, wanting to at least spare him the experience of being rejected in front of six other people.

"Actually, I was hoping we could talk right here." He rose from his seat.

"Um," Lucia said.

"I don't think that's a good idea." Elisa stood, too. "Let's just go into my room to talk, okay?"

"Dude, *listen to her*," Camila whispered.

He didn't.

Elisa began to leave the table and head toward her bedroom door, but Colin was faster, reaching her and taking her wrist in his hand, stopping her in her tracks.

"Elisa Benitez..."

"Oh my *God*," Maria said.

"Elisa, I have been pursuing your affections for almost a year now," he said. "I know, this may come as a shock to you."

"It doesn't," Lucia said, since Elisa was too flabbergasted to say a word.

He stammered for a second before he could use actual words again. "I really enjoy spending time with you, and I think you and I would be very well-matched. We're both intelligent, ambitious people, and we both enjoy fine literature and a good movie. Furthermore, my apartment is only a fifteen-minute drive away from yours, so we would always be in close proximity, and the fact that we are both college students would give us plenty to talk about. Now, I know you've turned me down before—"

"That's right." She finally found her voice, and when she found it, it came out sharp. "I have. Multiple times. So why on earth are you asking me again?"

He faltered, for just a moment. "B-because," he said, "because I very much like you. And I believe that I could make you very happy, if you'd allow me to try."

"I *don't* allow it," she said, wrenching her wrist out of his grasp. "And even if I did, you and I would *never* work as a couple."

The color drained from Colin's face. "Wh-why don't we step out?" he said, eyes darting nervously to the table. Mom was very still, eyes wide and horrified. Julieta, Maria, and Charlene all looked like they wanted to sink through the floorboards. Camila and Lucia were practically watching with popcorn.

Elisa let out a mirthless laugh. "Ohhh, no. I gave you the chance to avoid this, and you *blew it*. You put me on the spot and ask me out in front of my whole family—you get shot down in front of my whole family. Come to think of it, I gave you the chance to avoid it the first two times I rejected you. Or was it the first *three* times?"

"Um…"

"Whatever, it doesn't matter. The point is—I have tried and tried to be nice when turning you down," she said, "but it appears nothing less subtle than a baseball bat to the head will work with you. Colin, I don't like you. And I never will. And I don't just mean I don't like you *like that*. I mean, I don't like you, *period*."

Colin looked like he'd been slapped. Charlene made a heroic effort to intervene.

"Um, maybe we should get the table cleared off—"

"I'm not done," she said. "Here's a little tip for you, Colin. When a girl says she can't go out with you because she's busy but doesn't specify a time when she's *not* busy—she's rejecting you. When a girl opts to dance with someone she hates over dancing with you—she's rejecting you. When a girl has her best friend intervene repeatedly to avoid spending time with you—she's rejecting you. And if you want the next poor girl you try to inflict yourself on to *not* reject you, here are some handy pointers."

Her mother tried to intervene next. "Elisa, I think he gets it."

"No, Mom, I don't think he does. First tip: if you want people to like you, maybe talk about something other than yourself. Second tip: stop hugging and touching people without their permission. Third tip: stop acting like you take care of and provide for yourself. Your mom pays for everything. We all know it. Fourth tip: learn to take a rejection the first time you hear it. Because, you know, if you'd backed off earlier, maybe we could've at least been friends. But now, I don't want anything to do with you, romantically or otherwise. Because you, Colin Burger, are an obnoxious, self-centered creep who won't take no for an answer, and if you ever come over here again, I'll beat your ass and I'll enjoy doing it!"

With that, Elisa was done, and the room was so quiet, the noise from the apartment across the hall seemed loud. Elisa hadn't raised her voice—much—but she felt like she'd been screaming for a thousand years. Colin stood there, face pale, staring at her. Her mother had buried her face in her hands, and even Camila and Lucia looked like they'd stopped enjoying the show.

"I...understand," he finally said, after an unbearably long pause. "I'll, um, just...just show myself out, then. Thank you for dinner, Ms. Bello. Um..."

He hesitated, then went for the door.

Elisa turned on her heel, and went into her bedroom, slamming the door behind her.

A couple minutes later, Camila poked her head in.

"You okay, Lisa?" she asked tentatively.

She sighed, tugging anxiously at her dark hair. "I think so. I didn't exactly enjoy that."

"Kind of seemed like you did," Camila said. She sat down on Julieta's bed, facing Elisa.

She rolled her eyes. "Well, I mean, I'd been holding that back for about a year now," she said. "But spelling out everything I hate about somebody isn't my idea of fun."

"Are you kidding? You're practically the Ohio state champ." She smoothed her skirt. "You were a bit...harsh."

"Oh, come on. I was nice the first couple times I turned him down. He did this to himself."

"I guess, but—"

"The way I see it, once a guy refuses to take no for an answer, you don't have to be nice to him anymore." She flopped down onto her bed, staring up at the cracked ceiling.

"I'm not sure Mama will agree with you on that front," Camila warned.

She groaned. "Crap. I spent all that time trying to keep her from realizing Colin was interested..." She turned her gaze toward her sister. "Guess she knows, huh?"

She scrunched her face up in sympathy. "Looks that way."

"Well, she can get over it," she said. "Because I'm never going to like Colin Burger. Ever."

"Yeah, I'm... I'm pretty sure you made that clear, Lisa."

"Mostly, I just feel sorry for whatever poor woman he manages to trick into marrying him five or ten years from now..."

Interlude: In Which Colin Becomes Self-Aware

Unable to stand the intensely awkward silence that had overtaken the room after Colin left and Elisa stormed off, Charlene decided now was the time to excuse herself.

"I better head home now," she said, rising from the dinner table. She rinsed off her dishes in the sink as quickly as she could manage. "Thank you for having me over, Alejandra."

"Always a pleasure, dear," she said. She looked about ready to pass out.

Charlene quickly left, closing the door behind her and feeling *extremely* glad she wasn't going to be part of the discussion that was about to happen. Her long, red hair fell into her face, forcing her to push it away as she headed toward the elevator. When it arrived, she pressed the button for the first floor. And, as always, said a small prayer that today wouldn't be the day the elevator broke down.

Coffee. Coffee was something that she needed. Even if it was seven at night—getting a nice boost was the only way she'd be able to distract herself from the…experience she'd just had.

When she stepped out of the front door of Longbourn, she was surprised to see a familiar face sitting on the bench by the curb, looking quite miserable.

"Colin?" she said, approaching him slowly.

He looked up, then quickly looked away, rubbing his eyes. "Charlene, hi. I was just…um, my car's in the shop, so I'm waiting on an Uber."

"Oh."

She hesitated. She *could* just walk away now and leave him to mope. And yet…

"You okay?" she asked. It was a stupid question; of course he wasn't. But asking him still felt like the right thing.

He nodded, rubbing his eyes again. "Yeah, yeah. I mean, I've been better, of course, but…this too shall pass. That's the saying, right?"

She sat on the bench next to him. "Yeah. But that doesn't mean you have to be okay right away. I mean, Elisa had a right to turn you down, but that was…brutal."

"Yeah, that's, uh…that's one word for it."

There was a brief pause, during which she pretended not to notice Colin sniffling and wiping his nose on his jacket sleeve.

Then, he asked, "Was she right? Have I been acting like a creep?"

Charlene hesitated. "Um… Well, I mean, you did come on pretty strong."

"Well, yeah, but I thought girls wanted you to be forward," he said. "And then I thought maybe she was playing hard-to-get, so I tried again."

"And again," she pointed out.

"Well, yeah. I mean… I guess now that I think about it, she was giving off some hints that she wasn't into it," he admitted.

"Like?" she prompted.

"Like...always excusing herself early whenever I was over for dinner...always cutting me off whenever I talked..." He frowned. "And always suddenly needing to be somewhere else when I tried to talk to her alone..."

And then, she saw it on his face: the slowly dawning sensation of self-awareness.

"Never responding to my messages...the fact that whenever I called, I'd always get sent to voicemail after a ring or two..." Colin continued slowly. "Stiffening up whenever I touched her...without explicit permission... Outright... rejecting me when I asked her out, aaaaaaaaaaand I'm a goddamn idiot."

"*There* it is," Charlene said.

"I am *such* a goddamn idiot," he said again, face flushing red as he covered it with his hands. "I'm a member of the *honors* fraternity, and I couldn't figure that out?"

"You were blinded by your feelings. And also your massive, insufferable ego."

Much to her surprise, he actually snorted. He took his hands down from his face. His eyes lacked their usual, cheerful glint, and were now clouded with doubt.

"She's right."

"Yeah," she said. "I don't think you're a bad guy, Colin, but...you kind of made a mess of this one."

"No kidding," he said. "Do you think it's worth apologizing to her?"

"It never hurts to try," she said with a shrug. "But I'd wait until she's had a couple of days to calm down. Elisa was pretty fired up."

"You're right, I'll... I'll give her space. Maybe I should send her a very respectful text message..."

"Give it a couple of days," Charlene said firmly.

"Right, right, you're right..." Colin sighed, running a

hand through his sandy brown hair. "Where are you headed, anyway? I thought you lived here, too."

"I do," she said. "I was just going for some coffee."

There was a pause.

"Did Elisa really have you intervene so she wouldn't have to spend time with me?" he asked, tilting his head as he looked at her.

Charlene didn't answer with words. She just made a noise and a face.

Colin understood perfectly and groaned.

"So, everyone knew she hated me except me?"

"Yeah. Sorry."

"Don't be." He sighed. "I think I may have brought this on myself."

"'Think,' nothing," Charlene said. "You *absolutely* did." Then, her expression softened, just a bit, and she patted him on the knee. "But it's not too late to say you're sorry. I don't know if you and Elisa can ever be friends, exactly, but a sincere apology can work wonders."

"And she'll get one," he said. "After she's had time to become less…murderous… At least that'll give me time to write up a first draft."

"Wait, wait—you make drafts of your apologies?" she asked, unable to hide her amusement.

"I make drafts of *everything* important I have to say." Colin reached into his pocket for his phone and pulled up the notes app, showing it to her. "This one from yesterday is from when I had to call my advisor to ask her a question… This is from two weeks ago from when I had to schedule a doctor's appointment."

"What's that one?"

"That was telling my mom that it was actually me that broke her Ming vase when I was seven and I blamed it on the dog."

"And this one's…"

"What I was planning to say to Elisa today? Yeah…"

Charlene sighed, glancing over the note. Sure enough, the first part was word-for-word of what Colin had said at dinner. It appeared he hadn't been halfway through before Elisa cut him off.

"Well, if you need someone to proofread your apology, I'm available," she said.

"Thanks. I'm probably going to start on it once I get home."

"Speaking of which…" Charlene pointed to the road in front of them, just as a red car pulled up in front of Longbourn. "I think your chariot awaits."

Colin glanced at his phone. "Yeah, that's my ride." He got up from the bench. "Well…thanks for talking to me. I'll message you once I have a first draft."

"Okay. I'd say, 'have a good night,' but, well… I think I'll settle for 'have a good tomorrow.'"

"Nowhere to go but up."

He made his way over to the car, climbing into the backseat. Before the car could pull away, he rolled his window down.

"There's a coffee shop in my apartment complex," he called.

"I know," she called back.

"Care to join me at that one? My treat."

Charlene paused. *Okay, this is a guy who was interested in your best friend until literally five minutes ago, and he's sort of an idiot—probably the smartest idiot you've ever met, but still.*

Noticing her hesitation, he quickly began to backpedal.

"I mean—only if you want, if you don't want to, that's fine—"

But he does seem to want to be better. And there's no rule saying I'm not allowed to be friends with him. It's not weird. Is it?

Nah.

"Move over, I'm coming," she said, hopping up from the bench.

Colin opened the backdoor for her, and she hurried over, not wanting to keep the driver waiting any longer than they already had.

Why she'd agreed, she had no idea. He was absolutely ridiculous, even if he was harmless, and most of his awkwardness was weirdly endearing.

What am I doing? It wasn't that she felt sorry for him. He had been a jerk in so many ways.

But when he wasn't droning on about things, he was nice.

What was the harm in going for a cup of coffee with him?

Still, she had no idea why she'd accepted his invite.

Nope. Not weird at all.

Chapter Eleven

In Which Parental Support Is... Lacking

"Elisa Jane Benitez, I order you to call Colin right now and tell him you're sorry."

"I'm *not* apologizing. I have nothing to apologize *for*."

Elisa and her mother had been having this argument ever since Charlene left. She was still sitting on her bed, refusing to dignify the argument by standing up. Her mother, meanwhile, hadn't stopped pacing since she came in.

"Colin Burger could be very good for you, Elisa," Mom said, trying to force her daughter to see reason. Or, more accurately, *her* version of reason.

"I don't *like* him, Mom," she said, throwing up her hands in exasperation. "He's a jerk."

Mom stopped pacing long enough to give her a stony stare. "A jerk with a huge bank account and a very good family."

"You can't *stand* his family. You threw a tray of brownies at his mom at a PTA meeting when I was twelve."

"I am willing to put all that unpleasant business behind

me," she said.

"If you like Colin, you can have him. I won't touch him with a ten-foot pole."

"Why not?"

"Because I don't like him," she said through clenched teeth. "What part of that don't you get?"

"Don't you take that tone with me, Elisa Jane."

"Sorry," she snapped in a tone that indicated that she wasn't.

"Elisa, I *order* you to apologize and agree to give him a chance."

She crossed her arms. "You can't force me to go out with him," she said.

"If—if you don't—" Her mother was sputtering, trying to find something she could say to sway her. "If you don't apologize and give him at least one date, God as my witness, I'll never speak to you again."

"Promise?"

She glared at her but didn't say anything. Elisa rolled her eyes. Her mother was bluffing, and they both knew it. She'd threatened to never speak to her again when she got suspended for calling her old sociology teacher a "sexist, racist, backward-thinking, limp-dicked idiot," too. After twelve hours or so, she'd cracked and admitted that Elisa hadn't been entirely wrong, though she still felt that bringing his dick into it was a bit uncalled for. This would be no different, she was sure. She just had to wait it out.

Elisa got to her feet and stormed out of her bedroom, not bothering to see if Mom was following. "Well, as long as you're giving me the silent treatment," she said, grabbing her jacket, "I'm going to Papa's for a couple of hours. See you later."

"Elisa, you get—" She cut herself off.

"Bye."

She left the apartment, slamming the door behind her.

Her father lived in a small house with two roommates, a married couple named Stella and Yvonne, but they never seemed to mind when she came over unannounced. Luckily, it was only a twenty-minute walk. The cold autumn air nipping at her heels, Elisa hurried over to her father's house, thinking of all the ways her mother would probably make her life difficult for the next couple of weeks.

When she arrived, Stella answered the door. She was a short woman, even shorter than Elisa, and had dyed her hair a violent shade of purple.

"Is Papa here?" Elisa asked, shivering a bit from the wind.

"Yeah," she said. She stepped aside to let Elisa in, yelling up the stairs. "Miguel, Daughter Number Two is here to see you."

"Coming," he yelled back.

The small house's living room was stacked, wall-to-wall, with books. About 90 percent of them belonged to Elisa's father. Back when he still lived in Longbourn, most of the living room's floor space had been dedicated to his extensive library. Now that he'd moved out, it had grown exponentially. She swore it gained at least ten new books every time she came over.

Miguel Benitez dashed down the stairs, smiling once he saw his daughter. In spite of the awful day she'd been having, she smiled, too.

"Hey, Lisa," he said, wrapping his arms around her as soon as he reached her. As usual, his clothes smelled like the newspaper factory in which he worked. He pulled back to look at her face. His dark eyes, which he'd passed on to Elisa, glinted with thought as he looked her over. "Let's see…" he said, half to himself. "It's after dinnertime, you didn't call before coming over, you didn't bring a bag, meaning you left quickly... Your mom pissed you off."

"Bingo," she said.

"What happened?"

As they spoke, he began leading her up the stairs. The staircase, which creaked with every move they made, was also a storage space for more books. Stacks of dog-eared paperbacks rested at the bottom of the steps. If she hadn't already known they were there, she might have tripped over them. The house was just big enough for three people, but they had to make the best of the relatively small space they had been granted.

"Colin Burger asked me out," she said.

Her dad did a double take.

"That obnoxious kid you used to be in book club with?" he asked. His lip instinctively curled in disgust, earning a small grin from his daughter.

"The same," she said.

"What'd you say?"

She rolled her eyes. "What do you *think* I said?"

"Did he cry?"

"Not while I was there. I kind of let him have it," she admitted.

"How bad was it?" he asked. They reached the door to his room, which probably could've come off its hinges if someone breathed on it too hard. He pushed it open carefully, stepping aside to let her in.

Elisa tossed her bag onto his desk chair. "Um...the phrases 'obnoxious, self-centered creep' and 'I'll beat your ass' may have been thrown around."

"So, a pretty standard Benitez family dinner?"

"*Papa.*"

"Sorry. Colin Burger's rich, isn't he?"

"Seriously rich," she confirmed. "He's related to the Fitzgeralds."

"Damn. I take it your mother wasn't too thrilled you let a rich, single man slip through your fingers," he said. He sat down on his bed, which was really too small for a man of his height. The tiny room functioned as a combination bedroom/office, and the furniture setup was much closer to a game of Tetris than a page out of *Better Homes and Gardens*.

"More like 'forcefully threw a rich, single man directly into the trash can where he belongs.'" She sighed, leaning against the wall. "Mom said she won't speak to me ever again if I don't go out with him."

"God as her witness?"

"God as her witness."

Miguel rolled his eyes. "That sounds about right," he said. "I give her six hours before she caves. She can't force you to like him, and I think she knows that. And if you ever feel the temptation to give in, just remember: Alex may never speak to you again if you don't go out with him, but *I'll* never speak to you again if you *do*."

She laughed. "Woe is me," she said. "No matter what I do, I'll lose one of you."

He smiled. "Don't worry too much about this whole thing," he said. "There are plenty of Colins out there, but there's only one you. Your mom will get over it soon enough. Especially since Jules is dating that Robert person. Are they still together?"

Elisa nodded. "Yeah, it seems to be going pretty well. Mom's been so psyched about their relationship status that she's forgotten to hassle me about mine. You know, until Colin ruined that for me."

"Maybe you could bribe Julieta into having a fight with *her* friend. That should keep your mother distracted."

She snorted. "Unlikely. Jules likes him too much. And I'm not sure Bobby is *capable* of being disagreeable."

"Oh yeah, isn't he the one that let you stay in his house

for half a month?"

She nodded, having a seat next to her father on the bed. "Yep."

He let out a laugh. "Maybe you should've started squatting there."

"Now, you sound like Mom."

She glanced at his bedside table and the framed picture there of herself and her sisters at Julieta's community college graduation, all standing arm-in-arm in front of the stage. They were all laughing, giddy, Julieta in a cap and gown, everyone else in sundresses for the occasion. It was one of the only pictures Elisa had seen in the past few years where Maria was smiling.

That had been a pretty good night. Their parents had spent the entire ceremony and the party back at the apartment in proximity of each other, and nothing exploded. Camila and Lucia had been kind enough to put their usual antics to rest, meaning Elisa hadn't run herself ragged looking after them. Even Alejandra's parents and Miguel's parents, who normally couldn't be in the same city without someone getting slapped or yelled at, had managed to put their feud aside for the sake of Julieta's graduation.

That was one advantage, Elisa supposed, to being the family darling—*no one* wanted to be the one that ruined her special day. She could only hope that this would still be true when she got married. As the presumptive maid of honor, she was pretty sure it was her job to murder any troublemakers, and it would make things super awkward if the troublemakers turned out to be her own grandparents.

"You seen Cam and Lulu lately?" she asked, finger running over the wooden frame of the picture. Miguel saw her and Julieta fairly frequently, and Maria often came over to his house to study when the apartment was too loud. Back when they were younger, he'd spend time with all of them nearly every week. But as the girls got older, he acquired two roommates to help with the rent, and he took on more responsibilities at work, the arrangement had changed from "Papa comes and gets us and we stay with him on the weekends" to "we all have a key and are free to come over whenever we like." Now that all the sisters were old enough to walk over to his house on their own, this was okay in theory, but in practice, it just led to Camila and Lucia falling through the cracks.

Personally, Elisa thought the reasons her father had given for changing the arrangement were pretty lame. But she wasn't sure how to breach the topic without starting a massive argument.

He shifted awkwardly where he sat. "I IM'd Lucia last night," he offered.

She sighed. She loved her father, but she'd never been a fan of his "hands-off" approach when it came to her two youngest sisters. Julieta, Elisa, and Maria were usually okay with minimal interference from their father, but the other two needed all the help they could get.

"They know my door is always open to them," he said, sensing his daughter's exasperation.

"It feels like they're getting wilder all the time," she said, because she didn't dare question his parenting style directly. *Indirectly*, however...

"That's not surprising. I always feel the average level of silliness go up whenever they're around."

Elisa shot him a *look*, the kind that she'd learned from her mother.

"I mean that with love," he added quickly. "You know I don't always mesh well with those two, but I do love all my girls."

"I know," she said.

"And Cam and Lucia know it, too."

"Yeah," she said, even though she wasn't sure that was always true.

Miguel hastily changed the subject. "Do you want to crash on the couch tonight, or are you going to go home and brave Hurricane Alex?"

She sighed, rubbing the back of her neck. "I should probably just go and face it. Once she decides she's speaking to me again, she'll probably want to yell."

"You sure you don't want to hide out here for a little while longer?" he asked.

"Maybe just an hour or two."

"I have some reruns of *Law and Order* on the DVR."

"Sold."

• • •

Her mother had gone to bed by the time Elisa came home, for which she thanked her lucky stars. When she tiptoed in, closing the door as quietly as she could, she was surprised to see her youngest sister lounging on the couch, texting. Lucia looked up as the door shut.

"Hey, sis," she said, sitting up slightly.

"Lucia, it's getting late," she whispered, moving to sit on the couch with her. "Don't you have plans tomorrow morning?"

"It's fine, I can chug a Red Bull on the way there," she said with a shrug. "I just wanted to make sure you got home."

Elisa wrapped an arm around her shoulders, giving her a quick squeeze. "You didn't need to wait up for me."

"I know. But if it got to be two and you hadn't texted or anything, I was gonna wake up Mom."

"Well, thank you for restraining yourself long enough for me to get here," she chuckled. "She still mad?"

"A little bit," she said.

"Great."

"How was Papa?"

"The same as ever," she said. "You talk to him lately?" She wasn't sure why she was asking when she already knew the answer. Maybe just to gauge her reaction.

Lucia tugged on a lock of her hair, one of the strands that had been dyed. Everyone had been expecting their mom to hit the roof the day she came home with bright pink streaks in her black hair, but Mom had taken it remarkably well. She'd told Elisa privately that she thought it looked ridiculous, but, "It's hair—it'll grow out. Besides, my hair looked much stupider in the eighties."

"We messaged for a bit last night," she said, not meeting her eyes.

"You miss him, don't you?"

Lucia attempted a laugh. "Don't be dumb. He doesn't live even half an hour away."

"I miss Charlene even when she's only a few apartments over. I know you can miss Papa."

"He doesn't get me. Not the way Mom and Cam do."

"Yeah, but you still love him, and he still loves you," she said gently. If she couldn't push Miguel into reaching out, maybe she could push Lucia. "If you want to spend more time with him, invite him to do something."

"He's my dad," she said. "Isn't he supposed to do the inviting?"

"It can be a two-way street," she said, though she'd privately thought something similar.

"Yeah." She didn't look convinced, but she didn't say anything else on the subject. Instead, she got to her feet. "Well, now that I know that you didn't get stabbed on your way home, I'm headed to bed."

"Okay." Elisa got up as well. "Good night."

Lucia disappeared behind the room divider, and Elisa

headed to her bedroom, moving quietly so she wouldn't wake Julieta. She slipped under the covers, absentmindedly reaching for her phone. The events of the day still had her wired—maybe some social media stalking would help dull the mind and senses.

She'd spent an embarrassing amount of time scouring all of Wick's social media pages. Scrolling through his Instagram, taking great care to not accidentally like something from years ago, had become routine, and tonight was no different.

She'd been looking over his profile for about ten minutes when she saw something she'd never noticed before. A picture from four years ago, with the caption:

#tbt to when we were kids!! love ya, @missfitzgerald

The picture was of a young Wick, maybe twelve years old or so, grinning, braces on his teeth. And he was standing arm in arm with what was definitely, undoubtedly, a young Darcy Fitzgerald.

Chapter Twelve

In Which Wick Makes Elisa Hate Darcy Even More (Yes, That's Possible)

Three days later, as promised, Elisa showed up at the Hangover at seven p.m. Wick was late. Okay, not by much, but just enough that she was checking her messages or glancing at the clock every ten seconds. Still, once he did arrive, his smile was more than enough for her to let it slide.

"Sorry I'm late, Elisa," he said. "Traffic."

"It's cool," she said. She gave him a quick hug that left her feeling a bit fuzzy inside before they headed into the bar.

They filled the first half hour or so with polite small talk, chatting about her classes and his job, then Wick finally said, "You want to hear about Darcy."

She cringed slightly. "Has it been that obvious?"

He chuckled. "I get it. I have been sort of teasing you, haven't I?"

"Well, can you blame me for wanting to know?" Elisa asked. "I mean, it must be serious if you two used to be friends."

Wick raised an eyebrow. "How'd you know that?"

"Um—uh…" She stammered, unable to think of a good excuse. "Um—did you know Instagram sometimes randomly shows you pictures from years ago? Weird, right?"

He tilted his head, amused. "Methinks the lady's been cyberstalking someone."

She blushed. "Okay, fine. I may have been scrolling through your Instagram history and stumbled across a picture of you and Darcy. But don't flatter yourself—I do that to everyone."

He grinned. "Oh, come on, there's no shame in it. I dug pretty deep into your pictures, too. Your sisters are all gorgeous, by the way. Must be a family trait."

Her blush deepened, but she just said, "Don't let Lucia hear you say that. You'd never get rid of her."

"You really want to hear what went down between me and Darcy?"

She nodded.

"Okay. But first…" As a waiter went by, Wick flagged him down and handed him his glass. "Could I have a refill on this? I will definitely need booze for this conversation."

Once the waiter brought him another drink, he took a long sip before beginning. Elisa tried her best not to look too eager.

"So the first thing you need to know is that my dad went to military school with Darcy's dad," Wick said. "Winchester Military Academy, in Columbus."

"Wow," Elisa said. She didn't know much about military schools, but even she knew Winchester was supposed to be one of the best in the country, right behind West Point.

"I always wanted to go to Winchester," he continued, "just like my dad. And Darcy's dad and I were super tight—I mean, I was over at their house practically every day when Darcy and I were kids. So, Mr. Fitzgerald said that, when I was old enough, if I still wanted to go and I couldn't pay my way, he'd pay my tuition for me."

"That's so nice."

"It was."

"How the hell did *he* produce Darcy?"

Wick snorted. "A question I ask myself daily. Anyway, Darcy's mom and dad died when she was fourteen and I was seventeen. Car crash. It was… It was rough. On all of us." He let out a small sigh, shaking his head. "Darcy and her sister were left money, of course, but they couldn't actually touch it until they were eighteen. So it was put in a trust, and Darcy and her sister went to live with her uncle." He took a sip of his drink. "When it came time for me to go to Winchester, I asked her if I'd still be able to go. She said that she'd talk to her family and see to it that I would. So, next thing I know, one of her aunts has paid all four years of my tuition ahead of time, and I'm at Winchester, doing what I'd always wanted to do since I was a kid. And then…"

"And then?" she asked.

"And then I was expelled."

Her eyebrows shot up. "For what?"

"That's the thing," he said. "I have no idea. One day, I was top of my class, doing great, and the next, I'm told to get off of campus immediately. I was confused, not to mention totally crushed—and I asked the dean what happened. No one gave me a straight answer, which only made me more suspicious. Finally, the dean slipped up and mentioned Darcy had come by."

Elisa gasped. "No," she said. "*Seriously?* I knew Darcy was mean, but to get someone expelled…"

"To this day, I'm still not sure what the actual grounds for expulsion were," he said. "I assume Darcy threw her money at them until they invented one. Her parents were two of Winchester's biggest donors. I hadn't seen Darcy in a while by this point—I was in school, and so was she, you know how it is—but I called her, mainly to ask, 'What the hell?' But she wouldn't tell me why she did it, either. She just said, 'You know damn well why.'"

"You two didn't have some kind of falling out or anything?"

"Not that I know of." He sighed. "This happened pretty soon after Darcy turned eighteen and had full access to her money."

"You think she was planning to do this all along?"

"Who knows? And honestly, at this point, who cares?" Wick shrugged. "I'm just glad she's out of my life."

"I care!" Elisa shouted. She flushed with red when she suddenly realized people had turned to look at them. Lowering her voice, she said, "I mean, that's horrible. Especially since you two were so close…"

He nodded ruefully. "Honestly, I don't know why I haven't deleted that picture you found," he said. "I guess I just miss the way things were before."

"I'm sorry I brought all that back up," she said. "I didn't mean to barge into your personal issues, I was just… curious."

"I get that," he said. "Besides, I'm glad you know. Gotta keep as many people on alert as possible, right? Especially since your sister is dating Darcy's new BFF." He rolled his eyes. "Bobby's a nice guy, but he can be…intentionally oblivious sometimes."

"Does he know what happened?"

"Doubt it. I never told him, and Darcy wouldn't. But he does tend to kinda…avoid seeing the bad in anybody. No matter what."

Elisa fiddled with her straw, wondering if she should tell Bobby what happened. Of course, what happened between Wick and Darcy really wasn't any of her business—she was lucky he had told her at all—but wouldn't Bobby want to know? She decided she'd at least tell Julieta. Not that she wasn't planning to anyway, if she were being totally honest. Then Julieta could decide whether or not Bobby needed to know.

"Enough about my dark and troubled past," Wick said, waving his hand. "Let's hear about you."

Elisa shrugged. "No dark and troubled past to speak of," she said. "Divorced parents, but that's for the best. Neither of my parents have been murdered by a six-fingered man or a genocidal wizard yet. I'm not the last of my kind. I don't even have a secret affair to be ashamed of."

"I could change that."

She rolled her eyes, grabbing the drinks menu and smacking him playfully on the arm. "I don't know if you could call this an affair, much less a secret one."

"What are your requirements for an affair, then?" he asked.

"I'm not telling you that."

"And why not?"

"Because one of them is that you have to figure them out for yourself."

Wick laughed. "Ouch. Did I just get dumped on our first date?"

"Not dumped," she said, smiling. "Just put in your place."

"I like that."

"Good. Because snide comments and sniping at people I like is kinda my thing."

He grinned. "You *like* me?"

"Shut up, Sedgdick."

"Gee, never heard that one before."

"Sue me, I don't work well under pressure."

• • •

Julieta was waiting up for her when she got home.

"How was the date?" she asked as Elisa entered their bedroom, closing the door.

"It was…interesting," she said, tossing her purse onto the floor and flopping back on the bed.

"Did he kiss you?"

"Yeah, when we were leaving. It was…okay, I guess."

Julieta frowned. "Just 'okay'?"

She shrugged. "It wasn't horrible or anything. Objectively, it was pretty good. But it was just kind of… I dunno, I didn't see fireworks or feel all sparkly inside, or any of that stuff that's supposed to happen when you kiss. Not this time, anyway."

"Dating isn't always as perfect as the movies make it out to be," Julieta reminded her. "Sometimes it can take a couple dates to really click with someone."

"But not you and Bobby."

"Well, no, but…"

"No 'buts,'" Elisa said. She rolled over onto her side to face her sister. "I know what happened with you and Bobby is, like…one in a million. But it's what I'm looking for. Fireworks, sparkles, sparks, whatever you want to call it…I want *that*."

She smiled. "And you'll get it. But not with Wick, huh?"

"Doesn't look like it," she said with a shrug. "I did find out what happened between him and Darcy, though."

"Oh?"

"Get this." She sat up. "When they were kids, Darcy and Wick were actually friends. And Darcy's dad said he'd pay for Wick to go to college. But a few years after Wick started going to Winchester, she got him kicked out."

"What'd he do?" she asked.

"He has no clue. The school wouldn't tell him. All he knows is that after Darcy talked to them, he was out."

Julieta looked skeptical. "They seriously just booted him without even telling him why? I'm not sure that's even *legal*."

"You forget that the Fitzgeralds are rich enough to buy out God," she said. "Darcy probably bribed them."

"Even if that was the case," she said slowly, "wouldn't it have made more sense for them to make a reason up? To cover themselves. Because, seriously—if they expelled a student with no given reason or evidence, I'm pretty sure that's grounds to sue."

"Maybe Wick thought it'd be worse if he tried," she suggested.

"Maybe..."

Julieta still didn't look convinced, which annoyed her some, but she didn't say anything about it. She just said, "I just can't believe Darcy would do that to someone she used to be so close with. Even for her, that's cold."

"Yeah, almost...uncharacteristically cold."

"You cannot seriously be on Darcy's side after this."

"I'm not on anyone's side," she said. "We don't even know what Darcy's side *is*."

"Because she refused to give it."

"Is it just me, or are you more into having another reason to hate Darcy than you are into Wick himself?" Julieta asked with a small smirk. "You think you'll go out with him again?"

Elisa shrugged. "I dunno," she admitted. "Maybe, if he asks. I meant what I said. I want a connection, something *real*. But... I mean, not everyone falls in love at first sight like you and Bobby did."

Julieta blushed, looking away. "'Love at first sight' is a bit strong."

"Is it?"

"I really, really like him," she said. "But I'm not dropping the L-bomb just yet. I've always said it first, and it's always blown up in my face."

"Bobby doesn't seem like the type to run for the hills."

"Yeah, that's what I thought about Damon. And Matt. And Zach..."

"Fair point." She sighed. "I think you're being smart, playing it cool. Throwing yourself at him will probably make him lose interest. Not to mention make you look desperate."

"But I *am* desperate." Julieta laughed.

"Yeah, but you don't want *him* to know that."

"Okay, Mom."

"*Hey.*"

Elisa chucked a pillow across the room at her sister, who swatted it away with a laugh.

"Mom will be so disappointed when I tell her about Wick," she said, sighing. "Here I was hoping it'd be great, and that would get her to forgive me for rejecting Colin."

"Nah," she said. "You said Wick isn't rich. I think to get Mom to forgive you now, you'd have to marry Darcy."

"Ah, damn. Guess this means I'll die alone *and* motherless."

Chapter Thirteen

In Which Darcy's Relatives Are Actually Really Cool

October left in a whirlwind of Halloween candy and midterms, leaving colder weather and Christmas music on the radio in its wake. By the time November rolled around, Mom had finally quit bringing up the Colin Incident, for which she was grateful. It totally would've wrecked her Christmas to still be fighting over this. Besides, the holiday season was stressful enough as it was.

The end of the fall semester was advancing on her so fast, she found herself having dreams about literary analysis. She had begun work on her final papers, and before she knew it, it had been nearly a month since she went out with Wick. They'd texted, but he hadn't so much as hinted at the possibility of another date, and she didn't intend to, either. It wasn't that she disliked him, but with school and everything, she wasn't about to pursue a relationship she didn't feel very strongly about. She had better things to do than go on mediocre dates and obsess over Wick's history with Darcy.

At school, Darcy hadn't said much, which was a relief.

She'd worried that she'd ask about her date, and she didn't want to give her the satisfaction of admitting it hadn't worked out. The only time they'd interacted was when the professor had paired them together to read over and evaluate each other's papers on *Animal Farm*.

She was both impressed and annoyed with Darcy's paper. Impressed, because it was really, really good. Annoyed, because it was better than hers.

Even so, Darcy had returned her paper with only a couple of irritatingly helpful comments, and a message scribbled at the bottom. *Good job.*

Two words of lukewarm praise from someone she hated may not have seemed like much, but even so, she felt a bit of pride flooding in despite herself.

A couple of days after Thanksgiving, Julieta rapped on the inside of the bedroom door. Elisa looked up from where she was working on a biology paper.

"What's up?" she asked.

"Bobby called me and asked if we wanted to come over," Julieta said. "He's having a few friends over for a small party before everyone has to go back to school for finals."

"When?"

"Now. I knew if I mentioned it too early, Lucia would find out, and well..."

Elisa nodded. "I completely understand. Sure, I'll come. I've earned a break, anyway."

She hadn't, but that didn't stop her from closing her laptop and grabbing her coat off her bedroom floor. It felt like she'd been nowhere except her room for the past few days. Not helping matters was that the weather had become cold, wet, and gray. Most of the leaves had fallen from the trees, now just brown clumps on the sidewalk. Everything outside looked dead. She hoped they'd get some snow soon; she didn't much care for it, but at least it would make the outdoors a bit prettier.

She hadn't been back to Bobby's mansion since her overly long stay at Netherfield Park in early October, and the size of the place still caught her off-guard. Despite it not yet being December, they'd already begun putting up Christmas decorations. Generally speaking, the Benitez family only put up their Christmas tree on December 24th—usually after coming back from the sole church service most of them attended each year. But it looked like the Charles family liked to get a head start.

Bobby's idea of a "small" party was very different from Elisa's. There was a bar, complete with a bartender serving people drinks, and at least forty people, most of whom she had never met. One of the few people she did recognize, of course, was Darcy.

"I'm gonna go find Bobby, okay?" Julieta said. "Will you be okay on your own?"

"I'm fine, Jules. You don't have to babysit me." She waved her hands. "Go on."

Julieta smiled, before disappearing into the crowd, leaving her alone. She wandered around a bit, helping herself to some of the snacks that had been set out, mingling a little bit with the other guests. She was just about to find a corner to hide in with her phone so she could text Charlene, when a girl she'd never met before pulled her aside.

She was a tall, pretty girl, with dark brown skin and hair pulled up into an afro puff, and a gold necklace hanging around her neck. Something about her looked oddly familiar, but Elisa couldn't quite place it. She was sure they'd never met before, but she couldn't shake the feeling she'd seen her face somewhere.

Before she could ask about it, though, the girl said, "You play euchre?"

Elisa blinked, surprised. "No."

"You willing to learn?" she asked. "We only have three people, and we'd like to play." She smiled. "I'll even be your partner."

She shrugged. "Okay. But I'll probably suck."

"That's fine. We're not playing for money. Not yet, anyhow."

The girl took her by the arm and led her into a sitting room a few doors away from the main party. She almost laughed when she saw that there was a massive Christmas tree in here, too. It appeared the Charles family had bought and chopped down an entire forest to accommodate their decorating plans. At the side of the room, there was a small table where two other people were waiting.

"I'm Willow, by the way," the girl said. She indicated the other two players as she and Elisa sat down at the table—a tall girl with curly, dyed-red hair, and a smaller, skinnier person who had four piercings in each ear. "She's Christina, they're Keegan."

"Found someone else who doesn't know anyone?" Keegan asked, beginning to deal cards. Keegan wore what was quite possibly the most ridiculous sweater Elisa had ever seen. It *lit up*, for God's sake.

"We all just moved here recently," Christina added. "We're sharing an apartment and starting at the community college next semester."

"Oh, I go there," Elisa said. She reached for the cards they had slid toward her. Upon looking at them, she realized she didn't have a clue if her hand was good or bad. "I know a couple people here, but honestly, I'm just here because my sister is. Did you guys seriously just move out here for the college?"

Willow laughed. "Well, we all have ulterior motives. I'm here because my parents made it very clear that while they were fine with a gap semester or two, when I got to be twenty-one, it was time to either get a job or start getting a degree."

"Okay, see, you say that like they're being totally unreasonable," Christina said, rolling her eyes.

Keegan finished dealing and asked, "How long we playing for? First to ten points wins?"

"Uh…" Elisa blinked. "Sure?"

"She doesn't know how to play," Willow explained. "So, I vote we hold off on the betting, at least for now."

Christina rolled her eyes. "Willow, no one ever wants to gamble besides you, anyway. You're the only one of us that has anything worth betting on."

She ignored her, instead opting to give Elisa a quick crash course in the rules of the game. She nodded along, trying her best to look like she understood. She didn't. At all. Willow seemed pretty nice, but she wasn't the best teacher—it seemed for every rule she gave her, she added, "Wait, no, actually…" and then proceeded to completely contradict herself. Christina and Keegan weren't much better. Finally, they agreed to just start playing, and explain to Elisa as they want. This didn't strike her as the best strategy, but she didn't argue.

Willow set down her first card. "Anyway," she said, "I picked this college because of these two. Keegan's moving here to be closer to the girlfriend. Christina's here because we worked out that sharing the rent of an apartment with the two of us and attending a community college would be cheaper than going to OSU and living in the dorm."

Elisa snorted, setting down a card of her own. No one said anything, so she assumed that she was doing this right. "That sounds about right. I looked into OSU, but it was way too expensive. Better to just keep living at home, where the food and rent is free."

"It's just as well," Christina said. By now, they'd gone around the table once, and she felt like she *sort of* knew what to do. "My parents are having *another* kid. They'll be glad to have one less person living there."

"Oh, you're from a huge family, too? I'm the second of five."

Christina smiled. "I got you beat. First of seven, soon to be eight."

"Holy *shit*."

"Her parents are very 'make love, not war,'" Keegan said. They set down a card, saying, "And that's a trick for Christina and me."

"Enjoy it while it lasts," Willow teased. "We'll catch up, won't we Elisa?"

"Uh…no promises."

"I suppose having a big family is better than having parents that argue all the time," Christina said, with a slight grimace.

"I'm an only child," Keegan said, "and I like it that way."

"I'm an only, too," Willow added, "but, I mean, I was raised with Darcy and Gianna, so it's almost like having sisters."

Elisa looked over at her, so surprised she forgot it was her turn to put down a card until Christina nudged her. "Darcy and Gianna?" she repeated.

"Oh yeah, you wouldn't know, would you?" Willow said, shuffling through her cards. "Darcy and Gi are my cousins. They live with my parents and me. Darcy's been up here visiting Bobby, but Gi still lives with us—probably will until she finishes college. My parents don't mind, though; they're crazy about her."

"You look like you've seen a ghost," Keegan said, poking Elisa on the arm with an amused smile.

Elisa just stared at Willow. "Um…this is gonna sound weird, but is your last name Fitzgerald?"

She nodded, not seeming to find the question odd at

all. "Yeah," she said. "I mean, Darcy's family are like, *the* Fitzgeralds—I'm just the extended family."

"I know Darcy."

Willow looked up from her cards, then. "Oh, are you a friend of hers? What's your name?"

"'Friends' is probably the wrong word for it," she snorted. "I'm Elisa."

Now it was Willow who forgot to put down a card. "Elisa Benitez?"

"She's mentioned me?"

"Uh...once or twice."

Elisa groaned. "Please disregard everything she said. We don't exactly get along."

She laughed. "It hasn't been anything *bad*."

"Are you a friend of Bobby's, too?" Elisa asked.

"Eh." She shrugged. "I like him, but we don't see each other much. I think he just invited me because I'm new in town and he felt sorry for me. He hates the idea of someone being in town for more than a week without making a new friend."

"Well, see, we did okay," Christina said, nodding toward Elisa.

"How's Gianna doing on that front?" Keegan asked. "Aaaand another trick for me and Chris..."

Willow cringed. "Not so hot. Last time I saw her, she was talking to her internet friends on her phone in a coat closet. I was really hoping this party would encourage her to make some real friends, even just for one night."

"Internet friends *are* real friends," Keegan said.

"Well, yeah—but I'd hate for her to only be able to talk to someone through a computer screen. That's not good for her." Willow glanced at Elisa, and quickly explained. "Gianna's super-shy. She's always been like that—she's the sweetest girl, but I don't think she has any friends she didn't meet online. Unless you count her music teacher. *And* she's homeschooled, on top of everything else."

"Were you and Darcy homeschooled, too?" Elisa asked, as she set down a card that she somehow knew wasn't going to help them win.

Willow shook her head. "Nah. We both went to Columbus School for Girls. Gianna went there up until eighth grade, but after that…" She let out a small sigh. "Being around crowds got really hard for her. It was stressing her out just to get to class each morning, so eventually, my mom decided to teach her at home."

"That's not just shyness," Christina said. "That's diagnosable."

Willow nodded, setting down a card. "Honestly, if she even speaks to someone besides me and Darcy at this party, I'll be happy. Even if it's just to say, 'pass me that hors d'oeuvre, please.'"

"You can't force her to socialize. I think that'd just make matters worse," Keegan said.

"Yeah," Elisa said. "I don't know Gianna, but in my experience, forcing socially awkward people into situations with a lot of people usually doesn't end well."

"Exhibit A: every party Darcy's ever gone to," Willow sighed. She glanced at her. "I can't promise she'll actually talk to you, but I think Gianna would like to meet you."

"Me? Why?" she asked, tilting her head.

"She's heard Darcy talk about you a lot for the past few months. She's curious." Willow smiled. "So was I."

She rolled her eyes with a small grimace. "Wanted to see if the horror stories were true, huh?"

Willow smiled. "Not *horror* stories. Just stories. Anyway—after this game, I'll introduce you to Gianna."

"From what you've said, she's not much like her sister."

"Oh, absolutely *nothing*."

...

After the euchre game was finished—Keegan and Christina won; Willow and Elisa crashed and burned—Willow led Elisa away from the table, saying, "Now, if I know Gianna, she'll be hiding out someplace until me and Darcy are ready to go."

"Looks like being an introvert runs in the family," she said, weaving her way through the maze of people. "Besides you, anyway."

"Darcy's kind of shy and awkward, but she can usually manage," she said. "Gianna's been better in the past year or so, but it's still a work-in-progress. Just don't comment on it, okay?"

"Don't worry—I won't say a word."

"Knew I could count on you."

They found Gianna in another sitting room—how many did one house need? She was by herself on a couch, texting someone. The second she saw her, Elisa knew she had to be Darcy's sister—they looked almost exactly alike. Gianna was tall and slender, with long, wiry, dark brown hair and an angular face. Seeing the two of them together also made her realize why Willow's face had seemed so familiar—they had the exact same nose and eye shape. She was darker skinned than either Gianna or Darcy, but she could've passed herself off as a sibling, easily.

Gianna's only company was a couple on the other couch in the room making out, clearly not noticing that she was there. To be fair, she didn't seem to notice them, either—her eyes were glued to her phone.

"Hey, Gi," Willow said, sitting down next to her. She pulled Elisa with her. "Look who I found."

Gianna glanced up. Her dark eyes widened a bit when she saw them, but she still offered a quick, nervous smile and wave. Elisa smiled back.

"This is Elisa," Willow continued. "You know, Darcy's classmate?"

"It's great to meet you," Elisa said.

"Y-you, too." Her voice was so quiet, if she hadn't been listening for it, she almost certainly would've missed it. Gianna hesitated before forcing something else out. "Are— are you enjoying the party?"

Elisa nodded. "Yeah. Once I met Willow, anyway. What about you?"

She gave a wordless shrug.

"I'm gonna go see if I can find something to eat," Willow said, hopping up. "You two have fun."

Elisa turned around to stare at her. "Wait, wh—aaaaaand she's gone."

Judging from the look on Gianna's face, she hadn't been expecting to be set up on an impromptu playdate, either. But she didn't move, and neither did Elisa. Willow left the room, leaving the two of them alone except for the couple on the opposite couch, who were starting to run the bases without a hint of shame.

"Uh…" She grasped for a topic. The only thing she knew for sure they had in common was Darcy—and she couldn't exactly speak her mind there. Gianna *was* her sister, after all. "Darcy mentioned you take music lessons. How's that going?"

"V-very well. Thank you. I, um, I'm… I'm learning Chopin's number one in C Minor." She smiled suddenly, looking down at her lap. "Darcy pre-ordered a new piano for my Christmas gift. I'm not… I'm not supposed to know yet. I found the receipt by mistake."

"I won't tell," Elisa said. She couldn't quite picture Darcy giving anyone such a nice, extravagant gift, but somehow, the thought made her smile—just a little. "You and your sister are close, then?"

She nodded. "Ev-ever since Mom and Dad died, she's been half-sister, half-parent. I mean... Aunt Lila and Uncle Freddie are great, and I'm—I'm close to them, but without Darcy..."

"I can't imagine what that'd even be like. Especially as young as you guys were. How old are you, anyway?"

"Fif-fifteen."

Elisa tilted her head as she looked at her. "I have a sister a little younger than that," she said. "She's *nothing* like you."

"I-is that good, or...or...or bad?"

"Neither, I guess. I love Lucia, she's just exhausting."

She smiled slightly. "I'm pretty low maintenance, I guess."

"There are worse things to be."

There was a pause, Gianna nervously fidgeting with the hem of her sweater, not quite meeting her eyes. Finally, Elisa said something.

"We don't have to talk, if you don't want. I am perfectly fine with just sitting here texting in silence and watching the lovebirds over there."

Gianna glanced up at her. "Are you sure? I wouldn't want to be rude."

"Trust me, it's no problem," she said. "I've been social for almost a full hour. I need a break, anyway."

Gianna gave an uneasy grin before reaching for her phone again. Elisa followed suit. They sat in a surprisingly comfortable silence, now that the burden of conversation had been lifted. Although she looked just like her sister, Elisa was stunned at how different she seemed in personality.

While Darcy came off as exceedingly proud, it was clear that Gianna was just exceedingly, *painfully* shy. But she liked her. She seemed like a sweet girl, and she sort of reminded her of Maria when she was younger. And, hey, Willow seemed pretty nice, too. Between the two of them and what little she knew of Darcy's parents, it seemed more and more like Darcy was an anomaly in the Fitzgerald family. A snide, haughty, aloof anomaly.

After a little while, during which the couple finally decided to find someplace more private, much to her relief, Elisa said, "I'm gonna grab a drink. Do you want to go with me?"

Gianna hesitated then nodded, getting to her feet. She didn't say anything; she just trailed after her. They followed the noise back to the huge room where most of the party was being held. Elisa led her back toward the bar, which wasn't quite as packed as it had been before.

"What do you want?" she asked.

"Coke is fine." Glancing at the bar, Gianna nudged her. "Th-that's your sister, right...?"

Elisa turned to look where she was gesturing. Julieta sat on a barstool, talking to a man she recognized as one of Bobby's coworkers. He was obviously rather drunk, and Julieta's eyes were darting around the room, trying to find an escape route.

"Y-you are...you are soooo pretty," the man was saying. "I've—I've ne'er met a girl as pretty as you."

"Thank you. You're very kind," she said. She was smiling, but the corners of her mouth were shaking.

"You know—you know, I have a boat. I have a boat, Julia."

"Julieta."

"I have a *boat*, Julieta."

"That's nice," she said, turning away, curling in on herself a little bit.

Even though she was flashing every possible nonverbal *I am not interested* sign, the man kept talking. "I should totally take you out on my boat sometime. Y-you'd love it."

"Yeah," was all she said in response.

"Can I get your numberrrrr?"

This was Elisa's cue to intervene. Muttering to Gianna, "Give me a minute," she hurried over to the bar, grabbing Julieta's arm. "Oh my gosh, I've been searching for you everywhere," she said, faking concern. "Mom called, she said she needs to talk to you right now."

Looking very grateful for her sister's arrival, Julieta quickly threw up a mask of worry. "Is something wrong?"

"I dunno, but she sounded pretty upset."

Julieta turned to the drunk guy, who looked like he was two shots away from passing out. "I am so sorry," she lied, hurrying away. Elisa watched as she dashed across the room and out into the hallway, where she'd probably hide for a few minutes to keep up the ruse.

Julieta had gotten stuck in similar situations countless times before. Where Elisa was more likely to tell a guy to piss off when he wouldn't take a hint, Julieta would wind up humoring them for hours if no one swooped in to rescue her. She was living proof that one could, in fact, be *too nice*. She hated turning anyone down, even if she really, really wanted to.

With Julieta having escaped, Elisa sat down on the barstool that her sister had just occupied. Gianna took the empty one next to her, barely managing to whisper, "Coke, please," when the bartender asked what she wanted. When he left to get their drinks, she turned to Elisa again. "Th-thanks for sitting with me," Gianna said. "I'm trying to work on—on the whole—the whole...social interaction thing. But I'm not very good at it."

"That's okay," she said. "I don't mind hanging out with you at all."

"You don't?"

"Of course not. I like you."

Gianna smiled. "I like you, too."

"Are you and Darcy close to Willow?"

She nodded. "Willow likes to get under Darcy's skin—not that it's hard, I guess—but we're all really good friends on top of being cousins. And Willow's parents have been really good to us ever since we moved in."

"She said you were homeschooled."

"Yeah—yeah, regular school was, uh…not working out…" She twiddled with a button on her sweater. "Homeschooling is nice, but I know Darcy doesn't think I get out enough."

Elisa had to laugh. "I don't know if you've noticed, but your sister's not the most social person herself."

She laughed, too. "No. But she apparently still thinks there's hope for me."

"Talking about me?" a voice said.

They both turned and were surprised to see Darcy sitting a few stools away. She'd apparently been there a while—Elisa wondered how they'd missed her. She then wondered if she'd witnessed the whole fiasco with Julieta and the drunk guy, and why she hadn't tried to intervene herself.

"Darcy, hi," Gianna said, her face brightening. "I was starting to wonder if you'd gone up to your room for the night."

"I wouldn't have left without saying good night," she said, sipping at her drink.

"I met Elisa."

"I see that. Are you having fun?"

Gianna nodded.

"Good." Darcy then addressed Elisa directly. "I suppose I don't need to tell you that this is my sister."

"No, Willow already covered that when she introduced us," Elisa said.

"Where is Willow, anyway?"

She shrugged. "Your guess is as good as mine. After she introduced me to Gianna, she sort of took off."

Gianna spoke up. "Prob-probably playing cards with

Keegan and Christina again."

Darcy rolled her eyes. "I wish she wouldn't. She always wants to gamble."

"It's not like she can't afford it," Gianna pointed out.

"I know, but it's not *proper*."

Gianna slid off the stool. "I—I can go look for her, if you want."

"You want me to come with you?" Darcy asked.

She shook her head. "I'll be okay."

"Okay. I'll be here."

Gianna turned to Elisa. "It was great to meet you," she said. "Can I message you on Twitter or something?"

Elisa smiled, nodding. "Please do. It was great to meet you, too."

She grinned then scampered off.

Elisa took a sip of her drink before glancing at Darcy. "She's a really sweet girl."

She nodded. "I know. Too sweet for her own good sometimes."

She sighed, thinking of Julieta. "I know what you mean." There was a pause before she suddenly remembered what Wick had told her about Darcy. Feeling her chest tighten, she was unable to resist asking. "So—I had dinner with George Sedgwick a few weeks ago."

Darcy's grip on her own glass tightened. "I really, really wish you hadn't done that," she muttered.

"Does the phrase 'Winchester Academy' ring a bell?" she asked.

She glared at her. "I don't know what he told you, but rest assured, it wasn't the truth."

"Why should I believe you? It's your word against his."

"Why should you believe *him*?"

Elisa opened her mouth to argue, but nothing came out. So she sat there, stewing in silence a moment before getting to her feet. She wanted to put distance between them, and not just because of the mess with Wick. Darcy was infuriating in many ways, one of which, if Elisa were to be honest, was how, on paper, Darcy was exactly the sort of person she would've had a crush on—completely gorgeous, but also smart as hell. Even with the attitude problem, it was sort of hard to tear her gaze away sometimes.

Like a train wreck. A hot, hot train wreck.

"Leaving so soon?" Darcy asked.

"I want to check on Julieta," she said.

"Fine." She shrugged. "Thank you for being nice to my sister."

"Anytime." She hurried off before she could get trapped in another conversation.

She really did like Gianna and Willow. Honestly, she had difficulty grasping the fact that they were so close to Darcy. Had they *met* her? Maybe some attachment was unavoidable, since the three of them were raised together. But they seemed to genuinely like her—not just love her, but *like* her. She was almost certain the two of them didn't know what she'd done to Wick.

Then again, maybe they did, but loved her too much to care?

Elisa shook her head. That couldn't be it. If Charlene or Julieta pulled something like that, she wouldn't be able to get past it without a damn good reason, or at least some serious action taken to make up for it.

No, some things couldn't be excused.

Chapter Fourteen

In Which... *What*?!

The fall semester was over. Right after the Thanksgiving break, Elisa's life had been nothing but cramming for finals, taking her finals, and waiting for her grades to be posted after finals.

I never want to hear the word "finals" again.

The last couple weeks of the term flew by in a flurry of papers and multiple-choice tests. She didn't quite remember all of it, but she didn't care—she'd passed all three classes she was taking and had even managed a ninety-four on her Introduction to Literature final.

She hoped, realizing it was petty even as she hoped it, that she did better than Darcy.

Christmas had been as chaotic as she'd come to expect from her family. Her mother had invited her father over to open presents and have dinner—which wound up being from the nearest Thai place after they realized Mom had forgotten to thaw the chicken. Eating fried rice out of a delivery container, Elisa had laughed as she listened to her father recount the story of his and Alejandra's first Christmas together. She knew it by heart, from them getting snowed in at the house he'd been renting, to the lights in the living room sparking and starting a small fire, thanks to his bad job repairing the wiring. Her mother had to beat the flames out with the coat he'd just given her.

"And that is why Alex officially forbade me from handling anything electrical ever again," was how he always finished it.

Her mother would then add, "That is *also* why Miguel didn't get his security deposit back."

When Elisa took to social media to wish her extended family well, a picture of the Fitzgeralds popping up in her feed made her pause. Darcy, it appeared, had gone back to Columbus for the holiday. The photo showed her, Gianna, and Willow sitting on the floor in front of an elaborately and gorgeously decorated tree, each wearing matching Santa hats. Willow and Gianna were each giving the camera a warm, sunny smile, but Darcy simply stared with an exaggerated look of comical disdain.

In spite of herself, Elisa smiled as soon as she saw it.

• • •

Two days after Christmas was Charlene's birthday, and it was a big one: her twenty-first. Elisa knew her parents and sister would want to see her for most of the day, especially since she didn't have a party planned, so she'd have to squeeze any BFF time in early. Elisa was awake, dressed, and heading over to her apartment before the sun was even up. Despite the obscenely early hour, she didn't doubt that Charlene was awake. She was the only person she knew who woke up before sunrise of her own accord.

Elisa had a spare key to Charlene's apartment, as well as a standing invitation, and she frequently let herself in without knocking. The kitchen light was on. Good, that meant Char was awake. Or at least, she had been not too long ago.

As she walked through the still-dark living room toward the bedroom door, she called out, "Happy birthday, Char!"

"Elisa?" came the sleepy response.

"I figured your parents would want custody of you today, so I came by early," she said, nearly tripping over the coffee table. She cringed slightly, though she was more surprised than hurt. No matter how often she was over here, she was never any good at maneuvering in the dark.

"*Elisa.*" This came with a slight gasp, and she suddenly sounded much more awake than she did a moment ago.

Elisa pushed open the door, feeling around for the light switch. "*Haaaaaappy birthday tooooo yoooou—*"

She found the switch, and instantly, light flooded the bedroom. Charlene was still in bed and wasn't dressed yet. This wasn't much of an issue, since she and Elisa had seen basically all of each other over the years.

What *was* an issue, however, was that Charlene wasn't alone. And it wasn't like Elisa had walked in on her best friend in bed with a complete stranger. No, this was way, *way* worse than that.

Colin Burger sat up on the other side of Charlene's small bed, rubbing his eyes.

Then he looked up and saw that they had company.

Elisa and Colin both began screaming.

"Oh my God," she shrieked, rooted to her spot.

"This wasn't how I wanted you to find out," Charlene said, face as red as her hair.

"Oh my *God.*"

"Maybe we should all take a moment to calm down—"

"*Oh my God.*" Elisa stumbled, moving to sit on the chair in the corner. "Charlene—you—you're—this—*this has happened before*?"

"It's been happening for the last three weeks or so, actually," Charlene admitted.

Elisa buried her face in her hands. "Oh my Gaaaaaaawd…" she groaned.

Charlene reached for her bathrobe, pulling it on. Once she'd covered up, she sat on the arm of the chair next to Elisa. "Do you need a drink? A blanket? A Xanax?"

"You have a—a boyfriend, or a booty call, or *something*— and you didn't tell me?" she asked, the words spilling out of her before she could even consider them.

"He's a boyfriend, Elisa. And I didn't want you to freak out." She let out a small sigh, glancing over at Colin, who was blushing furiously. "I probably should've just told you up front. But hindsight is twenty-twenty."

"No *shit*. And—Charlene, come on. Colin? *Colin*?"

"Heyyyyy," Colin said. Fortunately, he'd remained in the bed, a blanket covering all the important bits.

Elisa had thought that that one time she'd walked in on her parents had been traumatizing.

"It's bad enough that you had a secret boyfriend," she screeched, voice approaching a range only audible to dogs. "But *Colin Burger*? Are you *serious*?"

Before Charlene or Colin could reply, there was pounding on the wall and a man's voice yelling, "SHUT THE *HELL* UP OVER THERE, OR I'LL SHUT OFF YOUR HOT WATER."

Charlene rolled her eyes. "I live next door to the landlord, remember?"

"Right. Sorry."

Colin spoke up again. "Look, Elisa, we knew you might be skeptical about our relationship. That is why I've prepared a speech, with an accompanying PowerPoint, to assure you that I will treat your best friend very, very well. My first point—"

Elisa raised her hand. "Okay, if there's anything that could possibly make me want to hear your speeches any less, it's you delivering them while *naked*."

"Oh. Right."

"Colin, you get dressed," Charlene said, standing up. "Elisa and I will talk out in the living room."

Elisa followed her out, closing the bedroom door behind her.

Charlene began immediately. "Okay, before you say anything—I asked *him* out. He didn't talk me into this or wear me down, and no one pushed me into this because of his money or whatever. This was my choice. *My* choice, Elisa. *Mine*. Do you understand what I'm getting at here?"

She didn't answer the question. She just said, "Charlene you can do so much better than that idiot."

She crossed her arms. "This may come as a shock to you, Elisa, but I actually *like* 'that idiot.'"

"You do?"

"I do."

"Why?"

Charlene threw up her hands in exasperation. "Well, *I* didn't put together a PowerPoint on it. He's smart—despite what you may think, he *is* really smart—and he's kind. He's passionate about what he does, and he knows what he wants to do with his life, which is more than any other guy I've dated can say, and he gets along great with Molly—"

"Your kid sister knows, but I didn't?"

"And he doesn't judge me for not having a degree, and... and... Elisa, the fact of the matter is, I can't always eloquently explain why I like him. I just *do*."

Elisa ran a hand through her hair. "I can't believe this."

"Believe it. Colin's my boyfriend now, Elisa."

"But he's—he's pretentious, and he talks too much, and he's not a good listener, and his mom is, objectively, the worst.

Sure, he's smart, but not nearly as smart as he thinks he is, and...and...and... And he listens to *Nickelback*..."

"That's all true," Charlene said.

"And you *still* like him?"

"Yes."

"Christ."

"This isn't the end of the world, Elisa," Charlene snapped. "Would it *kill* you to be happy for me?"

Elisa winced. "I'm sorry," she said. "I just—I just... I don't get it."

"I'm not asking you to get it. I'm asking you to be supportive."

"Who else knows? Is this a secret, or are we allowed to mention this to other people?"

Translation: can I tell Julieta so we can spend at least two hours discussing, in great detail, how completely and totally insane this is?

"So far, only you, my parents, and my sister know," she said. "But we don't intend to keep it a secret forever. We were just waiting for the right time to break the news. The real issue is Colin's mother."

"What about her?" she asked. "I mean, I know Catherine is kind of hard to deal with, but..."

"When I asked Colin about introducing me, he said that his mother doesn't like him dating outside of the family's 'social circle.'"

"So, no one poor."

"Right." Charlene sighed, sitting on the couch. Elisa sat next to her. "He says he thinks he can talk to her, but he's still working out what he wants to say. I mean, he also said it's not like she can force him to dump me—but we'd both prefer to avoid an explosion, if at all possible. So, until then, we're keeping this from her."

"I didn't know he was even capable of lying to his beloved

mother."

"Yeah, me neither. Though, it's been more lying by omission than anything. He skipped their last bridge game to go to a movie with me—he said he was going to see a screening of an important film at the college. The movie theater *was* on campus, and when you like comics as much as he does, the latest superhero movie *is* an important film…"

"I can't believe Colin's managed to keep this off of social media," she said. "Normally, he shares everything."

"It hasn't been easy," Charlene admitted. "I've had to prevent a few photos from making their way to Instagram because he wasn't thinking. But he's learning." She glanced at Elisa. "And he *is* really sorry for the way he treated you, by the way."

"Why hasn't he said that himself, then?"

"Because he was afraid you'd *eat* him."

Elisa sighed. "That's probably fair."

"Look. You don't have to like him. But can you please let me have this? I'm—he makes me happy, Elisa. Really, *really* happy."

Part of her wanted to argue, wanted to argue until Charlene came to her senses.

But from the look in her eyes that wasn't gonna happen, no matter what she said.

So instead, she said, "Okay. I—I want you to be happy."

The bedroom door opened, and Colin emerged, now fully dressed. *Thank God.*

"Can I come out now?" he asked.

"Yeah, hon," Charlene said, waving him to join her and Elisa on the couch. "Now—since you two are both here, why don't we all go grab breakfast someplace before I meet up with Mom and Dad?"

Elisa and Colin both nodded. He looked about as uncomfortable as she felt.

"Great. I'll go get dressed."

Charlene quickly left, leaving Elisa and Colin alone.

"So..." she said, after an unbearably long pause. "You and...you and Charlene, huh?"

He nodded. "I was just as surprised as you when she asked me out." He hesitated, then glanced at her face. "I do really like her. More than like her, probably." He gave her a meaningful look. "Don't tell her I said that. I think she's still kind of a flight risk."

"From the way she was just sticking up for you, I don't think you have to worry about her taking off," Elisa said. "But I won't."

"So you're okay with us dating?"

She shrugged. "It's not my call," she said. "I trust Charlene's judgement."

"Your endorsement melts the heart."

"Sorry." Elisa picked a piece of lint off of the ugly Christmas sweater Maria had gotten her. "I just—I can't think of a single thing you two have in common. That wasn't meant to be an insult, by the way."

"Finding common ground was hard at first," he admitted. "But it's there, if you know where to look. We're both smart, driven people. We're both so organized, it irritates other people. We both tend to prefer the independent parties to the two big ones, we both like classic cinema, and we're both Slytherins."

"I always thought of you as more of a Hufflepuff."

"It was a toss-up." He shrugged. "My point is—it's not like we're building this relationship off of nothing. And we're finding more common ground every day." He paused. "She's also the first girlfriend I've had that hasn't gone through my phone."

"That's sad."

"Yeah. There are many, many reasons my previous

relationships haven't lasted long… Many of which were probably my own fault…"

She hesitated. "I hope what you and Charlene have lasts."

He looked surprised. "Really?"

"I want Char to be happy. And if you make her happy—and she makes you happy—then I'd be the worst friend in the world to *not* want you guys to work out."

Colin smiled. "Thank you, Elisa."

Charlene emerged from her bedroom, wearing a heavy sweater and a pair of jeans, and a necklace that Elisa was sure Colin had given her. She rarely wore jewelry, except for a pair of stud earrings and a knockoff designer watch at work. But now, she wore a beautiful, sparkling necklace, with a heart-shaped pendant.

"Ready to go?" she asked.

Elisa nodded, getting up from the couch. "Ready."

Colin went to get the door for the girls, and the three began heading down to where he had parked his car overnight. While they held hands, Elisa just watched them, baffled, and trying to get adjusted to the new reality.

Colin Burger and Charlene Locke were dating. Willingly.

Somewhere, Elisa was sure, a herd of pigs was taking off.

Chapter Fifteen

In Which Elisa Goes Back to School

Elisa arrived at her first class of the new semester—
Communications I—in a bad mood. Even though she had
driven there, she'd still had to walk across the tundra that
was the student parking lot, and some idiot in a pickup truck
had splashed her with freezing water when he went through
a puddle.

She'd managed to protect the textbook she was carrying,
but her jeans and shoes were soaked. If it weren't the first day
of term, she would've just gone home to change. Not helping
matters was the fact that she'd gotten into an argument with
her mother that morning. Her mom found out Colin and
Charlene were dating and was back to giving her grief for
turning him down—now with added complaints about letting
Charlene "swoop in" and get him.

She arrived in the classroom shivering but still on time,
hoping her mood didn't show. She managed a genuine smile
when she saw a familiar face sitting in the back row.

"Willow," she said, approaching her quickly.

Willow looked up. In the month or so since they'd met, she'd gotten a lip piercing. "Hey, girl," she said. "I was wondering if I'd run into you."

Elisa took the chair next to her. "How've you been?"

"I've been good. Starting on the track to that currently-undeclared major," she said. "Christina and Keegan are both going for education."

"How are they?"

"Keegan broke up with their girlfriend last week."

She cringed. "Oh, I'm sorry."

"Eh, don't be," she said with a shrug. "I didn't tell you this when we met because Keegan still liked her back then—but she *hated* their dog. She pretended like she didn't, but Christina and I both knew. Finally, she got sick of pretending, and she told them, 'it's me or the dog.' So, they said, 'it was nice knowing you.' It's for the best."

She shook her head, chuckling. "Has saying 'it's me or the dog' to anyone *ever* worked? I mean, really?"

"It sure as hell won't with Keegan. They love that dog."

Elisa cast a glance around the room. People were trickling in quickly, grumbling about being wet and cold. She had to laugh a little bit. At least she wasn't alone.

"Is Darcy taking any classes here this semester?" she asked, hoping against hope they didn't have any together.

Willow shook her head. "No. She's staying with Bobby for a while longer, but she didn't sign up for any classes. I guess she's planning on heading back to Columbus soon. Well—I mean, we grew up just outside the city."

"Oh," was all Elisa could think of to say. She supposed she should've been relieved, but...

Arguing with Darcy or stubbornly ignoring her had become routine over the course of the past few months. Not a *pleasant* routine, but a routine. It was weird to imagine her days without it.

If Willow noticed how deflated she was, she didn't comment on it. She just said, "Yeah. I think she misses Gianna. They've never been apart for this long before."

"Darcy still living with your parents?"

"Nah. After she turned eighteen, she inherited her parents' old place—before that, it belonged to another relative, technically. She moved back in there—until she came up here to stay with Bobby, anyway. She said it was to get out of Mom and Dad's hair, but I think she just missed where she grew up. Gi thought about going with her, but she's super close to my parents, so she decided to stay put. But, I mean, my parents' place is only a ten-minute walk from Darcy's parents' old place, anyway."

"Is Darcy's place like Bobby's?"

"*Mine* is like Bobby's," Willow said, fiddling with one of her many gel pens. "Darcy's is much, *much* bigger. Our ancestor built it on land he owned—Darcy's side of the family owns the entire surrounding area, which is about as big as all of Netherfield Park. I mean, there's Bobby's money, and then there's *her* money."

"Holy Hell," Elisa said. "I knew your family was rich, but…"

She gave a nonchalant shrug. "Darcy's dad's company wasn't on the Fortune 500 for nothing."

Before she could reply, the professor, an elderly man who had clearly had this job for *way* too long, entered, and launched straight into his first lecture. They quickly shut up, though not before Elisa had the chance to whisper, "Let's grab a drink from the commons after this."

Willow smiled and nodded.

· · ·

The student commons coffee tasted more like boiled water

that had had a brown crayon dipped in it than anything actually digestible by humans, but it was caffeinated and hot—good enough. The commons themselves were packed, with no seats available, leading Willow and Elisa outside. They walked aimlessly around the campus, trying to keep moving enough that they wouldn't get too cold.

"Do you have any other classes this semester?" Elisa asked. A gust of wind passed between them, making them both shiver.

"Just one. Introduction to ASL," Willow said, sipping her coffee. She grimaced at the taste. "It's a Tuesday/Thursday course, though."

"I'm taking Art History—that starts in about an hour, actually," she said. "I'm also in Chem I. I figure if I get all the math and science out of the way early, I can use my last couple of semesters on classes I *don't* hate."

"I'm just gonna take a bit of everything," she admitted. "I'm trying to find something I could actually do for the rest of my life. Or at least the rest of my education."

Elisa was about to say she wished she had the option of just trying things out, instead of needing to get a degree and out of college as quickly as possible, when she spotted something across the green.

George Sedgwick, holding hands with another girl. They were laughing, heading toward Wick's car. The girl looked just as charmed as Elisa had been when she first met him. She stopped walking, just staring after them.

Willow turned around when she realized Elisa was no longer at her side and tilted her head curiously at her. "What's that look on your face?" she asked.

Wordlessly, she pointed.

As soon as she saw Wick, Willow's lip curled in disgust. "*Ugh*," she said. "You know Wick?"

"We went out," she said, moving to stand next to her

again. Wick and the girl had gotten into his car and were now driving away.

She frowned slightly. "Was it serious?" she asked, voice more weighted than Elisa had ever heard it.

Elisa sighed, shaking her head. "No. I—I really have no right to be upset. We went on one date. It wasn't terrible, but it wasn't great. After that, we texted, but then…we just sort of lost contact. It was mutual. I really shouldn't be mad. I mean, I'm not *mad*, I'm just…"

"I get it," Willow said. "But trust me—I've known Wick for years, and you can do better."

They reached a bench and sat down. "You sound like Darcy," Elisa said. "She told me to stay away from Wick, but she wouldn't tell me why."

She looked away, focusing on her coffee for a moment, before saying, "It's not my place to say why. I can tell you Darcy's right, though. I know you don't always get along with her, but trust me on this. She was trying to help you."

Elisa frowned. It was perfectly in character for Darcy to clam up and be annoyingly cryptic—but if even *Willow* was radio silent on the matter? That was weird.

Sensing her confusion, Willow said, "It's…it's a really personal family thing. I'd tell you, but it's not my story to tell."

"I understand," she said, though she wasn't quite sure she did.

Before, she'd been certain Willow hadn't known anything about Darcy getting Wick expelled. Now, she wasn't so sure.

• • •

Elisa got home after her art history class, inwardly reciting what she was going to say to her sister. Her class would be making a trip to Columbus over spring break, spending the entire week there touring the Alexandra Pemberley Museum of Classical Art. Pemberley was extremely old, and one of the highest-regarded art museums in the country. The place was massive, with dozens of exhibits. Even the week-long trip wouldn't be enough time to see it all. Elisa had always wanted to visit. However, due to travel and hotel expenses, the students' portion of the cost was a hundred dollars each.

It wouldn't be the end of the world if she couldn't go on the trip. After all, it wasn't mandatory. But she still really, really wanted to. Unfortunately, she was broke, and asking her mother for the money was out of the question. It wasn't that her mother wouldn't want her to go—it was that Elisa wasn't sure she'd be able to pay for it.

Julieta, however...

Part of her felt bad for even *thinking* of asking. But the other part of her knew that visiting Pemberley every day for a week would be so expensive, not even counting travel expenses, that the class trip would be the only way she'd be likely to go.

She knocked on the inside of the bedroom door.

"Am I interrupting?"

Julieta glanced up from her laptop. "Oh no, not at all," she said, smiling. "I was just taking a break, actually. How was the first day?"

"It was pretty good, mostly. I have a class with Willow." She set her backpack on the floor and sat on her unmade bed.

"Darcy's cousin?"

"Yep."

"She seemed nice."

"She is. I also saw Wick."

"Oh yeah?" Julieta asked. "What'd he say?"

"I said I saw him," she said. "I never said he saw me. He has a new girlfriend."

Julieta winced. "Oh, I'm sorry," she said.

She shrugged. "Don't be. I mean, I was never super into

him." She moved on, not wanting to dwell on the matter of George Sedgwick for longer than she had to. "My art history class is taking a field trip to Pemberley during spring break."

"Oh, that's great. That's in Columbus, right?"

Elisa nodded. "Yeah. The only issue is, um…it's a hundred bucks a head."

She bit her lip, immediately seeing the problem. "When is the money due?"

"In two weeks."

"Damn. I'm sure Mom would be able to put away twenty dollars every week until there was enough, but a hundred all at once is kind of a huge hit."

"I know," she said. "I know she'd want me to go, but I wouldn't feel right asking. Especially since I think I overheard her arguing with the bank again last night." She tugged guiltily at her hair. "I was kind of hoping *you* could lend me the money."

Julieta looked apprehensive. "You know I would in a heartbeat, but…"

"I'd take it as a loan, not a gift," she hastily added. "I'll pay you back as soon as I can."

Probably by borrowing money from Papa. Her financial situation was an endless cycle of borrowing from other people.

"E, I *know* you can't afford that."

She sighed. "Yeah. If you can't afford it, I get it. It's not a required trip."

"But you obviously really want it."

"I do," she admitted.

It wasn't even just about wanting to see Pemberley—though that was a big part of it. A lot of it was just not wanting to be the only student that didn't go. Growing up, Elisa and her sisters had missed out on field trips or been the only ones not able to get a souvenir or lunch out when they *could* go, and it had always sucked.

Even when no one was judging, even when no one noticed, it was impossible to not be embarrassed. Logically, she knew that she could always claim she had work or a family obligation during spring break, and no one would be likely to question it. But that didn't take away from the embarrassment of not being able to afford things her classmates could.

Julieta thought it over. "Tell you what. I haven't bought your birthday present yet. What if *this* is your present? I mean, a couple months early, but..."

"I'll take it," Elisa said. "But—but only if you're sure. I know you're kind of strapped for cash right now."

"I'll be fine," she said. "It's not like I have rent to pay. Besides, I've gotten a couple more clients recently. A few months ago, I probably wouldn't have been able to help you."

Elisa got up from her bed, walking over to hug her older sister.

"Thank you so much," she said, grinning.

"Happy birthday. *Very* early," Julieta replied. She gave Elisa a tight squeeze before pulling away. "Hopefully, this trip will be worth it."

Chapter Sixteen

In Which Bobby Goes MIA

Elisa would be the first to admit her experience with romantic love was limited at best. She didn't have any firsthand knowledge on what it was like to dating someone, or how a relationship could change your life and perspective. All she really had to go off of was what she'd observed of her friends and family. One thing she'd noticed was that when they were dating the guy or gal of their dreams, people tended to be a bit more...oblivious than normal. Not dumb, maybe, but definitely more blind to what was going on outside their happy little bubble. That was, at least, until life came along and bitch-slapped them back into reality.

It was a surprisingly warm January afternoon when Julieta got sent back to reality.

She and Elisa had been driving down to the mall near Netherfield Park. They intended to just walk around, more interested in getting out of the apartment than actually buying anything. They were almost to the highway when Julieta said, "Wait—actually, drive by Bobby's house. Maybe he'll want to come with us."

"You haven't seen him in a while, have you?" Elisa asked.

She sighed, shaking her head. "No, not since the party where you met Willow. We've been texting like usual, but between my job and his, plus all the holiday craziness... I haven't even gotten a chance to give him his gift yet."

As she spoke, she touched the gorgeous sterling silver bracelet she was wearing. It had shown up in the mail a couple days before Christmas, along with a note that had made her blush. Elisa attempted to sneak a peek at it but was immediately caught. Personally, she thought Bobby should've come by and delivered the gift in person, but Julieta had been too happy with it for her to complain much.

"I'm sure he understands," Elisa said. "Let's go see him."

So, she pulled into the driveway of Bobby's mansion, following Julieta to the front door.

A maid answered the door. "Can I help you?"

"Hi, Emily," Julieta said, smiling warmly. "Is Bobby in?"

The maid frowned. "Mr. Charles hasn't been here for a week," she said, confused. "I'm sorry, Julieta, I assumed someone told you."

Her face fell, but she forced herself to smile again a moment later. The corners of her mouth were shaking, though. Elisa frowned, glancing worriedly from her sister to the maid and back again.

It's probably nothing.

"Did he say where he was?" Julieta asked.

"At his vacation home in Massachusetts."

"Massachusetts?" Elisa said, before she could stop herself.

"Yes, he has a lovely home on the beach in Cape Cod."

"It's *winter.*"

Julieta was determined to keep up her sunny attitude, but she could tell she was faltering. "Did Bobby say when he'll be coming home?"

"Mr. Charles said he'd be in Cape Cod indefinitely," the maid said with an apologetic shrug.

Wow. Okay. So. Not "nothing."

"Where's Darcy?" she asked, before she even had a chance to consider why she wanted to know.

"Back home in Columbus, I'd assume. She didn't mention where she was going."

What did you expect? It's not like she's just lurking in the shadows, waiting for me to show up.

"Th-thank you," Julieta said. "Um...thanks. Have a great day. Thanks."

The two made their way back to the car, Elisa climbing into the driver's seat. Julieta stumbled into the passenger's side, looking like a deer in the headlights.

"Jules?" she asked quietly, looking over to her older sister.

"L-let's...let's just go on over."

"Julieta..."

"Come on, we're already out." She forced a smile. "It'll be fun."

Elisa bit her lip. "Okay," she finally said. "But I understand if you just want to go home."

"I need to...need to... I just want to have a little fun before I think about this, okay?"

• • •

They had been wandering around the mall, trying on clothes they couldn't really afford, for about an hour when Julieta finally hit her "happy face" limit. One moment, they had been squeezed into a tiny dressing room, Elisa helping her zip up an evening gown. The next, she was leaning against the wall and crying her eyes out.

"Oh, *honey*," Elisa said, reaching to pull her sister into a hug. "Oh, Julieta, I'm so sorry."

"How could he just leave without telling me?" she asked through her tears. "I thought he... I thought we..."

"Maybe it was an emergency?" Even as she suggested it, she didn't believe it.

"How do you forget to text your girlfriend for a full *week*? If...if I ever was his girlfriend..."

"Yes, you were," Elisa said. "You *are*. This isn't a breakup, it's..."

"Don't be naive." Julieta sniffled. "It's a breakup without the title. He went seven hundred miles away and didn't even say goodbye to me... I think that sends a message, loud and clear." She gave a mirthless laugh, wiping her tears. "I wasn't even worth the time it would've taken to say 'it's been fun, but it's over.' Forget a face-to-face breakup. He didn't even send me a goddamn text message."

"Bobby's an asshole," she said. She ran a hand over Julieta's hair; the only comfort she could provide. "You deserve better."

"How could he *do* this?" she asked again.

"I don't know. I really don't..."

Julieta was slowly regaining her composure, breathing steadying again, but her eyes were still red and watery. "I'm... Oh, I'm sorry, I didn't mean to freak out like that, I just..."

"Don't apologize," she said gently. "You have every right to freak out. I mean, this just doesn't seem like Bobby. He never struck me as the flakey type."

"He also didn't strike me as my next ex-boyfriend. I thought..." Julieta trailed off. She swallowed a lump in her throat, rubbing her eyes, before finding her voice again. "I thought maybe he and I had something real. I thought we had a future. But here we are."

"Here we are..."

Julieta took a deep breath, trying to find some semblance

of dignity. "I'm going to change back into my own clothes," she said. "Then, you and I are getting pretzels from the food court. *Then*, we're going home, and I'm going to have a good, old-fashioned breakup bonfire."

Elisa managed a small smile. "Ask for Lulu's help. She's the family expert at burning stuff." She reached for the dressing room door. "I'll see you out there."

"Okay."

She slipped out of the dressing room and was met with the concerned, questioning eyes of two employees, who had clearly heard everything.

"Is your sister okay?" one of them finally asked, apparently deciding it wasn't worth denying that they'd been listening.

"She will be." She sighed. "I hope."

· · ·

While Elisa waited at a table in the food court for Julieta to return with their pretzels, she decided that, yes, she was desperate enough to do this. The food court was mobbed, which would hopefully buy her enough time to make the call before she got back. Three text messages to Willow later, she had the phone number she needed.

She took a deep breath, before swallowing her pride and dialing the number.

"Hello, Darcy Fitzgerald speaking."

Elisa's next words were out before she even had a chance to consider them.

"What the hell is *wrong* with Bobby?"

There was a confused pause on the other end, before, "Should I start with his appearance or his personality, or...?" Then, suddenly, realization set in. *"Elisa?"*

"Listen, my sister and I just popped over to Bobby's

house to pay him a visit, and he's up and vanished with no explanation. So *you're* gonna explain for him. Why the hell has Bobby just run off to Cape Cod? In *January*."

"Cape Cod is actually quite lovely in the winter."

"Darcy, I *swear to God*."

There was a pause long enough that she briefly wondered if she'd been hung up on. Finally, Darcy spoke. "Something came up, that's all."

"You're a shitty liar," she said. "Listen, I've checked all of Bobby's social media, and he hasn't said a word about leaving Steventon, much less about going to Massachusetts. You know what that makes me think?"

"Oh, pray tell," she droned.

"I think he didn't just not tell Julieta he was leaving. He was making *sure* she wouldn't know. He must've known she'd catch on eventually, but thanks to his little media blackout, she didn't figure it out until he was too far away for her to strangle him."

"Don't be so dramatic," Darcy said. "He just realized he has obligations elsewhere."

"Give me one good reason why I shouldn't drive up to Cape Cod and kick his ass."

"Well, for one thing, his home up there has an extensive security system. For another, he's quite a bit taller than you, and probably in much better physical shape—"

Elisa groaned. "Stop holding out on me and tell me what happened."

"I told you. Bobby realized he had obligations outside of Steventon and your sister. It's nothing personal."

"He left a girl he's been dating for months without even saying 'see ya.' How in the hell is that *not* personal?"

"Believe what you want," she said. Elisa could almost see her condescending scowl.

"You know something, don't you?"

"Even if I did, I wouldn't be at liberty to reveal it."

"Just tell me why he left," Elisa snapped, exasperation making her voice squeak a bit.

"*Obligations*. That's all I'll say."

She ran a hand through her hair. "What about you? Where'd *you* run off to? You have *obligations*, too?"

"No," she said. "I'm just back home in Columbus. You are welcome to come and visit if you're ever in the area. There's always a guest room available to you."

Elisa took a deep breath to force herself to keep her temper. "Yeah. Great. Thanks. Bye," was all she could bring herself to say before hanging up on her.

She slammed her phone onto the table, slumping back in her chair. Well, *that* had been a dead end. She was certain Darcy knew more than she'd let on, but she was also certain it wouldn't do any good to keep asking.

She forced herself to hide her anger as Julieta approached, a tray of food in her hands. Things were already miserable enough. It wouldn't do any good to stew.

She would, however, absolutely be joining in on that breakup bonfire.

Chapter Seventeen

In Which Life Goes On

Lucia tossed a Polaroid of Bobby and Julieta into the trash can. "I'm totes glad you came to me for this," she said. "I'm the family expert at burning stuff. Now, are you *sure* you don't want to throw some of the stuff he left here into the burn pile?"

Julieta shook her head. "I told you, I'm sending it to him in Cape Cod."

"Oh, come on, what's the point of a breakup bonfire if you don't burn some of your ex-boyfriend's shit while you're at it?" she asked. "It's feminism."

Elisa rolled her eyes, fighting a small smile. "Lucia, for the last time, property damage is *not* feminism."

"Anything can be feminism if you play Beyoncé in the background while you do it. Speaking of which, do you have the music ready?"

She said, "This is ridiculous," but reached into her pocket for her phone anyway. They were standing in the alleyway behind Longbourn with a small fire-safe trash can, a lighter, a can of gasoline, and every picture and memento Julieta had of her and Bobby's relationship.

Despite her insistence that she wanted to burn the items and move on with her life, it had taken some prodding to get Julieta to actually follow through. Every time Elisa asked, she said, "No, no, not *yet*." She'd spent a week crying and looking at the photos, presents, and knickknacks, before deciding it was time to finally get rid of them. The bracelet she'd received for Christmas, however, remained in her top dresser drawer. Elisa had never intended to destroy that—it was worth nearly $500. She could be furious and pragmatic at the same time. Julieta had said she'd mail it to him, ignoring Maria's suggestions that she pawn it. But instead, it was hidden away in her bedroom, clearly not about to go anywhere. Elisa had found the bracelet while cleaning that morning and had very nearly called her on it.

But then she'd seen the tears in her sister's eyes as she gathered up the items she intended to burn, and she just couldn't do it. If Julieta wanted one reminder of the romance, one little piece of nostalgia to hang onto, she deserved to have that much.

Lucia had been happy to help, especially since Elisa had told her that beating Bobby to a pulp was "sadly, not an option." Of course, since most of the pictures were on the internet, and Julieta had vetoed burning anything that actually belonged to Bobby, the pile was rather small. But the idea of destroying it was still oddly satisfying.

Elisa started playing the song Lucia had picked out for the occasion. She had to admit that the music did make the image of Julieta drenching the pile in gasoline before lighting it on fire a touch more epic. The fire was small, easily controlled, and ate up the pictures in mere seconds.

Lucia bounced up and down on her feet. "Don't you feel better already?"

Julieta smiled weakly. "A little," she admitted. "I've never done this before. This is more your area."

"Well, all your other relationships have ended mutually," Elisa pointed out. "Nothing bonfire-worthy."

"What Bobby did wasn't just bonfire-worthy," Lucia insisted. "It was arson-worthy. Seriously, are you sure you don't want to burn one of his shirts? If he left it here, it obviously isn't *that* important to him."

"No, I'm sending his stuff up to him," she said firmly. "Besides, that way he'll know I know what he did."

Assuming Darcy didn't already tell him about my call.

They put the fire out before a cop could stumble across three Latina girls in a poor neighborhood burning things in an alleyway and inevitably haul them over to the nearest police station.

Elisa could just imagine *that* phone call. *"Hey, Mom, I know you're at work, but can you come and bail us out? Oh, we're in for arson..."* Though, when she'd heard what Bobby had done, their mom had looked about ready to burn something herself—or, more accurately, some*one*.

She wondered if Bobby knew how lucky he was he'd managed to get out of Steventon before he got knifed by a very angry Alejandra. Since *that* wasn't an option, she had settled for ranting to anyone that would listen about how Robert Charles II was a lying bastard that didn't deserve her daughter.

It didn't matter how rich you were. If you made one of her daughters cry, you were officially dead to her.

Elisa had to appreciate that.

It was still a nasty shock. Bobby had seemed like a genuinely nice, upstanding kind of guy. The kind who never forgot to call and would always do his breakups face-to-face. Julieta hadn't been the only one to see a future for them—Elisa had seen it, too. In her eyes, Bobby had been the man that might have finally deserved her older sister.

But first impressions, she reflected as she and her sisters went back into the apartment, were often wrong.

• • •

By early February, Elisa was almost used to Colin being around Charlene's apartment. Since he was still keeping the relationship hidden from his mother, hanging out at his place wasn't an option, apparently. Catherine Burger had a key and was prone to unannounced visits.

Elisa barely even wanted to vomit anymore when they cuddled on the couch, holding hands, or even kissing. Colin was still a question mark, but she did like the way Charlene's eyes lit up whenever he laughed at something she said, or the way she smiled whenever reading his texts. She was happy, and he was treating her well.

Valentine's Day fell on a Friday, and the happy couple was planning to spend it in a cabin Colin's family had in the woods about two hours away. Much to Elisa's surprise, however, they weren't planning to go alone. They had invited her and her sisters, and a couple other friends, too.

"I thought you two would be playing honeymooners all weekend," Elisa said. "You really want to spend your first Valentine's Day as a couple with a bunch of other people in the woods?"

"Valentine's Day is about love of all kinds," Colin said. "Romantic, familial, platonic…"

"And my parents said they'd be infinitely more comfortable if we weren't alone," Charlene added.

He blushed. "That, too."

"What can they do?" Elisa asked. "You live alone, and you're twenty-one."

She shrugged. "If I didn't agree, I was worried my dad

would have an aneurysm."

"Well, I'll be glad to go," she said, pulling her feet up onto the couch. The three of them were in Charlene's apartment, watching a classic sci-fi movie marathon. It was the only genre all three of them liked, and Elisa and Colin were both doing their best to avoid any conflict, no matter how minor. "It'll give me something to do besides watch my mom mope about how it's yet another Valentine's Day where all five of her daughters are single."

"How's Julieta doing?" Charlene asked. She reached for a handful of popcorn from the bowl on the coffee table. "I still can't believe Bobby did that."

"She's...coping. I catch her stalking his social media sometimes," Elisa sighed. "But she's stopped crying. She's mostly focusing on work. It's a good distraction—time-consuming and stable."

"Ah yes. Men may be fickle, but at least her job and her money won't wake up one day and randomly decide to run off to Cape Cod."

"That's the idea."

"I tried asking Darcy if she knows what happened," Colin said, pulling his gaze away from the screen, "but she wouldn't tell me anything. She just told me to keep my head up my ass and out of her business." He paused. "Her words."

Elisa snorted. "That sounds about right."

"So, yeah, dealing with that all weekend will be fun..."

She paused the TV, turning to stare at him. *"Darcy's* coming?"

Colin cringed. "When I asked Mother if I could use the cabin this weekend, I said I was bringing some friends out there. She made me invite Darcy. I didn't *want* to. And I didn't expect her to actually say *yes.* She's coming up from Columbus to meet us at the cabin on Friday night."

Elisa groaned. *"Dammit."*

On the one hand, maybe it'd be easier to grill her about Bobby's behavior if they were in the middle of nowhere and she couldn't run away.

On the other, being around Darcy usually left Elisa flustered, sputtering, and riled up. It was an unusual feeling for her, and she didn't think she liked it. Sure, she'd had people she didn't get along with before, but they never intruded on her thoughts quite as much as Darcy did. And it was all kinds of aggravating to realize that, with her beauty and all they had in common, Elisa might have actually liked her in another life.

Is there such a thing as a hatecrush?

"B-but," Colin said quickly, "I also invited Willow, so she's coming, too. Hopefully she can balance things out."

She sighed, unpausing the movie. It was an old-school space opera from the sixties about a team of astronauts who landed on an uncharted planet full of evil, somehow sentient robots and beautiful women who weren't too bright. It was the worst movie she had seen in months, and she loved it. "Well, if you were planning a romantic weekend, it appears your plan has been foiled. I cannot think of a single mood killer more effective than Darcy."

• • •

At dinner that night, Elisa told her sisters they were all invited up to the cabin—though she left out the Darcy part. She *so* did not want to think about it.

"I can't go," Lucia said. "I have a date. He's a *senior*." She smiled proudly.

Maria rolled her eyes. "He's too old for you."

"He's only seventeen."

"But *still*." She sighed. "I can't go, either. Lane's birthday is on the fifteenth, she's having a party."

Lucia did a double take. "*You* got invited to a party?"

"Oh, shut up, Lulu."

"I'll go," Camila said brightly. "I haven't got any other plans, and I'd like to see if you kick Colin's ass."

"If she does, film it," Maria said. "For posterity."

Lucia grinned. "We could totally sell that footage to some clickbait site. *Angry English Major Body-slams BFF's Boyfriend.*"

Elisa snorted and rolled her eyes. "Thanks, guys. What about you, Julieta?"

Julieta, who hadn't said a word throughout dinner, looked up from her food. "I...have a date, too."

Everyone turned to stare at her.

"What?"

"You got a new boyfriend, and you didn't think to mention that earlier?" Lucia asked.

She blushed. "He's not a boyfriend. He's just a guy at the coffeeshop I talk to sometimes. He asked me out for dinner, and I kind of thought, you know, 'Why not?'"

Mom looked concerned. "Honey, are you sure? You only broke up with Bobby a couple weeks ago..."

Julieta shook her head, forcing a smile that didn't fool anybody. "I'm fine."

"Still, I can't help but hope that maybe he'll come to his senses and—"

Her smile faded away and was replaced with a small scowl. "And *what*, Mom? Come back? Beg forgiveness? Get real." She sighed, picking at her food. "Bobby's made how he feels *very* clear. He's not coming back, and he's not going to make a big, romantic speech about how much he loves me and misses me anytime soon. Probably never. He's not gonna ride up on a white horse and marry me, Mom. We gave it a shot, okay? I thought it was working, but I was wrong."

Alejandra watched her eldest daughter, eyes sad. Elisa

wasn't sure what to do or say. Watching Julieta in pain was grueling for her mother. Elisa was sure it wasn't just losing the opportunity to marry into money—she had a feeling that Mom had stopped caring about that a long time ago. She had half a mind to drive up to Cape Cod and give Bobby a piece of her mind for what he'd done to her sister. She had been through breakups before, sure, but not like this. Never like this.

"Okay," Mom said quietly. "I want you to move on. And if dating again will help..."

"It will," Julieta said. "Can we just drop it, please? Let's talk about something else. Elisa, how was class today?"

Elisa gave an answer she barely even thought about. She didn't really care about school, and she doubted Julieta did, either. Valentine's Day would seriously suck for her this year—so soon after being dumped. She was sure her sister was only going out with this guy, whoever he was, as a distraction.

But who was she to judge? If a rebound was what she needed in order to forget about Bobby, then Elisa was all for it.

• • •

"Have fun, okay?" Julieta said, as Elisa and Camila finished getting ready for their trip. After checking their bags one final time, they'd headed down to the lobby to meet Colin and Charlene, and then, they'd be off. Colin would drive all four of them up, so Mom wouldn't be without a car all weekend. Elisa wasn't sure she wanted to spend the whole two-hour drive with him, but at least his car was sure to be more comfortable than the Benitez minivan.

"We will," Camila said, going to kiss her sister on the cheek. "And tell me all about this guy when we get back."

"I promise," she said. "Now, you know what to say if

someone offers you drugs or alcohol, right?"

"Yes, I say, 'One at a time, please.'"

Both of her older sisters glared at her.

"I'm *kidding.*"

Elisa sighed. "I'll keep her out of trouble," she promised. "Don't worry about us."

Julieta smiled. "Have a good time. Don't let Darcy ruin a fun weekend. And…if she says something about Bobby… I, um. I probably don't want to know, okay?"

She nodded. "I get it." She hugged her. "See you Sunday night."

They said goodbye to their other sisters and their mother before heading downstairs to meet Colin and Charlene. Elisa decided to do her absolute best to heed Julieta's advice. The cabin would be nice, and the forest it was in was beautiful. And it'd be nice to hang out with Willow and Charlene.

As they got into the car, Elisa told herself that this weekend would be fun. But still, she couldn't help but feel like the other shoe was about to drop.

Chapter Eighteen

In Which the Other Shoe Drops (...And Then Some)

Elisa lost her phone signal about half an hour away from the cabin. She decided that this was a good thing—it'd keep her from obsessively checking Lucia's social media every five minutes to make sure she was staying out of trouble. The cabin was tucked away in the woods next to a stream, which was frozen, and a couple rarely used nature trails. The ground was still rock-solid, but most of the snow had melted, and it wasn't too windy.

"It can get really cold out at night," Colin said, parking the car and turning it off. "But the cabin has heating and electricity. A small kitchen, a bathroom with a shower... only two bedrooms, but the couches fold out into beds."

"It's so cute," Camila said, getting out of the car. The others were quick to follow, stretching their legs and shoulders. "Do you come out here much?"

"My parents and I spend a couple weeks out here every summer," he said, "and my dad comes here with his old college buddies for a couple nights every winter."

"Any idea when other people will start arriving?" Charlene asked.

"Last text I got before we lost the signal was from Darcy—she's about half an hour behind us, and she has Willow with her. My friend Tom's driving, since Darcy doesn't have her license and Willow's is suspended again. Eddie and Freya are supposed to show up in maybe an hour and a half. Freya didn't get off work until about fifteen minutes ago."

"Let's get inside," Charlene said, bouncing up and down a bit to keep warm. "I'm freezing, and it'll take a while for the heater to warm up the entire cabin."

The inside was wood walls, floors, and furniture, even wood-colored decorations. What little wasn't varying shades of brown were varying shades of green. There was also a large deer's head hanging over the fireplace.

"It's fake," Colin said, noticing her look of disgust as he went to start a fire. "My dad's tried hunting, but it's always a disaster. He has many talents—aim is not one of them. After he accidentally shot Uncle Todd, Mother made him promise to never hold a gun ever again. After he accidentally shot Uncle Bill, she said arrows weren't allowed, either. But he insisted that the cabin wouldn't be complete without the head of a dead animal."

"Charming," she said. "I don't mind when people hunt for food, but people hunting for sport or decoration just leaves a bad taste in my mouth."

"I personally agree with you, but my dad and his brothers consider hunting to be the epitome of manhood." He rolled his eyes. "My uncles were always disappointed that my dad sucked, but they were even more disappointed when I wouldn't even *try*."

He stepped back as the fireplace flickered, flames warming Elisa's chilled fingers from where she stood. As he went to find the thermostat, she looked around the rest of the cabin. Heading up the stairs, she found that there was a master bedroom, and two smaller ones down the hall. Charlene had already parked her and Colin's bags in the master. Elisa smiled. Apparently having guests wouldn't stop them from playing honeymooners, after all.

"Has anyone claimed the other rooms?" she called down the stairs.

Colin yelled back from the kitchen. "Eddie and Tom are sharing one, and Darcy called dibs on the other. But she'd probably be willing to share with you."

"Pass." She began heading back downstairs. "I'll just share a couch with Willow."

Camila pouted. "You wouldn't share a couch with me? I'm shocked and insulted."

She smirked. "You snore."

"So do you."

"*And* you kick."

Colin got a huge bag of marshmallows and an even bigger bag of chocolate and placed them on the counter. "It's too cold to do this outside, and I don't know how to start a fire out there, anyway, but we can make s'mores in the fireplace, I think. The only correct way to do s'mores is outside over an open fire, but the fireplace will make for decent knockoffs."

"I always did 'em in the microwave," Charlene said.

He laughed. "Only the *finest* knockoff s'mores here."

Elisa turned away as he leaned in to kiss her. They weren't so bad together, she admitted, but their kissing could sometimes be…sloppy.

It would've been cute if it wasn't borderline nauseating.

Still, she was glad Charlene was so happy. After twenty years' worth of crappy Valentine's Days, she deserved it. She just hoped nothing would happen this weekend that could screw things up.

• • •

It was well past dark, and the last of the guests had arrived three hours prior. Eddie, Tom, and Freya, as it turned out, were three of Colin's classmates from the college he went to. Elisa found them all to be a bit pretentious, but very likable. Willow had arrived with a deck of cards, a karaoke machine, and a cooler full of beer, plus a huge bottle of vodka, while Darcy had arrived with a frown and a book. Elisa had brought a book, too, but was saving it for when everyone else had passed out—she always had difficulty falling asleep in an unfamiliar place.

By nine, Freya—who, as it turned out, was quite the lightweight—was passed out facedown on the couch. Elisa, Darcy, and Camila, all of whom were sober, kept an eye on her while watching everyone else get anywhere from mildly tipsy to stupidly, falling-down drunk. Darcy sulked in the corner with her book, while Elisa watched, laughing, as Camila and Willow sang duet after duet on the karaoke machine. By song number fifteen, Darcy had gone up to her room.

"And that was our interpretation of *Toxic* by Britney Spears," Willow announced, taking a bow as the rest of the cabin applauded. "Thank you."

She dropped the mic she was holding. Camila dove to catch it.

Willow plunked herself down on the couch next to Elisa, Camila quickly following. She was flushed with nervousness, never having been one to get up on stage, even in a small group. Even so, she was smiling widely. She'd been hesitant to join in at first, but Willow, who was completely unafraid to make a fool of herself, had worn her down.

"Having fun?" Willow asked, happily drunk.

"I am," Elisa said. "I'm glad Colin invited you."

"Me too. 'Sssspecially since I'm getting to know one

of your sisters." She shook Camila's shoulders. "Best duet partner ever."

"Well, I knew if I didn't go, you'd start harping on Darcy to join you," Camila said. "And then she probably would've cried or something."

Elisa rolled her eyes. "Please, I don't think Darcy's species is capable of tear production. She'd probably peel her skin off and sprout horns."

Camila snickered, but Willow turned to face her again, placing her hands on her face.

"Lisa. Lisa. Lisa. Look at me. Lisa. Lisa. Look at me, Lisa."

"I'm literally staring right at you."

"*Elisa.* Listen to me, Lisa. Darcy's—Darcy's not as bad as you think. Scout's honor."

"I thought you told me you got kicked out of Girl Scouts for sabotaging the other girls' cookie sales," Camila said.

"*Shhhhh.*" Willow waved one of her hands in her face. "My point is… The point is…"

Elisa smiled. "Look, I know you love Darcy. You two are family. But she's just so…"

"Look, look, look. No one knows how annoying she can be better than me. But she's…she's got a good heart."

"Uh-huh."

"She totally does," she insisted. "If you're her friend, and she thinks you're in danger of being hurt—*wham*! She's *there*. You don' even have to ask. Like—like, for example…uh…oh. *Oh*, Bobby. You kinda knew Bobby, right?"

"I thought I did," Elisa said. Now, she was paying attention. Camila, too, had sat up the rest of the way and was watching her intently.

Willow continued, oblivious to the sudden shift in mood. "I dunno all the details, but apparently, he was dating this girl who was, like, a level-five gold digger—but he, like, really liked her. So he didn't realize. Love makes you stupid. But, like, Darcy totally realized what kinda person that girl really was, so she pulled Bobby aside and told him the truth. I mean, it seriously hurt the poor guy, but, like, Darcy knows that a harsh truth is better than a lie to spare someone's feelings."

"And then Bobby went to Cape Cod," Elisa said slowly.

Willow nodded. "Right. He was kinda reluctant to give up on the gold digger, but Darcy convinced him that—that it was the best thing he could do for himself. Don't try to fix things, don't try to ration'lize the problem away. Just *go*."

"So...*Darcy*...broke them up."

"What was the girl's name?" Camila asked. Maybe Willow had it all wrong, or there was somehow another girl involved. Maybe this had happened years ago. Maybe she was thinking of a different Bobby. Maybe...

"Uhhh... Julianne, or Juliet. Something like that."

"Julieta," she said quietly.

Willow nodded, snapping her fingers. "*That's* it."

Camila looked like she was going to be sick. Elisa's hands were balled up into fists, nails digging into her palms.

Willow's smile was slowly dropping, as if she were being gradually eased into a bath of ice.

"You two...have a sister named Julieta, don't you...?" she said, the full truth of the matter slowly dawning on her.

Elisa nodded.

"Oh. Oh. *Oh*..." Then, it hit her. *"Oh shit."*

Willow looked absolutely mortified. Camila had buried her face in her hands, trying to process what she'd just learned.

Elisa's breath became shaky, her hands clenched into fists through no will of her own. She opened her mouth, but no words came out. There was nothing to say, nothing that would make this better. She got up from the couch, grabbing her coat off the hook, ignoring Willow's plea for her to sit back down. The others were in the center of the living room, playing a board game, oblivious to the conversation Elisa, Camila, and Willow were having. Darcy was still up in her room.

"I'm going for a walk," she announced, pulling her snow boots on. "I need some fresh air."

"Want some company?" Colin asked, beginning to get to his feet. "It's dark out there, you'll get lost."

"I'll be fine," she snapped. Then, a breath in, a breath out, trying to level herself. "I just—I kind of need some alone time."

He sat back down, nodding. "Okay. But if you're not back in an hour, I'm coming after you."

"Fine." Sixty minutes wouldn't be enough to clear her head, but she wasn't sure any amount of time would do the job.

She stepped out of the cabin and into the winter's night, trying her best not to slam the door behind her. Even with her coat, gloves, scarf, and hat, she began shivering almost immediately. Hopefully it'd get better if she kept moving.

What little snow remained crunched underneath her feet, the only noise in an otherwise silent forest. Most of the animals were hibernating and would be for another month, and it appeared the group back at the cabin were the only ones who'd decided to come out here this weekend. She walked aimlessly for nearly forty-five minutes, going in circles, going down the same path again and again, not wanting to get too far from the cabin, but not wanting to go back inside. Finally, she reached the edge of the frozen stream, and stood there, staring at the darkened landscape, inwardly fuming over what Willow had told her.

Even for Darcy, this was low. First what she'd done to Wick, and now this.

It was official, Elisa decided. Forget the idea that she'd been too harsh or judged too quickly. Darcy Fitzgerald was the most conceited, most vile, most insufferable person on the planet. She was stuck-up, and cruel, and…and…and…

"Elisa."

She let out a yelp, before turning around.

Darcy was standing there, blue pea coat with matching boots, looking apprehensive. Had someone told her what Elisa had found out? If she was here to try and apologize, she would have to restrain herself from tossing her onto the ice.

"Colin told me you'd gone for a walk. I followed your footprints," Darcy said. "I have an important matter to discuss with you."

"Did he tell you I want to be alone?" Elisa asked, voice shaking a bit, furious just from the sight of her.

"Yes. But I need to talk to you when we're alone, and we may not get another chance this weekend. That was… actually the entire reason I agreed when Colin invited me on this trip. I wanted to see you."

"Darcy, I promise you, whatever you have to say, I don't want to hear it."

"I have a present for you."

She blinked. "Um. What?"

Darcy reached into her pocket and produced a small, heart-shaped box of chocolates, handing it to her. Elisa took it, mainly because she was at a loss as to what else she could do. This wasn't one of the cheap boxes they sold at the drugstore—these were expensive. Fancy. When she took a closer look, she saw that Darcy had scribbled a message in Sharpie on the front.

For Elisa Benitez. I hope you enjoy these as much as I've enjoyed knowing you.—Darcy Fitzgerald.

Slowly, Elisa raised her head to look at her again. She was shuffling nervously on her feet, clearly waiting for some kind of reaction. When Elisa didn't speak, she filled the silence for her.

"I agonized over whether to get those for you," she admitted. "I knew I wanted to get you something for Valentine's Day, but I was worried the chocolates might be cliché. But then I thought to myself, they became cliché for a reason, and I know you enjoy chocolate, so I decided to just go for it."

"Um...thanks, I guess, but—" She was so confused, she had nearly forgotten she was mad at her. "Why are you... Why are you giving me a Valentine's Day present at all?"

Darcy took a shaking breath before stepping closer to her.

"Elisa, I have struggled in vain for the past few months. Ever since the day you and I met, really. But it cannot go on like this. I have something to say to you, and I ask that you listen to me. I admire you greatly, Elisa, and please believe me when I say that I most ardently love you."

Elisa dropped the box of chocolates. She stood frozen, staring at Darcy, searching her face for any sign that she was kidding. She found none. Finally, Elisa managed to force out a response.

"*What?*"

"Hear me out. I... I planned a speech."

"You planned a *speech* for—?"

"Listen. I wanted to confess to you long before today, but, a combination of my own shyness and how nervous I get around you, and the fact that your family is highly inappropriate in social situations, particularly those involving those of us with a higher social standing—"

"*Excuse* me?"

Darcy kept talking, apparently not noticing that she was about three seconds away from being slapped. "Please let me finish," she said. "In spite of your lower financial status, and your...frankly embarrassing family, I have been extremely taken by you since the day we met in Professor DeCaro's class. In spite of everything my brain has been telling me, my heart has been stolen away. By you."

Darcy stopped talking, watching Elisa's face, big brown eyes shining expectantly.

What am I even supposed to say to all that? Her brain was in "blue screen of death" mode.

Finally, she found her voice.

"Well, today your brain gets to say, 'I told you so,' because believe me, Darcy, your feelings are *not* mutual," she said. "In fact, they're about as far from mutual as it's possible to be."

She hadn't actually slapped Darcy, but judging from the look on her face, she might as well have.

"Wh...what?"

"You can't honestly be surprised by this," Elisa snapped, throwing up her hands. "You're cold and snotty and condescending. You're pretentious and talk like you're in a bad period piece. You've never said a nice thing about me—"

Darcy was staring at the ground, bottom lip trembling. If it had been anyone else, she would've felt sorry for her. "That is not true," she whispered.

"Oh, right, you said I was *fine*, you supposed. Were you expecting a prize for that?"

"Elisa—"

"You act like a complete bitch all the time. Not just to me—to *everyone*. Even Bobby, your so-called best friend."

Darcy licked her lips. "I... I admit, my social awkwardness can sometimes manifest in ways that makes me come off as... less than friendly," she said quietly. "Bobby has known me for years. He knows what I am really trying to say, and that I truly do care about him, even when I'm being...standoffish. I suppose I forget that not everyone is used to me, and I don't always... I don't always put forth the effort to be more sociable."

"Is that your excuse?"

"It's not an excuse, it's the truth."

"Also, who in their right mind asks out a girl by *insulting her family*? And that's not even getting into what you did to Julieta. How could you break up her and Bobby? *How*?"

Darcy glanced up at her, eyes slightly widened, but she didn't try and deny it.

"I was trying to protect Bobby."

"Protect him from what? Julieta has never hurt a soul in her life."

"And now that I've pulled Bobby away from her, she gets to keep that flawless track record," she said, crossing her arms. "Look, Elisa, I understand that your judgment may be somewhat clouded when it comes to your sister. I know the two of you are close. But believe me when I say that what I did was for the best. It was obvious to me that Julieta was not as invested in the relationship as Bobby was. It's not that she wasn't kind or friendly, but she behaved toward him the exact same way she behaved toward everyone else. Every man I ever saw try to advance on her while we were all out together, she gave the same smiles and patience she gave Bobby."

"That's because she's *nice*!" Elisa yelled. When had she begun shouting? She honestly wasn't sure.

"If Julieta wished to keep her relationship with Bobby casual, that is her right. It is even possible she thought that was clear and was unaware her actions would ever hurt anybody. But I didn't want his heart to get broken when he inevitably realized he was far more invested in the relationship than she."

"Julieta loved him, she—she would've *eloped* if he asked."

"Oh, I'm sure she would have," she said, voice laced with venom.

"What. The hell. Does that mean?"

"Oh, don't be naive, Elisa. It's obvious to me—to everyone—that marrying Bobby would be incredibly advantageous to Julieta and, by extension, your whole family."

"If you're calling my sister a gold digger, I *swear to God—*
"

"I'm not saying she was *only* after Bobby's money. I don't think she's that cold-hearted. But your youngest sister and *especially* your mother—they have both made it very clear that the financial gain is the biggest reason they encouraged the relationship."

Elisa stared at her in silence for a few moments, breathing shallow, tears stinging her eyes, whether from anger or sadness on her sister's behalf or just sheer frustration.

Upon seeing her tear up, Darcy's gaze softened, and she stepped forward, raising a shivering hand and reaching to wipe Elisa's eyes. She stopped just before she actually touched her, as if waiting for permission. Elisa didn't give it to her. She just took a step back and shook her head. Fortunately, she accepted that and quickly lowered her hand.

"I'm sorry," Darcy said. "I shouldn't have—I shouldn't have put it all quite like that. This isn't how I wanted this to go. I never meant to bring you pain."

"Julieta was in love with him," Elisa said. "Everyone knew it. Everyone, apparently, except for you, and Bobby's dumb ass."

She tore her gaze away, but her eyes were more regretful than angry. "Then why didn't she *say* so?"

"I don't know, maybe the same reason you've spent the past six months acting like a complete bitch." Even as she spoke, her voice was shaky.

Darcy glared at her, Elisa's comment sending her back on the defense. "It's just as well," she said. "Bobby's family never would've approved of him marrying into yours. You and Julieta, they liked fine, but your three youngest sisters— *especially* Lucia." She let out a cold laugh. It didn't suit her. In spite of everything, it didn't suit her. "I know she embarrasses you. Don't deny it. I've heard you reprimand her or complain about her countless times."

"She's my sister. That's my *job*," Elisa snapped. "And don't you *dare* talk about Lucia that way. You barely even know her. Lucia is a kind, caring, beautiful girl, and she doesn't need approval from spoiled girls who don't know how to function outside their sphere of privilege."

"Your sister, a beauty? I'd sooner call George Sedgwick a gentleman," she scoffed.

At this point, it felt less like an argument, and more like a contest to see who could upset the other more. She hated the fact that Darcy was winning.

"Oh, right, I didn't even get into what you did to Wick," Elisa said. "You ruined his future. What's your excuse for that?"

"Oh, yes, Wick's life has been *nothing* but suffering," she said dryly. "Rest assured, Elisa, all pain he's endured, he's brought on himself."

"What'd he do to deserve you getting him expelled for no reason?"

Darcy tilted her head. "So *that's* what he told you."

"Do you deny it?"

"In part. I saw that he was expelled, but I had my reasons."

"Knowing you, your reason was probably 'I got bored,'" she said. "Darcy, from the very first day I met you—maybe even the first moment—you've been nothing but rude, condescending, and cold. I thought you were an insufferable snob from the very start." She let out a small, biting laugh. "Well, it's always nice to be right."

Darcy's eyes were slightly watery, but Elisa pretended not to notice. "I thought it was you who once told me that first impressions could be misleading."

"Well, in this case, my first impression was dead-on. From the very start, I knew you were the last person I could *ever* fall in love with."

Elisa's bold declaration seemed to knock all the words right out of Darcy, and she stood in silence for a moment, staring at the ground. Finally, she took a deep breath, and her words came out clear, calm, and even.

"So, this is what you think of me." She shoved her hands in her pockets. "I apologize for any pain I caused you. I wish things were different. I wish…" Whatever it was that Darcy wished, she didn't say. After a few more seconds of silence, she raised her gaze to meet Elisa's once more. "Happy Valentine's Day. Goodbye."

Darcy turned on her heel and left, leaving her standing there, mind reeling. She had absolutely no clue what she was supposed to do now. No one told you how to handle this sort of thing. It wasn't every day you received a declaration of love, and it certainly wasn't every day you received a declaration of love from someone you despised.

Someone who, up until now, you assumed despised you just as much.

The sound of a car in the near distance snapped her out of her thoughts.

Frowning, she hurried back toward the cabin, wondering who on earth could've shown up now, especially so late.

When she reached the cabin, she saw a new car out in front—a Rolls Royce.

Then, she heard shrieking from inside the cabin.

Panicking, every horror movie she'd ever seen flashing through her brain, Elisa grabbed a large stick from off the ground and ran inside.

There was a new addition to the cabin, someone standing at the top of the stairs, holding open the door to the bedroom where Colin and Charlene were staying. It wasn't Freddy Kruger, or Jason, or whatever the monster was from *It Follows*. No, it was much, much worse.

"I'm sorry, Colin," Tom yelled up the stairs, standing at the foot of them. "We tried to stop her."

Catherine Burger. Colin's mother. The only person that hadn't known her son was dating Charlene. And, apparently, she'd just walked in on them.

Dearly hoping for Charlene's sake that they hadn't gotten past first base, Elisa ran up the stairs to join Catherine—or, more to the point, to back her friend up. She didn't put the stick down, though. She could already tell that this was going to get ugly. Charlene and Colin had taken some clothes off and were scrambling to get them back on, and he was talking a mile a minute. He stumbled to stand in the doorway as if trying to shield Charlene from his mother.

"M-Mother, I didn't know you'd be joining us. Would you like a s'more? Or maybe a hot dog? I think we still have some tortilla chips left… Uh, anyway, th-this is Charlene. You know Charlene, don't you? She and I are…are…"

Catherine's face twisted up in a way that made her look like a prune crossed with a bulldog.

"Colin."

"Mother, I…"

"Ignatius."

"Please don't—"

"*Burger.*" She reached forward to grab her son by the shirt, pulling him forward like a vulture swiping up its meal. "You and I are going to have a serious talk. Tell your little girlfriend to wait downstairs."

Colin faltered for a moment before swallowing a lump in his throat. He looked like he was trying to appear angry, but his eyes gave away his fear.

"No."

"Excuse me?"

"I said, no. If we're going to discuss my relationship with Charlene, then that discussion should *include* Charlene."

Catherine stared her son down for a moment. Elisa held her breath, waiting for Colin to falter, but he never did. He was visibly nervous, but he stood his ground, maintaining eye contact and refusing to budge.

This was probably the most Elisa had ever liked him.

Finally, Catherine spoke.

"Fine. But she, the one with the stick," she said, pointing a talon-like finger at Elisa, "is to go downstairs. And after this conversation, everyone in this cabin is to leave. Holiday's over."

She shoved her way past Colin and stormed into the room. Elisa hesitated. She wasn't sure she wanted to be a part of the conversation the others were about to have, but she didn't exactly want to abandon Charlene to be shrieked at by Catherine Burger. True, Colin would be there, and he was showing a surprising amount of spine, but he still looked shell-shocked as he leaned against the doorframe, mentally preparing himself for what was to come.

Charlene seemed to sense her worries because she said, "Go on, Lisa. Tell the others to start packing. We'll be down in a few."

"Okay." She glanced at Colin. "Good luck in there, buddy."

She headed down the stairs, and the door to their room closed as she went. The others, including a now-awake Freya, were at the bottom of the steps, waiting for a report.

"Mrs. Burger wants everyone out," she announced. "And, we, uh…depending on how the conversation going on upstairs goes, we, um, may also never see Colin again."

Everyone hastily began throwing their things into their bags, trying to clean up the area as best they could on such short notice. Elisa kept casting nervous glances back upstairs, half expecting to see Charlene and Colin running for their lives.

Darcy hadn't said a word since they got back to the cabin, even as everyone else was muttering about how pissed their roommates would be that they were back two days early or theorizing all the various ways Catherine could kill Colin. She'd simply dashed upstairs to get her bag out of the other bedroom, avoiding eye contact with Elisa.

That was fine. After this night, Elisa hoped she would never see or speak to Darcy again.

Interlude: In Which a Hangover is the Least of Charlene's Problems

Charlene had only had two and a half bottles of beer, but she was still too drunk for this conversation. Of course, she wasn't sure she'd *ever* be sober enough for it. She sat on the bed, massaging her temples as Colin paced nervously and Catherine started on her laundry list of why she was completely unsuited for her little boy.

"How could you keep this from me, Colin? How *could* you?" she hissed. "And stop that incessant pacing." She reached out, grabbing him by the arm to keep him in place.

"We were going to tell you eventually," he said.

I wasn't.

"What are you even doing here?" he asked. "I thought you had plans with Dad."

"They finished a few hours ago," Catherine said. "And I knew you were hiding something from me. I know you better than anyone. You asking to use the cabin over Valentine's Day weekend only confirmed it. I had you invite your cousin so she could keep an eye on things and report back—but it's a good thing I came myself, anyway, since *that* proved to be utterly useless. She wasn't even *here* when I arrived."

He groaned, hiding his face in his hands.

"How *could* you?" she asked again. "Colin, I have told you time and time again, we have a certain circle to which we restrict ourselves. Burgers marry wealth and prestige, not trailer trash like her."

Charlene flinched, but she managed to bite her tongue.

"Mother, only marrying people of a certain economic standing is the reason my grandparents are *cousins*," Colin said. "And if we're going to have this discussion, then I'm going to have to ask that you *don't* to refer to my girlfriend as trash."

"This isn't a discussion," she said venomously. "She's nothing but a disgusting gold digger—they *all* are."

Charlene spoke up, then. "Believe me, Mrs. Burger, your son's money is the last thing on my mind."

"If I want you to speak, I'll *ask* you," Catherine barked.

"No one asked *you* to speak, you know," Charlene said.

She turned back to her son. "Listen to me, Colin—girls like that, they'll ruin you. They'll take everything you've got and then run off to the next one. She'll lose interest as soon as someone richer comes along."

"Oh, please," Charlene snapped. "Colin's the first guy I've dated in three *years*. I knew about his money *long* before I was ever interested."

"Mother, listen..." He reached for Catherine's hands. "I'm sorry I hid this from you. It was stupid of me. But please, please give her a chance. Get to know her. I think you may actually like her."

Charlene was certain it would be a cold day in Hell before they ever got along, and from Catherine's expression, they were, for once, thinking the same thing.

"You two have more in common than you'd think," he added with a note of desperation.

"I," Catherine said, "have nothing in common with that uneducated, lice-ridden—"

"I may be poor," Charlene said, voice shaking, "but I am *not* a second-class citizen. You *cannot* talk to me like that."

"I can talk to the woman who's exploiting my youngest child *any way I like.*"

"Even *if* that were true," Colin said, "*which it's not*—it's not your decision, Mother. I'm twenty, nearly twenty-one. Charlene and I are both consenting adults—there is nothing you can do or say to keep us from being together."

Catherine looked him over.

"Fine. If you feel that strongly, if you think you're so independent—you can keep her around for as long as you like. But don't expect my financial or emotional support while you do."

Charlene rose to her feet now, eyes widening. "You hate me so much that you'd *cut him off?*"

"Children should obey their parents."

"He's your son, not your *property.*"

He clenched and unclenched his fists. "You can't use the money to control me, Mother. If you're going to force me to choose between you and Charlene, you are going to *lose.*"

"This shouldn't be a competition," Charlene said, growing more distressed with every passing second. "Your mom and I don't have to like each other, but—I mean, surely we can reach some sort of compromise?"

"This is my compromise," she said coolly. "Colin, if you come to your senses now, you won't have anything to worry about. If you don't... Well, you can say goodbye to your apartment, your tuition, your car...and everything else I've ever paid for."

Colin took a deep breath. Charlene braced herself for

what was to come.

"Fine," he said. "I'll be out of the apartment by Monday night."

His mother looked about as blindsided as Charlene felt. She was so sure that Colin would ultimately choose his relationship with his mother over her, and Catherine's face told her she'd been expecting the same thing.

The prospect of Colin suddenly being homeless and possibly having to drop out of college was utterly horrifying. The idea of him losing his family over her was also enough to make her feel nauseous. And yet, there was one voice—one horrible, selfish, wonderful voice in the back of her head— that almost allowed her to smile in spite of it all.

He chose me.

Catherine was absolutely fuming.

"You'd throw away everything—your prestige, your wealth, your education, your very *future*—all for this undeserving piece of filth?"

"Mother, I am going to tell you again to not talk about Charlene that way," Colin said, visibly struggling to keep his tone steady.

"She's *using* you, Colin. Once I cut you off, see how fast she leaves."

"Mother, *stop it*."

"I will not stand by and watch you get taken in by a worthless piece of sh—"

"I TOLD YOU TO *SHUT UP!*"

No sooner had Colin raised his voice than Catherine reached forward again, pulling her son toward her with one hand, the other flying at his face. Charlene moved quickly, dashing to him and pulling him back. Catherine hadn't slapped him, exactly—the more accurate term would be "clawed." She slashed her nails across his face, hard enough to draw some blood, leaving bright pink tracks across her son's skin.

He seemed more stunned than hurt and had a very blank look on his face. Realizing he was at his capacity, Charlene quickly said, "If you're going to be violent, you're going to have to leave."

Catherine stepped back, surveying her work. Satisfied with what she'd done, she said, "Fine. I'll leave. I wonder how long it'll take him to come crawling back. My little boy can't function without me."

Colin raised his head to look at her, then.

"Yes, I can," he said quietly. "And I *never* want to see or speak to you again."

She stared him down for a second, before letting out an irritated huff. She collected herself before saying, "I want everyone out of my cabin in five minutes. And you're out of that apartment by Monday night. Remember—you promised."

"I remember," Colin muttered.

Catherine left, slamming the door behind her. As soon as she was gone, Charlene quickly dashed to the dresser, grabbing some tissues to wipe up the blood.

"There's a first aid kit in the bathroom," he said, grimacing slightly as she touched where his skin had been broken. "I don't think it's that bad, but wouldn't that be just what I need? To get an infection, too?"

Charlene nodded, and grabbed the first aid kit. Using a baby wipe to clean up his face, she said, "Are you okay, babe?" She sighed, shaking her head. "Stupid question. Of course, you're not. But, I mean—"

"I'll live," he said grimly. He raised a hand to touch where he'd been clawed, murmuring, "Mother hasn't done anything like that in a long time…"

"Well, it'll be the last," she said. "I know it's not my place to say, but even if you ignore our relationship—I think you did the right thing. I mean, there's hating your son's girlfriend, and then there's emotional blackmail."

"Yeah..." He sighed. "Once we get to where we have a phone signal again, I'll call some of my cousins in the area. Some of them may be on Mother's side, but one of them is bound to let me crash on their couch until I find an apartment. Hell, maybe I can move into Longbourn."

Charlene hesitated.

"I understand if you don't want to, so early in the relationship," she said gently, "but you could always move in with me."

He looked up at her, surprised. "Are you sure?"

She nodded. "Yeah. I mean, this is kind of my fault, the least I could do is—"

"This isn't your fault, Char. I don't want you to offer just because you feel guilty."

"It's not just that," she said quickly. "I could use a roommate. And, you know, I guess I like having you around. I *guess*." She tried for a playful smile.

"Thank you. Thank you," Colin said, before leaning in to give her a peck on the lips.

She smiled wider. "Is that a 'yes'?"

He nodded. "Yeah. Yes, it is. And I promise, I'll find a way to help pay the rent." He bit his lip, obviously thinking very hard. "She already paid for this term of school, so she can't take that back—I've never applied for scholarships or financial aid before, but I can learn... I have about $5,000 in my bank account at the moment—and we took her off the account when I turned eighteen, so that's safe. She's still making payments on my car, so that's still hers... Shit, how am I even going to get to school now? I can't Uber every day."

"Your school is on a bus line. It's a fifty-minute trip each way, but you don't have to switch buses, so it evens out," Charlene said.

"I've...never taken the city bus."

She sighed. "Well, like you said—you can learn. You can finish up this term, and then when summer comes, you can look for a job. If you can only go half-time next fall, or even take a semester off, it's not the end of the world."

"I'm only on campus on Mondays and Wednesdays this term, so I may be able to find something now. I can apply for all the fast food places, retail, delivery—wait, no, you need a car for that..."

"Have you ever had a job?"

"I worked at a fast food place in sophomore year. Mother wouldn't pay for a game I really wanted. Too much blood and guts for her little boy's sensitive eyes. So, I got a job to pay for it myself."

Charlene brightened a bit. "Well, that's something."

He grimaced. "Not really. I got fired in two and a half days."

"How did you—?"

"Long story."

The two hastily packed up what little had been taken out of their bags and headed down the stairs. The others had finished packing, and Catherine was waiting outside for everyone to leave.

Charlene found Elisa and Camila. Colin followed close behind.

"Can you drive?" she asked Elisa. "I'm a bit buzzed, still, and Colin's..." She trailed off.

"I can't focus on the road right now," he said.

Elisa nodded. "No problem. Is everything okay?"

Charlene faltered, her eyes pricking with tears for the first time that night. "Nothing's okay. But it will be. We'll figure it out." She took a breath. "Colin's moving in with me."

She stared at them, but it only took three seconds for her to piece it together.

"She kicked you out?" she whispered to him, stunned. He shrugged wordlessly.

Charlene nodded. "*And* cut him off."

"*Christ.*"

"I've got some money put away," Colin said, "but once that runs out, I'm broke."

Elisa touched his arm sympathetically. "Welcome to the dark side," she said, trying to joke. "And if you need any help getting moved in, or applying for financial help, or finding a job—call me. My family's perfected the art of surviving while broke."

Colin, Camila, and Charlene followed Elisa to the car— the car that would be Catherine's again by the end of the weekend. Catherine stared her son down as he passed her, but he didn't even look her way. He definitely knew she was there, though. Charlene saw his bottom lip shake and how hard he was fighting to keep his gaze straight ahead. She squeezed his hand in solidarity.

Once they were in the car, Elisa hooked up her phone to the speakers and put on some music, correctly guessing that no one was in the mood to talk. Charlene leaned her head against Colin's shoulder, closing her eyes. She just wanted to sleep forever—or at least until this godawful day was over.

Chapter Nineteen

In Which Elisa Brings Charlene Up to Speed

Elisa and Camila returned home on Friday night—or, more accurately, early, early Saturday morning. Alejandra had never liked Colin much, but when her daughters told her what happened, she'd immediately gone into "mama bear" mode. She'd been happy to give him some pointers on how to create a budget. Although $5,000 was far more than she had in the bank, she understood that when you didn't have any income, whatever money you had suddenly didn't seem like so much. When she heard that he still had some things left in his old room at Catherine's house, she'd downright insisted on going to retrieve them herself.

"So you can focus on getting out of your old apartment," she said. Elisa, however, knew the truth: she didn't want to make him see his mother.

Elisa was glad. She hadn't asked how Colin had gotten that scratch on his face, but she could guess. Her own mother often drove her crazy, but as she watched her drive off in the minivan to go get his things from the dragon's den that was the Burger estate, she was suddenly feeling pretty lucky.

Colin had managed to load almost everything from his apartment into his car, though it was packed so tightly, he'd had to use some bungees to hold the doors shut. It took them about half an hour of working together to get everything out. Finally, though, all the boxes were sitting on the front desk of Longbourn's lobby, and he called his father to come and collect the car.

Mr. Burger took the keys from his son and gave him a sad look and a hug. He said, "You'll be fine," before driving away.

He didn't, Elisa noticed, apologize for what Catherine had done, or make any move to stop what was happening.

Once Mr. Burger, and Colin's beautiful Mercedes, disappeared over the horizon, they began the tedious process of moving each box up to the apartment. That took the better part of an hour, the elevator being as slow as it was. But finally, they got the last box off the counter and could start unpacking. This wasn't how Elisa had planned to spend her Saturday afternoon, but she doubted this was how they had planned to spend theirs, either.

"We're making two piles," Charlene said. "Stuff we want to keep and put away, and stuff that I already have, or we just don't need. We'll try to sell that stuff first and give it to Goodwill if we can't."

"Makes sense," Elisa replied, pushing the apartment door open with her foot. Her arms were full with a box labelled: BOOKS, NONFICTION—1/4. Colin had almost as many books as her father. She was sure there would be a bit of debate about how many he *really* needed to keep. Charlene was a reader herself, but, well...limited floorspace.

"Thanks for helping us out, Elisa," Colin said.

"No problem. I'm just sorry you're in this position."

He sighed. "Yeah, me too. But it's for the best. If she acted like that when we're just dating, imagine what she'd be like wh—if we got married."

Charlene leaned over to look in her own box, which conveniently hid her grin. "Okay, hon, do you *really* need the candelabras?"

"They could class up a Friday night dinner."

"Of ramen and diet root beer?"

He considered this. "Fine, we can sell them."

She began moving the candelabras to the "get rid of" pile, saying, "You heard from your mom at all?"

He shook his head. "Not a peep. This whole thing is a mess." He tried to smile. "Congrats on dodging that bullet, Elisa."

Elisa snorted. "I'd laugh if this wasn't all shot to hell."

He nodded in agreement, sorting through his own box (button-up shirts, casualwear). "In all seriousness—I'm so sorry about all that. About how I acted. I was a jerk."

She patted his shoulder. "Thanks. I actually like you a lot better now that you're into someone else."

"Eyyy, she's talking about me," Charlene said with a cheesy grin in her boyfriend's direction.

Elisa smiled then went back to the box she was digging through. "What was your mom even doing there, anyway?" she asked. "She said you could have the cabin, right?"

Colin groaned. "Ugh, I should've known—she'd figured out I was hiding something. I don't know how I ever thought I'd get away with it for long. I mean, I asked to borrow our secluded, romantic cabin over *Valentine's Day*. She knew something was up. That's why she had me invite Darcy, too. She was supposed to be a spy for her, but she sort of failed at that." He rolled his eyes, muttering to himself, "Darcy giving us a heads-up would've been nice, but *nooo*…"

"You know, I was expecting an exciting weekend, but this isn't what I had in mind," Elisa said. She opened a new box and found herself faced with a collection of Beanie Babies.

This was somehow both surprising, and not even slightly surprising at all.

"Did you at least have fun before everything went to shit?" Charlene asked. "I've been so preoccupied with this, I nearly forgot there were other people there."

"Uh, it was...interesting," Elisa said, opening another box. "Willow and Cam sang karaoke, I lost a game of euchre, Willow told me Darcy broke up Bobby and Julieta, Darcy told me she's in love with me, I found a stick that I could use to hit Cath—"

She was cut off by Charlene and Colin saying, "What the *hell*?" at the exact same time.

"Oh yeah, I forgot to tell you—Darcy broke up Bobby and Julieta, and she's in love with me." She was trying to be casual, trying to hide how much her mind was reeling.

"She said she loves you?" Charlene said, eyes wide. "Like, her words?"

She nodded. "Her words."

"What did you say?"

She rolled her eyes. "What do you think I said? I shot her down. Hard." She glanced at Colin. "Congrats on dodging *that* bullet."

"You shot me down pretty hard," he pointed out.

"Yeah, but compared to how I was with Darcy, I was downright pleasant." She sighed. "She opened up this whole thing by saying she hates my family, that they're embarrassing, that our social standing is *so* inferior to hers."

"Wow, I never knew Darcy was a romantic," Charlene said.

"*And* she didn't deny what she did to Wick. *Or* what she did to Jules. I mean, she seemed *proud* of that. She's convinced Jules is a gold digger, so she pulled Bobby away from her."

"Does Julieta know?"

Elisa shook her head. "No. Cam and I talked about it before we went to bed last night. Julieta was already hurt by Bobby leaving. The full truth would *kill* her. And if Mom knew, she'd kill Bobby *and* Darcy."

"I mean...would that really be so bad?"

"Only because I'd like to keep Mom out of jail."

"Oh, please. Your mom would take over within a week, and we all know it."

She snorted. "I'd rather not find out. So, we're keeping it to ourselves. Cam hasn't even told Lucia. They normally tell each other everything, but, well...if Radio Lulu knows something, so does all of Longbourn and the entirety of Steventon Public High."

"I can't believe this all happened *yesterday*," Charlene said. "It feels like we've all aged about ten years overnight."

"I knew she liked you," Colin said, "but I had no clue about her breaking up Bobby and Julieta. I thought it was obvious Julieta really, really liked him..."

She stared at him. "You knew Darcy liked me?"

"I knew she had a crush." He shrugged. "Willow told me."

"*Willow* knows?"

"And so does Bobby." He paused. "And Gianna, probably."

Elisa groaned. "Wait, is that why you didn't stop her from following me?"

He nodded, looking guilty. "I didn't realize just how much you hated her, or what she did to your sister. I told her you wanted to be alone, but then she told me she had a present for you, and I thought, you know, if you two got together, it could be...cute."

"You wanted someone to double-date with, didn't you?"

"*So* much."

She snorted. "Well, you'll have to keep looking, because

me and Darcy is *never* gonna happen." She straightened from where she'd been hunched over a box of ceramic figurines. "Char, do you have any coffee?"

"No. I ran out yesterday."

"I'm gonna pop over to my apartment to get some, then. I didn't get nearly enough sleep last night."

"Hurry back," Colin said.

Elisa slipped out of the apartment, heading down two floors to her own.

Stepping out of the elevator, she saw just about the last thing she expected or wanted outside her apartment door.

Darcy Fitzgerald, in the flesh.

"Oh, come *on*," she groaned.

Darcy jumped, glancing up. She'd been bent over and looked quite undignified as she scrambled to her feet. She shrunk away slightly as Elisa approached her.

"What are you doing here?" she asked, words sharp.

"I—um, I…" Darcy stammered, which was a side of her she had never seen. "I was delivering this."

She held out an envelope with Elisa's name in loopy cursive writing on the front.

"A letter?" she asked, confused. She didn't take it.

"Don't worry. It's not a repeat of last night's… embarrassment. It's just to clear a few matters up. You—you… you don't have to take it if you don't want to. I understand if you don't. I just…um…" She trailed off, still holding the envelope in front of her.

Elisa let out a huff and snatched the letter from her, not sure if she intended to open it or not, but taking it would get her to leave faster. "Anything else?" she asked, crossing her arms.

"No. No. I, uh…no. Goodbye."

Darcy began to leave, and Elisa called after her, "How'd you find my address?"

She turned back to face her. "After Willow began to sober up this morning, I told her what had happened. It was her idea that I write a letter for you, and she knew where you lived. I hope you don't mind she shared the address with me."

"No, it's...fine," Elisa said with a sigh. *Dammit, Willow.* "So she knows? About this whole...whatever the hell this is."

Darcy nodded. "She actually helped me write this letter."

"Colin told me he knew, too," she said. "About your... feelings."

She sighed, shifting uneasily on her feet. "I could've killed Willow when she told me she told him."

"So, everyone in your...group...knew you..."

"Knew I was pining away over you? Yes."

"I was gonna say 'had a thing for me.'"

Darcy tucked a lock of hair behind her ear. "Willow said that the only reason she had not yet attempted to, quote, 'hit that' was because she was aware of my feelings."

Elisa briefly considered saying that had Willow asked, she probably would've taken her up on the offer. Then she realized she really didn't hate Darcy *that* much. So instead, she said, "Anything else? Or are you just gonna stand there all day?"

She winced. "I'm sorry. I'll go," she said. "Tom's supposed to drive me back down to Columbus in an hour."

"Have a safe trip," she said, because she couldn't think of anything else to say.

"Thank you. I'm—I'm sorry I bothered you."

Darcy practically ran away, leaving Elisa with the envelope in her hands. She leaned against the wall outside her apartment, debating whether to open it. She wasn't convinced she wanted to hear anything Darcy had to say.

But the curiosity was killing her.

Finally, before she could talk herself out of it, she ripped open the envelope and unfolded the letter.

Chapter Twenty

In Which the World Gets Turned on Its Head

Dear Elisa Benitez,

I have spent the past few hours thinking of nothing but our last conversation. About what I said to you. About your rejection of me. About your reasons for rejecting me. About your accusations against me.

About things I could've done or said differently.

This letter is not intended to change your feelings toward me in any way. I understand that the odds of your feelings changing are highly unlikely, if not outright impossible. It is only intended to deliver my side of the story on both crimes of which you have accused me. I realize, as Julieta's sister and an acquaintance—or possibly more—of George Sedgwick, you may have an incomplete view of things. Not always false, but incomplete. I wish to provide you with information you may not have, so you can draw your own conclusions. You are, of course, not obligated to read this letter. Given your dislike of me, I wouldn't blame you for not wanting to hear anything I have to say, and I respect that. So, this will be my last communication with you for the foreseeable future, unless you are the one to initiate it. That's a promise.

If you've gotten this far, I'll assume you've decided to at least grant me the time it will take for you to read this. You do not have to reply to it, unless you wish to do so. Feel free to tear it up, burn it, make it into a papier-mâché project if you wish. But please, please hear me out.

Your first accusation: that I broke up Bobby and your sister. This is true. I stand by what I did. However, upon further contemplation, I've realized that if anyone were to know the true depth of Julieta's feelings, it would be you. Perhaps I was wrong, about Julieta's apparent lack of affection for my friend. I am willing to concede that your sister may have indeed had real, genuine feelings for him. But this, ultimately, doesn't change a thing. If Bobby was so easily swayed, then maybe I was wrong about the depth of his feelings, too. In any case, I think telling them the truth of what happened would only cause them both more heartache. Bobby's moved on with his life, and from what I've heard, Julieta has, too.

Now, on to your second accusation: that I had Wick kicked out of school for no reason. This is a lie—with one tiny nugget of truth buried within it. I don't know what details—or rather, his version of all the details—

Wick told you, so I'll start from the beginning.

Wick's father went to military school with my own. Although the Sedgwicks were of a lower social standing, they were often over at our home as I was growing up. Dinners, playdates, game nights, parties, even just to hang out—Wick and his parents were a frequent presence in our lives. He was about three years older than me, but I never let that stand in the way of our friendship, and neither did he. He was practically a brother to me. He always talked about how he wanted to go to Winchester Military Academy in Columbus, where we were living, like his father. But it was expensive, more than the Sedgwicks could afford. So, my father promised Wick that, when he was old enough, he would pay to send him.

My parents died when I was fourteen. Wick was seventeen at this point. Gianna and I were in the custody of Willow's father—my father's brother—and our parents' finances were divided between my aunt, my uncles, my sister and myself, although Gianna and I were not to access our funds until we were eighteen. So, when it came time for Wick to start at military school, my Aunt Catherine asked me if I still wished for his way to be paid. I said yes. I didn't hear from Wick again after that.

At first, I tried to tell myself that he was simply busy. He was in college now, preparing for his future. However, as I continued to reach out and he remained silent, it gradually became clear to me that he had moved on—and that his future, apparently, didn't include me. It hurt, but I survived. I'd known Bobby all my life, but this was when we really became close.

He was there when I was reeling from the loss of both my parents and my surrogate brother. I'll always love him for that.

My sister is very smart. She's always been two steps ahead of me, intellectually, and was among the most advanced in her class, which itself was for "gifted and talented" students. Her true area of expertise is music. When I was seventeen, Gianna was in junior high, and was permitted to take music classes at the college. I was worried about her being mixed in with people so much older, since she's always been so shy, even around her peers, but I couldn't be the one who held her back.

Gianna began attending a class at the college twice a week. The other students all took very well to her— they all treated her like the entire class' baby sister. Gi didn't mind this; she actually liked it. She felt like she was part of the group, and I think that, in her own way, she was. One day, she called me to say that she'd been invited out for post-midterm celebrations with the rest of the class. I knew they'd be going to a bar, but I trusted her to not do anything stupid, and her classmates to keep an eye out for her, so I told her to go and have fun.

This next part of the story is the hardest of all for me to recount. I want to start by saying that I've talked to Gianna about what happened, and she's fully aware of this letter and its contents. She's given me permission to share this information with you. I would never reveal it if she hadn't.

After that outing, I noticed a gradual shift in Gianna's

personality and actions over the course of a few months. She became more secretive, more private, even around me. She was constantly texting someone and got irritable if anyone got too close to her phone. She also began eating far less, and often seemed on-edge and stressed out. Willow and I asked her about it countless times, but she insisted we were imagining things. But I know my sister, and something was very, very wrong.

It was Willow that found out. She overheard Gianna on the phone one night, after everyone else in the house was asleep, and she distinctly heard her address the other caller by name: "Wick." She told me what she'd heard the next morning, and I immediately pulled Gianna aside to ask her about it. It took a few minutes of pestering, but once it became clear I knew something was going on and wouldn't drop it until I knew the full truth, she broke down and told me. She'd met Wick that night at the bar. They hadn't spoken in years, but he'd been his usual friendly, charming self. He'd told her he wanted to be friends again. But that friendship quickly turned into something more.

She and Wick had been together, sexually, and romantically (if you can call it that—I'm not sure I could stomach it), but she had known that the relationship was illegal, given her age, so she kept it secret. He, of course, had been fine with that. I told her that she had to break up with him and cease all contact. I told her that any grown man willing to pursue a relationship of that nature with a teenager is not a man you want around.

She was reluctant. She fought me. She said he loved

her, and she loved him, and that they'd get married as soon as she was old enough. She said I just didn't understand him, or her. I realized she wouldn't listen to me easily, so I told her that if she didn't, I'd tell our aunt and uncle, who would definitely call the police.

Looking back, what I regret most is not doing that from the start. But I didn't. I was horrified by Wick's actions, and at the time, I was only focused on getting Gi out of that relationship as quickly as possible.

Over the next few weeks, she slowly began to open up, though she was angry at me for quite a while. I found out she had tried to end the relationship twice previously, but Wick had always convinced her to come back. He made her feel like only he saw her as the mature, intelligent adult she so desperately wanted to be. I found out he hit her at least once during an argument. I found out he'd also been sending her lewd images and text messages, even during periods where she'd broken up with him. I did not, however, find out if he ever outright forced her into sex. I'm certain there was some coercion, and given their respective ages, the consent involved is dubious at best, but I've never been able to bring myself to ask for all the details, and Gianna doesn't seem to want to talk about it.

Finally, she realized that Willow and I had done the right thing, trying to pull her away from Wick. We had made every effort to make sure they couldn't see each other, but finally, Gi said she would terminate the relationship for good, and press charges against him for statutory rape. We began the process of pressing charges (including telling my aunt and uncle, both of whom were appalled Willow and I hadn't come to them for help right away). But, well…

I'm sure you've heard what it can be like for victims who try to bring their abusers to justice. The system is harsh on them. They're often scared or intimidated into silence. Gianna, unfortunately, was one of them. I don't hold this against her; the way the officers talked to and about her upset even me, and they went out of their way to assure her that the trial would be long and grueling, and even with proof, it was unlikely Wick would get convicted of anything serious, thanks to the fact that she didn't come forward right away and his stellar reputation. (I'm almost certain Gianna wasn't the first girl he's done this with, but if there are others, they never came forward, either. His record is flawless; not even a parking ticket.)

The stress was making her physically ill and causing her to have panic attacks, and finally, she decided to drop all charges. We tried to talk her out of it, but she was so distressed that eventually, we realized forcing her to continue would be cruel. He hadn't tried to contact her in a month or so, and she had no desire to see or speak to him again, so my aunt and uncle decided to simply focus on her recovery. She's been in counseling ever since, and that's when they began homeschooling her.

I couldn't stand the thought of him walking away scot-free. I had to make him pay somehow. What I really wanted was to lock him in a cage and throw away the key, but if Gianna wouldn't press charges, that plan wasn't happening anytime soon. So, I decided to do the only thing I could think of—put the fact that I was now eighteen and had full access to my money to good use. I went to Winchester with the proof we had against Wick and told them that if he wasn't expelled by the end of the day, I'd make them regret it. My family's one of the biggest donors Winchester's ever had, and my father's company could easily buy out the school and sell it back for twice its value, so they knew I wasn't kidding. (I think they were also worried I'd go to the press if they didn't do anything. I wouldn't have, because of Gianna, but I was fine with letting them believe I would.) I don't normally approve of blackmail, but to get Wick out of that school, I was more than happy to make an exception.

I hope now you understand why I did what I did. I got Wick expelled, yes, but I had a good reason. You don't have to take my word for it. You can ask Willow, Bobby, and Gianna—they'll tell you everything. I hope you also understand why I tried to dissuade you from pursuing a relationship with him. And why I couldn't tell you the whole story.

Again, this is my last attempt to contact you unless you contact me first. I regret some things, but not everything—I hope this letter is an adequate explanation for some of my actions. Please take care of yourself and have a good rest of term. If you wish to see me, I'll be at the Fitzgerald Estate in Columbus. You can also, of course, contact me through Willow or Colin.

I wish you nothing but happiness.

Sincerely,
Darcy Fitzgerald

Elisa read the letter again. And again. And then she read it two more times.

So many different emotions were swirling inside of her, getting all mixed up and tangled. Mostly, there was shock. And anger. And the horrible, sinking feeling in the pit of her stomach, of realizing she'd been completely and totally *wrong*.

Chapter Twenty-One

In Which Elisa Realizes She May Have Been Wrong

Charlene and Elisa were sitting on the couch, the letter on the coffee table in front of them, and they were both staring at it like it was a bomb about to explode. Or maybe one that had already went off. Colin had left the apartment to talk to her mom about places he could apply for a job. The second he was gone, she had burst, telling Charlene about the letter. She had practically shoved it into her hand, telling her to read it. Once she had finished, they'd both sat there in total silence. Elisa felt like she was stumbling through an endless fog, like she was sleepwalking and had yet to wake up.

"Holy shit," Charlene finally said.

"I know."

"I can't... I don't even know Gianna *or* Wick, and I still want to find him and kick his ass."

"I know them both, and my thoughts are a bit more... stabby." Elisa ran a hand over her hair. "I mean...holy shit. Gianna's only a little older than *Lucia*. For Wick to do that to her..."

"How are you feeling?" she asked. "About… everything."

"Well, Wick only kissed me once, but I still want to wash out my mouth with holy water," she said. "You won't tell anyone else about this, right? Not even Colin."

"Of course not," she assured her.

"Thanks. I'm not even sure I should've told *you*, to be honest… I just—I've only known for half an hour, and I can already feel it weighing on me. I can't imagine how Gi and Darcy must feel."

"Well," she said, reaching out to touch Elisa's arm gently, "I can help you carry the load."

Elisa ran a hand through her dark hair. "I think… I think I may have been too hard on Darcy."

Charlene nodded. "Yeah. I mean, it's not your fault—you couldn't have known."

"Still. I… I'm still mad at her for breaking up Bobby and Julieta," she admitted. "Although what she said about him being pulled away so easily is an…annoyingly good point. But the situation with Wick—I had it *all* wrong."

And she honestly couldn't believe *how* wrong she'd been. She'd spent months happy to believe Darcy was the sort of person to ruin someone's life for no reason, but now that she knew the truth, she was frankly shocked she had managed to be so restrained. If it were Elisa's sister, she wasn't sure she would've been able to keep herself from running him over in the street on sight.

Darcy was still an annoying, stuck-up jerk. But she was also someone that would do anything to protect her little sister. And her best friend. Even though she had been wrong about Julieta, she *did* seem to sincerely believe she was protecting Bobby.

She still couldn't say she liked Darcy, but Elisa could feel the last of her hatred for her slowly draining away.

• • •

Elisa spent the rest of Saturday and all of Sunday rereading the letter and restraining herself from either calling Wick and screaming at him or calling Gianna to apologize endlessly for ever having believed what he had said. As tempting as both those options were, from what she had read, Darcy's sister was finally starting to move on, and Elisa didn't want to bring it all back.

Still, she couldn't stop thinking about Gianna—fidgety, jumpy, nervous Gianna—and all she'd been through and what seeing her sister in that position must've done to Darcy. Despite their history, Elisa would've needed a heart of stone to not sympathize with her for that.

It was still on her mind as she got to Communications I on Monday morning. After the weekend she'd had, she'd almost forgotten about school and that she had to return to reality. But Monday came, and return, she did.

She took her usual seat next to Willow, and the first thing she said was, "Did you read the letter?"

Elisa nodded. "Yeah. About twelve times." She fidgeted nervously with her pencil. "Willow... You read Darcy's letter before she came to deliver it to me, didn't you? She...she said you helped her write it."

"Yeah, I, uh, supervised."

She hesitated, glancing around the room to see if anyone else paying any attention to them. No one was. Scooting closer, Elisa spoke in a lowered voice.

"Was everything she said about her sister and Wick true? I mean, I can't imagine even Darcy would lie about something like that—not with her own sister—but...I thought I got to know Wick pretty well, and...I'm kind of in shock, reading that he'd do something like that with... To a fifteen-year-old girl. I believe her, I just..."

Willow nodded. "I get it. It's hard to process. But it's all true."

"Gianna's only *fifteen*..."

"Oh, it's worse than that," she said, her lips twisting into a small scowl. "I know the letter didn't mention an exact timeframe, but this was about a year and a half ago. Gianna was thirteen when they began...uh."

"Dating?" Elisa offered, stomach churning even as she did.

She shook her head. "I'm sure Gi thought of it as dating, but I think the proper term for what Wick was doing is 'grooming.'"

"How—how old was he?"

"When he and Gianna began seeing each other? About twenty, twenty-one by the time Darcy got him kicked out."

She stared at the floor. "I think I'm gonna be sick."

Willow patted her arm. "I actually *was* a bit sick, when I found out. I mean, you hear about this shit all the time—secondhand stories from other people, the news, PSAs, you see it in the movies...but when it's someone you know, when it's someone you love as much as I love Gianna... It's almost too much to handle."

"But you did."

"I did. I think Gianna and Darcy are both still in the process of handling it. For Gianna, I'm not sure the process will ever end."

Class began after that, but Elisa barely even pretended to pay attention. School was, for once, the last thing on her mind.

...

Elisa's sisters had been confused when she told them she wanted to talk to all of them, but had agreed when she added, "It's super important."

All five Benitez sisters were crammed into her room, Elisa on her feet, pacing back and forth nervously.

"Okay, look—what I'm going to say may sound a bit weird," she said. "But I need you all to listen. You all remember that I was kind of going out with George Sedgwick a few months ago?"

"Sure, but didn't that only last for like, one date?" Maria asked.

She nodded. "Yeah. Look, I've just found out something about Wick's past, and it's... Let's just say I'm now very glad I am no longer in contact with him. I need you all to promise you won't go near him. Promise that if he tries to talk to you, or even looks at you, you'll walk away. And I—I know it sounds strange, but you can't ask me why."

Camila frowned, concerned. "Did he do something to you?"

"No—no, not me, specifically. Just... He's bad news. *Really* bad news. And I can't sleep easy until you all know to keep away."

"I don't know why you can't tell us," Maria said slowly, "but if it really means that much to you, then...I promise."

Camila nodded. "I promise, too."

"Why can't you tell us?" Lucia asked, tilting her head curiously.

"Because a lot of it... A lot of it, I was asked to keep private, and a lot of it involves people I barely know, and a lot of it is super personal and sensitive information about someone you guys have never even met. I'm trying to respect the other people's boundaries, but...I had to warn you about him."

"Fine. I promise," Lucia said, though she still seemed confused.

Elisa let out a relieved sigh. "Thank you. I know this is weird and awkward for you guys, but you all just took a load off my mind."

Chapter Twenty-Two

In Which No One Listens to Elisa, As Usual

As promised, Elisa didn't hear from Darcy again after she'd delivered the letter. She popped up now and again in Willow or Gianna's social media feeds, but she didn't call, text, or even like one of Elisa's posts. She wasn't sure if that was good or bad. Before reading the letter, she would've been eager to hold Darcy to her promise, but now that she had...

Now she couldn't explain *how* she felt. She and Darcy weren't friends, but she understood her a bit better. If nothing else, she certainly knew that she wasn't heartless, as she'd once believed. And, whether she liked it or not, she definitely felt her absence.

She could not get Darcy out of her head. And she wasn't even sure she wanted to anymore.

Because, apparently, the world has just gone completely insane.

It had been over a month since Elisa received the letter. February and March both passed in the blink of an eye, like her entire life was on fast-forward until she suddenly realized it was early April. She only had a week before midterms began, and after that, it'd be spring break, and she'd be spending the week at the Alexandra Pemberley Museum of Classical Art.

Elisa wasn't the only Benitez sister with big spring break plans. The night before, Lucia had come home bouncing off the walls because her on-and-off BFF Vivian Forester was going to Daytona Beach and had invited her to come along.

Let's hope they're still in the "on" phase by the time the trip actually gets here.

Elisa was sitting on her bed, going over the review packet her Communications I professor had handed out, while Lucia hung out in the room with her, babbling on and on. She was talking about all the things she wanted to do and see in Daytona Beach, but Elisa wasn't paying much mind until her ears picked up on the words, "Vivi's turning sixteen, so this trip is her present—her parents promised to leave her alone and let her do her thing as long as she promised to call every night…"

Elisa looked up. "Wait, wait, *wait*. Vivian's parents aren't going?"

Lucia looked like a deer caught in the headlights. "Um…"

"Lulu, no. No. You can*not* go. Not to Daytona Beach without any adult supervision."

"It's not without *any* adults," she protested. "Vivi's aunt lives in Daytona Beach, she's getting us at the airport. We're just, y'know…part of the gift is that we get to stay in a hotel instead of with the aunt, but she'll be around some of the time."

"*Some* of the time? Oh, great. *Great.*"

She crossed her arms. "Jeez, I'm not a three-year-old."

"Daytona Beach is totally nuts during spring break. It's not safe."

"I'll have my phone and pepper spray with me the whole

time," she insisted. "Besides, that's why Vivi's parents told her to bring a friend—so we can look out for each other."

"That would be a hell of a lot more comforting if I didn't know your track record."

"Mom already said I could go."

"What?"

"Look, I already talked to Mom, and I promised to be super-responsible and extra-careful. Video chats every night, updates every time we go someplace new—she'll always know where we are. We have to touch base with Vivi's aunt at least once a day, and I swore not to leave Vivi's side the entire time," Lucia said. "I only didn't tell you because I *knew* you'd be like this."

"Because, apparently, I'm the one with all the common sense in this family."

Without another word to her sister, Elisa got up from her bed and stormed into the kitchen, where Alejandra was working on dinner.

"Mom."

"Yes, dear?" she asked, not looking up from what she was doing.

"Did you *seriously* tell Lucia she could go to Daytona Beach?"

She sighed. "I was wondering when you'd flip out about this. Yes, I did. And don't try to change my mind—Julieta already did."

"Mom, you know how Lulu is. She could get hurt."

"You can get hurt doing most anything," she said. "Hand me the pickled jalapeños."

Elisa grabbed the jar out of the fridge, handing it to her mother as she said, "Lucia's not mature *or* responsible enough for this. I wouldn't trust her to go to Cleveland alone, let alone Daytona Beach."

"I used to go on vacation with friends all the time when

I was a girl," she said with a nostalgic smile. "Remember the stories?"

"Yes, Mom. Those stories were usually prefaced with, 'If you ever do this, I'll beat your ass.'"

"Don't you think you're being a bit dramatic? It's not as if I'm letting them run off completely by themselves—I'm not an idiot."

"Have you ever even met Vivian's aunt?"

Her mother deflated, admitting, "Well, no. But I *have* met her parents, and I trust them. So long as they see her aunt at least once a day, and she sees them to their room every night, I don't see the harm in letting them stay in a hotel. Especially not if Vivi's parents are paying."

"Oh yeah, Lulu with unsupervised access to a building full of young, male tourists, a hot tub, and unlimited room service. That can only end well."

Mom glared at her. "You watch your mouth. Your sister should get to have a bit of fun, and I've made it very clear that if she betrays my trust on this trip, there will never be another."

"There shouldn't be a first."

"Elisa, *I'm* her mother. Not you."

Mom went back to cooking, effectively ending the conversation.

She couldn't believe her mother was being so incredibly stupid. Exasperated, Elisa left the kitchen and stepped outside the apartment, fishing her phone out of her pocket. Leaning against the wall in the hallway, she dialed her father's number.

"Hello?"

"Papa, it's Elisa—I need your help."

"Is something wrong?" Miguel asked.

"Not yet. Look, it's kind of a long story, but the short and short of it is that Lucia's going to Daytona Beach with her friend over spring break, and her friend's parents aren't going with them. I mean, her friend's aunt will be there, but they're not staying with her, they'll be in a hotel on their own, and... and I don't know, I just have a bad feeling about this."

Miguel paused. "Does your mother know about this?"

"Yeah. I tried to talk to her, but she's fine with it. I thought maybe if you talked to her—"

"Lisa, you know your mom." He sighed. "How do you think she'd take it if her ex-husband called to talk her out of something he wasn't even supposed to know about—but did, thanks to one of her daughters asking him to interfere on an issue she'd already decided?"

"I know, I know, but...I'll tell her it was all my idea. I'll make sure she yells at me and not you. Just—just stop this."

"What makes you think I can?"

"You're Lucia's *father*. If Mom won't listen to me, maybe she'll listen to you."

"I agree with you completely. I think this is a terrible idea. But both Lucia and your mother are *incredibly* stubborn. And even if I managed to persuade Alex not to let her go, we'd never hear the end of it. You know how long Lulu can hold a grudge."

Elisa was appalled. "So you won't even *try*?"

"I don't see how I could do any good."

She groaned. "Forget it."

"I'm sorry, Elisa."

She massaged her forehead. "I'm—I'm being dumb, right? It'll be fine." Even as she said it, she didn't believe it. Lucia going to Daytona Beach with limited supervision was more than a terrible idea. It was a ridiculous, awful, potentially lethal, piece-of-shit idea.

"I'm sure it will be," Miguel said, sounding as unconvinced as she felt. "Try not to worry too much about it. Your sister's getting older—she's not a baby anymore."

"I... I know. I guess I'm just... I love Lulu too much to

not worry about her, you know?"

"I get it. But you'll have to stop fussing over her sometime," he said gently. "Try to just relax and enjoy your own spring break. You're going to that museum, right?"

"Yeah," Elisa said. "I'm, uh, I'm going to Pemberley with my art class."

"I went to Pemberley once, back when I still lived in Columbus. You'll love it."

Elisa smiled a bit, despite the situation. "I'll send you a postcard from the gift shop. We can see what gets back to Steventon first—it or me."

"I'm looking forward to it. Look, Elisa, I better go—I'm meeting a friend for dinner. He says if I'm late, he'll make me pick up the tab."

"Okay. Love you, Papa."

"I love you, too."

Elisa hung up, but remained out in the hallway for a while longer, trying to tell herself that her father was right. She couldn't baby Lucia forever. Maybe Lucia would prove her wrong. Maybe everything would be fine.

She didn't actually believe it, of course. But she had to keep telling herself that. The only alternative was to worry.

Chapter Twenty-Three

In Which Elisa Arrives at Pemberley

The Alexandra Pemberley Museum of Classical Art was beautiful, and well worth the two-hour drive. The tour guide told them that the architecture was inspired by the old Baroque style, and the place was elegant, sophisticated, and *massive*. Steventon had an art gallery, but it was small—local artists and the occasional traveling exhibit, if they got especially lucky. One could easily get through the entire museum in an hour or so. But Pemberley? You could get lost in Pemberley. According to the tour guide, he actually had.

"Now, you will all receive a tour of one exhibit every morning," he said, walking backward as he led them through a hall full of sculptures by local artists, somehow avoiding bumping into anything. "You are, of course, free to visit the rest of the museum on your own time if you wish. Now, we can get anywhere from a handful to a couple thousand visitors each day—attendance spikes when we open a new exhibit, as well as on Sundays and holidays, when admission is free. We've been very fortunate to have some extremely generous donors and volunteers that allow us to keep the museum accessible for everyone."

He kept talking while Elisa and her classmates wandered the room, gazing at each sculpture. They were all beautiful—her favorite was one made of blown glass in the center of the room, which resembled an odd, colorful bouquet. She was reading the plaque about the artist when she heard the door to the museum open and the lady at the desk greet the newest guest. This wouldn't have caught her attention at all if she hadn't picked up the familiar names.

"I didn't know you'd be coming today, Miss Fitzgerald—oh, and you brought Mr. Charles with you. Always a pleasure."

No. *Way.*

Elisa spun around so quickly it drew the attention of her classmates, looking back toward the entrance.

She spoke before she could think.

"Darcy?"

Darcy looked like she'd been struck by lightning when she saw Elisa. Bobby froze behind her, eyes wide. They stood there in the doorway staring at Elisa while she stood there in the gallery, staring right back. Together, the three of them must have looked like the world's most surprised wax figures.

Now the rest of the class was watching them, but Elisa was too shocked to care.

The tour guide didn't seem to notice anything was amiss and, in fact, approached Darcy with a broad, genuine smile.

"Darcy," he said. Elisa couldn't help but gawk; the whole situation was just *way* too weird. "I didn't realize you had a friend in this tour group. Why didn't you tell me?"

"I didn't know," she said faintly.

The tour guide turned to the class. "This is Darcy Fitzgerald," he explained. She waved awkwardly. "Alexandra Pemberley was her great-great-grandmother."

Of course she was.

"Her mother used to be the director here," the tour guide continued. "The family's been heavily involved in the museum's operation since its opening."

"Wait—wait, Darcy, is he saying you...*you* run this place now?" she said, blindsided.

Darcy found her voice. "No, no. I, uh, I'm too young for that, and I'm quite sure I have no talent for it. A family friend is the director now. I'm only involved because my ancestor's name is on the building."

The tour guide smiled. "Darcy's too modest," he said. "She's on the board of trustees."

Darcy looked like she wanted to sink into the floor. "Again—just because of my family. It's practically a figurehead position in my case."

"You know more than you let on," he said, squeezing her shoulder. "I mean, you practically grew up here. I've known you since you were small enough to fit inside a backpack."

"Thomas, please—you're making me blush."

"Okay, okay, I'll let you go." He chuckled, watching Darcy hustle away, Bobby close behind.

As she reached the end of the room, Darcy glanced over her shoulder at Elisa, hesitating just for a moment, brown eyes flickering with an emotion Elisa couldn't name, and then left.

"How do you know Darcy?" the tour guide asked her. The rest of the class had turned their attention away from Elisa and back to the sculptures—thank goodness.

"I—uh—we had a class together last semester," she said, not wanting to get into the full truth of the matter with a complete stranger.

"Oh, when Darcy was staying up in Steventon, right?"

"Yeah."

"Well, I'm glad she's made some friends," he said. "We all love her, but she's not always the most sociable with people her age."

"Who's 'we'?"

"Oh, the rest of us who work here at Pemberley. I wasn't exaggerating when I said she grew up here. Her mom used to bring her and her sister with her at least once a week. I remember board meetings where Darcy would sit in the corner with her books waiting for her mom to finish up. Now she's on the board herself, and she always tries to contribute as much as she can. She's always been such a nice girl."

"Uh...yeah."

Even though she didn't wish Darcy was dead anymore, she was still stunned to hear someone willingly describe her as "nice." Though now that she thought about it, maybe it made a little sense. As rude as she could be toward her peers, Elisa had never once seen Darcy talk down to any of the servants at Netherfield, or even so much as snap at a waiter. Maybe Darcy simply thought to put forth more of an effort with people working for or with her.

The tour moved on, the guide pointing out where the gift shop, the café, and the restrooms were, but all Elisa could think about was Darcy.

She had known Darcy lived in Columbus, but she'd figured—it was a big city; what were the odds of bumping into her? But she didn't just live in the general area. Her family had founded the very museum Elisa was here to see, and apparently, she was around a *lot*. And Bobby was with her, too. She wondered when he'd come back from Cape Cod—after the whole vanishing-act fiasco, she'd unfriended and unfollowed him on all social media, not trusting herself to not write, "What the hell is wrong with you?" on his wall where everyone could see it.

So much for a relaxing spring break.

• • •

Before the class headed back to the hotel for supper, Elisa ducked into the gift shop to find a postcard to send to her father. She supposed she shouldn't have been surprised when she saw Darcy in there, too.

At this point, she could probably crash land on a desert island and Darcy would have a summer home there.

"Darcy," she said quietly. "Hey."

She seized up, and her voice came out quiet and awkward. "Hey," she said. "I'm...uh... You look lovely."

Dressed in an old "Go Bucks" T-shirt and a pair of jean shorts, with her ugliest, most comfortable boots, Elisa certainly didn't feel lovely. But somehow, she could tell that Darcy meant it, and that made her smile, even if only a little.

"Thank you," she said. "You do, too." Darcy pretty much *always* looked great. Back before the letter, she had found that to be one of the most obnoxious things about her.

"I—I didn't—I didn't realize you were going to be here," she stuttered. "I hope I'm not making things awkward or unpleasant, or..."

Elisa shook her head. "Don't worry about it. I'm visiting with my art history class."

"Are you—are you here for the entirety of your break?"

She nodded. "We're seeing one exhibit per day. Won't cover the entire museum, but..."

"That's a shame. The entire museum is beautiful. I couldn't pick just a handful of places to show you."

"Too bad you're not our tour guide, huh? Hey, maybe that's a job for you here," she said, laughing, trying to sound casual.

"If you..." She cleared her throat. "If you want to see anything that's not on your schedule, let me know. I know this place like the back of my hand. I'd be happy to...to... Um, but, no pressure. If you don't want to, that's—"

"No. No, I'd... I'd like that," she said, and she was

surprised to find that she really meant it. "I never knew your family was into this stuff. Art, I mean."

"My mother lived for this museum." Darcy chuckled. "She adored my father, but I think Pemberley was her true love."

"That's sweet, in a way," she said. "Passion like that for your work is...is hard to find."

Darcy nodded. "That's what I think, too." She paused, before adding, "Gianna would probably be thrilled to see you, by the way. She thinks you're the greatest thing since sliced bread."

Elisa blushed. "Wish my *actual* sisters thought of me that way."

"Would you like to come over for lunch sometime while you're here?"

"Sure. That'd be... That'd be really nice. I'd love to see Gianna."

"How does tomorrow work?"

"Tomorrow works great."

Darcy's face broke out into a smile. A radiant, relieved grin. She'd never actually seen Darcy smile before.

It hit her that she'd do almost anything to keep that smile there, now that she'd seen it.

"What time will you be free tomorrow?" Darcy asked.

"The school stuff is set to end around twelve thirty."

"How about we meet back here after that, then?"

"It's a date," she said.

Before Darcy could reply, Bobby emerged from the bathroom, approaching them.

"Hey, are you ready to— Elisa?" Bobby said, suddenly noticing her. He still looked surprised to see her here. Maybe he was just surprised to find Elisa and Darcy having a civil conversation. *To be fair, it surprised me, too.*

"Hey, Bobby." Her words came out clipped, almost cold.

She had moved past the stage of homicidal fury, but that didn't mean she wasn't still irritated with him for what he did to Julieta. Darcy may have intervened, but he didn't have to listen.

"How have you been? It's been a while."

"Yeah. It has. I'm… I'm good. Been better, but I'm good."

"How's… How's Julieta?" The way Bobby said Julieta's name, Elisa knew that had been all he'd been wanting to ask from the moment he saw her.

"She's fine."

"I… I'm sorry things didn't work out between us—between me and Julieta, I mean. I've wanted to call her, but the way things ended… I figured she wouldn't want to hear from me. But, um, how's her job going? Does she—does she have a boyfriend now, or—"

Elisa cut him off. She didn't want to hear this.

"Bobby, if you want to know how Julieta's been doing, you should *talk* to her. Given your track record, you could use the practice."

He promptly shut up, averting his gaze. There was an awkward pause before Darcy cleared her throat again, saying, "S-so, um… Bobby and I were just about to head home. I'll—I'll meet you here tomorrow at twelve thirty, right, Elisa?"

She nodded. "Right."

"See you tomorrow, then."

They turned to go, leaving Elisa alone in the gift shop. She wasn't sure what to make of the last few minutes. Not only did she have a conversation with Darcy that didn't leave her wanting to kill something, but she'd agreed not just to have a meal, but also tour Pemberley with her. And she was actually looking *forward* to it.

I'm just glad to be making nice. Nothing more to it.

Yeah, a second voice in her head said. *You keep telling yourself that…*

Chapter Twenty-Four

In Which Elisa and Darcy Warm Up (Just a Bit)

"You came," Darcy said, surprised when Elisa approached her in the gift shop the next afternoon. Most of the museum's guests had left for the day, save for a few stragglers who were looking at Pemberley's many souvenirs.

"I said I would," she replied.

"Yeah, I just… After everything, I wasn't sure if…"

Elisa gave her a small smile. "Look—what's past is past," she said. "Let's try to start over. Clean slate. We both screwed up and said stupid things, and… I'm trying my hand at not going solely off my first impression."

Darcy nodded, attempting a smile of her own. "Clean slate," she repeated.

She led her out to the parking lot, where a car waited for them. The two got into the back seat, climbing awkwardly over each other as they tried to get themselves settled.

"How has Willow been?" Darcy asked when they were finally seated. "She texts me quite frequently, but I wouldn't put it past her to not tell me if she's been causing trouble."

Elisa laughed. "Willow's great. Our Communications prof loves her, and she's getting pretty good at ASL, too. Oh, but apparently, she's going to Miami over spring break to defend her title of 'Kween Kush of Bal Harbour Beach.' So, the vacation pics should be interesting."

Darcy snorted. It was both very un-Darcylike, and very adorable. "She told me about that. I tried to get my aunt to stop her, but she just said, 'If you think I can control Willow, you haven't been paying attention for the past nineteen years.'"

As they talked, the car whisked them away from the crowded, busy part of the city and then past it. Elisa remembered what Willow had said about her and Darcy not living in the city. They went through a suburb, the houses become larger and farther apart the longer they drove.

Finally they came to a huge gate, and the driver leaned out the window to reach a small, computerized panel. He put in a long and complicated security code as Darcy said, "The main house is a bit farther back. Sometimes during the nice weather, I like to bike out of here instead of taking a car, but when it gets too hot, it's murder."

"Wow," Elisa said, still staring out the window. "Willow told me your property was huge, but I had...*no* idea."

"It's been in my father's family for years," Darcy said. "I honestly can't imagine living anyplace else. It's home."

"You said 'the main house.' What else is there?"

"Oh—there's a guest house, a pool, a tennis court, a stable—though my family hasn't owned horses in years... There's the gardens, and the family graveyard."

Elisa stared at her.

"It's a bit morbid," she admitted. "I hardly ever go down there anymore. I mostly stick to the main house—and my guests tend to be ones I like to stay there with me, rather than out in the guest house. Actually, the most use the guest house ever got was when my parents were arguing and my mom felt that staying in there would make her point more easily than having my father sleep on the couch."

The house was visible in the distance a few minutes before they actually reached it. It was even bigger than Pemberley, and even more beautiful. Elisa couldn't keep her eyes off of it. She'd imagined what Darcy's home might look like many times, but nothing she'd dreamed up with had even come close. It was made of white marble, seeming both modern and ancient, with several balconies and a long flight of stairs leading up to the entrance.

The driver stopped, letting them out of the car. Elisa stood at the bottom of the stairs, still staring at the house.

"Do you really own this place?" she asked.

Darcy nodded. "Technically. I'm still learning the ins and outs of owning this much property, but my uncle and aunt help me out. We always knew I'd have to learn eventually, of course. Traditionally, it would've gone to the oldest son or the oldest daughter's first son, but my father said, 'It's the twenty-first century, for Christ's sake.' None of us really expected me to be in charge this early, but..." She trailed off, coming to stand next to Elisa.

"And you live here by yourself?" Elisa asked, finally turning to look at Darcy's face.

"Not entirely. Some of the staff members live here, too. Some prefer to commute from the city, but the ones that live here like it."

"Don't you get lonely?"

Darcy's eyes flicked down to her feet for a moment. "Sometimes," she admitted. "I wish Gianna had moved back here when I did. But I understand why she wanted to stay with our aunt and uncle. And she's here all the time."

They headed up the stairs, and someone was waiting to get the door. Darcy gave the older, silver-haired woman that took her jacket a warm smile, asking, "Is Gianna here yet?"

"She arrived about half an hour ago," the maid said. She took Elisa's coat, too. "She's in the music room."

"Thank you, Rachel. This is Elisa." She gestured towards her. "Elisa, this is Rachel."

"Hi," Elisa said, still a little surprised to see Darcy smiling of her own volition.

"Oh, you're Darcy's friend," Rachel said. "She mentioned you were coming over for lunch. It's so nice to finally meet you."

As Darcy led her to the music room, she said, "Rachel's been here for longer than I've been alive. I never had a governess, but she was close."

"She said it was nice to 'finally' meet me." She nudged her playfully. "What have you been saying?"

Darcy blushed. "All good things," she promised.

Elisa could hear someone playing a familiar tune she couldn't quite place as they headed toward a huge room at the end of a long, empty hall

"Is that Gianna playing?" she asked.

Darcy nodded. "Must be. She comes by here for her music lesson once a week—our aunt and uncle are paying for the lessons, but I think they want her to have to leave the house every now and then. Even if it's just to come to my house. Well, it's our house. The tutor meets her here, and then I'm banned from that room for two hours until they finish. She practices here every chance she gets, too."

"She's really good."

"She is."

Darcy knocked gently on the door as she pushed it open. The music room was huge and had not just the grand piano at which Gianna sat, but a shelf full of music books, some recording equipment, and a few other instruments. Gianna was concentrating on the sheet music propped in front of her, the music seeming to pour out of her almost effortlessly. Sat at the piano, doing what she loved, she was barely recognizable as the near-silent, jumpy girl Elisa had met.

"Hi, Gianna," Darcy said, once she reached the end of the piece.

She grinned, getting up to hug her sister. "Hi," she said. Now that she wasn't surrounded by strangers, her voice was much louder, much clearer. She turned to Elisa, a little more bashful now, but still smiling. "Elisa—I'm so glad you could make it. It's been forever."

Elisa smiled. "Yeah, it has. How've you been?"

"I've been good. Homeschooling is going...well, it's going. And my music lessons are great."

"I can tell. Darcy told me you were good, but—wow."

"Do you play at all?" Gianna asked.

"Only a little bit. I played piano in the school orchestra for one of my art credits," she said. "I sucked, but so did everyone else. Reviewers described my performance as 'satisfactory.'"

They both chuckled. "Not much of an art person?" she asked.

"Not that kind of art," she said. "I'm much more into literature and writing."

"Oh yeah. Darcy told me you're a great writer after she heard some of your essays in that class you guys took."

Darcy cast Gianna a look that plainly said, *Shut up.*

She grinned. "I'm not sure I'd call myself a great writer. But it's nice to be appreciated."

"You were, trust me. Darcy wouldn't shut up about your essay on *Go Set a Watchman* for two solid days, it was actually kind of annoying—"

"Lunch," Darcy said quickly, cutting her sister off. "Let's, uh—let's all go have lunch."

• • •

Darcy and Gianna said it would be silly to have lunch in the
main dining room, since there were only three of them, and
instead suggested they eat in one of the many lounges. The
three of them ate fish and chips, making small talk about
Gianna's lessons and what Darcy had been up to since leaving
Steventon.

"Mostly attending board meetings and taking some
courses at OSU," she said.

"What's your major, anyway?" Elisa asked.

"I'm going for a Bachelor's in English, and then I'll go to
law school if everything goes the way I hope it will," she said.
"I'd like to go into family law."

"Don't you need a pre-law degree?"

"Not necessarily," she said. "But I am taking a pre-law
course now. Mainly just to see if I actually like it before I go
through with applying to law school."

"And do you like it?"

"Very much." She smiled. "Gianna wants to go to
Julliard."

Gianna blushed a bit. "It'd be nice," she said. "I'm not
sure I can make a career of playing, though. I get awful stage
fright."

"For what it's worth," Elisa said, "I think Julliard would
be lucky to have you."

Darcy smiled, reaching over to muss her younger sister's
hair. She laughed, swatting her hand away. Elisa laughed,
too, still surprised at how much she was enjoying herself. She
caught Darcy's eye and gave her a small smile, which grew
into a grin when she blushed and looked away.

Darcy left a few minutes later, saying she needed to have
a word with one of the groundskeepers before she forgot,
leaving the other two alone. There was a slight pause before
Elisa decided to just say it.

"Hey," she said gently. "Your sister...um, she told me.

About Wick."

Gianna tensed slightly. "I know," she said quietly. "I'm… I'm actually kinda glad. Sometimes I… Sometimes I feel like such a failure for not being able to go through with the trial and everything. I feel like I owed it to any other girl he may go after, but I… I just couldn't. But at least now, someone else knows what he is."

Elisa reached to touch her arm. "You're not a failure. I can't imagine being in that position, and I can't even begin to understand how hard it must've been. Not pressing charges doesn't make you weak or make what happened to you less real."

Gianna smiled a little bit. "You sound like my sister," she said. "I could tell she wanted me to go forward with it, but… she also said she'd support my choice. And I made it."

"Darcy does support your choice," she said. "I'm sure of that. She loves you. Even back before I really got to know her, I could tell she loved you a lot." She sighed. "Honestly, I'm… I kind of feel like I should apologize to you, too. For believing Wick's word over hers."

Gianna shook her head. "Don't worry about it," she said. "I know how charming he can be. He says all the right things to make you feel special…then you want to believe everything he tells you."

Her stomach twisted into a knot. "That sounds about right."

"Wick is… Wick is an awful person, but he's not the main person in my life anymore, thank God," she said, fiddling with her napkin. "He's a douchebag I used to date, and he's a creep who took advantage of me once. But he's not the person I base myself on anymore. Sometimes I catch myself missing him, but…honestly, I'm glad to be rid of him. Let's just be glad he's out of our lives."

Elisa let out a snort, raising her glass of lemonade. "I'll

drink to that."

. . .

After lunch was over, they headed back to Pemberley so
Elisa could get her promised, not-on-the-itinerary tour. She
had Darcy take her to the hall of arms first, mainly to shut
Colin up, before the two passed a room with a plaque outside
the door. The plaque read, "The Pemberley Family, Past and
Present."

"What's this?" she asked, gesturing toward the door.

"Oh—that's where they have portraits and photos of all
the close relatives of Alexandra Pemberley, plus the family
tree and the history of how she founded this place, pictures
from the opening... I hardly ever go in there—it hasn't
changed much over the years."

"Let's check it out," Elisa said, pulling open the door.

There was a painted portrait of Alexandra Pemberley
herself at the start of the room. In it, she was in her mid-fifties
or so, with an elegant, almost standoffish air. Maybe it was
just her imagination, but Elisa could've sworn she saw a bit of
Darcy in her eyes.

"She never married," Darcy said. "She said matrimony
would one day end, but art would last forever. That, and
marriage was basically legal slavery."

Elisa chuckled. "Maria would've liked her."

She looked over each photo and painting, each depicting
a relative or a group of relatives, ranging from Alexandra's
nephew, who took over running the museum when she died,
to a gaggle of cousins who, according to the plaque next to
the photograph, were minor members of the nobility. At the
end of the room, the most recent photograph hung on the
wall.

It depicted a small family of four—a tall black man in a

military uniform, his arm around a blonde white woman in a lovely navy-blue dress, and, in front of them, a pair of girls about four years apart. One was about ten, smiling shyly for the camera, and the other, about fourteen, was…

"This is you and your parents," Elisa said quietly as Darcy came to stand next to her.

She nodded, staring at her father's image with a slightly glazed look in her eyes. "This was taken about six months before they passed."

Elisa watched her for a moment before saying, "You miss them a lot, don't you?"

"More than words can say." She raised a hand as if she were about to touch the photograph, but stopped herself, retracting it quickly. "You would've liked them, I think. They were always so welcoming to everyone. My mom, it seemed, never met a stranger."

"You look so much like both of them," she said, turning her gaze back to the photo. "And—wow, Gianna looks a *lot* like your mom…"

Darcy cracked a smile. "She talks like her, too. Their speech patterns and the way they word things—it's uncanny."

They remained in front of the photo, a sort of melancholy filling the room before, finally, Darcy said, "Come on. I want to show you the topiary garden."

Elisa didn't argue, following her out. She'd heard of the garden—landscaped to look like a famous painting she could never remember the name of, it was free and open to the public even when the museum was not. There were several people there, walking their dogs or having picnic lunches, but it was quiet and peaceful.

"What's your family like, Elisa?" Darcy asked, as they wandered through the garden, which was perfectly picturesque. Bushes clipped into the shapes of people in period clothing, with a lovely pond and an abundance of colorful, stunning flowers. "I... I know I've met them, but... I'm realizing now that my initial impressions of them may have been unfair."

Elisa smiled, a light breeze brushing against her skin, carrying the scent of all the flora surrounding them. "You haven't met my dad, but I think you two would get along. You actually remind me of him."

"Is that a good thing?"

"It's a great thing," she said. "He likes books and sarcasm and avoiding emotional conversations."

Darcy smiled. "Okay, I can see that. Do he and your mother embarrass you with all the PDA like mine embarrassed me, or are they more reserved?"

She looked away, nervously rubbing her arm. "They, uh... They actually split up when I was nine."

"Oh. I'm—I'm sorry, I didn't—"

"Don't be," she said, shaking her head. "It's for the best. I thought they were the perfect couple when I was a kid, but now that I'm older, I can see the cracks in the relationship from back then..." She sighed, forcing the conversation into calmer waters. "Mom is funny. Hotheaded. Meddling. Kind of ridiculous, but really, really loving. She'd do anything for us."

"What about the rest of your family? Extended family, I mean."

"I don't really see them much. My mom's brother lives in Chicago, but he calls when he can. He's cool, as far as adults go. Gives good presents, tells bad jokes. Mom's parents come over for holidays and birthdays, but it's always kind of... awkward. Between the language barrier and the generational differences, I never know how to talk to them."

"Language barrier?" Darcy asked. "So they speak Spanish at home?"

Elisa nodded. "Yeah. I speak some, but I'm not fluent

like Mom and Papa are. Their families are both Mexican immigrants. Mom's parents came over when her older brother was a toddler—she's the only one who was born here. Papa's family has been in the States for four or five generations. My parents actually get along pretty well—I mean, as well as you can expect a divorced couple to—but their families have been like the Montagues and the Capulets since they began dating. Except instead of a double suicide, the story ends with a visit to Mr. Divorce Lawyer and some awkward family dinners. So it's better."

"That must make Thanksgiving tense," Darcy said.

"You have no idea. Julieta's the only one who can get them to stop fighting. She's always been the family peacekeeper—her and Camila." A small gust of wind blew her hair into her eyes. Shoving it away, she said, "Cam is a little wild sometimes, but she has such a good heart. So do Maria and Lucia, really. They irritate the hell out of me, but they're all really nice, once you get to know them."

"I hope I get the opportunity to get to know them better." Elisa smiled. "I do, too."

She stopped walking when they reached the top of a hill, giving them a perfect view of the entire garden. Standing there in silence, Elisa felt her breath catch in her throat for a moment. She took in the sight, wanting to permanently freeze this image in her memory.

"Do you... Do you like it here? At Pemberley, I mean?" Darcy asked, watching her closely.

She smiled, nodding excitedly. "This entire place is beautiful. I can't believe your family is the one that started it. You're so lucky."

Darcy blushed. "I am," she admitted. "What time do you need to back at the hotel?"

Elisa's heart dropped into the pit of her stomach as she realized she'd have to rejoin her classmates eventually.

"Dinnertime—six."

She actually liked her professor and classmates. But she'd been having such a nice time, she didn't want the afternoon to end. She wanted to keep hanging out with Darcy.

Now that's something I never thought I'd say.

"Would you want to meet up again tomorrow?" Elisa asked.

Darcy looked up, surprised, but nodded. "If you're willing."

"I am. More than willing, actually."

• • •

The next day, Elisa and Darcy met up—same time, same place. They had lunch at the Fitzgerald Estate again, though Gianna didn't join them that time. After the meal was over, the two didn't head back to Pemberley right away, but instead wandered the empty halls. Eventually, they found themselves on one of the balconies overlooking the rest of the grounds.

"I think I can actually see the museum from up here," Elisa said, hoisting herself up to sit on the railing. Her feet dangled several meters off the ground. Darcy hesitated before joining her.

"I remember when we were kids, Bobby and I used to try to stand on these," she said. "Nothing ever happened, but our parents always gave us an earful for being so stupid."

"How is Bobby, anyway?"

Darcy fidgeted. "He's…" She sighed. "He's okay, mostly, but lonely. He misses your sister."

Elisa stared down at the ground. "I'm not nearly as mad anymore," she said quietly, "but I really wish you hadn't broken them up."

She ducked her head as if trying to hide her face. "Me, too," she said. "It was… It was a really stupid thing to do.

I thought I was protecting him, but..." She licked her lips. "I've thought about telling Bobby I was wrong, but...but I'm worried that meddling any further will only make matters worse."

She nodded. "Yeah, I... I can understand that. After I found out you broke them up, I wondered if I should tell Julieta, but she seemed so desperate to move on."

"Bobby really hurt her, didn't he?"

"Yeah. I don't think he's a bad guy, but... But seriously, he's a grown man. Why would he let his best friend just run his love life?" Elisa said, frustrated. "I understand taking your advice into account, but—he should've known how much Julieta loves him."

"Do you think it's too late for them?" she asked quietly.

Elisa looked at her, then. "I don't think it's ever too late," she said. "But I think if things are going to get better between those two, it'll be up to them to initiate it—not us."

"I... I'm so used to meddling when I think something is wrong. It'll take some unlearning," Darcy said, trying to laugh.

"Well, meddling isn't *always* bad. I mean, getting Wick expelled definitely counts as meddling, but it had to be done."

"It was either that or corner him in an alley with a baseball bat," she said dryly. "I have a terrible swing, so I decided to just throw my money at the problem until it went away. Or, more accurately, threaten to take my money *away* from the problem until it went away."

"How long did it take them to cave?"

"About an hour and a half of arguing, three if you count how long it took the dean of students to agree to see me." Her face twisted into a scowl. "He tried to say that because Gianna wouldn't press charges, it wasn't his problem."

"No matter how long it took, it's pretty impressive that you got them to listen to you."

"Well, it also took throwing around phrases like 'I can buy and sell you,' and 'PR nightmare,' and 'buy out this academy and turn it into a liberal arts college.'" She let out a small, quiet laugh, but it faded quickly. Her eyes were clouded, not really looking at Elisa. "Thinking about that whole thing is... Most of it is awful. One of the worst periods of my entire life," she said. "Even worse than when Mom and Dad died. I had my aunt and uncle and the rest of my family to lean on when that happened—as terrible as it was, I always knew that I'd survive. But if something even worse had happened to Gianna? I'm... I'm not sure I would've been able to survive that."

Elisa, purely on instinct, reached for her hand, squeezing it gently. Darcy met her eyes, plainly surprised. The touch ignited a warmth in her, which spread from her fingertips to her chest. It was both the strangest and the most natural thing in the world.

"You're a good sister," Elisa said quietly. "And a good friend. And I'm... I'm really glad we're getting this chance to start over."

Darcy, to her surprise, didn't pull her hand away or avert her gaze.

"Me, too," she murmured.

Interlude: In Which Lucia Makes a Huge Mistake

Lucia was wandering a club in Daytona Beach. Vivi always had at least three fake IDs, and she could get them made for other students—for a price. No one questioned the process—they just paid her and let her work her magic. But she'd gotten Lucia a free one for this trip. As tall as she was, the bouncer had only taken a quick glance at the ID before deciding that she was, in fact, of age.

As promised, she'd texted her mother every time she and Vivi changed locations.

Off the plane. Vivi's aunt Erin is waiting for us at baggage claim. —L

At the hotel. Gave Erin your number. —L

Going to dinner. —L

And it was true. They had grabbed dinner someplace. She just conveniently left out the fact that that place happened to be a dark, loud, crowded club, after the resident adult had left their hotel room and gone back to her place for the night. It was Mom's fault if she didn't ask, she told herself.

She'd gotten separated from Vivi. More specifically, the two had gotten into an argument in the bathroom, and Vivi had stormed off, leaving her alone. Although she'd been annoyed when she'd been promised to stay at her friend's side the entire trip, now that she'd left, she felt a bit more aware of all the staring, leering eyes and strange men surrounding her.

Vivi never stays mad for long. We'll touch base and talk this out back at the hotel.

Lucia hadn't seen her in about an hour and a half but had been trying to distract herself by doing what she'd come out here to do—dance and have fun. She'd been on the dance floor, song after song, in the middle of a pack of guys who said they were from the University of Georgia. One in particular, who seemed to be their leader, had taken a real liking to her. Now, exhausted, she stood at the edge of the dance floor trying to catch her breath, and found the guy had followed her.

"You want to get out of here?" he asked, leaning in to whisper in her ear.

Lucia froze. The guy seemed nice enough, but something in her was warning her to stay away. So she said, "Uh—I don't think so. Not tonight."

"Come oooon, I've got a great hotel room with room service."

"That sounds nice and all, but I've got to catch up with my friend. I had a great time dancing with you, though. Have a good night."

She patted his chest awkwardly before starting to make her way to the exit. Or at least trying to. She was stopped when the guy grabbed her wrist.

"What's the rush?" he asked. "Since when are you so

shy?"

"I'm… I'm just…" She was trying to think of what she'd been taught to say in this situation, but all her words seemed to have vanished when she needed them. Her eyes began to fill with tears. "I… Let *go* of me."

The guy began to pull her closer, instead. Lucia tried to reach into her purse, fumbling around for her pepper spray, which she'd never actually had to use before. But then, a miracle occurred.

A second guy, tall and formidable, appeared beside her.

"Hey, buddy, she said *no*," he said. "I work as a bouncer back home. I hit harder when I'm drunk, and I've had three shots of tequila, so I suggest you back the hell up."

The guy she had been dancing with hesitated, considering his options, then dropped her wrist, muttering a four-letter word she had never been called in her life as he walked away.

Lucia let out a shaking breath, turning toward her rescuer. "Thank you," she said.

"Hey, no problem," he said, gray eyes glinting as he smiled. "I can't stand guys like that."

"Do you *really* work as a bouncer?"

He laughed. "Yep. I get paid to stand there, read a list, and look intimidating. Nice work if you can get it."

"You ever had to beat anybody up?"

"It comes with the job."

She chuckled, wiping her eyes.

"Hey, hey, don't cry," he said. "Can't stand to see a pretty girl crying. Want to sit down?"

She nodded. "Yes, please. A-and thank you, again."

They found a couch in a relatively quiet corner of the club and settled on it. Lucia looked her rescuer over. He was good-looking, athletically built. He also seemed oddly familiar, but Lucia couldn't place where she'd seen him before.

"Where are you from?" Lucia asked.

"Steventon, Ohio. Kind of a boring city about two hours from—"

"From Columbus," she finished. "I know. I, um, I live there, too. I'm down here for spring break."

"No way. What are the odds?" he asked, smiling. "Do you sneak into bars underage there, too?"

Lucia flushed. "Um…"

He laughed. "I work at clubs, remember? You learn to pick out teenagers with fake IDs pretty quick." He nudged her gently. "Don't worry, I won't tell. How old are you, really?"

She glanced around to make sure no one was listening. "Fourteen," she said.

"Really? I thought you were sixteen, at least."

"It's the height," she shrugged. "I'm taller than my oldest sister, and she's in her twenties. How old are you?"

"Twenty-two. I've been standing guard at nightclubs for longer than I've actually been allowed to go *into* them."

"Do you like it?"

"It pays the bills. Hey, you mentioned to that other guy that you were looking for your friend. Want me to go get her?"

She shook her head, not wanting him to leave. "No, no. I mean, I am here with a friend, but, um… I'm kinda mad at her right now. I'd rather hang out with you."

He grinned. "You flirting with me?" he asked playfully.

Lucia rolled her eyes to cover up the fact that she was blushing. "Shut up."

"You know, if you don't want to hang around here, I was thinking of going for a walk down the beach. Want to come with?"

She paused. "Okay," she said.

Just as they got to their feet, her phone went off, with a new text message from her mother.

Location update?

Lucia hesitated, before texting back.

Going back to the hotel for bed. Love you. —L

"Who was that?" the guy asked as she put her phone back into her purse.

"Uh...nothing important. I'm Lucia Benitez, by the way," she said, extending her hand for a shake. "What's your name?"

He took her hand, shaking it.

"George Sedgwick. Call me Wick."

Chapter Twenty-Five

In Which the World Ends

Elisa awoke Friday morning with an odd twinge of sadness. She and the rest of her class would hit the road for Steventon the next night. She'd had one of the best spring breaks ever while she'd been at Pemberley, and she didn't want to go back to "the real world." She'd been having fun with Darcy—and wishing they'd been able to get along like this right from the beginning.

On Friday afternoon, they had planned to walk around the grounds of the Fitzgerald estate, but a good, old-fashioned April rainstorm dashed that plan. So, the two stayed inside, walking aimlessly, just talking.

Darcy was showing Elisa the extensive family library, saying, "I don't think it's possible for one person to read all of these, even if they read a book a day their entire life."

"How many have you read?" Elisa asked.

"Most of the ones in the classic fiction section—except for the ones by Kerouac. I could never get into his style. I didn't get far in *War and Peace*, either, and I've tried at least four times. I've read a lot of the poetry, about half the plays... A couple nonfiction, but not many. It's like...we have books so we can *escape* from reality. Why would I want to read *more* about it?"

Elisa laughed, a finger running over the spines of the antique books on the shelf labelled *Collector's*. There were ladders and small stairwells leading to more and more shelves of books, and lots of tables and comfy seats for reading. Her father would go nuts in this place.

"What are you doing over the summer break?" Darcy asked. "I know you'll have finals and stuff to deal with after spring break ends, but maybe we could get together after finals."

Elisa smiled. "I'll probably be taking a course online, but I'll definitely be able to hang out some."

"If it wouldn't give you flashbacks to your stay at Netherfield Park, you're always welcome to visit me here. I have more than enough room, and I haven't had guests in quite a while." She paused, quickly adding, "A-and your family is invited as well, of course."

"Don't let my mother hear you say that. She'd never leave. But I'd like that. It could be a fun vacation. Less expensive than Disney."

She blushed. "I can't promise it'll be as fun as Disney, though. I'm not great at entertaining guests, I admit."

"You're doing all right."

Darcy opened her mouth to say something else, but the ring of Elisa's phone interrupted.

She glanced at the caller ID. "It's Jules," she said. "I should probably take this."

"Go ahead."

Elisa answered. "Hello?"

"Oh, thank God—I was worried I wouldn't be able to reach you," Julieta said on the other end. Her voice was high-pitched, shaking. Elisa had never heard her sound like this before. "You need to get home right away."

"Wait, what? What happened?" Silence. "Julieta, *what happened*?"

"It's Lucia."

Elisa's stomach twisted in on itself, visions of her baby sister lying in a hospital bed flashing through her mind. "Oh God—oh God, is she hurt?"

Darcy looked up, approaching her but saying nothing.

Julieta was audibly fighting to hold back tears.

"Vivian went out to get them some food this morning. When she got back to the hotel, all of Lulu's stuff was gone, and she left a note. *Don't panic, I'm safe. George will look after me. Don't know when or if I'll be home. Love you.*"

"She—she ran off?" Elisa stumbled, sitting down. Her hands were shaking. "How long has she been gone?"

"At least four hours. She's not answering her phone, and she hasn't posted anything on social media since early this morning. I've tried to call about a hundred times, but it goes straight to voicemail. She must have shut it off…"

Julieta sniffled then went on. "Vivi called the police after she called us, but they haven't found anything, either. And—and Vivi's aunt says she hasn't seen her since last night. The last people to see her were the staff at the hotel—they said she returned her room key and got into a car, but they couldn't tell who was driving. There—there was a camera outside the hotel, of course, but the footage doesn't show the driver's face, and the license plate isn't visible, either."

"Shit. Shit. *Shit*." Elisa trembled from head to toe, trying not to break down sobbing. "I'm coming home. I'm coming home right now. I'll—I'll, um, I'll try to get a ride, and if I can't—"

"I can get you home," Darcy said softly.

Elisa nodded, then realized Julieta couldn't see her. "I

have a ride. I'll text you as soon as I'm on the way. I'll see you soon. I love you."

"I love you, too."

Julieta hung up, leaving Elisa sitting there, phone still in hand, staring straight ahead. Rain continued to pelt the roof, the only sound other than her racing heartbeat.

"Elisa?" Darcy whispered. She sat down next to her and hesitantly offered her hand. Elisa took it without thinking, lacing their fingers together and squeezing tightly. They sat there for a moment, Elisa trying to keep her breathing steady, before Darcy tried asking again. "Elisa, what happened?"

"Lucia's... Lucia, um...she..." She took a shaking breath, trying to focus on the feeling of her hand in Darcy's. "She went down to Daytona Beach with a friend, and—and this morning, she ran off from the hotel, leaving a note to say she's with someone named George and she doesn't know if she's coming home, and—and..."

Darcy frowned. "George," she said quietly. "Not George Sedgwick?"

Elisa looked over at her, heart freezing. "You don't think...?"

"It'd be one hell of a coincidence, but...given Wick's history..."

"Oh no, no, no..." She pulled up Twitter on her phone. "I unfollowed him, but his privacy settings let anyone see his profile. Stupid piece of shit."

She pulled up Wick's profile and looked at the most recent post.

It was geotagged from Daytona Beach.

"*Fuck.*" Elisa dropped her phone into her lap, burying her face in her hands. "I could've prevented this, I should've fought harder to keep Lucia from going, I should've told her the full truth about Wick..."

"And I should've warned more people what he is," Darcy

said gently, rubbing Elisa's back. "There's a lot of *could'ves* and *should'ves*. We can't dwell on those. We're no good to your sister like that."

Elisa nodded, feeling numb. "You're right. I, um, I have to get back to the hotel and tell the prof I'm leaving…" She began to stand. Darcy followed her.

"No," she said. "Go home now. I'll have someone drive you from here. Give me your room key, and I'll get your things out of your room and have them sent to you. I'll explain everything to your professor, and you can email him when you get home."

Elisa nodded again, following Darcy out of the library.

Five minutes later, the two girls dashed down the front steps. The rain poured down harder than ever, soaking them both as a car pulled up to whisk Elisa away.

"It'll be all right," Darcy said. Elisa didn't know if she actually believed it, or if she was just trying to comfort her. She decided to go with the former.

"I… Darcy, thank you so much."

"Don't thank me. It's nothing."

"No, no. It's not nothing. It's so far from nothing."

Elisa hesitated, then threw her arms around Darcy, pulling her into a hug. She was surprised but reciprocated. For a brief second, they stood there, holding each other, and time stopped. For just a moment, all the panicked noise in Elisa's head went quiet, leaving her with only the patter of the rain hitting the sidewalk and the sound of their breathing. Finally, they pulled away, tears escaping Elisa, at last.

"You better get going," Darcy said softly. "You're already soaked to the skin."

"Yeah, yeah, I… I know."

She took a step back, wiping her eyes to no avail.

She almost said, "Come with me."

Instead, she said, "It's crazy."

"What is?"

"This whole thing. Lucia, Wick…you and me."

"You and me?"

"I can't believe how wrong I was about you."

Darcy smiled, but it didn't reach her eyes. She just said, "Go. And if you need anything, don't hesitate to call me. I'm here for you."

If she'd said anything else, Elisa definitely would've burst into tears on the spot. So she just nodded, before getting into the car. Water dripping from her clothes and onto the fine leather seat, she turned to gaze out the window as the engine revved. The driver, having been told it was urgent, peeled away from the house, and Darcy disappeared from view within a minute. The last Elisa saw of her, she stood out on the sidewalk in front of the estate, completely drenched and shivering, brown eyes watching the car speed away.

She leaned back into her seat, trying to regulate her breathing. It would do no good to panic. No good whatsoever.

She panicked anyway.

Chapter Twenty-Six

In Which Things Fall Apart

About an hour into the two-hour trip, Elisa got a phone call. It wasn't Julieta again, or, as she hoped, Lucia. It was Willow.

Willow began talking as soon as she picked up.

"Darcy told me the situation," she said. "I'm driving over to Daytona Beach from Miami. I doubt Wick is still there, but it's something."

"You don't have to," she said.

"Yes, I do. You're my friend."

"Thank you, Willow." She sighed, rubbing her eyes. "Sh-she's probably not hurt, is she? I mean—I mean, physically hurt. Wick wouldn't...?"

"I don't think he'd kill her, if that's what you mean."

Elisa was torn between appreciating how direct she was and breaking down sobbing at the very idea. "She's only been gone for five hours now. That's..."

"That means we still have plenty of chances to find her," Willow said. "Okay, I'm about to get on the highway, so I should probably hang up. I'm headed for Daytona Beach until I hear something that tells me I should go someplace else. If there's any place down south you think she might be, give me a call."

"I will. Thank you. Thank you."

Willow hung up, leaving Elisa once again alone with her thoughts. The driver had correctly guessed she wouldn't be in the mood for small talk. She leaned her head against the window, trying to find something to do besides panic. She could barely see anything—the rain hadn't let up a bit.

Knowing nothing would've changed since the last time she did it, Elisa pulled up Lucia's profile on her phone.

Nothing.

. . .

Thanks to a combination of unusually good luck with traffic lights, a relatively non-busy road, and a total disregard of speed limits when the driver thought he could get away with it, Elisa was back home at Longbourn faster than Google Maps said was technically possible. She half wondered if Darcy had bribed him to get her there as quickly as he could, laws of physics be damned. Or maybe he just somehow understood how important this was.

"Would you like me to walk you up?" the driver asked, pulling up in front of the apartment complex.

"No, thank you," Elisa said, fumbling to get the door open. "Thank you for driving me out here—and tell Darcy I said thank you, too."

"I will."

She got out of the car and hurried into the building without looking back.

Her hands shook by the time she reached her apartment.

Inside, things were more crowded than they'd been in years. Both her parents were there, which was unusual in itself. Her mother was on the phone, screaming at someone (probably the police), while her father was sitting at the kitchen table with Maria, both in the process of contacting all of Lucia's friends. Julieta was where Lucia had put her room, tidying things up, as if that could somehow convince their little sister to come back. The divider, Elisa noticed, had been folded up and pushed aside, placing Lucia's bed right in the middle of the room.

Colin and Charlene had both shown up, which was the only thing that made her feel even slightly better. Charlene flitted her way through the kitchen, fixing everyone drinks and snacks, since none of the Benitezes were in the right frame of mind to remember to eat and drink. Colin, meanwhile, was on the couch, rubbing Camila's back. She was crying, trying to speak, but unable to get the words out.

"Anything?" was the first thing Elisa said when she shut the door behind her. She tossed her hoodie on the small mountain of jackets that had formed on the kitchen table.

"No," Charlene said, squeezing past Maria to bring Alejandra a drink. "But it's—it's still early. Most missing persons cases get solved within the first week, and most of those are within the first twenty-four hours. Most of the time, you have to give it a full twenty-four hours, but we knew right away, so we've got a head start. She'll be okay."

Elisa got the impression she'd Googled these statistics in the hopes of calming the family, and herself.

"I've searched all her social media and her planner a thousand times to see if she mentions a George anyplace," Julieta said, fingers quickly flipping through Lucia's magazine collection. "She would've told us if she had a boyfriend, right?"

Elisa's stomach churned. "It's George Sedgwick."

Charlene stared at her, hazel eyes going wide. "Are you sure?" she asked, color draining from her face.

She nodded. "It fits his pattern, and I checked his social media. He is—or was—in Daytona Beach at the same time Lulu was."

"His pattern? What are you talking about?" Julieta asked, getting to her feet.

Everyone was staring at her, now. Elisa took a shaking breath, knowing that the cat was out of the bag.

Gianna and Darcy will understand. I hope.

"Darcy told me he...he abused her younger sister, who's about Lucia's age," she said, having to force the words out.

"Abused how?" her dad asked, but the look on his face told her he already had an idea.

"Abused as in dated her when he was twenty and she was thirteen. And—and hit her, at least once, and...and they were sleeping together. Darcy isn't sure if her sister had a choice, but even if she technically did...she was still thirteen."

"Son of a..." He trailed off, one of his hands coming up to massage his forehead.

Her mother looked like she was going to throw up, and Camila began crying even harder. Julieta just stood there, watery eyes staring straight ahead as she whispered, "Oh no, no, no..."

"B-but if we know who she's with, that's a good thing, right?" Charlene said, trying to keep her voice level.

Mom nodded, but she still looked like she was about to break down completely. "Elisa, you'll have to—have to tell the police all that, so they know who to look for."

Elisa nodded. "I can do that." At least it made her feel less useless.

"Did Darcy's sister charge him with anything?" Maria asked. "If he has priors, it'd be easier to find him, right?"

Elisa sighed, sitting at the table next to her father. "She tried to, but the police scared her—between that and her anxiety, she never would've been able to handle the trial.

She and her aunt and uncle decided it'd be better to cut their losses and just work on helping her after the shitshow Wick put her through."

"The police scared her into letting him walk away?" Maria said, shocked. "But they're police. Locking him up is their *job*."

"It happens all the time," her father said grimly.

"I'll call the police so you can make a statement," Mom told Elisa, getting on the phone once again.

"She's been frantic ever since Lulu's friend called her," her father said, as he watched their mother. "Julieta is the one that told me what was going on. I came over right away."

"How are you *not* frantic?" she asked.

"I think I've gone on autopilot," he admitted. "I'll probably panic later. So, you know, that'll be a fun surprise." He ran a hand over his hair, before making eye contact with his second-eldest daughter. "She's okay, Elisa. I know she is. If she wasn't—we'd feel it. *I'd* feel it."

She nodded, trying to believe him. "I hope you're right."

. . .

The policeman assigned to Lucia's case was named Officer Nathanson. He smelled like bad cigars and cheap coffee, and his desk was cluttered and covered in papers from a thousand other cases. Elisa's father had driven her down to the police station so she could tell them about Wick. They'd offered to come to the apartment, but it was crowded enough as it was.

"So, this…Wick—does he have any prior charges, to your knowledge?" he asked. He'd taken out a pen and notepad and was scribbling as Elisa spoke.

"No, but—but only because Gianna was scared into dropping them."

She'd relayed the entire Gianna/Wick story to him and

told him about Wick being in Daytona Beach. He didn't seem like he thought she was *lying*, but he didn't seem to be as scared as Elisa was.

"You said Wick is your ex-boyfriend?"

"Not exactly. We went on one date," Elisa said. "It didn't work out. What does this have to do with my sister?"

"If she is with him, it may explain why he targeted her—*if* he targeted her. Was he angry with you when the relationship didn't work out?"

"I—I mean, I don't *think* so," she said. She cleared her throat, trying to force herself to sound more levelheaded and less panicky. "There wasn't a fight or anything, we just stopped texting, and that was it. He didn't seem any more interested in me than I was in him."

She realized, now, bile rising in her throat, that she was probably too old for him.

"Well, we'll definitely look into him," he said. "Do you know where he works?"

Elisa nodded. "He said he works as a bouncer at all the local clubs—Eclipse, Cat's Eye, and the Parlour, I think."

"I'll ask if any of his coworkers know where he is. Does he have any friends nearby?"

"He must, but I don't know who they are."

He took a deep breath, setting his notepad down. "Okay. Thank you for coming down here, Elisa." They got to their feet, and the officer gave her what she assumed was supposed to be a comforting look. "We're going to do everything we can to find Lucia. Kids her age, they... They want a taste of adventure, of being grown-up, and they do stupid things. Things they *think* they want, before they realize it's not what they pictured. Most of the time, we can get 'em home before anyone gets hurt."

"*Most* of the time," she repeated.

He hesitated, before saying, "My point is, I've seen a lot

of cases like this, and it nearly always comes out right in the end. I know you're scared for your sister, but try to remember, she's probably just fine."

"Yeah." The word came out brittle and unconvinced.

Dad was waiting outside the room for her, and they headed back to the car.

"Well?" he asked.

"Well, I told them everything I know. He said they'd look into it, but he didn't seem convinced."

"I'm not surprised. If he has no record, they're inclined to believe he's innocent."

"I hate him," she whispered, hands balling into fists. "I hate him *so much*."

"*You* hate him?" Miguel said, trying to joke, trying to cheer her up, even a little. "Hell, he better *hope* they lock him up. If your mom and I get ahold of him first, the last thing he'll ever see is Alex with a machete."

Elisa laughed, mainly to keep herself from crying. They headed back to Longbourn, and she tried to tell herself, over and over and over, that Lucia would be fine. It had been a little over seven hours since she ran off. And Daytona Beach was crowded—if people knew to look for her, someone would see her eventually.

Sooner or later, someone would find her. And then she'd have to come home.

Right?

Chapter Twenty-Seven

In Which Things Put Themselves Back Together

One week, three days, and one hour since Lucia had gone missing.

Elisa was beginning to lose steam.

Every day, she went through the motions. Get up. Check Lucia's social media. Call all her friends. Share the "missing" post she'd made once again. Try to call Lucia. Wait for any word from the police. She would walk around town for any sign of her sister, while her parents would drive around, and Julieta managed things that could be done from home. Come home. Try to sleep.

Nothing. Nothing. Nothing.

After the first day, she didn't even have the option of calling Wick's cell every hour anymore. Soon, the calls had started going right to voicemail, and then, she'd started getting an automated "the number you have dialed is not in service" message. She shouldn't have been surprised he had experience in slipping off the grid, even if only temporarily.

The trail had gone completely cold, it seemed.

She'd done her best not to break down crying in front of anyone else, no matter how hard it got. Things were stressful enough. She didn't need to pile on. She had to just keep pushing through, keep looking until they found her.

She missed Darcy.

It was a strange thing to think, in the middle of a crisis, but she really, really missed Darcy. She wanted to cry, and she wanted to cry to someone who had been through this, too—and come out the other side. She wanted to hear her reassure her that it was all going to be fine.

She wanted to believe it was all going to be fine.

Elisa blew off school—she'd emailed her professors explaining why, but she hadn't bothered to check to see if they'd answered yet. If they understood, great. If not, who cared? There were worse things than having to repeat a course. They'd alerted Lucia's high school. Maria and Camila had returned there when spring break ended. Elisa was grateful her senior year of high school was at college.

Apparently, other students had found out pretty quick that Lucia was gone, and they had to endure questions, stares, and whispers. Cam, in particular, was having a hard time. Even though they were in different grades, Lucia was her constant companion at school as well as at home. She was barely getting through the day.

Elisa did her best to comfort her, but it was hard, especially when she felt like crying half the time herself.

Charlene and Colin had both been forced to return to work and school but were over at the apartment with Elisa every chance they got. Her father had practically moved back in, sleeping on the couch, and promised he wouldn't leave until Lucia was found. Willow had scoured all of Daytona Beach and the surrounding areas but hadn't come across a single clue as to where Lucia and Wick may have gone from there—just that they'd either left or were doing a remarkably good job at hiding. She was now back in Steventon and offered to skip class so she could be around to help, but Elisa wouldn't let her.

On the third day of Lucia's disappearance, her mother had said six words that she'd never, ever expected to hear her say of her own free will: "I should have listened to you."

They'd been fixing a haphazard dinner of microwave pasta and the cheapest garlic bread money could buy. Elisa almost dropped the plate she was holding, certain she hadn't heard her correctly.

Her mother continued, "Ever since we got that call, I haven't been able to stop thinking about how Lulu is off doing who-knows-what with that creep, and how I could've stopped it from happening if I just…"

"Mama, don't beat yourself up," she said gently, reaching to touch her shoulder. "I mean, I knew Wick was a predator, but I didn't tell anybody. I wanted to protect my friend's privacy, so I just…didn't warn her, even though I should have. I thought I was doing the right thing. Look where that's gotten us."

She sniffled. "Still. I'm her mother. I should've had better instincts. I should've been more vigilant."

"There are a lot of 'could'ves' and 'should'ves,'" Elisa said, remembering Darcy's words to her just before she left for home.

"Yeah. Like I should've listened to you. I'm sorry, Elisa."

"It's okay. I'm sorry, too."

Personally, she was in no mood to gloat. She'd never been less happy to be right in her entire life.

She had spent an irritating amount of time on Wick's social media pages, hoping against hope he'd slip up and reveal something. He was posting semi-regularly, presumably from a new phone, but nothing was geotagged, and he never mentioned where he was—not even a state. He was smart, smarter than he acted—smarter than she had given him credit for.

She was about to make the usual rounds to Lucia's favorite hangouts, on the off-chance she'd gone to any of them, when there was a knock at the door.

Alejandra, Miguel, and Elisa all practically tripped over each other to answer it, but Elisa got there first. She threw open the door, but it wasn't Lucia.

"Bobby?" she said, unable to hide her surprise.

"Hey—Darcy told me what happened," he said, stepping inside. His blue eyes were shining with concern. "I came as soon as I could. I wanted to see if there was anything I can do to help."

"Nothing comes to mind," Mom said, "but we appreciate you coming, anyway."

Julieta emerged from her room and stopped. Elisa tensed, wondering what she would say or do upon seeing her ex for the first time since he ditched her. She tried not to cringe as her sister's mouth opened, preparing herself for an explosion.

"Bobby. You're here," she said.

Wait, *what*?

He nodded quickly, too quickly. "Yeah, I… I had to come and see if there was anything I could do to help."

"Thank you."

She sounded like she meant it, but her voice was just a touch cooler than it ever had been around him before. Bobby definitely noticed but didn't say anything in reply. His eyes just darted nervously from Julieta to the floor and back again. Elisa hoped one of them would speak to the other, but neither of them did.

"I was just about to walk around town to see if anyone's seen her," Elisa finally said, partially just to fill the awkward silence. "I could use a ride. I can cover more ground that way."

Bobby nodded, tearing his gaze away from Julieta. "Okay. Sure. I can do that. Anything you need. I—I can't imagine how awful this must be for all of you."

In Bobby's bright red Lexus, checking all of Lucia's favorite places only took about an hour and a half, and most of that was Elisa hopping out of the car and running inside each location to see if anyone had seen her sister. All the cashiers and managers knew the situation and had promised they'd call if they saw Lucia, but she couldn't resist going to ask in person anyway. Just in case.

"That's the last place on my list." Elisa sighed, slumping back into the passenger's seat, having just come out of Lucia's favorite store in the mall. "No one's seen or heard a thing."

"And her social media's still silent?" Bobby asked, looking at Elisa with concern in his eyes. She tried her best to stop herself from sniffling.

"Not a word since the morning she vanished," she confirmed.

He took a slightly trembling breath. "I don't want to scare you," he said, "but are you sure that note she left was really—?"

Elisa nodded. "We already thought of that," she said. "We gave the cops her planners and old diary to compare the handwriting. Definitely hers."

She wiped away some newly-formed tears with the back of her hand. He pretended not to notice, turning on the car again.

"When Wick was with Gianna, he'd take her to motels sometimes," he said slowly. "Gianna told her sister she was going to the library or the mall, but…" He trailed off, shaking his head. "You know. It couldn't hurt to check out some motels nearby. See if she's with him in any of them…"

Elisa nodded, trying her best not to dwell too much on that image.

"Yeah. Yeah. Let's—let's go."

. . .

They hit every hotel and motel in Steventon but found no sign of Lucia. This wasn't really a surprise; Wick would have to be pretty dumb to bring Lucia back here. It had been a longshot, and they both knew it. So, when Bobby suggested they drive over to a nearby town to see if maybe they were hiding out there, she agreed. She didn't know if it would do any good. She had to be doing *something*. Doing nothing was a fast-track to insanity.

"Just twenty more minutes of driving, then we'll be in Wylit," Bobby said. The town was nearby, a little nothing of a community, easily accessible via the highway. Elisa couldn't imagine why anyone would stay there—unless, of course, they didn't want to be found.

She sighed, nodding, leaning her head against the window.

"Thank you for doing this," she said. "I really appreciate it. I know my parents and sisters do, too."

"You're welcome. I'm just sorry I couldn't get here earlier." He sighed, fingers nervously drumming on the steering wheel. "I wanted to come as soon as Darcy told me, but I was trapped at a work thing—actually, I'm still supposed to be there. But Jules was texting me updates the entire time—and when it had been a week and still nothing… I couldn't stay away another minute."

Elisa glanced over at him, surprised. "You've been talking to Julieta?"

He blushed. "Yeah, I mean, after she turned me down, she said we could be frie—"

"*What?*"

He went even redder. "I thought she would've told you

by now."

"Well, she didn't. But now, you have to. You can't leave me with that."

Elisa wasn't sure how much of her interest was her being genuinely invested in the relationship, and how much was just her wanting to distract herself.

Bobby ran a hand through his blond hair, letting out a long breath.

"After I saw you at Pemberley," he said, "I realized I couldn't go on without Julieta like I had. I missed her so much it was like my arm had been cut off. I thought about calling her a thousand times, but…I was scared. When Darcy told me she thought Julieta wasn't into it, I panicked. I cut her off before I could think it through. I figured doing it that way would save me the heartache, but…" He licked his lips, trying to find words. "The further back I pulled from Julieta, the more I realized how much I wanted to be with her. Within two weeks of leaving, I was kicking myself for ever listening to Darcy."

"Why did you?" Elisa asked quietly.

"Like I said, I panicked. I've never felt this way about anyone—I've loved women before, sure, but…not like this. The idea that maybe it was all one-sided was…was terrifying. And Darcy's never done me wrong, at least, not on purpose. I knew she wouldn't suggest Julieta didn't love me back unless she truly believed it. So, I panicked, and like an idiot, I left behind the best thing that ever happened to me."

Elisa listened to him.

And to think Julieta had thought she'd meant nothing to him.

"By the time I was ready to accept I'd made a huge mistake, it seemed like it was too late," Bobby said. "Especially since she was going out with other people."

"How'd you know that?"

He flushed with red. "Look, internet-stalking your ex is a very important part of the healing process. Before she unfriends you, I mean."

Elisa snorted. "If it makes you feel any better, the guy she went out with for Valentine's Day was a rebound if I ever saw one."

"That actually *does* make me feel a bit better," he admitted. "Anyway, I was trying to get over her—and failing miserably. And then I saw you at Pemberley. After you told me to talk to her myself, I decided you were right."

"I usually am."

"I drove over to Steventon that night and showed up at the apartment. Fortunately, Julieta was home alone—I think your mother may have killed me on sight for what I did. Not that I blame her. Jules was surprised to see me, but she agreed to get a bite to eat someplace. I explained everything. I told her what Darcy had told me, and how I had been an idiot and listened to her instead of using my judgement, and how I regretted it every second we were apart, and that I wanted to try again. And…she turned me down."

"Wow," she said. She could scarcely imagine that.

"When I asked her out again, she said…she said, 'How do I know you won't run off again?' I said, 'Because Darcy won't pull anything like that again.' And she asked, 'How can I date a man who can't make his own choices?' And I realized…she was right. I told her I loved her, and she called me an idiot.

She said I blew it, and then walked out on me to prove it. I went home, hating life, but the next morning, I woke up to a long email from Julieta. She said that she'd meant what she said the night before, but that she still missed me, and didn't want to throw away what we'd had. She said she wasn't sure if it could ever be fixed, but she wanted to try. But she didn't want to start dating again—she wanted to be friends. She said that we can be friends, and if it grows into something more, great, but it's a long way off, and in the meantime, maybe we should see other people."

"*Are* there other people?"

He laughed. "No. At least not on my side. I'm not pushing anything with Jules, though. I'm just glad she's willing to talk to me now. And she's a good friend."

"She is." Elisa reached over to pat his arm. "She does still love you, you know. Fixing things may not take as long as you think. But if you *ever* pull a disappearing act like that *ever* again, I *will* bury you alive."

"I'll hand you the shovel."

• • •

Elisa and Bobby were almost at the last hotel in Wylit when the call came.

"It's Mom, I should take this," she said, grabbing her cell phone out of her pocket. She answered the call. "Hello?"

"Lucia's home."

"What?" She began smacking Bobby on the arm, and he let out an *"ow!"* with each slap. "She's home?"

"She's home," Mom said. She sounded like she'd been crying.

"Oh, thank *God*… Is she hurt at all?"

"She has a busted lip and a bruise on her cheek. I'm grateful it's only that."

"Yeah—yeah, me too."

"You were right—she *was* with George Sedgwick. And she's pressing charges."

"Oh good. Was he with her?"

"No. She showed up alone."

"We're headed over right now," Elisa said.

"No, go to the police station. Your father and I are about to take her over."

"Okay. Okay, we'll go to the station… Bobby and I are in Wylit. We thought she might be hiding out here."

"You were close," she said. "She said she and Wick were in Parkersburg."

Parkersburg was about two towns away from Steventon, barely an hour's drive. Elisa kicked herself for not thinking to check there sooner.

"I'll be there soon," she said. "Can I talk to Lulu?"

"I don't think a full SWAT team could pull her away from Cam right now."

"Okay, I'll wait my turn." She sighed. "See you at the station."

She hung up, bouncing up and down in her seat. The sheer relief now turned into tears, streaming down her cheeks even as she smiled. It felt like she hadn't done that in years. Her sister was home, and safe. And if things went well, Wick would never be able to go near another girl ever again.

"She's safe?" Bobby asked, having already turned the car around to head back to Steventon.

"She's safe." Elisa grinned. "We're not sure where Wick is, but she's decided to press charges, so hopefully the cops will find him."

"How do you feel?" he asked.

"Relieved," she said. "Like I've been coiled up impossibly tight for the past week, and now I can finally unravel."

Bobby drove as quickly as possible to Steventon, but as far as Elisa was concerned, no speed was fast enough.

• • •

"Where is she?" was the first thing Elisa asked when she arrived at the police station, and saw her entire family, sans Lucia, waiting in the lobby. They were all in various states of disarray, but they all looked much more at ease than they had been all week. Camila's makeup was smudged from crying, as she leaned against her father's shoulder. Elisa ran toward them, heart pounding. Bobby had come inside with her, but hung back, not wanting to interfere.

"She's giving her statement," her dad said. "Your mother and I offered to go in with her, but she insisted she'd be okay alone. We didn't want to push her…"

"She won't tell us the details of how she got home or what happened." Julieta sighed from where she sat on the floor with Maria. The bench in the lobby hadn't had enough room for the whole family. "She promised to tell the police everything, but she said she needs some time before she tells us."

"Personally, I'm willing to give her all the time in the world, but I would like to know…" Mom sighed. "The important thing is she's all right."

"Talking about me?" a small voice said.

Everyone looked up as Lucia emerged, accompanied by an officer.

What little remained of Elisa's dignity went out the window the second she saw her baby sister. She almost tripped over Maria in her hurry to run over to throw her arms around her. The tears were back, and more uncontrollable than ever.

"Oh, Lulu, I was so scared I'd never see you again," she said, blubbering like an idiot. She hugged Lucia tightly, too tightly, unable to fathom ever letting go.

"I'm here, Elisa," she said quietly. Her arms were wrapped tightly around her older sister, and she seemed to crumble a bit. "You were right. About Wick. About how I should stay away from him. You were right," Her voice broke. "I'm so sorry, Elisa…"

"Shhh, shh, it's okay. It's okay."

"No, it's not—no it's not, I scared everyone and ran off with someone you *tried* to tell me was bad news…"

Elisa pulled back to look her sister in the eye.

"Listen to me," she said gently, though she was still crying. "He's scum. This isn't your fault. He's the bad guy here, not you."

"But I—I went with him, I said yes. He never... he never forced me to do anything... At least, not to start with—"

"*He's* the adult. He should've known better. He *does* know better It was his responsibility to make sure nothing like this happened," she said. "He took advantage of you."

"I should've listened to you," Lucia repeated. "I—I met him in Florida, and—and he seemed so charming and nice and sweet, and, and...and I figured he couldn't have done whatever it was you thought he did, and...and the fact that you told me to stay away made me want him more because I'm such an *idiot*..." Her voice broke as a fresh wave of tears spilled down her face.

"You're not an idiot," she said. "I should've told you the full truth. I should've fought harder to protect you..."

"You can't always protect me from myself."

"No," she admitted, "but I can try."

Lucia managed a smile, though she was still crying, and hugged Elisa tightly once more.

Elisa wanted to stay here, with her little sister safe in her arms, forever.

Chapter Twenty-Eight

In Which There Are No More Secrets

The day after Lucia returned home, Elisa once again called a meeting with all her sisters, once again all crammed in her bedroom.

"I think if there's anything to be learned from all this," she said, "it's that keeping secrets is a bad, bad idea. If I'd told you all what Wick did to Gianna…" She trailed off then shook her head. "There's no point dwelling on what could've been. My point is…can we all agree, no more keeping secrets from each other if it could be a matter of someone's safety?"

Her sisters all nodded in agreement. They'd spent almost every waking moment together since Lucia had returned home safely. None of them had asked too many questions about what had happened. She had, as promised, told the police everything she could, and Alejandra said that she'd tell her family when she was good and ready. Elisa tried not to let herself get caught up in all the nightmare scenarios that had been flashing through her mind since she realized Lucia was with Wick.

About an hour after their little meeting, Lucia rapped on the inside of Elisa and Julieta's bedroom door.

"Can I talk to you alone for a bit, E?" she asked.

Elisa nodded, setting down her book. "Of course," she said. "Roof?"

Lucia nodded. It was the only place in Longbourn with relative privacy.

Hollering to their mother that they would be back in a few minutes, they headed to the top of the apartment complex. It was a hideous view, overlooking the ugliest part of Steventon, but it was quiet, and secluded. Lucia sat down with her back to the chain-link fence that had been installed a few years before to prevent falls.

Elisa sat with her. "What's up?" she asked.

Lucia was quiet for a moment. "I met Wick at a club in Daytona Beach," she finally said. "First night I was there. This guy was harassing me, and Wick…'rescued' me. After that, we hung out every night, and…and… We started sleeping together. I knew it wasn't a good idea, but he convinced me that our ages didn't matter for people like us, that he wasn't normally 'that guy,' but I was an exception, and…"

She reached for her hand. "You don't have to talk about this if you're not ready, Lulu."

"No, I… He said he was planning to take a road trip. And he wanted me to come with. He said he'd…he'd never felt this way about a girl. That I was special to him." Lucia's voice was trembling. "He actually got me to believe it…"

Elisa's eyes were filling with tears again, but she forced herself not to shed them. She had to be strong. For Lucia.

"After a couple days, I started to get homesick. I… I started thinking about Mom, and Camila, and…and I really missed you. So I asked Wick to take me home. He said, 'Lu, home for you is wherever I am.'"

"Ugh," Elisa said, grimacing in disgust.

"I know," she agreed. "But I ate it up. I bought the whole thing, hook, line, and sinker. So I stayed with him, even though I knew it was a bad idea. Even though…even though my gut was telling me to run away, I stayed. I…I can't even call myself a victim." Her small hands were bunching into fists, her voice heavy with disgust. "I had a choice, and I made the wrong one. I stayed. Even after he *hit me*, I stayed."

"Lu, that's not how it works," she said. She reached over to stroke Lucia's hair, but her younger sister flinched away. Retracting her hand, she said, "He's an adult. You're a child. He made you think he cared, even when he was doing awful things. You're not a bad person because you bought into it." She took a shaking breath before asking, "When…when did he hit you?"

"The first time? We got in an argument over…" She sighed. "He wanted me to go to this rager at a school his friend went to. I knew it'd be full of drunk frat boys and drug dealers and all kinds of shit, so I said I didn't want to go. He said I was being stupid. A *kid*. He said I was being a kid, and I called him a jackass…and that's when he punched me. See, a *smart* person would've left right then and there, but no. I stayed, because he was oh-so-sorry. That he'd just been caught up in the moment." She let out a raw, bitter laugh. "God, I even went to the fucking party. I'm like every other dumbass that lets her boyfriend walk all over her because he's cute. What's *wrong* with me?"

"Lucia, stop putting yourself down," Elisa said, voice firm. "You're not stupid, or less of a victim. Don't ever try and downplay what you've been through because you feel bad about yourself. Okay?"

Lucia didn't respond right away, but finally mumbled something that sounded like, "Okay." Slowly, she leaned her head against Elisa's shoulder.

She wrapped an arm around her. "I'm so glad you're

taking him to trial. And I'll be with you every step of the way."

Lucia tried to smile, but it didn't reach her eyes. Finally, she turned her gaze away from her.

"I was thinking about what you said, about not keeping secrets," she said. "I know you said it was mostly for when it was a matter of someone's safety... But what about a matter of someone's happiness?"

"What are you talking about?"

"Elisa, *Darcy* is the one that found me."

Elisa swore her heart froze for just a moment. It took nearly a full minute for her to find her voice again.

"What?"

"Darcy found me. Found us. She found us, and she got me to come home. She had someone drive me here, too. The reason I'm back home, it's... It's all her."

"But—but *how*—?"

"We talked a little bit while her driver took us back to Steventon. She told me about how she'd run into you at Pemberley while you were in Columbus, how she was there when you got the call that I... That I..."

Lucia trailed off, guilt stealing her voice away. When she found it again, it was quiet, but calm.

"Apparently, the only thing Darcy's done since you left Columbus was call every hotel, club, and bar in the area to find out if Wick had been in," she said. "She told me what he'd done to her sister, and that Gianna had told her all the places they'd gone together. She figured sooner or later, Wick would have to come back up here, if only to get his extra credit cards. She was right, too. He was running out of money, fast."

She was digging her nails into one of her arms, dragging them down, leaving tracks behind. On instinct, Elisa reached out to stop her.

"Anyway, we—we made it to Parkersburg, and Wick said

it should be fine so long as I didn't go back into Steventon and stayed in the hotel. He'd been posting stuff online the entire time, he said people would notice if he went silent right when I ran away. He said as long as he didn't let it tag his location, it'd be fine. Stupid asshole…" She sighed, licking her lips.

"Darcy was checking his social media, too, of course, but couldn't find anything that nailed down where he was. One night, when he went out to get a drink, he bumped into a friend, and posted a picture with them online. And, wouldn't you know it, Darcy saw, and showed it to Gianna. Gianna recognized the bar—I guess they'd been there together. So Darcy knew he was in Parkersburg and had someone drive her out. After that, it was only a matter of time before she found the hotel, since it's a pretty small place… She drove by and saw Wick outside our hotel room getting ice. I *told* him he wasn't careful enough…"

"What'd Darcy do?" Elisa asked.

"Well, she told me on the way back that she'd *wanted* to call the cops, but he saw her. She knew he'd run before the cops got there, so she had to deal with him herself. She kind of…forced her way into our hotel room. Wick kept telling her to get the hell out, but she stood her ground. She told me he'd done this before, that I was just the latest naive, vulnerable girl he was taking advantage of. I didn't want to believe her. I said he loved me. I think I even believed it."

"So why'd you come home?"

Lucia stared down at her lap, eyes watery.

"Darcy turned to Wick," she said. "And she said—she said, 'Okay, George. If you two are so in love, then I take it you told her all about Gianna.' And she told me the whole story. About how Wick had done the exact same thing to Gianna as he'd done to me. Found a girl that was too young for him, and told her she was so grown-up, that she was special." A couple biting laughs escaped her. "He even used the same lines on her. Darcy was standing there, reciting all the compliments and put-downs Wick had fed me, word-for-word. Like it was all just part of a script. And she said that he had hit her sister, too, and forced her into situations she didn't want. Everything he'd pulled on me—everything—he'd done to her."

"Did Wick try and deny it?"

"No. That was the worst part. He just told me that Gianna was a bitch, that's why he'd dropped her. But Darcy said, 'No, she dropped *you*. Because she realized she deserved better.' And she looked at me and said, 'Lucia, you deserve better, too.' I... I didn't know what to think. I asked him, if I told him to wait two years, until I was old enough to date him for real, would he? He said we didn't need to worry about some stupid law, but I said that...that if he loved me, if I wasn't just another Gianna to him, he'd be willing to wait."

"And he wasn't," she finished.

Lucia sighed. "And he wasn't. He said, 'I like you. But I'm only human, I'm not gonna wait around for some kid to grow up.' I told him to go to hell, and he just... He looked at Darcy and asked if she was gonna call the cops. And she said, 'Not if you get your ass out of here in the next minute.' So he did. He didn't even say goodbye to me."

"Oh, Lulu..." Elisa murmured. "Lulu, I'm so... I'm so sorry."

"I just stood there. I was too shocked to even cry at first. And Darcy... It was like she wasn't even the same girl I'd met before. She was quiet. Kind. She told me what happened wasn't my fault, and that it wasn't too late to come home. That I had people back home who really, really loved me."

"And she was right. You did. You *do*."

Lucia tried to smile. The two sat in silence for a few minutes, Lucia trying to collect herself, before Elisa said, "Darcy really came through. I... I can't believe it. I'm so glad she managed to get through to you."

"Me, too. I'm not sure anyone else *could* have gotten through like she did," she admitted. "She also said she can act as a witness at the trial, if she has to. She said she can't make any promises for Gianna, but she'll talk to her and see if she's willing."

"Why didn't you tell me before? Hell, why didn't Darcy tell me?"

Lucia hugged her knees to her chest. "She asked me not to tell you. I don't know how she expected to keep it from you forever—I mean, if nothing else, it was bound to come out during the trial."

"But why wouldn't Darcy want me to know?"

"She didn't say. I think she didn't want you to feel indebted to her."

"But I *am*," Elisa said. "I'm so, so grateful, and I owe her so much for this—"

"I think that's what she wanted to avoid," Lucia said carefully. "That she didn't want you to think she did this so you'd be grateful. Elisa, Darcy did this for... Well, I'm pretty sure Darcy did this just for *you*."

Elisa stared at her. Lucia kept talking.

"Whenever one of us mentioned you, Darcy's eyes just... lit up. I'd say she was lovesick if it wasn't *Darcy*. She obviously cares about you, more than you think. Elisa...I think she might love you."

Elisa laughed nervously. "Don't be dumb," she said. "I mean—I mean, Darcy asked me out a few months ago, but I shot her down. We're friends now, but... Just friends. She would've done this for any of her friends."

"Yeah, because clearly, vigilantism in the name of *friendship* is totally a thing that happens every day."

"Look, Darcy had feelings for me at one point, but..."

"Do you have feelings for *her* now?"

Elisa tried to respond, but all of her wit and words seemed to have deserted her when she needed them most, and she was left with inarticulate stammering.

Lucia grinned, a shadow of her old self.

"No," she said, too loudly. "Darcy and I are friends now, that's all."

"Uh-huh. That's *totally* how I react to one of my platonic *gal pals*."

Lucia got to her feet.

"I just thought you should know."

She headed back into the building, leaving Elisa sitting on the roof.

Elisa may not have ever felt sparkly inside or seen fireworks in her head over someone before, but she definitely did now. She also felt a bit dizzy, but she told herself that was because she didn't eat breakfast.

Her mind was instantly flooded with all the things she wanted to say to Darcy. Mostly, "Thank you." But also, "You're officially my favorite person," "Can I please hug you and never let go?" and, "Did you really do this for me?"

This was just the romantic in Lucia getting the best of her, right? She would've loved it if this had all been some big, grand romantic gesture for Elisa's sake, but...

No. No. Darcy didn't feel that way about Elisa anymore. Any feelings Darcy once had were gone by now. She'd made sure of it.

And then, there it was.

The feeling of regret.

Chapter Twenty-Nine

In Which Catherine Burger Tries to Sink Yet Another Ship

Bobby had come over almost every day since Lucia had returned home. He and Julieta had been hanging out a lot, going to the movies or for meals, insisting that it was "just as friends." No one really bought it, but they didn't call them on it for Julieta's sake. Elisa half hoped she'd forgive him soon so she could just date the idiot and be happy and half hoped she'd make him grovel a little more. It was clear that Bobby was sincerely sorry—even their mother had forgiven him—but Julieta was keeping her guard up high. It was difficult to blame her.

Elisa spent as much time with Lucia as she could, but still give her space, a balancing act that was anything but easy. When she wasn't with her sister, she was trying to ride out the rest of the semester in peace. She'd returned to school and was relieved to find out that her professors completely understood why she'd been ditching and were all fine with letting her make up assignments. Spring break had only been over for about two and a half weeks, but it felt like a lifetime ago.

She sat on Charlene's living room floor with her overdue chemistry assignments spread out in front of her. While it was nice to have something to think about that wasn't connected to the utter chaos Wick had caused, chemistry was enough to give Elisa a headache. It wasn't her strong suit at the best of times, and she hadn't done herself any favors by skipping class.

Not helping matters was the fact that she'd told Charlene and Colin what Darcy had done, mainly to get it off her chest. Now, after listening to their rambling on the matter for the last half hour, she wished she hadn't said anything.

"Darcy—she's like a superhero," Charlene said. "I mean, what she did was amazing, wasn't it?"

"Since when were you such a fan of hers?" Elisa asked, tearing her gaze away from the notes her lab partner had leant her—which was, admittedly, not that difficult.

"Since I found out she basically rescued your sister," she said.

"Have you called her?" Colin asked, perched on the couch behind Elisa. Charlene, meanwhile, was pacing. "I mean, you pretty much *have* to call her."

"He's right," she said. "I mean, you can't *not* call."

"I've been doing a splendid job at it for the past week," Elisa said dryly.

"Really, Elisa? You're seriously not gonna say anything?" she asked, incredulous.

"I didn't say that. I just… I need time to think about what I'm gonna say."

"I've found it helps to write up a draft," Colin said.

"What is there to think about?" Charlene asked. "Just say what you mean. 'OMG, thank you so much for finding and rescuing my baby sister.' Boom. Done."

"It's not that easy," she said, exasperated. "I mean—she

obviously didn't want me to know. She asked Lulu not to tell me."

"But now the cat's out of the bag. So you may as well call."

"Why wouldn't she want you to know?" Colin asked.

She sighed, tucking a lock of hair behind her ear. "Lulu has this ridiculous idea that it was so I wouldn't feel 'indebted' to Darcy. That Darcy did this for *me*, specifically."

"Is that *really* so ridiculous?"

"Yes," she said. "Look, we've become friends, and I'm really, really glad, but… But I'm not the sort of person you just drop everything to help."

"I think to Darcy, you are," Colin said.

"Not anymore," she said. "I… I think I blew it back at your cabin on Valentine's Day."

Charlene had stopped pacing and was now watching Elisa's face closely.

"Lisa. Do you…*regret* turning Darcy down?"

She forced herself to stare at her notes. "No. I mean everything I said back then. Or—or, I mean, I *did* mean it, at the time."

"But now?"

She fiddled with a pen. "Now things are different. Darcy and I are friends. *Just* friends." She stared at Charlene. "So don't get any bright ideas about…about locking us into a closet together or sending us each a love note signed by the other, or tricking us into getting engaged, or *whatever.*"

"Don't look at me. Look at Colin. He's been wanting you two to just make out already since you went to Pemberley."

Colin gave his girlfriend an exasperated look. "Narc." Even as he said it, he was smiling. "Well, if we're putting all cards on the table, I guess I should tell you that Darcy was asking about you."

She felt her face flush. "Really?" she asked, fighting to

keep her voice nonchalant. "When?"

"When you were looking for your sister. Literally every single day since you got back. I was kinda surprised, since she hardly ever calls me, but she didn't want to bother you. She figured you had enough to deal with, she didn't need to add to everything. So I promised to keep her posted."

"Oh."

She wished Darcy had gone ahead and bothered her.

"Of course," Colin said in a tone that he probably thought sounded casual, "since everything's getting back to normal, you could probably *call her* and let her know how you're doing yourself..."

Charlene met his eye with a grin while Elisa pretended not to notice. "Yeah. I mean, I'm sure she'd be glad to know that you're feeling better. She'd probably prefer to see you in person, but a *call* would be better than nothing."

Elisa lowered her head into her hands. "If I call her, will the two of you *shut up*?"

"*Yes*," they both said.

Elisa got her phone out of her pocket and dialed Darcy's number. It went right to voicemail.

"You've reached the personal cell phone of Darcy Fitzgerald. I am currently attending to family business in London and won't be back until early June. I prefer to not use my personal phone during family trips if at all possible. If it is urgent, you can reach me via the Wilder Hotel. If it is not urgent and you are a friend, please leave a message and I will get back to you as soon as I return to the States. If you are my doctor, please contact me via my personal email address. If you are a telemarketer, a politician, or my cousin Colin, I beg you to kindly piss off. Thank you and have a nice day."

Beeeeeeep.

"Uh—uh, Darcy, hi, it's—it's Elisa." Why was she suddenly so flustered by leaving a voicemail? "Um...look,

Lulu told me. What you did for us. For—for her, I mean. And, I, uh, wanted to call to say thank you. I can't possibly say that enough. Um…enjoy whatever you're doing with your family— if—if it's an 'enjoy' kinda thing. If not…my condolences? Uh. God. This call was a mistake, just—just call me back, please, thanks, *gotta go, bye*."

She hung up and threw her cell phone in front of her like it was a burning coal.

Colin and Charlene stared at her.

"Oh, shut up," Elisa said.

"We didn't say a word," Colin said.

She sighed. "Darcy's voicemail said she's in London, some family thing, and that she'd call when she got back. That if it was urgent, I could reach her at the hotel—"

"Okay, so look up the hotel's number," Charlene said, as if this was the most obvious thing in the world.

"No," Elisa said. "This isn't urgent. She'll call back when she has time. Now, can we talk about literally anything else? What'd you have for lunch today?"

"Oh, this new sandwich they have down at the sub shop— the Double Decker My Best Friend's an Idiot Who Needs to Call Darcy's Hotel Right Now." Charlene gave her the eyebrow.

Elisa stared at her. "That wasn't even witty. Love has dampened your sense of humor."

"I think it's enhanced it."

"You were so much more fun when you were single and bitter."

"Yeah, well, now I'm boring and happy. Suck it."

• • •

The day after Elisa's ill-fated call to Darcy, an unexpected visitor arrived at Longbourn.

"Elisa, darling, there's an old lady who looks like Sauron's unwashed bath towel asking for you," Alejandra said, sticking her head into Elisa's bedroom.

She looked up from the book she was reading, confused. "Mrs. Burger?"

Elisa got up, heading out into the living room, and, indeed, Catherine Burger was standing in the doorway. She wore a hat that made it look like something had died on top of her head, and her face was twisted into the ugliest frown imaginable.

"Mrs. Burger, if you're looking for Colin, he made it very clear he doesn't—" Elisa began to say, but Catherine cut her off.

"I'm not here to see my son," she said. "I'm here to speak to you. Alone."

"Uh…okay." She leaned in to whisper to her mother. "If I don't come back, avenge me."

"It's a promise."

Elisa stepped out into the hallway to talk to Catherine, leaning against her door.

"Don't slouch, Elisa, it's *most* unbecoming of a young lady," Catherine said.

"What did you want to speak to me about?" Elisa asked, slouching further.

"I have heard the most *disturbing* rumor, that you were romantically involved with my niece, Darcy Fitzgerald. You've always struck me as a smart one, so hopefully I don't need to tell you why a young woman of Darcy's stature dating a girl like you would be *wholly* inappropriate. If the rumor is true, I must urge you to terminate the relationship at once—"

Elisa cut her off. The look on Catherine's face told her she wasn't used to being cut off.

"It's *not* true."

"Oh. Well." She looked like she'd had an entire speech

planned and now wasn't sure what to say. "Good."

"Darcy and I are only friends, Mrs. Burger."

"Then I assume it will be no issue for me to ask you to *promise* that you will never let it become anything more than that."

Elisa stared at her, appalled by the sheer nerve she had.

"*Excuse* me?" she said, once she found her voice again.

"Promise me that, should Darcy ever have a lapse in judgement enough to ask you for a romantic relationship, you'll reject her."

It was obvious Mrs. Burger didn't realize why this was such an inappropriate and unbelievable demand to make of a girl she barely knew. Elisa just stood there, jaw dropped, unable to quite grasp that yes, Catherine really *did* have this much gall.

Finally, she said, "No. No, Catherine, I will *not* make that promise."

Catherine stared her down. "Why not?"

"I don't owe you an explanation. *Goodbye.*"

Elisa went back into her apartment and slammed the door.

She opened it again a second later.

"Actually, you know what—I don't owe you an explanation, but it's gonna bug me if I don't say this. I won't make that promise, because this isn't your life. This isn't some project you can micromanage. This is mine and Darcy's life."

"The concerns of my niece are concerns of mine," Catherine said. "And a low-class girl like you—a girl that lives in a dump like this, a girl with no wealth or prestige to her name, a girl who has nothing to offer to the relationship—can never make Darcy happy."

"You thought Charlene couldn't make Colin happy, but I was just over at their apartment, and let me tell you—your son is happier now than he *ever* was with you."

Catherine said nothing. Elisa took a step closer.

"And let me spell out what kind of girl I am, since you're so fond of dwelling on it. I'm a smart, determined girl who would do anything for her friends. So is Darcy. I'm a regular girl trying to figure out what to do with her life. So is Darcy. I'm a girl who's too independent, too determined to be her own person to listen to the unsolicited advice of a washed-up Charles Dickens villain. So is Darcy. So far, we're equals."

"You are the furthest thing from," Catherine squawked. "The Fitzgeralds are on a completely different level from your family."

"Why are you trying to run everyone else's lives?" Elisa asked, one of her hands clenching into a fist. She hadn't intended to lose her temper, but the second she'd started talking, all the words had rushed out of her like a waterfall. Despite the fact that Catherine looked like she was about ready to squish her like a bug, she felt nothing but relief at speaking her mind. "First Colin, now Darcy—and me. Why aren't you just content to let people do what they have to in order to be happy? None of us are hurting anyone. We're all just...people trying to live our lives. You're not trying to *help* us; you're trying to *control* us. Well, it's not going to work."

Catherine resembled a bleached prune, her lips moving but no sounds coming out.

"Darcy and I are adults," Elisa said. "If we decide we want our relationship to take that kind of turn, it'll be because we want it to. And if we decide we don't want it to, that'll be our choice, too. So, until you feel like being supportive, get the hell out of my apartment building. And stay away from Colin unless you want to act like a loving mother for once."

Elisa went back inside and slammed the door. For real this time.

Julieta and Alejandra were both staring at her.

"I'm going to the roof as soon as I think Lady Bracknell

out there has left," Elisa said.

She peered out the peephole and was glad to see the other woman was gone. She ran up to the roof. Julieta, to her surprise, followed her.

"What was that about?" she asked. "Mom and I heard shouting."

"Darcy's aunt heard a rumor we're going out," she said. "And when I told her we're not, she tried to make me promise to never go out with her. I kind of lost my temper."

Julieta let out a laugh. "Wow. I would've thought you would've *gladly* made that promise."

"Six months ago, I would have."

"Why not now?" she asked, approaching her younger sister. "You *hate* Darcy—don't you?"

And then, it all came out. Elisa told her everything. Darcy confessing her love. Seeing Darcy at Pemberley. Darcy rescuing Lucia. Calling Darcy and being both disappointed and relieved when she couldn't reach her.

By the time she was done, all the energy had completely drained from her body. And yet, a weight lifted off her shoulders. It was nice to not have to bottle everything up anymore. Julieta stood there, shocked, trying to take it all in.

"Wow. I...that's..." She trailed off, unable to find words.

Elisa stared at the ground below them, vision going slightly blurry.

"Julieta, I was—I was wrong about Darcy," she whispered. "I was so wrong."

"Elisa... Do you have feelings for her?" she asked gently.

Elisa sighed and turned her gaze toward the sky. "Back when she first told me she had feelings for me, I—I hated her, I said she was the last person I could ever love, and at the time, I meant it. But now—now I really think I could. I already might. I don't know. I'm not sure how love is supposed to feel, but..."

"If she has you thinking about it, that might mean something."

"Darcy told me she loved me three months ago. How could so much have changed in just *three months*?"

"You are different people now. You've both... It feels like you've grown up, all at once. Darcy became someone you could love, and you became someone who could love her back."

"And now she doesn't love me, right?" When did her voice become so shaky? "I mean, I... I rejected her, and maybe— maybe her being in London when I called was a *sign*..."

Julieta sighed. "Elisa, if I told you I got a sign from the universe to not be with Bobby, you would slap me upside the head until I saw sense. You'd say, 'Tell the universe to stay out of your business. Make your own decisions.'"

Elisa laughed, rubbing her eyes.

"Lisa, don't give up on Darcy just because you're scared. I'm scared, too, but... Bobby and I aren't giving up on each other, and look what we've been through. So don't give up on Darcy. If she would make you happy—*don't* give up on her."

Elisa shrugged helplessly. "It may not be my call anymore."

Julieta rubbed Elisa's back.

"Give her a chance to get back in the country and hear your message. I think she'll surprise you."

Interlude: In Which Catherine Tries Again (And Fails, Miserably)

Darcy was set to fly back to the United States in three days when her aunt called the Wilder Hotel. Darcy had never liked her Aunt Catherine much but endured her as best she could over the years. So, when the manager of the hotel called her room, telling her she had a call, she took it, dutifully.

"Hello?"

"Darcy." Aunt Catherine sounded very angry, indeed. "I have just been to see that dreadful Benitez girl."

"Which Benitez girl?" Darcy asked, confused.

"Elisa, of course. What other one could I possibly mean?"

"To my knowledge, there are five Benitez girls, none of whom are dreadful. What did you need to see Elisa for?"

"To address a rumor I heard that the two of you are… involved."

The blood rushed to her face, her cheeks burning. She hadn't told Catherine about her feelings. How could she possibly have found out?

She managed to keep an even tone and answered, "We're not."

"I know. She told me as much. But then she refused to promise she *wouldn't* become involved with you."

"Wait, what?"

"I know, the *audacity*. So now, I need your word, instead. Please, for the sake of your auntie's nerves—"

"Wait, wait, wait. You're telling me you tried to get Elisa to say she wouldn't go out with me if I were the last girl on earth—and she refused to?"

"Well, not in so many words, but... Darcy, what is the meaning of this?"

Darcy was grinning from ear to ear. "I gotta go, Aunt Catherine."

"Darcy? Darcy—"

She quickly hung up on her aunt and flopped back onto her hotel room's bed, almost embarrassed at how giddy she was. Her smile was so wide, it actually hurt a little bit, but she couldn't stop it. She felt like the door Elisa had slammed shut back in February had just opened again. Just a little bit, maybe just a crack, but wide enough for Darcy to go running through.

She tried not to let herself get too excited, telling herself that Elisa had never actually said she was interested, and that she may well have just been trying to get under Aunt Catherine's skin. But she couldn't help it. A warmth was spreading through her, and no amount of logic or cynicism could stop it now.

Chapter Thirty

In Which All Ends Happily

The third of June was Elisa's high school graduation. She hadn't actually been to the high school since last August, but her mother had insisted she attend the ceremony. Elisa would've been perfectly content to show up, collect her diploma, and peace the hell out. Mom also insisted on a small party back home after the ceremony was done. Her parents, her sisters, her grandparents, Charlene, Colin, Bobby, Willow, Gianna, and even Louise and Cora were all crammed into the apartment, eating chips and cake. They were all talking so much, Elisa couldn't hear herself think. She'd managed to find a semi-quiet corner in the kitchen and was chatting with Gianna and Lucia. Lucia had, amazingly, taken very well to the shy, soft-spoken Gianna, and had been keeping her company all night.

Elisa was glad. They both needed a friend who understood what Wick had put them through. Lucia's bruise was fading, and the spark was returning to her eyes, but she still had a long way to go. She'd taken the rest of the school year off and had enrolled in a summer school program to make things up. Their parents were also looking into counseling for her. Wick still hadn't been found, but Elisa was determined to keep up hope that he'd be arrested soon. He couldn't hide forever.

"It's too bad your sister couldn't come with you," Lucia said to Gianna, hoisting herself up to sit on the kitchen counter. "She's still in London, right?"

"Sh-she flew out this—this morning," she said.

Elisa glanced down at her feet, determined not to dwell too much on Darcy.

"Well, I'm glad you could come, Gi," Elisa said. "How have things been in Columbus?"

"They're—they're good, especially now that all the Wick drama is...well, I won't say *over*, b-but..."

Lucia sighed. "It's basically paused until the cops catch up to him. But he's bound to turn up sooner or later. He's not dumb, but he's not smart enough to just disappear."

"I... I hope I—I can get up the courage to test-testify," Gianna said. "At the trial, I m-mean."

"If you can't, that's okay," Lucia said. "Some of the stuff he sent me on my phone is enough to get him some time, if nothing else. I hope."

"And if the legal system fails us, we can always just kill him," Elisa said, shrugging casually.

Gianna cracked a smile. "S-sounds like a plan to me."

There was a knock at the door. She didn't pay too much attention until Mom came into the kitchen.

"Elisa, there's a Darcy looking for you?"

She looked up so quickly, she nearly gave herself whiplash. Lucia, meanwhile, could barely contain her glee, swinging her legs excitedly. Gianna just smiled, sipping innocently on her drink.

Elisa stared at her.

"You *didn't*."

"I did. Thank me later."

"*Oh* my God."

Elisa stood there for a second, more nervous than she'd been even when getting up onstage to get her diploma. She shook her head, trying to set herself straight. She took a deep breath, and then went to the door.

She'd never seen Darcy look so unkempt. Her hair was pulled back into a messy ponytail, there were bags under her eyes from a hard day of traveling, and she was in sweatpants and flip-flops. Elisa, still in the pink dress and jewelry she'd worn to her ceremony, for once felt a bit overdressed.

"I... I just came from the airport," Darcy said, not taking her eyes off her for a second.

"You look lovely," was all she could think of to say.

"Thank you."

There was a pause.

"Elisa, I got your voicemail."

Elisa blushed, finally tearing her gaze away. "I... I see," she said. "Do you want to talk alone?"

Darcy nodded. "Very much, yes."

She swallowed the lump in her throat and called out, "Be back in a few minutes." She and Charlene made eye contact across the room. Charlene's eyes widened when she saw who was with her, mouthing *"Oh my God, what?"* when Darcy wasn't looking. Elisa could only give a shrug and a silent *"I don't know"* in response. She tried her best to ignore the fact that Colin, Willow, and Gianna all looked annoyingly proud of themselves.

Elisa led Darcy up to the roof. When they got there, they both stood in awkward silence, Darcy rocking on her feet.

"I didn't intend for you to find out what I did," she finally said. "At least, not like that."

"That's what I don't understand," Elisa said. "You—you rescued my little sister, and I will always, *always* be grateful for that. I don't get why you didn't tell me."

She licked her lips, looking away.

"I was worried that you'd think that I—that I'd only done it to impress you. I... Elisa, my only thought when I helped Lucia was your happiness."

Astonished, she could only stare.

"I didn't care what I had to do or say to help you, I just—I had to. Because the idea of you being unhappy was intolerable. Even if you never knew that I helped, I would've been content, knowing that you were happy."

"Darcy..."

She looked at her now.

"And then, when I was in London, I got a call from my aunt, saying that she'd attempted to make you promise to not pursue a romantic relationship with me—and you refused her."

Elisa blushed. "Yeah. I shot her down pretty hard."

"Hearing that... Hearing that is what gave me hope," she admitted.

Through no conscious thought of her own, Elisa moved closer to Darcy, her heart pounding louder and louder, until she was close enough to see every detail of her face.

"Hope for what?" she asked.

They were standing mere inches apart now, their voices barely raised. The entire world had disappeared.

"I suppose it's not too much of a secret that—that my feelings are still the same as they were in February," Darcy said. "If anything, they've only grown since then. But—but if *your* feelings are still the same as they were at the time, please tell me so. One word, and I'll never bring this up again. But if your feelings are different now—"

Elisa cut her off, closing the gap between them and kissing her, her hands trailing into Darcy's hair. Darcy froze for a second, shocked, before leaning into it, kissing her back.

Elisa had imagined this moment an embarrassing number of times over the past couple of weeks. She'd imagined the softness of her lips, the feeling of Darcy's hands shaking—wait, maybe that was her—and the dizziness and the warmth and the sense that she was finally where she was supposed to be.

The real thing left all her fantasies behind.

They pulled away, Elisa still on tiptoe to reach Darcy's lips, trying to catch their breath.

Elisa spoke first.

"Does that... Does that bring you up to speed?" she asked.

Darcy laughed, leaning her forehead against hers. "You... I never thought, after everything that happened..."

"Everything *had* to happen," she said. "If we hadn't started off where we did, we wouldn't have changed into who we are now. And who knows—who knows where we'd be if we hadn't changed."

"I'd probably still be the ice queen you loved to hate," Darcy said, her arms wrapping around Elisa's waist. "You hated me so much, I can't believe that now, you...you..."

"I was an idiot," she said gently. "So were you. We *both* had a lot to learn."

"And what have you learned?"

Elisa kissed her again.

"I love you, Darcy Fitzgerald. Most ardently."

Darcy smiled against her lips, pressing another kiss to her mouth.

"I love you, too, Elisa Benitez," she said. "I was already halfway through falling in love with you before I knew I had even begun. Once I realized, I found I couldn't stop it. And soon, I found I didn't *want* to stop it. I love you *so* much. And I don't want us to have to ever be apart again. If...that's what you want, too?"

"It is."

They kept kissing, losing track of time, until footsteps approached, coming up the stairs. They both pulled back, heat flooding their faces as they turned toward the noise.

Her dad stood in the stairwell, eyebrows raised.

"Am I interrupting something?" he asked.

"I—I, uh, I'm going to—I'm gonna go find Gianna and see how she's doing," Darcy said quickly. "I'll—Elisa, you can…explain things to him— Hi, Mr. Benitez, I'm Darcy, I'm your daughter's…uh…*I gotta go*."

Darcy practically ran back down the stairs and down the hall, probably looking for the nearest hole to crawl into. Elisa laughed as she watched her, completely enamored.

Her father just stared at her, waiting for the explanation he had been promised.

"That was Darcy, my…my girlfriend."

Elisa had never been able to call someone her girlfriend before. She'd never been able to call anyone her anything before.

"I take it she's new?" he asked.

She nodded. "New as in…five minutes ago."

"What's she like?"

"Smart. Loyal. Kind of awkward, but…but so good. She's so good to me, and good *for* me."

"I take it you really, really like her," he said.

"Papa, I love her."

He smiled, stepping forward to wrap his arms around her.

"Then I'm happy for you, Elisa," he said. "This Darcy better be the woman you deserve."

"She is. I promise, she is. And if you want to get to know her, talk about books. She'll be all over that."

He chuckled, pulling away from their hug.

"All I want is for you to be happy," he said. "I'm glad you

found someone to help you with that."

"I am, too. And I like to think I make her happy, in return."

"You do. I think anybody can see that."

They rejoined the party, and Darcy had clearly told Willow everything, because she was practically glowing. Darcy grinned shyly, trying to make conversation with one of Elisa's grandmothers. Elisa stood by her side and dreaded the moment she'd have to leave.

• • •

"It's a bit unorthodox to have a 'the trial can proceed' party, but we're a bit unorthodox ourselves," Colin said, settling into the couch as the movie started.

None of them were really paying attention to the movie. Colin and Charlene were snuggling, Lucia and Gianna were going over Lucia's summer school homework, and Elisa and Darcy were talking, sitting on the other end of the couch. But the movie provided some background noise, and it was nice to have an excuse to hang out. And this *definitely* called for some kind of celebration, no matter how small.

Wick had been found in Cleveland and brought in by the police. The trial could start. Gianna had also submitted some screencaps she'd saved from the first time she'd attempted to press charges—screencaps that, combined with Lucia's own evidence, would hopefully be enough to send him away for a long time. And it wasn't just Lucia and Gianna; Darcy had been right, there *were* other girls. Two others, both about fifteen years old, had come forward, and were willing to testify.

Elisa wasn't entirely sure how the trial would pan out, but she was optimistic. So was Lucia, which was more than she had dared to expect.

Things weren't back to normal just yet, but they were definitely better.

"You didn't have to come all the way from Columbus," she said to Darcy, wrapping an arm around her.

"Hey, I'm up here any chance I get," Darcy said. "Sort of a side effect of a long-distance relationship. Well, medium-distance."

"I've actually been thinking about that," she said. "Maybe it shouldn't have to be medium-distance much longer."

"What do you mean?"

"I mean...how would you feel if I started at OSU, in Columbus?" She reached up to trail a couple fingers through her hair. "I wouldn't be able to go in the fall, but I could transfer in for the spring semester. Plus that gives me time to get financial aid in order...and talk Mom around on the idea."

Darcy grinned. "I would *love* that. And you're definitely smart enough to get scholarships, and you could live in the dorm."

"So, it looks like I have an application to start."

"It appears that you do," Darcy said, leaning up to kiss her lips. "Your mom will be sad to see you go."

"Maybe," Elisa admitted. "But she has four other daughters to torment. Us getting together has given her renewed hope for Jules and Bobby."

Alejandra had freaked out harder than anybody when Elisa told her she was dating a Fitzgerald. She'd asked her about ten times if she was kidding and had taken to Facebook to brag as soon as she realized it was true.

So now everyone Elisa had ever *met* knew, too.

Including Catherine Burger, who, according to Darcy, had blocked her, since this was apparently the next-best thing to disinheriting her.

"Good riddance," she said. Colin had agreed. Elisa

worried about him when his mother first cut him off, but he seemed to be handling the new reality incredibly well. She could tell he still missed her at times, but she was surprised at how much independence he'd shown. And he and Charlene were happier than ever.

Colin and Charlene were both over-the-moon for the new couple and insisted on taking a little credit. Colin had already begun planning potential double dates. *Another reason*, Elisa thought, *to hightail it out of Steventon*. When they told Julieta and Bobby, he'd simply handed Julieta twenty dollars.

Elisa herself had never imagined being this happy. She'd been content before, but it was nothing compared to this. She'd become the very lovesick, giddy sort of girl she used to make fun of. Not that this stopped her from snarking at her new girlfriend, of course. Darcy was slowly getting used to it and had even begun firing back.

And now, with the future wide open in front of her, Elisa was both exhilarated and terrified. Moving away from home to live in the dorms was a nerve-wracking thought, but she was ready. If she had Charlene, her sisters, even Colin, and *especially* Darcy, she was certain she was ready to take on almost anything.

It wasn't a happy ending, per se, but it was a very, very happy start.

Acknowledgments

Thanks to Candace, a truly fantastic editor, and the entire team at Entangled for helping make my dream a reality.

Thanks to Annie, both for being an incredible friend, and for giving me the first feedback that made this book actually readable. You're the best.

Thanks to Mom and Dad, for supporting me, all my gay-ass nonsense, and my dream of becoming a writer. And never once trying to talk me out of it. Also, thanks for, like, raising me and stuff.

And, perhaps most of all, thanks to Jane Austen, for giving us the classic romantic comedy that this novel ~~completely rips off~~ pays loving tribute to.

About the Author

Susan Mesler-Evans is a writer, college student, D&D enthusiast, theatre nerd, and horrific procrastinator. Born and raised in Columbus, Ohio, Susan now lives in Florida, and can often be found reading, scrolling through Tumblr until 2 AM, overanalyzing her favorite fictional characters and relationships, bingewatching comedies on Netflix, thinking about writing, and even, on occasion, actually writing. *Most Ardently* is her first full-length novel. You can find her at susanmeslerevanswrites.com.

Discover more New Adult titles from Entangled Embrace...

SHADOWS YOU LEFT
a novel by Jude Sierra & Taylor Brooke

ERIK:

For years he's been bouncing from city to city. But in Seattle, everything changed. River's an artist. A pretty boy. Someone so soft shouldn't be intrigued by Erik's rough edges.

RIVER:

His life was quiet, with a simple routine. Then Erik comes along, shrouded in mystery. Neither of them expected a relationship so complicated. They're both trying to escape a shadowed past. But the faster you run from shadows, the faster they chase you.

PROMISE ME
a novel by Samanthe Beck and Robin Bielman

Instead of soaking up the SoCal sunshine while house-sitting for my aunt, I'm dealing with a Pomeranian who thinks she's a pit bull, two half sisters who would happily prune me off the family tree, and *him*. Vaughn Shaughnessy. Hot model about to go nuclear, dangerously sexy flirt whose perceptive green eyes promise he's more than just a pretty face. I should avoid him, but that's impossible because he also happens to be my extremely lickable—I mean likable—neighbor. I don't dare risk it, but I'm not sure I can resist...

FALLING FOR THE PLAYER
a novel by Jessica Lee

Bad boy and former NFL running back Patrick Guinness is tired of meaningless sex. Ever since his scorching hot one-night stand three years ago, no one has interested him. So when Max Segreti wanders into his mechanic shop—and his life again—Patrick can't stop thinking about the totally-out-of-his-league law student and the possibility of getting him out of his system once and for all...

UNDER A STORM-SWEPT SKY
a novel by Beth Anne Miller

An eighty-mile trek across the stunning beauty of Scotland's Isle of Skye isn't something I imagined myself doing. Ever. This isn't a trail for beginners. Rory Sutherland, my guide on this adventure, is not happy. We clash with every mile, but we recognize a shared pain. The tension between us is taut with unsaid words. And hope. He's broken. I'm damaged. Together, we're about to make the perfect storm.